The season has opened for the year of 1814, and there is little reason to hope that we will see any noticeable change from 1813. The ranks of society are once again filled with Ambitious Mamas, whose only aim is to see their Darling Daughters married off to Determined Bachelors. Discussion amongst the Mamas fingers Viscount Bridgerton as this year's most eligible catch, and indeed, if the poor man's hair looks ruffled and windblown, it is because he cannot go anywhere without some young miss batting her eyelashes with such vigor and speed as to create a breeze of hurricane force. Perhaps the only young lady not interested in Bridgerton is Miss Katharine Sheffield, and in fact, her demeanor toward the viscount occasionally borders on the hostile.

And that is why, Dear Reader, This Author feels that a match between Bridgerton and Miss Sheffield would be just the thing to enliven an otherwise ordinary season.

LADY WHISTLEDOWN'S SOCIETY PAPERS, 13 APRIL 1814

Julia Quinn

THE VISCOUNT WHO LOVED ME

AVON BOOKS
An Imprint of HarperCollins*Publishers*

This is a work of fiction. Names, characters, places, and incidents are products of the author's imagination or are used fictitiously and are not to be construed as real. Any resemblance to actual events, locales, organizations, or persons, living or dead, is entirely coincidental.

AVON BOOKS
An Imprint of HarperCollins*Publishers*
10 East 53rd Street
New York, New York 10022-5299

For Little Goose Twist,
who kept me company
throughout the writing of this book.
I can't wait to meet you!

And also for Paul,
even though he is allergic to musicals.

Prologue

*A*nthony Bridgerton had always known he would die young.

Oh, not as a child. Young Anthony had never had cause to ponder his own mortality. His early years had been a young boy's perfection, right from the very day of his birth.

It was true that Anthony was the heir to an ancient and wealthy viscountcy, but unlike most other aristocratic couples, Lord and Lady Bridgerton were very much in love, and they saw their son's birth not as the arrival of an heir, but rather that of a child.

And so there were no parties, no fêtes, no celebration other than that of mother and father staring in wonderment at their new son.

The Bridgertons were young parents—Edmund barely twenty and Violet just eighteen—but they were sensible and they were strong, and they loved their son with a fierceness and devotion that was rarely seen in their social circles. Much to her own mother's horror, Violet insisted upon nursing the boy herself, and Edmund never subscribed to the prevailing attitude that fathers should neither see nor hear their children. He took the infant on long hikes across the fields of Kent, spoke to him of philosophy and poetry before he could possibly understand the words, and told him a bedtime story every night.

Because the viscount and viscountess were so young

and so very much in love, it came as no surprise to anyone when, just two years after Anthony's birth, he was joined by a younger brother, christened Benedict. Edmund immediately adjusted his daily routine to take two sons on his hikes, and he spent a week holed up in the stables, working with his leatherworker to devise a special pack that would hold Anthony on his back while he held the baby Benedict in his arms.

They walked across fields and streams, and he told them of wondrous things, of perfect flowers and clear blue skies, of knights in shining armor and damsels in distress. Violet used to laugh when they returned all windblown and sun-kissed, and Edmund would say, "See? Here is our damsel in distress. Clearly we must save her." And Anthony would throw himself into his mother's arms, giggling as he swore he'd protect her from the fire-breathing dragon they'd seen just *two miles down the road* in the village.

"Two miles down the road in the village?" Violet would breathe, keeping her voice carefully laden with horror. "Heaven above, what would I do without three strong men to protect me?"

"Benedict's a baby," Anthony would reply.

"But he'll grow up," she'd always say, tousling his hair, "just as you did. And just as you still will."

Edmund always treated his children with equal affection and devotion, but late at night, when Anthony cradled the Bridgerton pocket watch to his chest (given to him on his eighth birthday by his father, who had received it on his eighth birthday from *his* father), he liked to think that his relationship with his father was just a little bit special. Not because Edmund loved him best; by that point the Bridgerton siblings numbered four (Colin and Daphne had arrived fairly close together) and Anthony knew very well that all the children were well loved.

No, Anthony liked to think that his relationship with his father was special simply because he'd known him the longest. After all, no matter how long Benedict had known their father, Anthony would always have two years on him. And six on Colin. And as for Daphne, well, besides the fact that she was a girl (the horror!), she'd known Father a full eight years less than he had and, he liked to remind himself, always would.

Edmund Bridgerton was, quite simply, the very center of Anthony's world. He was tall, his shoulders were broad, and he could ride a horse as if he'd been born in the saddle. He always knew the answers to arithmetic questions (even when the tutor didn't), he saw no reason why his sons should not have a tree house (and then he went and built it himself), and his laugh was the sort that warmed a body from the inside out.

Edmund taught Anthony how to ride. He taught Anthony how to shoot. He taught him to swim. He took him off to Eton himself, rather than sending him in a carriage with servants, as most of Anthony's future friends arrived, and when he saw Anthony glancing nervously about the school that would become his new home, he had a heart-to-heart talk with his eldest son, assuring him that everything would be all right.

And it was. Anthony knew it would be. His father, after all, never lied.

Anthony loved his mother. Hell, he'd probably bite off his own arm if it meant keeping her safe and well. But growing up, everything he did, every accomplishment, every goal, every single hope and dream—it was all for his father.

And then one day, everything changed. It was funny, he reflected later, how one's life could alter in an instant, how one minute everything could be a certain way, and the next it's simply . . . not.

It happened when Anthony was eighteen, home for the summer and preparing for his first year at Oxford. He was to belong to All Souls College, as his father had before him, and his life was as bright and dazzling as any eighteen-year-old had a right to enjoy. He had discovered women, and perhaps more splendidly, they had discovered him. His parents were still happily reproducing, having added Eloise, Francesca, and Gregory to the family, and Anthony did his best not to roll his eyes when he passed his mother in the hall—pregnant with her *eighth* child! It was all a bit unseemly, in Anthony's opinion, having children at their age, but he kept his opinions to himself.

Who was he to doubt Edmund's wisdom? Maybe he, too, would want more children at the advanced age of thirty-eight.

When Anthony found out, it was late afternoon. He was returning from a long and bruising ride with Benedict and had just pushed through the front door of Aubrey Hall, the ancestral home of the Bridgertons, when he saw his ten-year-old-sister sitting on the floor. Benedict was still in the stables, having lost some silly bet with Anthony, the terms of which required him to rub down both horses.

Anthony stopped short when he saw Daphne. It was odd enough that his sister was sitting in the middle of the floor in the main hall. It was even more odd that she was crying.

Daphne never cried.

"Daff," he said hesitantly, too young to know what to do with a crying female and wondering if he'd ever learn, "what—"

But before he could finish his question, Daphne lifted her head, and the shattering heartbreak in her large brown eyes cut through him like a knife. He stumbled back a step, knowing something was wrong, terribly wrong.

"He'd dead," Daphne whispered. "Papa is dead."

For a moment Anthony was sure he'd misheard. His father couldn't be dead. Other people died young, like Uncle Hugo, but Uncle Hugo had been small and frail. Well, at least smaller and frailer than Edmund.

"You're wrong," he told Daphne. "You must be wrong."

She shook her head. "Eloise told me. He was . . . it was . . ."

Anthony knew he shouldn't shake his sister while she

sobbed, but he couldn't help himself. "It was *what,* Daphne?"

"A bee," she whispered. "He was stung by a bee."

For a moment Anthony could do nothing but stare at her. Finally, his voice hoarse and barely recognizable, he said, "A man doesn't die from a bee sting, Daphne."

She said nothing, just sat there on the floor, her throat working convulsively as she tried to control her tears.

"He's been stung before," Anthony added, his voice rising in volume. "I was with him. We were both stung. We came across a nest. I was stung on the shoulder." Unbidden, his hand rose to touch the spot where he'd been stung so many years before. In a whisper he added, "He on his arm."

Daphne just stared at him with an eerily blank expression.

"He was fine," Anthony insisted. He could hear the panic in his voice and knew he was frightening his sister, but he was powerless to control it. "A man can't die from a bee sting!"

Daphne shook her head, her dark eyes suddenly looking about a hundred years old. "It was a bee," she said in a hollow voice. "Eloise saw it. One minute he was just standing there, and the next he was . . . he was . . ."

Anthony felt something very strange building within him, as if his muscles were about to jump through his skin. "The next he was *what,* Daphne?"

"Gone." She looked bewildered by the word, as bewildered as he felt.

Anthony left Daphne sitting in the hall and took the stairs three at a time up to his parents' bedchamber. Surely his father wasn't dead. A man couldn't die from a bee sting. It was impossible. Utterly mad. Edmund Bridgerton was young, he was strong. He was tall, his shoulders were broad, his muscles were powerful, and by God, no insignificant honeybee could have felled him.

But when Anthony reached the upstairs hall, he could

tell by the utter and complete silence of the dozen or so hovering servants that the situation was grim.

And their pitying faces . . . for the rest of his life he'd be haunted by those pitying faces.

He'd thought he'd have to push his way into his parents' room, but the servants parted as if they were drops in the Red Sea, and when Anthony pushed open the door, he knew.

His mother was sitting on the edge of the bed, not weeping, not even making a sound, just holding his father's hand as she rocked slowly back and forth.

His father was still. Still as . . .

Anthony didn't even want to think the word.

"Mama?" he choked out. He hadn't called her that for years; she'd been "Mother" since he'd left for Eton.

She turned, slowly, as if hearing his voice through a long, long tunnel.

"What happened?" he whispered.

She shook her head, her eyes hopelessly far away. "I don't know," she said. Her lips remained parted by an inch or so, as if she'd meant to say something more but then forgotten to do it.

Anthony took a step forward, his movements awkward and jerky.

"He's gone," Violet finally whispered. "He's gone and I . . . oh, God, I . . ." She placed a hand on her belly, full and round with child. "I told him—oh, Anthony, I told him—"

She looked as if she might shatter from the inside out. Anthony choked back the tears that were burning his eyes and stinging his throat and moved to her side. "It's all right, Mama," he said.

But he knew it wasn't all right.

"I told him this had to be our last," she gasped, sobbing onto his shoulder. "I told him I couldn't carry another, and we'd have to be careful, and . . . Oh, God, Anthony, what I'd do to have him here and give him another child. I don't understand. I just don't understand. . . ."

Anthony held her while she cried. He said nothing; it seemed useless to try to make any words fit the devastation in his heart.

He didn't understand, either.

The doctors came later that evening and pronounced themselves baffled. They'd heard of such things before, but never in one so young and strong. He was so vital, so powerful; nobody could have known. It was true that the viscount's younger brother Hugo had died quite suddenly the year before, but such things did not necessarily run in families, and besides, even though Hugo had died by himself out-of-doors, no one had noticed a bee sting on his skin.

Then again, nobody had looked.

Nobody could have known, the doctors kept saying, over and over until Anthony wanted to strangle them all. Eventually he got them out of the house, and he put his mother to bed. They had to move her into a spare bedroom; she grew agitated at the thought of sleeping in the bed she'd shared for so many years with Edmund. Anthony managed to send his six siblings to bed as well, telling them that they'd all talk in the morning, that everything would be well, and he would take care of them as their father would have wanted.

Then he walked into the room where his father's body still lay and looked at him. He looked at him and looked at him, staring at him for hours, barely blinking.

And when he left the room, he left with a new vision of his own life, and new knowledge about his own mortality.

Edmund Bridgerton had died at the age of thirty-eight. And Anthony simply couldn't imagine ever surpassing his father in any way, even in years.

Chapter 1

The topic of rakes has, of course, been previously discussed in this column, and This Author has come to the conclusion that there are rakes, and there are Rakes.

Anthony Bridgerton is a Rake.

A rake (lower-case) is youthful and immature. He flaunts his exploits, behaves with utmost idiocy, and thinks himself dangerous to women.

A Rake (upper-case) knows he is dangerous to women.

He doesn't flaunt his exploits because he doesn't need to. He knows he will be whispered about by men and women alike, and in fact, he'd rather they didn't whisper about him at all. He knows who he is and what he has done; further recountings are, to him, redundant.

He doesn't behave like an idiot for the simple reason that he isn't an idiot (any moreso than must be expected among all members of the male gender). He has little patience for the foibles of society, and quite frankly, most of the time This Author cannot say she blames him.

And if that doesn't describe Viscount Bridgerton—surely this season's most eligible bachelor—to perfection, This Author shall retire Her quill immediately. The only question is: Will 1814 be the season he finally succumbs to the exquisite bliss of matrimony?

This Author Thinks . . .
Not.

LADY WHISTLEDOWN'S SOCIETY PAPERS, 20 APRIL 1814

"*P*lease don't tell me," Kate Sheffield said to the room at large, "that she is writing about Viscount Bridgerton again."

Her half-sister Edwina, younger by almost four years, looked up from behind the single-sheet newspaper. "How could you tell?"

"You're giggling like a madwoman."

Edwina giggled, shaking the blue damask sofa on which they both sat.

"See?" Kate said, giving her a little poke in the arm. "You always giggle when she writes about some reprehensible rogue." But Kate grinned. There was little she liked better than teasing her sister. In a good-natured manner, of course.

Mary Sheffield, Edwina's mother, and Kate's stepmother for nearly eighteen years, glanced up from her embroidery and pushed her spectacles farther up the bridge of her nose. "What are you two laughing about?"

"Kate's in a snit because Lady Whistledown is writing about that rakish viscount again," Edwina explained.

"I'm not in a snit," Kate said, even though no one was listening.

"Bridgerton?" Mary asked absently.

Edwina nodded. "Yes."

"She always writes about him."

"I think she just likes writing about rakes," Edwina commented.

"Of course she likes writing about rakes," Kate retorted. "If she wrote about boring people, no one would buy her newspaper."

"That's not true," Edwina replied. "Just last week she

wrote about us, and heaven knows we're not the most interesting people in London."

Kate smiled at her sister's naïveté. Kate and Mary might not be the most interesting people in London, but Edwina, with her buttery-colored hair and startlingly pale blue eyes, had already been named the Incomparable of 1814. Kate, on the other hand, with her plain brown hair and eyes, was usually referred to as "the Incomparable's older sister."

She supposed there were worse monikers. At least no one had yet begun to call her "the Incomparable's spinster sister." Which was a great deal closer to the truth than any of the Sheffields cared to admit. At twenty (nearly twenty-one, if one was going to be scrupulously honest about it), Kate was a bit long in the tooth to be enjoying her first season in London.

But there hadn't really been any other choice. The Sheffields hadn't been wealthy even when Kate's father had been alive, and since he'd passed on five years earlier, they'd been forced to economize even further. They certainly weren't ready for the poorhouse, but they had to mind every penny and watch every pound.

With their straitened finances, the Sheffields could manage the funds for only one trip to London. Renting a house—and a carriage—and hiring the bare minimum of servants for the season cost money. More money than they could afford to spend twice. As it was, they'd had to save for five solid years to be able to afford this trip to London. And if the girls weren't successful on the Marriage Mart . . . well, no one was going to clap them into debtor's prison, but they would have to look forward to a quiet life of genteel poverty at some charmingly small cottage in Somerset.

And so the two girls were forced to make their debuts in the same year. It had been decided that the most logical time would be when Edwina was just seventeen and Kate almost twenty-one. Mary would have liked to have waited until Edwina was eighteen, and a bit more mature, but that would have made Kate nearly twenty-two, and heavens, but who would marry her then?

Kate smiled wryly. She hadn't even wanted a season. She'd known from the outset that she wasn't the sort who would capture the attention of the *ton*. She wasn't pretty enough to overcome her lack of dowry, and she'd never learned to simper and mince and walk delicately, and do all those things other girls seemed to know how to do in the cradle. Even Edwina, who didn't have a devious bone in her body, somehow knew how to stand and walk and sigh so that men came to blows just for the honor of helping her cross the street.

Kate, on the other hand, always stood with her shoulders straight and tall, couldn't sit still if her life depended upon it, and walked as if she were in a race—and why not? she always wondered. If one was going somewhere, what could possibly be the point in not getting there quickly?

As for her current season in London, she didn't even like the city very much. Oh, she was having a good enough time, and she'd met quite a few nice people, but a London season seemed a horrible waste of money to a girl who would have been perfectly content to remain in the country and find some sensible man to marry there.

But Mary would have none of that. "When I married your father," she'd said, "I vowed to love you and bring you up with all the care and affection I'd give to a child of my own blood."

Kate had managed to get in a single, "But—" before Mary carried on with, "I have a responsibility to your poor mother, God rest her soul, and part of that responsibility is to see you married off happily and securely."

"I could be happy and secure in the country," Kate had replied.

Mary had countered, "There are more men from which to choose in London."

After which Edwina had joined in, insisting that she

would be utterly miserable without her, and since Kate
never could bear to see her sister unhappy, her fate had
been sealed.

And so here she was—sitting in a somewhat faded
drawing room in a rented house in a section of London
that was almost fashionable, and . . .

She looked about mischievously.

. . . and she was about to snatch a newspaper from her
sister's grasp.

"Kate!" Edwina squealed, her eyes bugging out at the
tiny triangle of newsprint that remained between her right
thumb and forefinger. "I wasn't done yet!"

"You've been reading it forever," Kate said with a
cheeky grin. "Besides, I want to see what she has to say
about Viscount Bridgerton today."

Edwina's eyes, which were usually compared to
peaceful Scottish lochs, glinted devilishly. "You're
awfully interested in the viscount, Kate. Is there something you're not telling us?"

"Don't be silly. I don't even know the man. And if I did,
I would probably run in the opposite direction. He is
exactly the sort of man the two of us should avoid at all
costs. He could probably seduce an iceberg."

"Kate!" Mary exclaimed.

Kate grimaced. She'd forgotten her stepmother was listening. "Well, it's true," she added. "I've heard he's had
more mistresses than I've had birthdays."

Mary looked at her for a few seconds, as if trying to
decide whether or not she wanted to respond, and then
finally she said, "Not that this is an appropriate topic for
your ears, but many men have."

"Oh." Kate flushed. There was little less appealing than
being decisively contradicted while one was trying to
make a grand point. "Well, then, he's had twice as many.
Whatever the case, he's far more promiscuous than most
men, and not the sort Edwina ought to allow to court her."

"*You* are enjoying a season as well," Mary reminded her.

Kate shot Mary the most sarcastic of glances. They all knew that if the viscount chose to court a Sheffield, it would not be Kate.

"I don't think there is anything in there that's going to alter your opinion," Edwina said with a shrug as she leaned toward Kate to get a better view of the newspaper. "She doesn't say very much about *him,* actually. It's more of a treatise on the topic of rakes."

Kate's eyes swept over the typeset words. "Hmmph," she said, her favorite expression of disdain. "I'll wager she's correct. He probably won't come up to scratch this year."

"You always think Lady Whistledown is correct," Mary murmured with a smile.

"She usually is," Kate replied. "You must admit, for a gossip columnist, she displays remarkable good sense. She has certainly been correct in her assessment of all the people I have met thus far in London."

"You should make your own judgments, Kate," Mary said lightly. "It is beneath you to base your opinions on a gossip column."

Kate knew her stepmother was right, but she didn't want to admit it, and so she just let out another "Hmmph" and turned back to the paper in her hands.

Whistledown was, without a doubt, the most interesting reading material in all London. Kate wasn't entirely certain when the gossip column had begun—sometime the previous year, she'd heard—but one thing was certain. Whoever Lady Whistledown was (and no one *really* knew who she was), she was a well-connected member of the *ton*. She had to be. No interloper could ever uncover all the gossip she printed in her columns every Monday, Wednesday, and Friday.

Lady Whistledown always had all the latest *on-dits*, and unlike other columnists, she wasn't hesitant about using people's full names. Having decided last week, for example, that Kate didn't look good in yellow, she wrote, clear as day: "The color yellow makes the dark-haired Miss Katharine Sheffield look like a singed daffodil."

Kate hadn't minded the insult. She'd heard it said on more than one occasion that one could not consider oneself "arrived" until one had been insulted by Lady Whistledown. Even Edwina, who was a huge social success by anyone's measure, had been jealous that Kate had been singled out for an insult.

And even though Kate didn't particularly want to be in London for a season, she figured that if she had to participate in the social whirl, she might as well not be a complete and utter failure. If getting insulted in a gossip column was to be her only sign of success, well then, so be it. Kate would take her triumphs where she may.

Now when Penelope Featherington bragged about being likened to an overripe citrus fruit in her tangerine satin, Kate could wave her arm and sigh with great drama, "Yes, well, I am a singed daffodil."

"Someday," Mary announced out of the blue, giving her spectacles yet another push with her index finger, "someone is going to discover that woman's true identity, and then she's going to be in trouble."

Edwina looked at her mother with interest. "Do you really think someone will ferret her out? She has managed to keep her secret for over a year now."

"Nothing that big can stay a secret forever," Mary replied. She jabbed her embroidery with her needle, pulling a long strand of yellow thread through the fabric. "Mark my words. It's all going to come out sooner or later, and when it does, a scandal the likes of which you have never seen is going to erupt all over town."

"Well, if I knew who she was," Kate announced, flipping the single-sheet newspaper over to page two, "I'd probably make her my best friend. She's fiendishly entertaining. And no matter what anyone says, she's almost always right."

Just then, Newton, Kate's somewhat overweight corgi, trotted into the room.

"Isn't that dog supposed to stay outside?" Mary asked. Then she yelped, "Kate!" as the dog angled over to her feet and panted as if waiting for a kiss.

"Newton, come here this minute," Kate ordered.

The dog gazed longingly at Mary, then waddled over to Kate, hopped up onto the sofa, and laid his front paws across her lap.

"He's covering you with fur," Edwina said.

Kate shrugged as she stroked his thick, caramel-colored coat. "I don't mind."

Edwina sighed, but she reached out and gave Newton a quick pat, anyway. "What else does she say?" she asked, leaning forward with interest. "I never did get to see page two."

Kate smiled at her sister's sarcasm. "Not much. A little something about the Duke and Duchess of Hastings, who apparently arrived in town earlier this week, a list of the food at Lady Danbury's ball, which she proclaimed 'surprisingly delicious,' and a rather unfortunate description of Mrs. Featherington's gown Monday last."

Edwina frowned. "She does seem to pick on the Featheringtons quite a bit."

"And no wonder," Mary said, setting down her embroidery as she stood up. "That woman wouldn't know how to pick out a dress color for her girls if a rainbow wrapped itself right around her neck."

"Mother!" Edwina exclaimed.

Kate clapped a hand over her mouth, trying not to laugh. Mary rarely made such opinionated pronouncements, but when she did, they were always marvelous.

"Well, it's true. She keeps dressing her youngest in tangerine. Anyone can see that poor girl needs a blue or a mint green."

"You dressed me in yellow," Kate reminded her.

"And I'm sorry I did. That will teach me to listen to a shopgirl. I should never have doubted my own judgment. We'll simply have to have that one cut down for Edwina."

Since Edwina was a full head shorter than Kate, and several shades more delicate, this would not be a problem.

"When you do," Kate said, turning to her sister, "make sure you eliminate the ruffle on the sleeve. It's dreadfully distracting. *And* it itches. I had half a mind to rip it off right there at the Ashbourne ball."

Mary rolled her eyes. "I am both surprised and thankful that you saw fit to restrain yourself."

"I am surprised but not thankful," Edwina said with a mischievous smile. "Just think of the fun Lady Whistledown would have had with *that*."

"Ah, yes," Kate said, returning her grin. "I can see it now. 'The singed daffodil rips off her petals.' "

"I am going upstairs," Mary announced, shaking her head at her daughters' antics. "Do try not to forget that we have a party to attend this evening. You girls may want to get a bit of rest before we go out. It's sure to be another late night for us."

Kate and Edwina nodded and murmured promises to that effect as Mary gathered her embroidery and left the room. As soon as she was gone, Edwina turned to Kate and asked, "Have you decided what you're going to wear tonight?"

"The green gauze, I think. I should wear white, I know, but I fear it does not suit me."

"If you don't wear white," Edwina said loyally, "then neither shall I. I shall wear my blue muslin."

Kate nodded her approval as she glanced back at the newspaper in her hand, trying to balance Newton, who had flipped over onto his back and was angling to have his belly rubbed. "Just last week Mr. Berbrooke said you are an angel in blue. On account of it matching your eyes so well."

Edwina blinked in surprise. "Mr. Berbrooke said that? To you?"

Kate looked back up. "Of course. All of your beaux try to pass on their compliments through me."

"They do? Whyever?"

Kate smiled slowly and indulgently. "Well, now, Edwina, it might have something to do with the time you announced to the entire audience at the Smythe-Smith musicale that you could never marry without your sister's approval."

Edwina's cheeks turned just the slightest bit pink. "It wasn't the entire audience," she mumbled.

"It might as well have been. The news traveled faster than fire on rooftops. I wasn't even in the room at the time and it only took two minutes for me to hear about it."

Edwina crossed her arms and let out a "Hmmph" that made her sound rather like her older sister. "Well, it's true, and I don't care who knows it. I know I'm expected to make a grand and brilliant match, but I don't have to marry someone who will ill treat me. Anyone with the fortitude to actually impress *you* would have to be up to snuff."

"Am I so difficult to impress, then?"

The two sisters looked at each other, then answered in unison, "Yes."

But as Kate laughed along with Edwina, a niggling sense of guilt rose within her. All three Sheffields knew that it would be Edwina who would snag a nobleman or marry into a fortune. It would be Edwina who would ensure that her family would not have to live out their lives in genteel poverty. Edwina was a beauty, while Kate was . . .

Kate was Kate.

Kate didn't mind. Edwina's beauty was simply a fact of life. There were certain truths Kate had long since come to accept. Kate would never learn to waltz without trying to take the lead; she'd always be afraid of electrical storms, no matter how often she told herself she was being silly; and no matter what she wore, no matter how she dressed her hair or pinched her cheeks, she'd never be as pretty as Edwina.

Besides, Kate wasn't certain that she'd like all the attention Edwina received. Nor, she was coming to realize, would she relish the responsibility of having to marry well to provide for her mother and sister.

"Edwina," Kate said softly, her eyes growing serious, "you don't have to marry anyone you don't like. You know that."

Edwina nodded, suddenly looking as if she might cry.

"If you decide there isn't a single gentleman in London who is good enough for you, then so be it. We shall simply go back to Somerset and enjoy our own company. There's no one I like better, anyway."

"Nor I," Edwina whispered.

"And if you do find a man who sweeps you off your feet, then Mary and I shall be delighted. You should not worry about leaving us, either. We shall get on fine with each other for company."

"You might find someone to marry as well," Edwina pointed out.

Kate felt her lips twist into a small smile. "I might," she allowed, knowing that it probably wasn't true. She didn't want to remain a spinster her entire life, but she doubted she would find a husband here in London. "Perhaps one of your lovesick suitors will turn to me once he realizes you are unattainable," she teased.

Edwina swatted her with a pillow. "Don't be silly."

"But I'm not!" Kate protested. And she wasn't. Quite frankly, this seemed to her the most likely avenue by which she might actually find a husband in town.

"Do you know what sort of man I'd like to marry?" Edwina asked, her eyes turning dreamy.

Kate shook her head.

"A scholar."

"A *scholar*?"

"A scholar," Edwina said firmly.

Kate cleared her throat. "I'm not certain you'll find many of those in town for the season."

"I know." Edwina let out a little sigh. "But the truth is—and you know this even if I am not supposed to let on in public—I'm really rather bookish. I'd much rather spend my day in a library than gadding about in Hyde Park. I think I should enjoy life with a man who enjoyed scholarly pursuits as well."

"Right. Hmmm . . ." Kate's mind worked frantically. Edwina wasn't likely to find a scholar back in Somerset, either. "You know, Edwina, it might be difficult to find you a true scholar outside the university towns. You might have to settle for a man who likes to read and learn as you do."

"That would be all right," Edwina said happily. "I'd be quite content with an amateur scholar."

Kate breathed a sigh of relief. Surely they could find someone in London who liked to read.

"And do you know what?" Edwina added. "You truly cannot tell a book by its cover. All sorts of people are amateur scholars. Why, even that Viscount Bridgerton Lady Whistledown keeps talking about might be a scholar at heart."

"Bite your tongue, Edwina. You are not to have anything to do with Viscount Bridgerton. Everyone knows he is the worst sort of rake. In fact, he's the worst rake, period. In all London. In the entire country!"

"I know, I was just using him as an example. Besides, he's not likely to choose a bride this year, anyway. Lady Whistledown said so, and you yourself said that she is almost always right."

Kate patted her sister on the arm. "Don't worry. We will find you a suitable husband. But *not*—not not not not not Viscount Bridgerton!"

At that very moment, the subject of their discussion was relaxing at White's with two of his three younger brothers, enjoying a late afternoon drink.

Anthony Bridgerton leaned back in his leather chair, regarded his scotch with a thoughtful expression as he swirled it about, and then announced, "I'm thinking about getting married."

Benedict Bridgerton, who had been indulging in a habit his mother detested—tipping his chair drunkenly on the back two legs—fell over.

Colin Bridgerton started to choke.

Luckily for Colin, Benedict regained his seat with enough time to smack him soundly on the back, sending a green olive sailing across the table.

It narrowly missed Anthony's ear.

Anthony let the indignity pass without comment. He was all too aware that his sudden declaration had come as a bit of a surprise.

Well, perhaps more than a bit. "Complete," "total," and "utter" were words that came to mind.

Anthony knew that he did not fit the image of a man who had settling down on his mind. He'd spent the last decade as the worst sort of rake, taking pleasure where he may. For as he well knew, life was short and certainly meant to be enjoyed. Oh, he'd had a certain code of honor. He never dallied with well-bred young women. Anyone who might have any right to demand marriage was strictly off-limits.

With four younger sisters of his own, Anthony had a healthy degree of respect for the good reputations of gently bred women. He'd already nearly fought a duel for one of his sisters, all over a slight to her honor. And as for the other three . . . he freely admitted that he broke out in a cold sweat at the mere thought of their getting involved with a man who bore a reputation like his.

No, he certainly wasn't about to despoil some other gentleman's younger sister.

But as for the other sort of women—the widows and actresses who knew what they wanted and what they were getting into—he'd enjoyed their company and enjoyed it well. Since the day he left Oxford and headed west to London, he'd not been without a mistress.

Sometimes, he thought wryly, he'd not been without two.

He'd ridden in nearly every horse race society had to offer, he'd boxed at Gentleman Jackson's, and he'd won more card games than he could count. (He'd lost a few, too, but he disregarded those.) He'd spent the decade of his twenties in a mindful pursuit of pleasure, tempered only by his overwhelming sense of responsibility to his family.

Edmund Bridgerton's death had been both sudden and unexpected; he'd not had a chance to make any final requests of his eldest son before he perished. But if he had, Anthony was certain that he would have asked him to care for his mother and siblings with the same diligence and affection Edmund had displayed.

And so in between Anthony's rounds of parties and horse races, he'd sent his brothers to Eton and Oxford, gone to a mind-numbing number of piano recitals given by his sisters (no easy feat; three out of four of them were tone deaf), and kept a close and watchful eye on the family finances. With seven brothers and sisters, he saw it as his duty to make sure there was enough money to secure all of their futures.

As he grew closer to thirty, he'd realized that he was spending more and more time tending to his heritage and family and less and less in his old pursuit of decadence and pleasure. And he'd realized that he liked it that way. He still kept a mistress, but never more than one at a time, and he discovered that he no longer felt the need to enter every horse race or stay late at a party just to win that last hand of cards.

His reputation, of course, stayed with him. He didn't mind that, actually. There were certain benefits to being thought England's most reprehensible rake. He was nearly universally feared, for example.

That was always a good thing.

But now it was time for marriage. He ought to settle

down, have a son. He had a title to pass on, after all. He did feel a rather sharp twinge of regret—and perhaps a touch of guilt as well—over the fact that it was unlikely that he'd live to see his son into adulthood. But what could he do? He was the firstborn Bridgerton of a firstborn Bridgerton of a firstborn Bridgerton eight times over. He had a dynastic responsibility to be fruitful and multiply.

Besides, he took some comfort in knowing that he'd leave three able and caring brothers behind. They'd see to it that his son was brought up with the love and honor that every Bridgerton enjoyed. His sisters would coddle the boy, and his mother might spoil him . . .

Anthony actually smiled a bit as he thought of his large and often boisterous family. His son would not need a father to be well loved.

And whatever children he sired—well, they probably wouldn't remember him after he was gone. They'd be young, unformed. It had not escaped Anthony's notice that of all the Bridgerton children, he, the eldest, was the one most deeply affected by their father's death.

Anthony downed another sip of his scotch and straightened his shoulders, pushing such unpleasant ruminations from his mind. He needed to focus on the matter at hand, namely, the pursuit of a wife.

Being a discerning and somewhat organized man, he'd made a mental list of requirements for the position. First, she ought to be reasonably attractive. She needn't be a raving beauty (although that would be nice), but if he was going to have to bed her, he figured a bit of attraction ought to make the job more pleasant.

Second, she couldn't be stupid. This, Anthony mused, might be the most difficult of his requirements to fill. He was not universally impressed by the mental prowess of London debutantes. The last time he'd made the mistake of engaging a young chit fresh out of the schoolroom in conversation, she'd been unable to discuss anything other than food (she'd had a plate of strawberries in her hand at the time) and the weather (and she hadn't even gotten *that* right; when Anthony had asked if she thought the weather was going to turn inclement, she'd replied, "I'm sure I don't know. I've never been to Clement.")

He might be able to avoid conversation with a wife who was less than brilliant, but he did *not* want stupid children.

Third—and this was the most important—she couldn't be anyone with whom he might actually fall in love.

Under no circumstances would this rule be broken.

He wasn't a complete cynic; he knew that true love existed. Anyone who'd ever been in the same room with his parents knew that true love existed.

But love was a complication he wished to avoid. He had no desire for his life to be visited by that particular miracle.

And since Anthony was used to getting what he wanted, he had no doubt that he would find an attractive, intelligent woman with whom he would never fall in love. And what was the problem with that? Chances were he wouldn't have found the love of his life even if he had been looking for her. Most men didn't.

"Good God, Anthony, what has you frowning so? Not that olive. I saw it clearly and it didn't even touch you."

Benedict's voice broke him out of his reverie, and Anthony blinked a few times before answering, "Nothing. Nothing at all."

He hadn't, of course, shared his thoughts about his own mortality with anyone else, even his brothers. It was not the sort of thing one wanted to advertise. Hell, if someone had come up to him and said the same thing, he probably would have laughed him right out the door.

But no one else could understand the depth of the bond he'd felt with his father. And no one could possibly understand the way Anthony felt it in his bones, how he simply knew that he could not live longer than his father had done. Edmund had been everything to him. He'd always aspired to be as great a man as his father, knowing that

that was unlikely, yet trying all the same. To actually achieve more than Edmund had—in any way—that was nothing short of impossible.

Anthony's father was, quite simply, the greatest man he'd ever known, possibly the greatest man who'd ever lived. To think that he might be more than that seemed conceited in the extreme.

Something had happened to him the night his father had died, when he'd remained in his parents' bedroom with the body, just sitting there for hours, watching his father and trying desperately to remember every moment they'd shared. It would be so easy to forget the little things—how Edmund would squeeze Anthony's upper arm when he needed encouragement. Or how he could recite from memory Balthazar's entire "Sigh No More" song from *Much Ado About Nothing,* not because he thought it particularly meaningful but just because he liked it.

And when Anthony finally emerged from the room, the first streaks of dawn pinking the sky, he somehow knew that his days were numbered, and numbered in the same way Edmund's had been.

"Spit it out," Benedict said, breaking into his thoughts once again. "I won't offer you a penny for your thoughts, since I know they can't possibly be worth that much, but what are you thinking about?"

Anthony suddenly sat up straighter, determined to force his attention back to the matter at hand. After all, he had a bride to choose, and that was surely serious business. "Who is considered the diamond of this season?" he asked.

His brothers paused for a moment to think on this, and then Colin said, "Edwina Sheffield. Surely you've seen her. Rather petite, with blond hair and blue eyes. You can usually spot her by the sheeplike crowd of lovesick suitors following her about."

Anthony ignored his brother's attempts at sarcastic humor. "Has she a brain?"

Colin blinked, as if the question of a woman with a brain were one that had never occurred to him. "Yes, I rather think she does. I once heard her discussing mythology with Middlethorpe, and it sounded as if she had the right of it."

"Good," Anthony said, letting his glass of scotch hit the table with a thunk. "Then I'll marry her."

Chapter 2

At the Hartside ball Wednesday night, Viscount Bridgerton was seen dancing with more than one eligible young lady. This behavior can only be termed "startling" as Bridgerton normally avoids proper young misses with a perseverance that would be impressive were it not so utterly frustrating to all marriage-minded Mamas.

Can it be that the viscount read This Author's most recent column and, in that perverse manner all males of the species seem to endorse, decided to prove This Author wrong?

It may seem that This Author is ascribing to herself far more importance than She actually wields, but men have certainly made decisions based on far, far less.

LADY WHISTLEDOWN'S SOCIETY PAPERS, 22 APRIL 1814

By eleven o'clock that evening, all of Kate's fears had been realized.

Anthony Bridgerton had asked Edwina to dance.

Even worse, Edwina had accepted.

Even worse, Mary was gazing at the couple as if she'd like to reserve a church that minute.

"Will you stop that?" Kate hissed, poking her step-mother in the ribs.

"Stop what?"

"Looking at them like that!"

Mary blinked. "Like what?"

"Like you're planning the wedding breakfast."

"Oh." Mary's cheeks turned pink. A guilty sort of pink.

"Mary!"

"Well, I might have been," Mary admitted. "And what's wrong with that, I might ask? He'd be a superb catch for Edwina."

"Were you listening this afternoon in the drawing room? It's bad enough that Edwina has any number of rakes and rogues sniffing about her. You cannot imagine the amount of time it has taken me to sort the good suitors from the bad. But Bridgerton!" Kate shuddered. "He's quite possibly the worst rake in all London. You cannot want her to marry a man like him."

"Don't you presume to tell me what I can and cannot do, Katharine Grace Sheffield," Mary said sharply, stiffening her spine until she'd straightened to her full height—which was still a full head shorter than Kate. "I am still your mother. Well, your stepmother. And that counts for something."

Kate immediately felt like a worm. Mary was all she'd ever known as a mother, and she'd never, not even once, made Kate feel any less her daughter than Edwina was. She'd tucked Kate into bed at night, told her stories, kissed her, hugged her, helped her through the awkward years between childhood and adulthood. The only thing she had not done was ask Kate to call her "Mother."

"It counts," Kate said in a quiet voice, letting her gaze fall shamefully down to her feet. "It counts for a lot. And you *are* my mother. In every way that matters."

Mary stared at her for a long moment, then started to blink rather furiously. "Oh, dear," she choked out, reaching into her reticule for a handkerchief. "Now you've gone and turned me into a watering pot."

"I'm sorry," Kate murmured. "Oh, here, turn around so no one sees you. There you are."

Mary pulled out a white square of linen and dabbed at her eyes, the exact same blue as Edwina's. "I do love you, Kate. You know that, don't you?"

"Of course!" Kate exclaimed, shocked that Mary would even ask. "And you know . . . you know that I . . ."

"I know." Mary patted her arm. "Of course I know. It's just that when you agree to be mother to a child you haven't borne, your responsibility is twice as great. You must work even harder to ensure that child's happiness and welfare."

"Oh, Mary, I do love you. And I love Edwina."

At the mention of Edwina's name, they both turned and looked out across the ballroom at her, dancing prettily with the viscount. As usual, Edwina was a vision of petite loveliness. Her blond hair was swept atop her head, a few stray curls left to frame her face, and her form was the epitome of grace as she moved through the steps of the dance.

The viscount, Kate noted with irritation, was blindingly handsome. Dressed in stark black and white, he eschewed the garish colors that had become popular among the more foppish members of the *ton*. He was tall, stood straight and proud, and had thick chestnut hair that tended to fall forward over his brow.

He was, on the surface at least, everything man was meant to be.

"They make a handsome couple, don't they?" Mary murmured.

Kate bit her tongue. She actually bit her tongue.

"He's a trifle tall for her, but I don't see that as an insurmountable obstacle, do you?"

Kate clasped her hands together and let her nails bite into her skin. It said a great deal about the strength of her grip that she could feel them all the way through her kid gloves.

Mary smiled. A rather sly smile, Kate thought. She gave her stepmother a suspicious look.

"He dances well, don't you think?" Mary asked.

"He is not going to marry Edwina!" Kate burst out.

Mary's smile slid straight into a grin. "I was wondering how long you'd manage to hold your silence."

"Far longer than was my natural inclination," Kate retorted, practically biting each word.

"Yes, that much was clear."

"Mary, you know he is not the sort of man we want for Edwina."

Mary cocked her head slightly to the side and raised her brows. "I believe the question ought to be whether he is the sort of man *Edwina* wants for Edwina."

"He's not that, either!" Kate replied heatedly. "Just this afternoon she told me that she wanted to marry a scholar. A scholar!" She jerked her head toward the dark-haired cretin dancing with her sister. "Does he look like a scholar to you?"

"No, but then again, you don't look particularly like an accomplished watercolorist, and yet I know that you are." Mary smirked a bit, which needled Kate to no end, and waited for her reply.

"I'll allow," Kate said through clenched teeth, "that one ought not judge a person merely on his outer appearance, but surely you must agree. From all that we have heard of him, he does not seem the sort to spend his afternoons bent over musty books in a library."

"Perhaps not," Mary mused, "but I had a lovely chat with his mother earlier this evening."

"His mother?" Kate fought to follow the conversation. "What has that to do with anything?"

Mary shrugged. "I find it difficult to believe that such a gracious and intelligent lady could have raised anything but the finest of gentlemen, regardless of his reputation."

"But Mary—"

"When you are a mother," she said loftily, "you will understand what I mean."

"But—"

"Have I told you," Mary said, the purposeful tone of her voice indicating that she'd meant to interrupt, "how lovely you look in that green gauze? I'm so glad we chose it."

Kate looked dumbly down at her dress, wondering why on earth Mary had changed the subject so suddenly.

"The color suits you well. Lady Whistledown shall not be calling you a singed blade of grass in Friday's column!"

Kate stared at Mary in dismay. Perhaps her stepmother had become overheated. It *was* crowded in the ballroom, and the air had grown thick.

Then she felt Mary's finger jabbing her directly below her left shoulder blade, and she knew something else was afoot entirely.

"Mr. Bridgerton!" Mary suddenly exclaimed, sounding as gleeful as a young girl.

Horrified, Kate jerked her head up to see a startlingly handsome man approach them. A startlingly handsome man who looked startlingly like the viscount currently dancing with her sister.

She swallowed. It was either that or let her jaw hang open.

"Mr. Bridgerton!" Mary said again. "How nice to see you. This is my daughter Katharine."

He took her limp, gloved hand and brushed an airy kiss across her knuckles. So airy, in fact, that Kate rather suspected he hadn't kissed her at all.

"Miss Sheffield," he murmured.

"Kate," Mary continued, "this is Mr. Colin Bridgerton. I met him earlier this evening while I was talking with his mother, Lady Bridgerton." She turned to Colin and beamed. "Such a lovely lady."

He grinned back. "We think so."

Mary tittered. Tittered! Kate thought she might gag.

"Kate," Mary said again, "Mr. Bridgerton is brother to the viscount. Who is dancing with Edwina," she added unnecessarily.

"I gathered," Kate replied.

Colin Bridgerton shot her a sideways glance, and she knew instantly that he had not missed the vague sarcasm in her tone.

"It is a pleasure to meet you, Miss Sheffield," he said politely. "I do hope you will favor me with one of your dances this evening."

"I— Of course." She cleared her throat. "I would be honored."

"Kate," Mary said, nudging her softly, "show him your dance card."

"Oh! Yes, of course." Kate fumbled for her dance card, which was tied prettily to her wrist with a green ribbon. That she had to fumble for anything actually tied to her body was a bit alarming, but Kate decided to blame her lack of composure on the sudden and unexpected appearance of a heretofore unknown Bridgerton brother.

That, and the unfortunate fact that even under the best of circumstances she was never the most graceful girl in the room.

Colin filled his name in for one of the dances later that evening, then asked if she might like to walk with him to the lemonade table.

"Go, go," Mary said, before Kate could reply. "Don't worry about me. I'll be just fine without you."

"I can bring you back a glass," Kate offered, trying to figure out if it was possible to glare at her stepmother without Mr. Bridgerton noticing.

"Not necessary. I really should get back to my position with all the other chaperones and mamas." Mary whipped her head around frantically until she spied a familiar face. "Oh, look, there is Mrs. Featherington. I must be off. Portia! Portia!"

Kate watched her stepmother's rapidly retreating form

for a moment before turning back to Mr. Bridgerton. "I think," she said dryly, "that she doesn't want any lemonade."

A sparkle of humor glinted in his emerald green eyes. "Either that or she's planning to run all the way to Spain to pick the lemons herself."

Despite herself, Kate laughed. She didn't want to like Mr. Colin Bridgerton. She didn't much want to like any Bridgerton after all she'd read about the viscount in the newspaper. But she allowed that it probably wasn't fair to judge a man based on his brother's misdeeds, so she forced herself to relax a bit.

"And are you thirsty," she asked, "or were you merely being polite?"

"I am always polite," he said with a wicked grin, "but I am thirsty as well."

Kate took one look at that grin, lethally combined with those devastating green eyes, and nearly groaned. "You are a rake as well," she said with a sigh.

Colin choked—on what, she did not know, but he choked nonetheless. "I beg your pardon?"

Kate's face flushed as she realized with horror that she'd spoken aloud. "No, it is I who should beg your pardon. Please forgive me. That was unforgivably rude."

"No, no," he said quickly, looking terribly interested and not a little bit amused, "do continue."

Kate swallowed. There was really no way to get out of it now. "I was merely—" She cleared her throat. "If I might be frank . . ."

He nodded, his sly grin telling her that he could not imagine her being anything *but* frank.

Kate cleared her throat yet again. Really, this was getting ridiculous. She was starting to sound as if she'd swallowed a toad. "It had occurred to me that you might be rather like your brother, that is all."

"My brother?"

"The viscount," she said, thinking it must be obvious.

"I have three brothers," he explained.

"Oh." Now she felt stupid. "I'm sorry."

"I'm sorry, too," he said with great feeling. "Most of the time they're a dreadful nuisance."

Kate had to cough to cover up her small gasp of surprise.

"But at least you were not comparing me to Gregory," he said with a dramatic sigh of relief. He shot her a cheeky, sideways look. "He's thirteen."

Kate caught the smile in his eyes and realized he'd been bamming her all along. This was not a man who wished his brothers off to perdition. "You're rather devoted to your family, aren't you?" she asked.

His eyes, which had been laughing throughout the conversation, turned dead serious without even a blink. "Utterly."

"As am I," Kate said pointedly.

"And that means?"

"It means," she said, knowing she should hold her tongue but speaking anyway, "that I will not allow anyone to break my sister's heart."

Colin remained silent for a moment, slowly turning his head to watch his brother and Edwina, who were just then finishing up their dance. "I see," he murmured.

"Do you?"

"Oh, indeed." They arrived at the lemonade table, and he reached out and took two glasses, handing one to her. She'd already had three glasses of lemonade that evening, a fact of which she was sure Mary had been aware before she'd insisted Kate have some more. But it was hot in the ballroom—it was always hot in ballrooms—and she was thirsty again.

Colin took a leisurely sip, watching her over the rim of his glass, then said, "My brother has it in his mind to settle down this year."

Two could play at this game, Kate thought. She took a sip of her lemonade—slowly—before speaking. "Is that so?"

"I would certainly be in a position to know."

"He is reputed to be quite a rake."

Colin looked at her assessingly. "That is true."

"It is difficult to imagine so notorious a rogue settling down with one woman and finding happiness in marriage."

"You seem to have given such a scenario a great deal of thought, Miss Sheffield."

She leveled a frank stare directly at his face. "Your brother is not the first man of questionable character to court my sister, Mr. Bridgerton. And I assure you, I do not take my sister's happiness lightly."

"Surely any girl would find happiness in marriage to a wealthy and titled gentleman. Isn't that what a season in London is all about?"

"Perhaps," Kate allowed, "but I'm afraid that line of thinking does not address the true problem at hand."

"Which is?"

"Which is that a husband can break a heart with far greater intensity than a mere suitor." She smiled—a small, knowing sort of smile—then added, "Don't you think?"

"Having never been married, I am certainly not in a position to speculate."

"Shame, shame, Mr. Bridgerton. That was the worst sort of evasion."

"Was it? I rather thought it might be the best. I am clearly losing my touch."

"That, I fear, will never be a worry." Kate finished the rest of her lemonade. It was a small glass; Lady Hartside, their hostess, was notoriously stingy.

"You are far too generous," he said.

She smiled, a real smile this time. "I am rarely accused of that, Mr. Bridgerton."

He laughed. Right out loud in the middle of the ballroom. Kate realized with discomfort that they were suddenly the object of numerous curious stares.

"You," he said, still sounding most heartily amused, "must meet my brother."

"The viscount?" she asked with disbelief.

"Well, you might enjoy Gregory's company as well," he allowed, "but as I said, he is only thirteen and likely to put a frog on your chair."

"And the viscount?"

"Is not likely to put a frog on your chair," he said with an utterly straight face.

How Kate managed not to laugh she would never know. Keeping her lips completely straight and serious, she replied, "I see. He has a great deal to recommend him, then."

Colin grinned. "He's not such a bad sort."

"I am much relieved. I shall begin planning the wedding breakfast immediately."

Colin's mouth fell open. "I didn't mean— You shouldn't— That is to say, such a move would be premature—"

Kate took pity on him and said, "I was joking."

His face flushed slightly. "Of course."

"Now, if you'll excuse me, I must make my farewell."

He raised a brow. "Not leaving so early, are you, Miss Sheffield?"

"Not at all." But she wasn't about to tell him she had to go relieve herself. Four glasses of lemonade tended to do that to a body. "I promised a friend I would meet her for a moment."

"It has been a pleasure." He executed a smart bow. "May I see you to your destination?"

"No, thank you. I shall be quite all right on my own." And with a smile over her shoulder, she made her retreat from the ballroom.

Colin Bridgerton watched her go with a thoughtful expression, then made his way to his older brother, who was leaning against a wall, arms crossed in an almost belligerent manner.

"Anthony!" he called out, slapping his brother on the back. "How was your dance with the lovely Miss Sheffield?"

"She'll do," was Anthony's terse reply. They both knew what that meant.

"Really?" Colin's lips twitched ever so slightly. "You should meet the sister, then."

"I beg your pardon?"

"Her sister," Colin repeated, starting to laugh. "You simply must meet her sister."

Twenty minutes later, Anthony was confident he'd gotten the whole story on Edwina Sheffield from Colin. And it seemed that the road to Edwina's heart and hand in marriage lay squarely through her sister.

Edwina Sheffield apparently would not marry without the approval of her older sister. According to Colin, this was common knowledge, and had been for at least a week, ever since Edwina had made an announcement to this effect at the annual Smythe-Smith musicale. The Bridgerton brothers had all missed this momentous statement, as they avoided Smythe-Smith musicales like the plague (as did anyone with any affection for Bach, Mozart, or music in any form.)

Edwina's older sister, one Katharine Sheffield, more commonly known as Kate, was also making her debut this year, even though she was reputed to be at least one and twenty. Such timing led Anthony to believe that the Sheffields must be among the less wealthy ranks of the *ton*, a fact which suited him nicely. He had no need of a bride with a great dowry, and a bride without one might have more need of *him*.

Anthony believed in using all of his advantages.

Unlike Edwina, the elder Miss Sheffield had not immediately taken the *ton* by storm. According to Colin, she was generally well liked, but she lacked Edwina's dazzling beauty. She was tall where Edwina was tiny, and dark where Edwina was fair. She also lacked Edwina's dazzling grace. Again, according to Colin (who, though recently arrived in London for the season, was a veritable font of knowledge and gossip), more than one gentleman had reported sore feet after a dance with Katharine Sheffield.

The entire situation seemed a bit absurd to Anthony. After all, who had ever heard of a girl requiring her sister's approval for a husband? A father, yes, a brother, or even a mother, but a sister? It was unfathomable. And furthermore, it seemed odd that Edwina would look to Katharine for guidance when Katharine clearly did not know what she was about in matters of the *ton*.

But Anthony didn't particularly feel like searching out another suitable candidate to court, so he conveniently decided this simply meant that family was important to Edwina. And since family was all-important to him, this was one more indication that she would make an excellent choice as a wife.

So now it appeared that all he had to do was charm the sister. And how difficult could that be?

"You'll have no trouble winning her over," Colin predicted, a confident smile lighting his face. "No trouble at all. A shy, aging spinster? She's probably never received attentions from such a man as you. She'll never know what hit her."

"I don't want her to fall in love with me," Anthony retorted. "I just want her to recommend me to her sister."

"You can't fail," Colin said. "You simply can't fail. Trust me, I spent a few minutes in conversation with her earlier this evening, and she could not say enough about you."

"Good." Anthony pushed himself up off the wall and gazed out with an air of determination. "Now, where is she? I need you to introduce us."

Colin scanned the room for a minute or so, then said, "Ah, there she is. She's coming this way, as a matter of fact. What a marvelous coincidence."

Anthony was coming to believe that nothing within five yards of his younger brother was ever a coincidence, but he followed his gaze nonetheless. "Which one is she?"

"In the green," Colin said, motioning toward her with a barely perceptible nod of his chin.

She was not at all what he'd expected, Anthony realized as he watched her pick her way through the crowds. She was certainly no ape-leading amazon; it was only when compared to Edwina, who barely touched five feet, that she would appear so tall. In fact, Miss Katharine Sheffield was quite pleasant-looking, with thick, medium brown hair and dark eyes. Her skin was pale, her lips pink, and she held herself with an air of confidence he could not help but find attractive.

She would certainly never be considered a diamond of the first water like her sister, but Anthony didn't see why she shouldn't be able to find a husband of her own. Perhaps after he married Edwina he'd provide a dowry for her. It seemed the very least a man could do.

Beside him, Colin strode forward, pushing through the crowd. "Miss Sheffield! Miss Sheffield!"

Anthony swept along in Colin's wake, mentally preparing himself to charm Edwina's older sister. An underappreciated spinster, was she? He'd have her eating out of his hand in no time.

"Miss Sheffield," Colin was saying, "what a delight to see you again."

She looked a bit perplexed, and Anthony didn't blame her. Colin was making it sound as if they'd bumped into each other accidentally, when they all knew he'd trampled at least a half dozen people to reach her side.

"And it's lovely to see you again as well, sir," she replied wryly. "And so unexpectedly soon after our last encounter."

Anthony smiled to himself. She had a sharper wit than he'd been led to believe.

Colin grinned winningly, and Anthony had the distinct

and unsettling impression that his brother was up to something. "I can't explain why," Colin said to Miss Sheffield, "but it suddenly seemed imperative that I introduce you to my brother."

She looked abruptly to Colin's right and stiffened as her gaze settled on Anthony. In fact, she rather looked as if she'd just swallowed an antidote.

This, Anthony thought, was odd.

"How kind of you," Miss Sheffield murmured—between her teeth.

"Miss Sheffield," Colin continued brightly, motioning to Anthony, "my brother Anthony, Viscount Bridgerton. Anthony, Miss Katharine Sheffield. I believe you made the acquaintance of her sister earlier this evening."

"Indeed," Anthony said, becoming aware of an overwhelming desire—no, *need*—to strangle his brother.

Miss Sheffield bobbed a quick, awkward curtsy. "Lord Bridgerton," she said, "it is an honor to make your acquaintance."

Colin made a noise that sounded suspiciously like a snort. Or maybe a laugh. Or maybe both.

And Anthony suddenly *knew*. One look at his brother's face should have given it all away. This was no shy, retiring, underappreciated spinster. And whatever she had said to Colin earlier that evening, it had contained no compliments about Anthony.

Fratricide was legal in England, wasn't it? If not, it damn well should have been.

Anthony belatedly realized that Miss Sheffield had held out her hand to him, as was only polite. He took it and brushed a light kiss across her gloved knuckles. "Miss Sheffield," he murmured unthinkingly, "you are as lovely as your sister."

If she had seemed uncomfortable before, her bearing now turned downright hostile. And Anthony realized with a mental slap that he'd said *exactly* the wrong thing. Of course he should not have compared her to her sister.

It was the one compliment she could never have believed.

"And you, Lord Bridgerton," she replied in a tone that could have frozen champagne, "are almost as handsome as your brother."

Colin snorted again, only this time it sounded as if he were being strangled.

"Are you all right?" Miss Sheffield asked.

"He's fine," Anthony barked.

She ignored him, keeping her attention on Colin. "Are you certain?"

Colin nodded furiously. "Tickle in my throat."

"Or perhaps a guilty conscience?" Anthony suggested.

Colin turned deliberately from his brother to Kate. "I think I might need another glass of lemonade," he gasped.

"Or maybe," said Anthony, "something stronger. Hemlock, perhaps?"

Miss Sheffield clapped a hand over her mouth, presumably to stifle a burst of horrified laughter.

"Lemonade will do just fine," Colin returned smoothly.

"Would you like me to fetch you a glass?" she asked. Anthony noticed that she'd already stepped out with one foot, looking for any excuse to flee.

Colin shook his head. "No, no, I'm quite capable. But I do believe I had reserved this next dance with you, Miss Sheffield."

"I shall not hold you to it," she said with a wave of her hand.

"Oh, but I could not live with myself were I to leave you unattended," he replied.

Anthony could see Miss Sheffield growing worried at the devilish gleam in Colin's eye. He took a rather uncharitable pleasure in this. His reaction was, he knew, a touch out of proportion. But something about this Miss Katharine Sheffield sparked his temper and made him positively *itch* to do battle with her.

And win. That much went without saying.

"Anthony," Colin said, sounding so deucedly innocent and earnest that it was all Anthony could do not to kill him on the spot, "you're not engaged for this dance, are you?"

Anthony said nothing, just glared at him.

"Good. Then you will dance with Miss Sheffield."

"I'm sure that's not necessary," the woman in question blurted out.

Anthony glared at his brother, then for good measure at Miss Sheffield, who was looking at him as if he'd just despoiled ten virgins in her presence.

"Oh, but it is," Colin said with great drama, ignoring the optical daggers being hurled across their little threesome. "I could never dream of abandoning a young lady in her hour of need. How"—he shuddered—"ungentlemanly."

Anthony thought seriously about pursuing some ungentlemanly behavior himself. Perhaps planting his fist in Colin's face.

"I assure you," Miss Sheffield said quickly, "that being left to my own devices would be far preferable to dan—"

Enough, Anthony thought savagely, was really enough. His own brother had already played him for a fool; he was not going to stand idly by while he was insulted by Edwina's sharp-tongued spinster sister. He laid a heavy hand on Miss Sheffield's arm and said, "Allow me to prevent you from making a grievous mistake, Miss Sheffield."

She stiffened. How, he did not know; her back was already ramrod straight. "I beg your pardon," she said.

"I believe," he said smoothly, "that you were about to say something you would soon regret."

"No," she said, sounding deliberately thoughtful, "I don't think regrets were in my future."

"They will be," he said ominously. And then he grabbed her arm and practically dragged her onto the ballroom floor.

Chapter 3

Viscount Bridgerton was also seen dancing with Miss Katharine Sheffield, elder sister to the fair Edwina. This can only mean one thing, as it has not escaped the notice of This Author that the elder Miss Sheffield has been in much demand on the dance floor ever since the younger Miss Sheffield made her bizarre and unprecedented announcement at the Smythe-Smith musicale last week.

Whoever heard of a girl needing her sister's permission to choose a husband?

And perhaps more importantly, whoever decided that the words "Smythe-Smith" and "musicale" might be used in the same sentence? This Author has attended one of these gatherings in the past, and heard nothing that might ethically be termed "music."

LADY WHISTLEDOWN'S SOCIETY PAPERS, 22 APRIL 1814

There was really nothing she could do, Kate realized with dismay. He was a viscount, and she was a mere nobody from Somerset, and they were both in the middle of a crowded ballroom. It didn't matter if she'd disliked him on sight. She *had* to dance with him.

"There is no need to drag me," she hissed.

He made a great show of loosening his grip.

Kate ground her teeth together and swore to herself that this man would never take her sister as his bride. His manner was too cold, too superior. He was, she thought a touch unfairly, too handsome as well, with velvety brown eyes that matched his hair to perfection. He was tall, certainly over six feet, although probably not by more than an inch, and his lips, while classically beautiful (Kate had studied enough art to regard herself qualified to make such a judgment) were tight at the corners, as if he did not know how to smile.

"Now then," he said, once their feet began to move in the familiar steps, "suppose you tell me why you hate me."

Kate trod on his foot. Lord, he was direct. "I beg your pardon?"

"There is no need to maim me, Miss Sheffield."

"It was an accident, I assure you." And it *was,* even if she didn't really mind this particular example of her lack of grace.

"Why," he mused, "do I find I have difficulty believing you?"

Honesty, Kate quickly decided, would be her best strategy. If he could be direct, well then, so could she. "Probably," she answered with a wicked smile, "because you know that had it occurred to me to step on your foot on purpose, I would have done so."

He threw back his head and laughed. It was not the reaction she'd been either expecting or hoping for. Come to think of it, she had no idea what sort of reaction she'd been hoping for, but this *certainly* wasn't what she'd been expecting.

"Will you stop, my lord?" she whispered urgently. "People are starting to stare."

"People started to stare two minutes ago," he returned. "It's not often a man such as I dances with a woman such as you."

As barbs went, this one was well aimed, but sadly for him, also incorrect. "Not true," she replied jauntily. "You are certainly not the first of Edwina's besotted idiots to attempt to gain her favor through me."

He grinned. "Not suitors, but idiots?"

She caught his gaze with hers and was surprised to find true mirth in his eyes. "Surely you're not going to hand me such a delicious piece of bait as that, my lord?"

"And yet you did not take it," he mused.

Kate looked down to see if there was some way she might discreetly step on his foot again.

"I have very thick boots, Miss Sheffield," he said.

Her head snapped back up in surprise.

One corner of his mouth curved up in a mockery of a smile. "And quick eyes as well."

"Apparently so. I shall have to watch my step around you, to be sure."

"My goodness," he drawled, "was that a compliment? I might expire from the shock of it."

"If you'd like to consider that a compliment, I give you leave to do so," she said airily. "You're not likely to receive many more."

"You wound me, Miss Sheffield."

"Does that mean that your skin is not as thick as your boots?"

"Oh, not nearly."

She felt herself laugh before she realized she was amused. "That I find difficult to believe."

He waited for her smile to melt away, then said, "You did not answer my question. Why do you hate me?"

A rush of air slipped through Kate's lips. She hadn't expected him to repeat the question. Or at least she'd hoped that he would not. "I do not hate you, my lord," she replied, choosing her words with great care. "I do not even know you."

"Knowing is rarely a prerequisite for hating," he said softly, his eyes settling on hers with lethal steadiness. "Come now, Miss Sheffield, you don't seem a coward to me. Answer the question."

Kate held silent for a full minute. It was true, she had not been predisposed to like the man. She *certainly* wasn't about to give her blessing to his courtship of Edwina. She didn't believe for one second that reformed rakes made the best husbands. She wasn't even sure that a rake could be properly reformed in the first place.

But he might have been able to overcome her preconceptions. He could have been charming and sincere and straightforward, and been able to convince her that the stories about him in *Whistledown* were an exaggeration, that he was not the worst rogue London had seen since the turn of the century. He might have convinced her that he held to a code of honor, that he was a man of principles and honesty . . .

If he hadn't gone and compared her to Edwina.

For nothing could have been more obvious a lie. She knew she wasn't an antidote; her face and form were pleasing enough. But there was simply no way she could be compared to Edwina in this measure and emerge as her equal. Edwina was truly a diamond of the first water, and Kate could never be more than average and unremarkable.

And if this man was saying otherwise, then he had some ulterior motive, because it was obvious he wasn't blind.

He could have offered her any other empty compliment and she would have accepted it as a gentleman's polite conversation. She might have even been flattered if his words had struck anywhere close to the truth. But to compare her to Edwina . . .

Kate adored her sister. She truly did. And she knew better than anyone that Edwina's heart was as beautiful and radiant as her face. She didn't like to think herself jealous, but still . . . somehow the comparison stung right to the core.

"I do not hate you," she finally replied. Her eyes were trained on his chin, but she had no patience for cowardice, especially within herself, so she forced herself to meet his gaze when she added, "But I find I cannot like you."

Something in his eyes told her that he appreciated her stark honesty. "And why is that?" he asked softly.

"May I be frank?"

His lips twitched. "Please do."

"You are dancing with me right now because you wish to court my sister. This does not bother me," she hastened to assure him. "I am well used to receiving attentions from Edwina's suitors."

Her mind was clearly not on her feet. Anthony pulled his foot out of the way of hers before she could injure him again. He noticed with interest that she was back to referring to them as suitors rather than idiots. "Please continue," he murmured.

"You are not the sort of man I would wish my sister to marry," she said simply. Her manner was direct, and her intelligent brown eyes never left his. "You are a rake. You are a rogue. You are, in fact, notorious for being both. I would not allow my sister within ten feet of you."

"And yet," he said with a wicked little smile, "I waltzed with her earlier this evening."

"An act which shall not be repeated, I can assure you."

"And is it your place to decide Edwina's fate?"

"Edwina trusts my judgment," she said primly.

"I see," he said in what he hoped was his most mysterious manner. "That is very interesting. I thought Edwina was an adult."

"Edwina is but seventeen years old!"

"And you are so ancient at, what, twenty years of age?"

"Twenty-one," she bit off.

"Ah, that makes you a veritable expert on men, and husbands in particular. Especially since you have been married yourself, yes?"

"You know I am unwed," she ground out.

Anthony stifled the urge to smile. Good Lord, but it was *fun* baiting the elder Miss Sheffield. "I think," he said, keeping his words slow and deliberate, "that you have found it relatively easy to manage most of the men who have come knocking on your sister's door. Is that true?"

She kept her stony silence.

"Is it?"

Finally she gave him one curt nod.

"I thought so," he murmured. "You seem the sort who would."

She glared at him with such intensity that it was all he could do to keep from laughing. If he weren't dancing, he probably would have stroked his chin in an affectation of deep thought. But since his hands were otherwise engaged, he had to settle for a ponderous tilt of his head, combined with an arch raise of his eyebrows. "But I also think," he added, "that you made a grave mistake when you thought to manage *me*."

Kate's lips were set in a grim, straight line, but she managed to say, "I do not seek to manage you, Lord Bridgerton. I only seek to keep you away from my sister."

"Which just goes to show, Miss Sheffield, how very little you know of men. At least of the rakish, roguish variety." He leaned in closer, letting his hot breath brush against her cheek.

She shivered. He'd known she'd shiver.

He smiled wickedly. "There is very little we relish more than a challenge."

The music drew to a close, leaving them standing in the middle of the ballroom floor, facing one another. Anthony took her arm, but before he led her back to the perimeter of the room, he put his lips very close to her ear and whispered, "And you, Miss Sheffield, have issued to me a most delicious challenge."

Kate stepped on his foot. Hard. Enough to make him let out a small, decidedly unrakish, unroguish squeak.

When he glared at her, though, she just shrugged and said, "It was my only defense."

His eyes darkened. "You, Miss Sheffield, are a menace."

"And you, Lord Bridgerton, need thicker boots."

His grasp tightened on her arm. "Before I return you to the sanctuary of the chaperones and spinsters, there is one thing we need to make clear."

Kate held her breath. She did not like the hard tone of his voice.

"I am going to court your sister. And should I decide that she will make a suitable Lady Bridgerton, I will make her my wife."

Kate whipped her head up to face him, fire flashing in her eyes. "And I suppose, then, that you think it is *your* place to decide Edwina's fate. Do not forget, my lord, that even if you decide she will make a *suitable*"—she sneered the word—"Lady Bridgerton, she might choose otherwise."

He looked down at her with the confidence of a male who is never crossed. "Should I decide to ask Edwina, she will not say no."

"Are you trying to tell me that no woman has ever been able to resist you?"

He did not answer, just raised one supercilious brow and let her draw her own conclusions.

Kate wrenched her arm free and strode back to her stepmother, shaking with fury, resentment, and not a little bit of fear.

Because she had an awful feeling that he did not lie. And if he really did turn out to be irresistible . . .

Kate shuddered. She and Edwina were going to be in big, big trouble.

The next afternoon was like any following a major ball. The Sheffields' drawing room was filled to bursting with flower bouquets, each one accompanied by a crisp white card bearing the name, "Edwina Sheffield."

A simple "Miss Sheffield" would have sufficed, Kate thought with a grimace, but she supposed one couldn't really fault Edwina's suitors for wanting to make certain the flowers went to the correct Miss Sheffield.

Not that *anyone* was likely to make a mistake on that measure. Floral arrangements generally went to Edwina. In fact, there was nothing general about it; every bouquet that had arrived at the Sheffield residence in the last month had gone to Edwina.

Kate liked to think she had the last laugh, however. Most of the flowers made Edwina sneeze, so they tended to end up in Kate's chamber, anyway.

"You beautiful thing," she said, lovingly fingering a fine orchid. "I think you belong right on my bedstand. And you"—she leaned forward and sniffed at a bouquet of perfect white roses—"you will look smashing on my dressing table."

"Do you always talk to flowers?"

Kate whirled around at the sound of a deep male voice. Good heavens, it was Lord Bridgerton, looking sinfully handsome in a blue morning coat. What the devil was *he* doing here?

No sense in not asking.

"What the dev—" She caught herself just in time. She would not let this man reduce her to cursing aloud, no matter how often she did it in her head. "What are *you* doing here?"

He raised a brow as he adjusted the huge bouquet of flowers he had tucked under his arm. Pink roses, she noted. Perfect buds. They were lovely. Simple and elegant. Exactly the sort of thing she'd choose for herself.

"I believe it's customary for suitors to call upon young women, yes?" he murmured. "Or did I misplace my etiquette book?"

"I meant," Kate growled, "how did you get in? No one alerted me to your arrival."

He cocked his head toward the hall. "The usual manner. I knocked on your front door."

Kate's look of irritation at his sarcasm did not prevent him from continuing with, "Amazingly enough, your butler answered. Then I gave him my card, he took a look at it, and showed me to the drawing room. Much as I'd like to claim some sort of devious, underhanded subterfuge," he continued, maintaining a rather impressively supercilious tone, "it was actually quite aboveboard and straightforward."

"Infernal butler," Kate muttered. "He's supposed to see if we're 'at home' before showing you in."

"Maybe he had previous instructions that you would be 'at home' for me under any circumstances."

She bristled. "I gave him no such instructions."

"No," Lord Bridgerton said with a chuckle, "I wouldn't have thought so."

"And I know Edwina didn't."

He smiled. "Perhaps your mother?"

Of course. "Mary," she groaned, a world of accusation in the single word.

"You call her by her given name?" he asked politely.

She nodded. "She's actually my stepmother. Although she's really all I know. She married my father when I was but three. I don't know why I still call her Mary." She gave her head a little shake as her shoulders lifted into a perplexed shrug. "I just do."

His brown eyes remained fixed on her face, and she realized she'd just let this man—her nemesis, really—into a small corner of her life. She felt the words "I'm sorry" bubbling on her tongue—a reflexive reaction, she supposed, for having spoken too freely. But she didn't want to apologize to this man for anything, so instead she just said, "Edwina is out, I'm afraid, so your visit was for nothing."

"Oh, I don't know about that," he replied. He grasped

the bouquet of flowers—which had been tucked under his right arm—with his other hand, and as he brought it forward Kate saw that it was not one massive bouquet, but three smaller ones.

"This," he said, putting one of the bouquets down on a side table, "is for Edwina. And this"—he did the same with the second—"is for your mother."

He was left with a single bouquet. Kate stood frozen with shock, unable to take her eyes off the perfect pink blooms. She knew what he had to be about, that the only reason he'd included her in the gesture was to impress Edwina, but blast it, no one had ever brought her flowers before, and she hadn't known until that very moment how badly she'd wanted someone to do so.

"These," he said finally, holding out the final arrangement of pink roses, "are for you."

"Thank you," she said hesitantly, taking them into her arms. "They're lovely." She leaned down to sniff them, sighing with pleasure at the thick scent. Glancing back up, she added, "It was very thoughtful of you to think of Mary and me."

He nodded graciously. "It was my pleasure. I must confess, a suitor for my sister's hand once did the same for my mother, and I don't believe I've ever seen her more delighted."

"Your mother or your sister?"

He smiled at her pert question. "Both."

"And what happened to this suitor?" Kate asked.

Anthony's grin turned devilish in the extreme. "He married my sister."

"Hmmph. Don't think history is likely to repeat itself. But—" Kate coughed, not particularly wanting to be honest with him but quite incapable of doing anything otherwise. "But the flowers are truly lovely, and—and it was a lovely gesture on your part." She swallowed. This wasn't easy for her. "And I do appreciate them."

He leaned forward slightly, his dark eyes positively melting. "A kind sentence," he mused. "And directed at me, no less. There now, that wasn't so difficult, was it?"

Kate went from bending lovingly over the flowers to standing uncomfortably straight in an instant. "You do seem to have a knack for saying the *exact* wrong thing."

"Only where you're concerned, my dear Miss Sheffield. Other women, I assure you, hang on my every word."

"So I've read," she muttered.

His eyes lit up. "Is that where you've developed your opinions of me? Of course! The estimable Lady Whistle-down. I should have known. Lud, I'd like to strangle the woman."

"I find her rather intelligent and quite on the mark," Kate said primly.

"You would," he returned.

"Lord Bridgerton," Kate ground out, "I'm sure you did not come calling to insult me. May I leave a message for Edwina for you?"

"I think not. I don't particularly trust that it would reach her unadulterated."

That was really too much. "I would *never* stoop to interfering with another person's correspondence," Kate somehow managed to say. Her entire body was shaking with rage, and if she'd been a less controlled sort of woman, her hands would surely have been wrapped around his throat. "How dare you imply otherwise."

"When all is said and done, Miss Sheffield," he said with annoying calmness, "I really don't know you very well. What I do know consists of your fervent avowals that I will never find myself within ten feet of your sister's saintly presence. You tell me, would *you* feel confident to leave a note if you were me?"

"If you are attempting to gain my sister's favor through me," Kate replied icily, "you are not doing a very good job of it."

"I'm aware of that," he said. "I really shouldn't provoke

you. It's not very well done of me, is it? But I'm afraid I just can't help myself." He grinned roguishly and held up his hands in a helpless manner. "What can I say? You do something to me, Miss Sheffield."

His smile, Kate realized with dismay, was truly a force to be reckoned with. She suddenly felt faint. A seat . . . yes, what she needed to do was sit down. "Please, have a seat," she said, waving at the blue damask sofa as she scrambled across the room to a chair. She didn't particularly want him to linger, but she couldn't very well sit without offering him a seat as well, and her legs were starting to feel *awfully* wobbly.

If the viscount thought oddly of her sudden burst of politeness, he did not say anything. Instead he removed a long black case off the sofa and placed it on a table, then sat down in its place. "Is that a musical instrument?" he queried, motioning to the case.

Kate nodded. "A flute."

"Do you play?"

She shook her head, then cocked her head slightly and nodded. "I'm trying to learn. I took it up just this year."

He nodded in reply, and that, apparently, was to be the end of the subject, because he then politely asked, "When do you expect Edwina to return?"

"Not for at least an hour, I should think. Mr. Berbrooke took her out for a ride in his curricle."

"Nigel Berbrooke?" He practically choked on the name.

"Yes, why?"

"The man has more hair than wit. A great deal more."

"But he's going bald," she couldn't resist pointing out.

He grimaced. "And if that doesn't prove my point, I don't know what will."

Kate had reached much the same conclusion about Mr. Berbrooke's intelligence (or lack thereof), but she said, "Isn't it considered bad form to insult one's fellow suitors?"

Anthony let out a little snort. "It wasn't an insult. It was the truth. He courted my sister last year. Or tried to. Daphne did her best to discourage him. He's a nice enough fellow, I'll grant you that, but not someone you'd want building you a boat were you stranded on a desert island."

Kate had a strange and unwelcome image of the viscount stranded on a desert island, clothes in tatters, skin kissed by the sun. It left her feeling uncomfortably warm.

Anthony cocked his head, regarding her with a quizzical gaze. "I say, Miss Sheffield, are you feeling all right?"

"Fine!" she practically barked. "Never better. You were saying?"

"You look a bit flushed." He leaned in, watching her closely. She really didn't look well.

Kate fanned herself. "It's a bit hot in here, don't you think?"

Anthony shook his head slowly. "Not at all."

She gazed longingly out the door. "I wonder where Mary is."

"Are you expecting her?"

"It's unlike her to leave me unchaperoned for so long," she explained.

Unchaperoned? The ramifications were frightening. Anthony had a sudden vision of being trapped into marriage with Miss Sheffield the elder, and it made him break out in a cold sweat. Kate was so unlike any debutante he'd ever met that he'd quite forgotten that they even needed a chaperone. "Perhaps she's not aware I'm here," he said quickly.

"Yes, that must be it." She sprang to her feet and crossed the room to the bellpull. Giving it a firm yank, she said, "I'll just ring for someone to alert her. I'm sure she won't want to miss you."

"Good. Perhaps she can keep us company while we wait for your sister to return."

Kate froze halfway back to her chair. "You're planning to wait for Edwina?"

He shrugged, enjoying her discomfort. "I have no other plans for the afternoon."

"But she might be hours!"

"An hour at most, I'm sure, and besides—" He cut himself off, noting the arrival of a maid in the doorway.

"You rang, miss?" the maid queried.

"Yes, thank you, Annie," Kate replied. "Would you please inform Mrs. Sheffield that we have a guest?"

The maid bobbed a curtsy and departed.

"I'm sure Mary will be down at any moment," Kate said, quite unable to stop tapping her foot. "Any minute now. I'm sure of it."

He just smiled in that annoying manner, looking terribly relaxed and comfortable on the sofa.

An awkward silence fell across the room. Kate offered him a tight smile. He just raised a brow in return.

"I'm sure she'll be here—"

"Any minute now," he finished for her, sounding heartily amused.

She sank back into her chair, trying not to grimace. She probably didn't succeed.

Just then a small commotion broke out in the hall—a few decidedly canine barks, followed by a high-pitched shriek of, "Newton! Newton! Stop that at once!"

"Newton?" the viscount queried.

"My dog," Kate explained, sighing as she rose to her feet. "He doesn't—"

"NEWTON!"

"—get along with Mary very well, I'm afraid." Kate moved to the door. "Mary? Mary?"

Anthony rose when Kate did, wincing as the dog let out three more earsplitting barks, which were immediately followed by another terrified shriek from Mary. "What is he," he muttered, "a mastiff?" It had to be a mastiff. Miss

Sheffield the elder seemed exactly the sort to keep a man-eating mastiff at her beck and call.

"No," Kate said, rushing out into the hall as Mary let out another shriek. "He's a—"

But Anthony missed her words. It didn't matter much, anyway, because one second later, in trotted the most benign-looking corgi he'd ever seen, with thick caramel-colored fur and a belly that almost dragged on the ground.

Anthony froze with surprise. *This* was the fearsome creature from the hall? "Good day, dog," he said firmly.

The dog stopped in its tracks, sat right down, and . . . Smiled?

Chapter 4

This Author was, sadly, unable to determine all the details, but there was a considerable to-do Thursday last near The Serpentine in Hyde Park involving Viscount Bridgerton, Mr. Nigel Berbrooke, both the Misses Sheffield, and an unnamed dog of indeterminate breed.

This Author was not an eyewitness, but all accounts seem to indicate that the unnamed dog emerged the victor.

LADY WHISTLEDOWN'S SOCIETY PAPERS, 25 APRIL 1814

Kate stumbled back into the drawing room, knocking arms with Mary as they both squeezed through the doorway at the same time. Newton was seated happily in the middle of the room, shedding on the blue-and-white rug as he grinned up at the viscount.

"I think he likes you," Mary said, somewhat accusingly.

"He likes you, too, Mary," Kate said. "The problem is that *you* don't like *him*."

"I'd like him better if he didn't try to accost me every time I come through the hall."

"I thought you said Mrs. Sheffield and the dog didn't get along," Lord Bridgerton said.

"They don't," Kate replied. "Well, they do. Well, they don't *and* they do."

"That clears things up immeasurably," he murmured.

Kate ignored his quiet sarcasm. "Newton adores Mary," she explained, "but Mary doesn't adore Newton."

"I'd adore him a bit more," Mary interrupted, "if he'd adore me a bit less."

"*So*," Kate continued determinedly, "poor Newton regards Mary as something of a challenge. So when he sees her . . ." She shrugged helplessly. "Well, I'm afraid he simply adores her *more*."

As if on cue, the dog caught sight of Mary and bounded straight over to her feet.

"Kate!" Mary exclaimed.

Kate rushed to her stepmother's side, just as Newton rose on his hind legs and planted his front paws just above Mary's knees. "Newton, down!" she scolded. "Bad dog. Bad dog."

The dog sat back down with a little whine.

"Kate," Mary said in an extremely no-nonsense voice, "that dog *must* be taken for a walk. Now."

"I had been planning to when the viscount arrived," Kate replied, motioning to the man across the room. Really, it was remarkable the number of things she could blame on the insufferable man if she put her mind to it.

"Oh!" Mary yelped. "I beg your pardon, my lord. How rude of me not to greet you."

"It is of no concern," he said smoothly. "You were a bit preoccupied upon your arrival."

"Yes," Mary grumbled, "that beastly dog. . . . Oh, but where are my manners? May we offer you tea? Something to eat? It is so kind of you to call upon us."

"No, thank you. I've just been enjoying your daughter's invigorating company while I await Miss Edwina's arrival."

"Ah, yes," Mary answered. "Edwina's off with Mr. Berbrooke, I believe. Isn't that so, Kate?"

Kate nodded stonily, not sure she liked being called "invigorating."

"Do you know Mr. Berbrooke, Lord Bridgerton?" Mary asked.

"Ah, yes," he said, with what Kate thought was fairly surprising reticence. "Yes, I do."

"I wasn't sure if I should have allowed Edwina to go off with him for a ride. Those curricles are terribly difficult to drive, aren't they?"

"I believe that Mr. Berbrooke has a steady hand with his horses," Anthony replied.

"Oh, good," Mary replied, letting out a much-relieved sigh. "You have surely set my mind at rest."

Newton let out a staccato bark, simply to remind everyone of his presence.

"I had better find his lead and take him for a walk," Kate said hurriedly. She certainly could use a bit of fresh air. And it would be nice to finally escape the viscount's fiendish company. "If you'll excuse me . . ."

"But wait, Kate!" Mary called out. "You cannot leave Lord Bridgerton here with me. I'm sure I'll bore him to tears."

Kate slowly turned around, dreading Mary's next words.

"You could never bore me, Mrs. Sheffield," the viscount said, debonair rake that he was.

"Oh, but I could," she assured him. "You've never been trapped in conversation with me for an hour. Which is about how long it will be before Edwina returns."

Kate stared at her stepmother, her jaw actually hanging open with shock. What on earth did Mary think she was doing?

"Why don't you go with Kate to take Newton for a walk?" Mary suggested.

"Oh, but I could never ask Lord Bridgerton to accompany me on a *chore*," Kate said quickly. "It would be beyond rudeness, and after all, he is our esteemed guest."

"Don't be silly," Mary answered, before the viscount could get even half of a word in. "I'm sure he wouldn't look upon it as a chore. Would you, my lord?"

"Of course not," he murmured, looking utterly sincere. But really, what else could he say?

"There. That settles it," Mary said, sounding inordinately pleased with herself. "And who knows? You may stumble across Edwina in your travels. Wouldn't that be convenient?"

"Indeed," Kate said under her breath. It would be lovely to be rid of the viscount, but the last thing she wanted to do was deliver Edwina into his clutches. Her sister was still young and impressionable. What if she couldn't resist one of his smiles? Or his glib tongue?

Even Kate was willing to admit that Lord Bridgerton exuded considerable charm, and she didn't even like the man! Edwina, with her less suspicious nature, would surely be overwhelmed.

She turned to the viscount. "You shouldn't feel you must accompany me while I walk Newton, my lord."

"I'd be delighted," he said with a wicked smile, and Kate had the distinct impression he was agreeing to go for the sole purpose of vexing her. "Besides," he continued, "as your mother said, we might see Edwina, and wouldn't that be a delightful coincidence?"

"Delightful," Kate returned flatly. "Just delightful."

"Excellent!" Mary said, clapping her hands together with joy. "I saw Newton's lead on the hall table. Here, I'll go and get it for you."

Anthony watched Mary leave, then turned to Kate and said, "That was very neatly done."

"I'll say," Kate muttered.

"Do you suppose," he whispered, leaning toward her, "that her matchmaking is directed toward Edwina or you?"

"Me?" Kate all but croaked. "Surely you jest."

Anthony rubbed his chin thoughtfully, gazing at the doorway through which Mary had just exited. "I'm not certain," he mused, "but—" He closed his mouth upon hearing Mary's footsteps drawing back near.

"Here you are," Mary said, holding the lead out to Kate. Newton barked enthusiastically and drew back as if preparing to lunge at Mary—undoubtedly to shower her with all sorts of unpalatable love—but Kate kept a firm hold on his collar.

"Here," Mary quickly amended, handing the lead instead to Anthony. "Why don't you give this to Kate? I'd rather not get too close."

Newton barked and gazed longingly at Mary, who inched farther away.

"You," Anthony said forcefully to the dog. "Sit down and be quiet."

Much to Kate's surprise, Newton obeyed, settling his plump bottom onto the rug with almost comical alacrity.

"There," Anthony said, sounding rather pleased with himself. He held out the lead toward Kate. "Shall you do the honors or shall I?"

"Oh, go right ahead," she replied. "You seem to have such an affinity for canines."

"Clearly," he shot back, keeping his voice low so that Mary could not hear, "they are not so very different from women. Both breeds hang on my every word."

Kate stepped on his hand as he knelt to fasten the lead to Newton's collar. "Oops," she said, rather insincerely. "I'm so sorry."

"Your tender solicitude quite unmans me," he returned, standing back up. "I might break into tears."

Mary's head bobbed back and forth between Kate and Anthony. She couldn't hear what they were saying but was clearly fascinated. "Is something wrong?" she queried.

"Not at all," Anthony replied, just as Kate gave a firm, "No."

"Good," Mary said briskly. "Then I'll see you to the door." At Newton's enthusiastic bark, she added, "Then again, maybe not. I don't really want to get within ten feet of that dog. But I'll wave you off."

"What would I do," Kate said to Mary as she passed her, "without you to wave me off?"

Mary smiled slyly. "I surely don't know, Kate. I surely don't know."

Which left Kate with a queasy feeling in her stomach and a vague suspicion that Lord Bridgerton might have been correct. Maybe Mary was playing matchmaker with more than just Edwina this time around.

It was a horrifying thought.

With Mary standing in the hall, Kate and Anthony exited out the doorway and headed west on Milner Street. "I usually stay to the smaller streets and make my way up to Brompton Road," Kate explained, thinking that he might not be very familiar with this area of town, "then take that to Hyde Park. But we can walk straight up Sloane Street, if you prefer."

"Whatever you wish," he demurred. "I shall follow your direction."

"Very well," Kate replied, marching determinedly up Milner Street toward Lenox Gardens. Maybe if she kept her eyes ahead of her and moved briskly, he'd be discouraged from conversation. Her daily walks with Newton were supposed to be her time for personal reflection. She did not appreciate having to drag him along.

Her strategy worked quite well for several minutes. They walked in silence all the way to the corner of Hans Crescent and Brompton Road, and then he quite suddenly said, "My brother played us for fools last night."

That stopped her in her tracks. "I beg your pardon?"

"Do you know what he told me about you before he introduced us?"

Kate stumbled a step before shaking her head, no. Newton hadn't stopped in *his* tracks, and he was tugging on the lead like mad.

"He told me you couldn't say enough about me."

"Wellll," Kate stalled, "if one doesn't want to put too fine a point on it, that's not entirely untrue."

"He implied," Anthony added, "that you could not say enough *good* about me."

She shouldn't have smiled. "*That's* not true."

He probably shouldn't have smiled, either, but Kate was glad he did. "I didn't think so," he replied.

They turned up Brompton Road toward Knightsbridge and Hyde Park, and Kate asked, "Why would he do such a thing?"

Anthony shot her a sideways look. "You don't have a brother, do you?"

"No, just Edwina, I'm afraid, and she's decidedly female."

"He did it," Anthony explained, "purely to torture me."

"A noble pursuit," Kate said under her breath.

"I heard that."

"I rather thought you would," she added.

"And I expect," he continued, "that he wanted to torture you as well."

"Me?" she exclaimed. "Whyever? What could I possibly have done to him?"

"You might have provoked him ever so slightly by denigrating his beloved brother," he suggested.

Her brows arched. "Beloved?"

"Much-admired?" he tried.

She shook her head. "That one doesn't wash, either."

Anthony grinned. Miss Sheffield the elder, for all her annoyingly managing ways, did have an admirable wit. They'd reached Knightsbridge, so he took her arm as they crossed over the thoroughfare and took one of the smaller pathways that led to South Carriage Road within Hyde Park. Newton, clearly a country dog at heart, picked up his pace considerably as they entered greener surroundings, although it would be difficult to imagine the portly canine moving with anything that might correctly be termed speed.

Still, the dog seemed rather jolly and certainly interested in every flower, small animal, or passerby that crossed their path. The spring air was crisp, but the sun was warm, and the sky was a surprisingly clear blue after so many typical London days of rain. And while the woman on his arm was not the woman he planned to take to wife, nor, in fact, was she a woman he planned to take to anything, Anthony felt a rather easy sense of contentment wash over him.

"Shall we cross over to Rotten Row?" he asked Kate.

"Hmmm?" was her distracted reply. She had her face tipped up to the sun and was basking in its warmth. And for one extremely disconcerting moment, Anthony felt a sharp stab of . . . *something*.

Something? He gave his head a little shake. It couldn't possibly be desire. Not for this woman.

"Did you say something?" she murmured.

He cleared his throat and took a deep breath, hoping it would clear his head. Instead, he simply got an intoxicating whiff of her scent, which was an odd combination of exotic lilies and sensible soap. "You seem to be enjoying the sun," he said.

She smiled, turning to face him with a clear-eyed gaze. "I know that's not what you said, but yes, I am. It's been so dreadfully rainy of late."

"I thought young ladies were not supposed to let sun on their faces," he teased.

She shrugged, looking only the slightest bit sheepish as she replied, "They're not. That is to say, we're not. But it does feel heavenly." She let out a little sigh, and a look of longing crossed her face, so intense that Anthony almost ached for her. "I do wish I could remove my bonnet," she said wistfully.

Anthony nodded his agreement, feeling much the same way about his hat. "You could probably push it back just a bit without anyone noticing," he suggested.

"Do you think?" Her entire face lit up at the prospect, and that strange stab of *something* pierced his gut again.

"Of course," he murmured, reaching up to adjust the

rim of the bonnet. It was one of those bizarre confections women seemed to favor, all ribbons and lace, and tied in such a way that no reasonable man could ever make sense of it. "Here, just hold still for a moment. I'll fix it."

Kate held still, just as he'd gently ordered, but when his fingers accidentally brushed the skin on her temple she stopped breathing as well. He was so very close, and there was something very odd about it. She could feel the heat of his body, and smell the clean, soapy scent of him.

And it sent a prickle of awareness straight through her.

She hated him, or at least she heartily disliked and disapproved of him, and yet she had the most absurd inclination to lean forward slightly, until the space between their bodies was squeezed into nothingness, and . . .

She swallowed and forced herself to draw back. Good God, what had come over her?

"Hold for a moment," he said. "I haven't finished."

Kate reached up with frantic fingers to adjust her bonnet. "I'm sure it's just fine. You needn't—you needn't worry yourself."

"Can you feel the sun any better?" he asked.

She nodded, even though she was so distracted she wasn't even sure if it was true. "Yes, thank you. It's lovely. I— Oh!"

Newton let out a loud stream of barks and yanked on the lead. Hard.

"Newton!" she called out, jerking forward with the lead. But the dog already had something in his sights— Kate had no idea what—and was bounding enthusiastically forward, pulling her along until she was stumbling over her feet, her entire body pulled into a diagonal line, with her shoulder decidedly in front of the rest of her. "Newton!" she called out again, rather helplessly. "Newton! Stop!"

Anthony watched with amusement as the dog barreled forward, moving with more speed than he would have ever guessed its short, pudgy legs could have managed.

Kate was making a valiant attempt to keep her grip on the lead, but Newton was now barking like mad, and running with equal vigor.

"Miss Sheffield, allow me to take the lead," he boomed, striding forward to aid her. It wasn't the most glamorous manner in which to play the hero, but anything would do when one was trying to impress the sister of one's future bride.

But just as Anthony caught up with her, Newton gave the lead a vicious tug, and it went flying from her grasp. Kate let out a shriek and dashed forward, but the dog was off and running, the lead snaking along the grass behind him.

Anthony didn't know whether to laugh or groan. Newton clearly did not intend to be caught.

Kate froze for a moment, one hand clasped over her mouth. Then her eyes caught Anthony's, and he had the worst sort of feeling that he knew what she intended to do.

"Miss Sheffield," he said quickly, "I'm sure—"

But she was off and running, hollering, "Newton!" with a decided lack of decorum. Anthony let out a weary sigh and began running after her. He couldn't very well let her chase the dog on her own and still presume to call himself a gentleman.

She had a bit of a head start on him, though, and when he caught up with her around the corner, she'd stopped. She was breathing hard, her hands on her hips as she scanned her surroundings.

"Where'd he go?" Anthony asked, trying to forget that there was something rather arousing about a woman who was panting.

"I don't know." She paused to catch her breath. "I think he's chasing a rabbit."

"Oh, now, well, *that* will make it easy to catch him," he said. "Since rabbits always stick to the well-trod paths."

She scowled at his sarcasm. "What are we to do?"

Anthony had half a mind to answer, "Go home and get

a *real* dog," but she looked so worried he bit his tongue. Actually, upon closer inspection she looked more irritated than worried, but there was definitely a bit of worry in the mix.

So instead he said, "I propose we wait until we hear someone shriek. Any minute now he's bound to dash right across some young lady's feet and scare her out of her very wits."

"Do you think?" She didn't look convinced. "Because he's not the scariest dog to look at. He thinks he is, and it's really quite sweet, actually, but the truth is, he's—"

"Eeeeeeeeeeeeeaaaaaaaaaahhhhhk!"

"I believe we have our answer," Anthony said dryly, and he took off in the direction of the anonymous lady's scream.

Kate hurried after him, cutting right across the grass toward Rotten Row. The viscount was running in front of her, and all she could think was that he must really want to marry Edwina, because despite the fact that he was clearly a splendid athlete, he looked most undignified dashing through the park after a rotund corgi. Even worse, they were going to have to run right across Rotten Row, the *ton*'s favorite spot for riding and driving.

Everyone was going to see them. A less determined man would have given up ages ago.

Kate kept running on after them, but she was losing ground. She hadn't spent much time in breeches, but she was fairly certain it was easier to run in them than in skirts. Especially when one was out in public and could not hitch them up above one's ankles.

She tore across Rotten Row, refusing to make eye contact with any of the fashionable ladies and gentlemen out with their horses. There was always the chance she wouldn't be recognized as the hoydenish miss racing through the park as if someone had set fire to her shoes. Not much of a chance, but a chance nonetheless.

When she reached the grass again, she stumbled for a second and had to pause to take a few deep breaths. Then horror dawned. They were almost to The Serpentine.

Oh, *no*.

There was little Newton liked better than to jump in a lake. And the sun was just warm enough that it might look tempting, especially if one happened to be a creature covered with thick, heavy fur, a creature who'd been running at breakneck speed for five minutes. Well, breakneck for an overweight corgi.

Which was still, Kate noted with some interest, fast enough to keep a six-foot-tall viscount at bay.

Kate hitched up her skirts an inch or so—hang the onlookers, she couldn't afford to be fussy right now—and took off running again. There was no way she'd catch up with Newton, but maybe she could catch up with Lord Bridgerton before he killed Newton.

Murder *had* to be on his mind by now. The man would have to be a saint not to want to murder the dog.

And if one percent of what had been written about him in *Whistledown* was true, he was no saint.

Kate gulped. "Lord Bridgerton!" she called out, intending to tell him to call off the hunt. She'd simply have to wait for Newton to exhaust himself. With four-inch-tall legs, that had to come sooner rather than later. "Lord Bridgerton! We can just—"

Kate stumbled in her tracks. Was that Edwina over there by The Serpentine? She squinted. It *was* Edwina, standing gracefully with her hands clasped in front of her. And it appeared that the hapless Mr. Berbrooke was making some sort of repair to his curricle.

Newton stopped short for one moment, spying Edwina at the same moment Kate did, and abruptly changed his course, barking joyfully as he ran toward his beloved.

"Lord Bridgerton!" Kate called out again. "See, look! There's—"

Anthony turned around at the sound of her voice, then

followed her pointed finger toward Edwina. So that was why the damned dog spun on its heel and made a ninety-degree change of course. Anthony had nearly slipped on the mud and fallen on his bum trying to maneuver such a sharp turn.

He was going to kill that dog.

No, he was going to kill Kate Sheffield.

No, maybe—

Anthony's gleeful thoughts of vengeance were broken by Edwina's sudden shriek of, "Newton!"

Anthony liked to think of himself as a man of decisive action, but when he saw that dog launch himself in the air and hurtle himself toward Edwina, he was quite simply frozen with shock. Shakespeare himself could not have devised a more appropriate ending to this farce, and it was all playing out right before Anthony's eyes as if at half speed.

And there was nothing he could do about it.

The dog was going to hit Edwina straight in the chest. Edwina was going to topple backward.

Straight into The Serpentine.

"Nooooooo!" he yelled, charging forward even though he knew all attempts at heroics on his part were utterly useless.

Splash!

"Dear God!" Berbrooke exclaimed. "She's all wet!"

"Well, don't just stand there," Anthony snapped, reaching the scene of the accident and charging forward into the waters. "Do something to help!"

Berbrooke clearly did not quite understand what that meant, because he just stood there, bug-eyed, as Anthony reached down, grasped Edwina's hand, and hauled her to her feet.

"Are you all right?" he asked gruffly.

She nodded, sputtering and sneezing too hard to answer.

"Miss Sheffield," he roared, seeing Kate skid to a halt

on the banks. "No, not you," he added, when he felt Edwina jerk to attention at his side. "Your sister."

"Kate?" she asked, blinking the filthy water from her eyes. "Where's Kate?"

"Dry as a bone on the embankment," he muttered, followed by a holler in Kate's direction of, "Rein in your bloody dog!"

Newton had cheerfully splashed back out of the Serpentine and was now sitting on the grass, his tongue hanging happily out of his mouth. Kate scurried to his side and grabbed the lead. Anthony noticed that she had no pithy comeback to his roared order. Good, he thought viciously. He wouldn't have thought the bloody woman would have had the sense to keep her mouth shut.

He turned back to Edwina, who, astoundingly, still managed to look lovely even while dripping with pond water. "Let me get you out of here," he said gruffly, and before she had a chance to react, he scooped her into his arms and carried her to dry ground.

"I've never seen anything like that," Berbrooke said, shaking his head.

Anthony made no reply. He didn't think he'd be able to speak without tossing the idiot into the water. What was he thinking, just standing there while Edwina was submerged by that pathetic excuse for a dog?

"Edwina?" Kate asked, walking forward as far as Newton's lead would allow. "Are you all right?"

"I think you've done enough," Anthony bit out, advancing upon her until they were barely a foot apart.

"Me?" she gasped.

"Look at her," he snapped, thrusting a pointed finger in Edwina's direction even while his full attention was focused on Kate. "Just look at her!"

"But it was an accident!"

"I'm really fine!" Edwina called out, sounding a little panicked by the level of anger simmering between her sister and the viscount. "Cold, but fine!"

"See?" Kate returned, swallowing convulsively as she took in the disheveled sight of her sister. "It was an accident."

He merely crossed his arms and arched a brow.

"You don't believe me," she breathed. "I can't believe you don't believe me."

Anthony said nothing. It was inconceivable to him that Kate Sheffield, for all her wit and intelligence, could *not* be jealous of her sister. And even if there was nothing she could have done to prevent this mishap, surely she must be taking a bit of pleasure in the fact that she was dry and comfortable while Edwina looked like a drowned rat. An attractive rat, to be sure, but certainly a drowned one.

But Kate clearly wasn't done with the conversation. "Aside from the fact," she scorned, "that I would never ever do anything to harm Edwina, how do you propose I managed this amazing feat?" She clapped her free hand to her cheek in an expression of mock discovery. "Oh, yes, I know the secret language of the corgis. I ordered the dog to yank the lead from my hand and then, since I have the second sight, I knew that Edwina was standing right here by the Serpentine, so then I said to the dog—through our powerful mind-to-mind connection, since he was much too far away to hear my voice at this point—to change his direction, head for Edwina, and topple her into the lake."

"Sarcasm doesn't become you, Miss Sheffield."

"*Nothing* becomes you, Lord Bridgerton."

Anthony leaned forward, his chin jutting out in a most menacing manner. "Women should not keep pets if they cannot control them."

"And men should not take women with pets for a walk in the park if they cannot control either," she shot back.

Anthony could actually feel the tips of his ears turning red with barely leashed rage. "You, madam, are a menace to society."

She opened her mouth as if to return the insult, but instead she just offered him an almost frighteningly devious smile and turned to the dog and said, "Shake, Newton."

Newton looked up at her finger, pointed right at Anthony, and obediently trotted a few steps closer to him before allowing himself a full-body shake, spraying pond water everywhere.

Anthony went for her throat. "I . . . am . . . going . . . to . . . KILL YOU!" he roared.

Kate ducked nimbly out of the way, dashing over to Edwina's side. "Now, now, Lord Bridgerton," she taunted, seeking safety behind her sister's dripping form. "It would not do to lose your temper in front of the fair Edwina."

"Kate?" Edwina whispered urgently. "What is going on? Why are you being so mean to him?"

"Why is he being so mean to *me*?" Kate hissed back.

"I say," Mr. Berbrooke suddenly said, "that dog got me wet."

"He got all of us wet," Kate replied. Including her. But it had been worth it. Oh, it had been worth it to see the look of surprise and rage on that pompous aristocrat's face.

"You!" Anthony roared, jabbing a furious finger at Kate. "Be quiet."

Kate held her silence. She wasn't foolhardy enough to provoke him any further. He looked as if his head might explode at any moment. And he'd certainly lost whatever claim to dignity he'd had at the beginning of the day. His right sleeve was dripping wet from when he'd hauled Edwina out of the water, his boots looked to be ruined forever, and the rest of him was spotted with water, thanks to Newton's expert shaking prowess.

"I'll tell you what we're going to do," he continued in a low, deadly voice.

"What I need to do," Mr. Berbrooke said jovially, clearly unaware that Lord Bridgerton was likely to murder the first person who opened his mouth, "is finish repairing this curricle. Then I can take Miss Sheffield home." He pointed at Edwina, just in case anyone didn't understand to which Miss Sheffield he referred.

"Mr. Berbrooke," Anthony ground out, "do you know how to fix a curricle?"

Mr. Berbrooke blinked a few times.

"Do you even know what is *wrong* with your curricle?"

Berbrooke's mouth opened and closed a few more times, and then he said, "I have a few ideas. Shouldn't take terribly long to figure out which is the actual problem."

Kate stared at Anthony, fascinated by the vein leaping in his throat. She had never before seen a man so clearly pushed to his limit. Feeling not a little apprehensive at the impending explosion, she took a prudent half step behind Edwina.

She didn't like to think herself a coward, but self-preservation was another matter entirely.

But the viscount somehow managed to keep himself under control, and his voice was terrifyingly even as he said, "This is what we're going to do."

Three pairs of eyes widened in expectation.

"I am going to walk over there"—he pointed at a lady and gentleman about twenty yards away who were trying not to stare but not succeeding—"and ask Montrose if I might borrow his carriage for a few minutes."

"I say," Berbrooke said, craning his neck, "is that Geoffrey Montrose? Haven't seen him for an age."

A second vein started leaping, this time on Lord Bridgerton's temple. Kate grasped Edwina's hand for moral support and held tight.

But Bridgerton, to his credit, ignored Berbrooke's exceedingly inappropriate interjection and continued with, "Since he will say yes—"

"Are you sure?" Kate blurted out.

Somehow his brown eyes resembled icicles. "Am I sure of what?" he bit off.

"Nothing," she mumbled, ready to kick herself. "Please continue."

"As I was saying, since as a friend and a gentleman"—he glared at Kate—"he will say yes, I will take Miss Sheffield home and then *I* will return home and have one of my men return Montrose's curricle."

No one bothered to ask which Miss Sheffield he was talking about.

"What about Kate?" Edwina inquired. After all, the curricle could only seat two.

Kate gave her hand a squeeze. Dear, sweet Edwina.

Anthony looked straight at Edwina. "Mr. Berbrooke will escort your sister home."

"But I can't," Berbrooke said. "Got to finish with the curricle, you know."

"Where do you live?" Anthony snapped.

Berbrooke blinked with surprise but gave his address.

"I will stop by your house and fetch a servant to wait with your conveyance while you escort Miss Sheffield to her home. Is that clear?" He paused and looked at everyone—including the dog—with a rather hard expression. Except for Edwina, of course, who was the only person present who had not lit a fuse directly under his temper.

"Is that clear?" he repeated.

Everyone nodded, and his plan was set into motion. Minutes later, Kate found herself watching Lord Bridgerton and Edwina ride off into the horizon—the very two people she had vowed should never even be in the same room together.

Even worse, she was left alone with Mr. Berbrooke and Newton.

And it took only two minutes to discern that of the two, Newton was the finer conversationalist.

Chapter 5

It has come to This Author's attention that Miss Katharine Sheffield took offense at the labeling of her beloved pet, "an unnamed dog of indeterminate breed."

This Author is, to be sure, prostrate with shame at this grievous and egregious error and begs of you, dear reader, to accept this abject apology and pay attention to the first ever correction in the history of this column.

Miss Katharine Sheffield's dog is a corgi. It is called Newton, although it is difficult to imagine that England's great inventor and physicist would have appreciated being immortalized in the form of a short, fat canine with poor manners.

LADY WHISTLEDOWN'S SOCIETY PAPERS, 27 APRIL 1814

By that evening, it had become apparent that Edwina had not come through her (albeit brief) ordeal unscathed. Her nose turned red, her eyes began to water, and it was apparent to anyone who glimpsed her puffy face for even a second that, while not seriously ill, she'd caught a bad cold.

But even while Edwina was tucked into bed with a hot water bottle between her feet and a therapeutic potion brewed up by the cook in a mug on her bedside table, Kate was determined to have a conversation with her.

"What did he say to you on the ride home?" Kate demanded, perching on the edge of her sister's bed.

"Who?" Edwina replied, sniffing fearfully at the remedy. "Look at this," she said, holding it forward. "It's giving off fumes."

"The viscount," Kate ground out. "Who else would have spoken to you on the ride home? And don't be a ninny. It's not giving off fumes. That's just steam."

"Oh." Edwina took another sniff and pulled a face. "It doesn't smell like steam."

"It's *steam*," Kate ground out, gripping the mattress until her knuckles hurt. "What did he *say*?"

"Lord Bridgerton?" Edwina asked blithely. "Oh, just the usual sort of things. You know what I mean. Polite conversation and all that."

"He made polite conversation while you were dripping wet?" Kate asked doubtfully.

Edwina took a hesitant sip, then nearly gagged. "What is *in* this?"

Kate leaned over and sniffed at the contents. "It smells a bit like licorice. And I think I see a raisin at the bottom." But as she sniffed, she thought she heard rain pattering against the glass of the window, and so she sat back up. "Is it raining?"

"I don't know," Edwina said. "It might be. It was rather cloudy when the sun set earlier." She gave the glass one more dubious look, then set it back on the table. "If I drink that, I *know* it will make me sicker," she stated.

"But what else did he say?" Kate persisted, getting up to check out the window. She pushed the curtain aside and peered out. It was raining, but only lightly, and it was too early to tell whether the precipitation would be accompanied by any thunder or lightning.

"Who, the viscount?"

Kate thought herself a saint for not shaking her sister senseless. "Yes, the viscount."

Edwina shrugged, clearly not as interested in the conversation as Kate. "Not much. He asked for my welfare, of course. Which was only reasonable, considering that I had just been dunked in The Serpentine. Which, I might add, was perfectly wretched. Aside from being cold, the water was most certainly not clean."

Kate cleared her throat and sat back down, preparing to ask a most scandalous question, but one which, in her opinion, simply had to be asked. Trying to keep her voice devoid of the complete and total fascination that was coursing through her veins, she asked, "Did he make any untoward advances?"

Edwina lurched back, her eyes growing round with shock. "Of course not!" she exclaimed. "He was a perfect gentleman. Really, I don't see what has you so excited. It wasn't a very interesting conversation. I can't even remember half of what was said."

Kate just stared at her sister, unable to fathom that she could have been trapped in conversation with that odious rake for a good ten minutes and it *didn't* make an indelible impression on her. Much to her own everlasting dismay, every single awful word he'd said to her was etched permanently on her brain.

"By the way," Edwina added, "how was your time with Mr. Berbrooke? It took you nearly an hour to return."

Kate shuddered visibly.

"That bad?"

"I'm sure he will make some woman a good husband," Kate said. "Just not one with a brain."

Edwina let out a little giggle. "Oh, Kate, you are awful."

Kate sighed. "I know. I know. That was terribly cruel of me. The poor man hasn't an unkind bone in his body. It's just that—"

"He hasn't an intelligent bone, either," Edwina finished.

Kate raised her brows. It was most unlikely Edwina to make such a judgmental comment.

"I know," Edwina said with a sheepish smile. "Now I am the unkind one. I really shouldn't have said a word, but truly, I thought I would perish on our curricle ride."

Kate straightened with concern. "Was he a dangerous driver?"

"Not at all. It was his conversation."

"Boring?"

Edwina nodded, her blue eyes slightly bewildered. "He was so hard to follow it was almost fascinating to try to figure out how his mind works." She let out a stream of coughs, then added, "But it made my brain hurt."

"So he's not to be your perfect scholar-husband?" Kate said with an indulgent smile.

Edwina coughed some more. "I'm afraid not."

"Maybe you should try a bit more of that brew," Kate suggested, motioning to the lonely mug sitting on Edwina's bedside table. "Cook swears by it."

Edwina shook her head violently. "It tastes like death."

Kate waited a few moments, then had to ask, "Did the viscount say anything about me?"

"You?"

"No, some other me," Kate practically snapped. "Of course *me*. How many other people may I correctly refer to as 'me'?"

"No need to get upset about it."

"I'm not upset—"

"But actually, no, he didn't mention you."

Kate suddenly felt upset.

"He had a lot to say about Newton, though."

Kate's lips parted with dismay. It was never flattering to be passed over for a dog.

"I assured him that Newton is truly the perfect pet, and that I was not at all angry with him, but he was rather charmingly upset on my behalf."

"How charming," Kate muttered.

Edwina grabbed a handkerchief and blew her nose. "I say, Kate, you're rather interested in the viscount."

"I did spend practically the entire afternoon trapped in conversation with him," Kate replied, as if that ought to explain everything.

"Good. Then you've had a chance to see how polite and charming he can be. He's very wealthy, too." Edwina let out a loud sniffle, then fumbled around for a fresh handkerchief. "And while I don't think that one can choose a husband based entirely on finances, given our lack of funds, I would be remiss not to consider it, don't you think?"

"Well . . ." Kate hedged, knowing that Edwina was absolutely correct but not wanting to say anything that might be construed as approval of Lord Bridgerton.

Edwina brought the handkerchief to her face and gave her nose a rather unfeminine blow. "I think we should add him to our list," she said, snuffling over the words.

"Our list," Kate echoed, her voice strangled.

"Yes, of possible matches. I think he and I would suit very well."

"But I thought you wanted a scholar!"

"I did. I do. But you yourself pointed out the unlikelihood of my finding a true scholar. Lord Bridgerton seems intelligent enough. I'll just have to devise a way to discover if he likes to read."

"I'd be surprised if that boor *can* read," Kate muttered.

"Kate Sheffield!" Edwina exclaimed with a laugh. "Did you just say what I think you said?"

"No," Kate said baldly, because of course the viscount could read. But he was just so awful in every other way.

"You did," Edwina accused. "You are the *worst,* Kate." She smiled. "But you do make me laugh."

A low rumble of distant thunder echoed in the night, and Kate forced a smile on her face, trying not to flinch. She was usually all right when the thunder and lightning were far away. It was only when they came one on top of each other, and both seemingly on top of her, that she felt as if she were about to burst from her skin.

"Edwina," Kate said, needing to have this discussion with her sister but also needing to say something that would take her mind off the approaching storm, "you must put the viscount from your mind. He is absolutely not the sort of husband who would make you happy. Aside from the fact that he is the worst sort of rake and would probably flaunt a dozen mistresses in your face—"

At Edwina's frown, Kate cut off the rest of her sentence and decided to expand upon this point. "He would!" she said with great drama. "Haven't you been reading *Whistledown*? Or listening to anything any of the other young ladies' mamas have to say? The ones who have been on the social circuit for several years and know what's what. They *all* say he is a terrible rake. That his only saving grace is how nicely he treats his family."

"Well, that would be a mark in his favor," Edwina pointed out. "Since a wife would be family, yes?"

Kate nearly groaned. "A wife isn't the same as a blood relative. Men who would never dream of uttering a cross word in front of their mothers trample all over their wives' feelings every day."

"And how would you know this?" Edwina demanded.

Kate's mouth fell open. She couldn't remember the last time Edwina had questioned her judgment on an important matter, and unfortunately, the only answer she could think of on such short notice was, "I just do."

Which, even she had to admit, really didn't pass muster.

"Edwina," she said in a placating voice, deciding to steer the topic in a different direction, "aside from all that, I don't think you would even like the viscount if you got to know him."

"He seemed pleasant enough while driving me home."

"But he was on his best behavior!" Kate persisted. "Of course he'd seem nice. He wants you to fall in love with him."

Edwina blinked. "So you think it was all an act."

"Exactly!" Kate exclaimed, pouncing on the concept.

"Edwina, between last night and this afternoon, I spent several hours in his company, and I can assure you, he was *not* on his best behavior with me."

Edwina gasped with horror and maybe a little titillation. "Did he kiss you?" she breathed.

"No!" Kate howled. "Of course not! Where on earth would you get that idea?"

"You said he wasn't on his best behavior."

"What I meant," Kate ground out, "was that he wasn't polite. Nor was he very nice. In fact, he was insufferably arrogant and dreadfully rude and insulting."

"That's interesting," Edwina murmured.

"It wasn't the least bit interesting. It was horrible!"

"No, that's not what I meant," Edwina said, thoughtfully scratching her chin. "It's very odd that he would have behaved rudely to you. He must have heard that I shall be looking to your judgment when I choose a husband. One would think he'd go out of his way to be nice to you. Why," she mused, "would he behave the churl?"

Kate's face colored a dull red—thankfully not so noticeable in the candlelight—as she muttered, "He said he couldn't help himself."

Edwina's mouth fell open, and for one second she sat utterly frozen, as if suspended in time. Then she fell back onto her pillows, hooting with laughter. "Oh, Kate!" she gasped. "That is splendid! Oh, what a tangle. Oh, I love it!"

Kate glared at her. "It's not funny."

Edwina wiped at her eyes. "It might be the funniest thing I've heard all month. All year! Oh, my goodness." She let out a short stream of coughs, brought on by her laughing fit. "Oh, Kate, I do believe you might have cleared out my nose."

"Edwina, that's disgusting."

Edwina brought her handkerchief to her face and blew her nose. "But true," she said triumphantly.

"It won't last," Kate muttered. "You'll be sick as a dog by morning."

"You're probably right," Edwina agreed, "but oh, what fun. He said he couldn't help himself? Oh, Kate, that is just rich."

"There is no need to dwell on it," Kate grumbled.

"Do you know, but he might be the very first gentleman we've met all season you haven't been able to manage."

Kate's lips twisted into a grimace. The viscount had used the same word, and they were both correct. She'd indeed spent the season managing men—managing them for Edwina. And she suddenly wasn't so sure she liked this role of mother hen she'd been thrust into.

Or maybe she'd thrust herself into it.

Edwina saw the play of emotion on her sister's face and immediately turned apologetic. "Oh, dear," she murmured. "I'm sorry, Kate. I didn't mean to tease."

Kate arched a brow.

"Oh, very well, I did mean to tease, but never to actually hurt your feelings. I had no idea Lord Bridgerton had upset you so."

"Edwina, I just don't like the man. And I don't think you should even consider marrying him. I don't care how ardently or how persistently he pursues you. He will not make a good husband."

Edwina was silent for a moment, her magnificent eyes utterly sober. Then she said, "Well, if you say so, it must be true. I have certainly never been steered wrong by your judgment before. And, as you said, you have spent more time in his company than have I, so you would know better."

Kate let out a long and ill-disguised sigh of relief. "Good," she said firmly. "And when you are feeling more the thing, we shall look among your current suitors for a better match."

"And maybe you could look for a husband, too," Edwina suggested.

"Of course I'm always looking," Kate insisted. "What

would be the point of a London season if I weren't looking?"

Edwina looked dubious. "I don't think you *are* looking, Kate. I think that all you do is interview possibilities for me. And there is no reason you shouldn't find a husband as well. You need a family of your own. I certainly can't imagine anyone more suited to be a mother than you."

Kate bit her lip, not wanting to respond directly to Edwina's point. Because behind those lovely blue eyes and perfect face, Edwina was quite the most perceptive person she knew. And Edwina was right. Kate hadn't been looking for a husband. But why should she? No one was considering her for marriage, either.

She sighed, glancing toward the window. The storm seemed to have passed without striking her area of London. She supposed she ought to be thankful for small favors.

"Why don't we see about you first," Kate finally said, "since I think we both agree that you are more likely to receive a proposal before I do, and then we'll think about my prospects?"

Edwina shrugged, and Kate knew that her deliberate silence meant that she did not agree.

"Very well," Kate said, rising to her feet. "I'll leave you to your rest. I'm sure you'll need it."

Edwina coughed as a reply.

"And drink that remedy!" Kate said with a laugh, heading out the door.

As she shut the door behind her, she heard Edwina mutter, "I'd rather die."

Four days later, Edwina was dutifully drinking Cook's remedy, although not without considerable grumbling and complaint. Her health had improved, but only to the point where she was *almost* better. She was still stuck in bed, still coughing, and very irritable.

Mary had declared that Edwina could not attend any social functions until Tuesday at the earliest. Kate had taken that to mean that they all would receive a respite (because really, what was the point of attending a ball without Edwina?), but after Kate spent a blessedly uneventful Friday, Saturday, and Sunday with nothing to do but read and take Newton for walks, Mary suddenly declared that the two of them would attend Lady Bridgerton's musicale Monday evening, and—

(Kate tried to interject a vehement argument about why this was not a good idea at this point.)

—that was *final*.

Kate gave in fairly quickly. There was really no point in arguing any further, especially since Mary turned on her heel and walked away directly after uttering the word, "final."

Kate did have certain standards, and they included not arguing with closed doors.

And so Monday evening she found herself dressed in ice blue silk, fan in hand, as she and Mary rolled through the streets of London in their inexpensive carriage, on their way to Bridgerton House in Grosvenor Square.

"Everyone will be very surprised to see us without Edwina," Kate said, her left hand fiddling with the black gauze of her cloak.

"You are looking for a husband as well," Mary replied.

Kate held silent for a moment. She couldn't very well argue that point, since, after all, it was supposed to be true.

"And stop crumpling your cloak," Mary added. "It will be wrinkled all evening."

Kate's hand went limp. She then tapped the right one rhythmically against the seat for several seconds, until Mary blurted out, "Good heavens, Kate, can't you sit still?"

"You know I can't," Kate said.

Mary just sighed.

After another long silence, punctuated only by the tapping of her foot, Kate added, "Edwina will be lonely without us."

Mary didn't even bother to look at her as she answered, "Edwina has a novel to read. The latest by that Austen woman. She won't even notice we're gone."

That much was also true. Edwina probably wouldn't notice if her bed caught on fire while she was reading a book.

So Kate said, "The music will probably be dreadful. After that Smythe-Smith affair . . ."

"The Smythe-Smith musicale was performed by the Smythe-Smith daughters," Mary replied, her voice starting to hold an edge of impatience. "Lady Bridgerton has hired a professional opera singer, visiting from Italy. We are honored simply to receive an invitation."

Kate knew without a doubt that the invitation was for Edwina; she and Mary were surely included only out of politeness. But Mary's teeth were beginning to clench together, and so Kate vowed to hold her tongue for the remainder of the ride.

Which wouldn't be so difficult, after all, as they were presently rolling up in front of Bridgerton House.

Kate's mouth dropped open as she looked out the window. "It's huge," she said dumbly.

"Isn't it?" Mary replied, gathering her things together. "I understand that Lord Bridgerton doesn't live there. Even though it belongs to him, he remains in his bachelor's lodgings so that his mother and siblings may reside at Bridgerton House. Isn't that thoughtful of him?"

Thoughtful and *Lord Bridgerton* were not two expressions Kate would have thought to use in the same sentence, but she nodded nonetheless, too awed by the size and grace of the stone building to make an intelligent comment.

The carriage rolled to a halt, and Mary and Kate were helped down by one of the Bridgerton footmen, who rushed to open the door. A butler took their invitation and admitted them, taking their wraps and pointing them toward the music room, which was just at the end of the hall.

Kate had been inside enough grand London homes not to publicly gape at the obvious wealth and beauty of the furnishings, but even she was impressed by the interiors, decorated with elegance and restraint in the Adam style. Even the ceilings were works of art—done up in pale shades of sage and blue, the colors separated by white plasterwork so intricate it almost appeared to be a more solid form of lace.

The music room was just as lovely, the walls painted a friendly shade of lemon yellow. Rows of chairs had been set up for attendees, and Kate quickly steered her stepmother toward the back. Truly, there could be no reason why she'd want to put herself in a noticeable position. Lord Bridgerton was sure to be in attendance—if all the tales about his devotion to his family were true—and if Kate was lucky, maybe he wouldn't even notice her presence.

Quite to the contrary, Anthony knew exactly when Kate stepped out of her carriage and entered his family home. He had been in his study, having a solitary drink before heading down to his mother's annual musicale. In a bid for privacy, he'd chosen not to live at Bridgerton House while still a bachelor, but he did keep his study here. His position as head of the Bridgerton family carried with it serious responsibilities, and Anthony generally found it easier to attend to these responsibilities while in close proximity to the rest of his family.

The study's windows looked out over Grosvenor Square, however, and so he had been amusing himself watching the carriages arrive and the guests alight. When Kate Sheffield had stepped down, she'd looked up at the facade of Bridgerton House, tipping her face up in much the same manner she'd done while enjoying the warmth of the sun in Hyde Park. The light from the sconces on either side of the front door had filtered onto her skin, bathing her with a flickering glow.

And Anthony's breath was sucked right out of him.

His glass tumbler landed on the wide windowsill with a heavy thunk. This was getting ridiculous. He wasn't self-delusional enough to mistake the tightening of his muscles as anything other than desire.

Bloody hell. He didn't even like the woman. She was too bossy, too opinionated, too quick to jump to conclusions. She wasn't even beautiful—at least not compared to quite a few of the ladies flitting about London for the season, her sister most especially included.

Kate's face was a touch too long, her chin a hair too pointed, her eyes a shade too big. Everything about her was too *some*thing. Even her mouth, which vexed him to no end with its endless stream of insults and opinions, was too full. It was a rare event when she actually had it closed and was treating him to a moment of blessed silence, but if he happened to look at her in that split second (for surely she could not be silent for much longer than that) all he saw were her lips, full and pouty, and—provided that she kept them shut and didn't actually speak—eminently kissable.

Kissable?

Anthony shuddered. The thought of kissing Kate Sheffield was terrifying. In fact, the mere fact that he'd even *thought* of it ought to be enough to have him locked up in an asylum.

And yet . . .

Anthony collapsed in a chair.

And yet he'd dreamed about her.

It had happened after the fiasco at The Serpentine. He'd been so furious with her he could barely speak. It was a wonder he'd managed to say anything at all to Edwina during the short ride back to her house. Polite conversation was all he'd been able to get out—mindless words so familiar they tripped from his tongue as if by rote.

A blessing indeed, since his mind most definitely had not been where it should be: on Edwina, his future wife.

Oh, she hadn't agreed to marry him. He hadn't even asked. But she fit his requirements for a wife in every possible way; he'd already decided that she would be the one to whom he would finally propose marriage. She was beautiful, intelligent, and even-tempered. Attractive without making his blood rush. They would spend enjoyable years together, but he'd never fall in love with her.

She was exactly what he needed.

And yet . . .

Anthony reached for his drink and downed the rest of its contents in one gasping gulp.

And yet he'd dreamed about her sister.

He tried not to remember. He tried not to remember the details of the dream—the heat and the sweat of it—but he'd only had this one drink this evening, certainly not enough to impair his memory. And although he'd had no intention of having more than this one drink, the concept of sliding into mindless oblivion was starting to sound appealing.

Anything would be appealing if it meant he wouldn't remember.

But he didn't feel like drinking. He'd not overimbibed in years. It seemed such the young man's game, not at all attractive as one neared thirty. Besides, even if he did decide to seek temporary amnesia in a bottle, it wouldn't come fast enough to make the memory of *her* go away.

Memory? Ha. It wasn't even a real memory. Just a dream, he reminded himself. Just a dream.

He'd fallen asleep quickly upon returning home that evening. He'd stripped naked and soaked in a hot bath for nearly an hour, trying to remove the chill from his bones. He hadn't been completely submerged in The Serpentine as had Edwina, but his legs had been soaked, as had one of his sleeves, and Newton's strategic shake had guaranteed that not one inch of his body remained warm during the windy ride home in the borrowed curricle.

After his bath he'd crawled into bed, not particularly caring that it was still light outside, and would be for a good hour yet. He was exhausted, and he'd had every intention of falling into a deep, dreamless sleep, not to be awakened until the first streaks of dawn touched the morning.

But sometime in the night, his body had grown restless and hungry. And his treacherous mind had filled with the most awful of images. He'd watched it as if floating near the ceiling, and yet he felt everything—his body, naked, moving over a lithe female form; his hands stroking and squeezing warm flesh. The delectable tangle of arms and legs, the musky scent of two bodies in love—it had all been there, hot and vivid in his mind.

And then he'd shifted. Just the tiniest bit, perhaps to kiss the faceless woman's ear. Except as he moved to the side, she was no longer faceless. First appeared a thick lock of dark brown hair, softly curling and tickling at his shoulder. Then he moved even farther . . .

And he saw her.

Kate Sheffield.

He'd awakened in an instant, sitting bolt upright in bed and shaking from the horror of it. It had been the most vivid erotic dream he'd ever experienced.

And his worst nightmare.

He'd felt frantically around the sheets with one of his hands, terrified that he'd find the proof of his passion. God help him if he'd actually ejaculated while dreaming of quite the most awful woman of his acquaintance.

Thankfully, his sheets were clean, and so, with beating heart and heavy breath, he'd lain back against his pillows, his movements slow and careful, as if that would some-how prevent a recurrence of the dream.

He'd stared at the ceiling for hours, first conjugating

Latin verbs, then counting to a thousand, all in an attempt to keep his brain on anything but Kate Sheffield.

And amazingly, he'd exorcised her image from his brain and fallen asleep.

But now she was back. Here. In his home.

It was a terrifying thought.

And where the hell was Edwina? Why hadn't she accompanied her mother and sister?

The first strains of a string quartet drifted under his door, discordant and jumbled, no doubt the warm-up of the musicians his mother had hired to accompany Maria Rosso, the latest soprano to take London by storm.

Anthony certainly hadn't told his mother, but he and Maria had enjoyed a pleasant interlude the last time she'd been in town. Maybe he ought to consider renewing their friendship. If the sultry Italian beauty didn't cure what ailed him, nothing would.

Anthony stood and straightened his shoulders, aware that he probably looked as if he were girding himself for battle. Hell, that's how he *felt*. Maybe, if he was lucky, he'd be able to avoid Kate Sheffield entirely. He couldn't imagine she'd go out of her way to engage him in conversation. She'd made it abundantly clear that she held him in just as much esteem as he did her.

Yes, that's exactly what he would do. Avoid her. How difficult could that be?

Chapter 6

Lady Bridgerton's musicale proved to be a decidedly musical affair (not, This Author assures you, always the norm for musicales). The guest performer was none other than Maria Rosso, the Italian soprano who made her debut in London two years ago and has returned after a brief stint on the Vienna stage.

With thick, sable hair and flashing dark eyes, Miss Rosso proved as lovely in form as she did in voice, and more than one (indeed, more than a dozen) of society's so-called gentlemen found it difficult indeed to remove their eyes from her person, even after the performance had concluded.

LADY WHISTLEDOWN'S SOCIETY PAPERS, 27 APRIL 1814

Kate knew the minute he walked in the room.

She tried to tell herself it had nothing to do with a heightened awareness of the man. He was excruciatingly handsome; that was fact, not opinion. She couldn't imagine that every woman didn't notice him immediately.

He arrived late. Not very—the soprano couldn't have been more than a dozen bars into her piece. But late enough so that he tried to be quiet as he slipped into a chair toward the front near his family. Kate remained motionless in her position at the back, fairly certain that he didn't see her as he settled in for the performance. He didn't look her way, and besides, several candles had been snuffed, leaving the room bathed in a dim, romantic glow. The shadows surely obscured her face.

Kate tried to keep her eyes on Miss Rosso throughout the performance. Kate's disposition was not improved, however, by the fact that the singer could not take her eyes off of Lord Bridgerton. At first Kate had thought she must be imagining Miss Rosso's fascination with the viscount, but by the time the soprano was halfway done, there could be no doubt. Maria Rosso was issuing the viscount a sultry invitation with her eyes.

Why this bothered Kate so much, she didn't know. After all, it was just another piece of proof that he was every bit the licentious rake she'd always known him to be. She should have felt smug. She should have felt vindicated.

Instead, all she felt was disappointment. It was a heavy, uncomfortable feeling around her heart, one that left her slumping slightly in her chair.

When the performance was done, she couldn't help but notice that the soprano, after graciously accepting her applause, walked brazenly up to the viscount and offered him one of those seductive smiles—the sort Kate would never learn to do if she had a dozen opera singers trying to teach her. There was no mistaking what the singer meant by that smile.

Good heavens, the man didn't even need to chase women. They practically dropped at his feet.

It was disgusting. Really, truly disgusting.

And yet Kate couldn't stop watching.

Lord Bridgerton offered the opera singer a mysterious half-smile of his own. Then he reached out and actually tucked an errant lock of her raven hair behind her ear.

Kate shivered.

Now he was leaning forward, whispering something in

her ear. Kate felt her own ears straining in their direction, even though it was quite obviously impossible for her to hear a thing from so far away.

But still, was it truly a crime to be ravenously curious? And—

Good heavens, did he just kiss her neck? Surely he wouldn't do that in his mother's home. Well, she supposed Bridgerton House was technically *his* home, but his mother lived here, as did many of his siblings. Truly, the man should know better than that. A little decorum in the company of his family would not be remiss.

"Kate? Kate?"

It may have been a small kiss, just a feather-light brush of his lips against the opera singer's skin, but it was still a kiss.

"Kate!"

"Right! Yes?" Kate nearly jumped half a foot as she whirled around to face Mary, who was watching her with a decidedly irritated expression.

"Stop watching the viscount," Mary hissed.

"I wasn't—well, all right, I was, but did you see him?" Kate whispered urgently. "He's shameless."

She looked back over at him. He was still flirting with Maria Rosso, and he obviously didn't care who saw them.

Mary's lips pursed into a tight line before she said, "I'm sure his behavior isn't any of our business."

"Of course it's our business. He wants to marry Edwina."

"We don't know that for sure."

Kate thought back over her conversations with Lord Bridgerton. "I'd say it's a very, very good bet."

"Well, stop watching him. I'm certain he wants nothing to do with you after that fiasco in Hyde Park. And besides, there are any number of eligible gentlemen here. You'd do well to stop thinking of Edwina all the time and start looking around for yourself."

Kate felt her shoulders sag. The mere thought of trying

to attract a suitor was exhausting. They were all interested in Edwina, anyway. And even though she wanted nothing to do with the viscount, it still stung when Mary said she was *certain* he wanted nothing to do with *her*.

Mary grasped her arm with a grip that brooked no protest. "Come now, Kate," she said quietly. "Let us go forward to greet our hostess."

Kate swallowed. Lady Bridgerton? She had to meet Lady Bridgerton? The viscount's mother? It was hard enough to believe that a creature such as he even *had* a mother.

But manners were manners, and no matter how much Kate would have liked to slip out into the hall and depart, she knew she must thank her hostess for staging such a lovely performance.

And it had been lovely. Much as Kate was loath to admit it, especially while the woman in question was hanging all over the viscount, Maria Rosso did possess the voice of an angel.

With Mary's arm firmly guiding her, Kate reached the front of the room and waited her turn to meet the viscountess. She seemed a lovely woman, with fair hair and light eyes, and rather petite to have mothered such large sons. The late viscount must have been a tall man, Kate decided.

Finally they reached the front of the small crowd, and the viscountess grasped Mary's hand. "Mrs. Sheffield," she said warmly, "what a delight to see you again. I so enjoyed our meeting at the Hartside ball last week. I am very glad you decided to accept my invitation."

"We would not dream of spending the evening anywhere else," Mary replied. "And may I present my daughter?" She motioned to Kate, who stepped forward and bobbed a dutiful curtsy.

"It is a pleasure to meet you, Miss Sheffield," Lady Bridgerton said.

"And I am likewise honored," Kate replied.

Lady Bridgerton motioned to a young lady at her side. "And this is my daughter, Eloise."

Kate smiled warmly at the girl, who looked to be about the same age as Edwina. Eloise Bridgerton had the exact same color hair as her older brothers, and her face was lit by a friendly, wide smile. Kate liked her instantly.

"How do you do, Miss Bridgerton," Kate said. "Is this your first season?"

Eloise nodded. "I'm not officially out until next year, but my mother has been allowing me to attend functions here at Bridgerton House."

"How lucky for you," Kate replied. "I should have loved to have attended a few parties last year. Everything was so new when I arrived in London this spring. The mind boggles at the simple attempt to remember everyone's name."

Eloise grinned. "Actually, my sister Daphne came out two years ago, and she always described everyone and everything to me in such detail, I feel as if I already recognize almost everyone."

"Daphne is your eldest daughter?" Mary asked Lady Bridgerton.

The viscountess nodded. "She married the Duke of Hastings last year."

Mary smiled. "You must have been delighted."

"Indeed. He is a duke, but more importantly, he is a good man and loves my daughter. I only hope the rest of my children make such excellent matches." Lady Bridgerton cocked her head slightly to the side and turned back to Kate. "I understand, Miss Sheffield, that your sister was not able to attend this evening."

Kate fought a groan. Clearly Lady Bridgerton was already pairing up Anthony and Edwina for a walk down the aisle. "I'm afraid she caught a chill last week."

"Nothing serious, I hope?" the viscountess said to Mary, in a rather mother-to-mother sort of tone.

"No, not at all," Mary replied. "In fact, she is nearly

back to sorts. But I thought she should have one more day of recuperation before venturing out. It would not do for her to suffer a relapse."

"No, of course not." Lady Bridgerton paused, then smiled. "Well, that is too bad. I was so looking forward to meeting her. Edwina is her name, yes?"

Kate and Mary both nodded.

"I've heard she is lovely." But even as Lady Bridgerton said the words, she was glancing at her son—who was flirting madly with the Italian opera singer—and frowning.

Kate felt something very uneasy in her stomach. According to recent issues of *Whistledown,* Lady Bridgerton was on a mission to get her son married off. And while the viscount didn't seem the sort of man to bend to his mother's will (or anyone's, for that matter), Kate had a feeling that Lady Bridgerton would be able to exert quite a bit of pressure if she so chose.

After a few more moments of polite chatter, Mary and Kate left Lady Bridgerton to greet the rest of her guests. They were soon accosted by Mrs. Featherington, who, as the mother of three unmarried young women herself, always had a lot to say to Mary on a wide variety of topics. But as the stout woman bore down on them, her eyes were focused firmly on Kate.

Kate immediately began to assess possible escape routes.

"Kate!" Mrs. Featherington boomed. She had long since declared herself on a first-name basis with the Sheffields. "What a surprise to see you here."

"And why is that, Mrs. Featherington?" Kate asked, puzzled.

"Surely you read *Whistledown* this morning."

Kate smiled weakly. It was either that or wince. "Oh, you mean that little incident involving my dog?"

Mrs. Featherington's brows rose a good half inch. "From what I hear, it was more than a 'little incident.' "

"It was of little consequence," Kate said firmly,

although truth be told, she was finding it difficult not to growl at the meddlesome woman. "And I must say I resent Lady Whistledown referring to Newton as a dog of indeterminate breed. I'll have you know he is a full-blooded corgi."

"It was truly of no matter," Mary said, finally coming to Kate's defense. "I'm surprised it even warranted a mention in the column."

Kate offered Mrs. Featherington her blandest smile, fully aware that both she and Mary were lying through their teeth. Dunking Edwina (and nearly dunking Lord Bridgerton) in The Serpentine was not an incident of "little consequence," but if Lady Whistledown hadn't seen fit to report the full details, Kate certainly wasn't about to fill the gap.

Mrs. Featherington opened her mouth, a sharp intake of breath telling Kate that she was preparing to launch into a lengthy monologue on the topic of the importance of good deportment (or good manners, or good breeding, or good whatever the day's topic was), so Kate quickly blurted out, "May I fetch you two some lemonade?"

The two matrons said yes and thanked her, and Kate slipped away. Once she returned, however, she smiled innocently and said, "But I have only two hands, so now I must return for a glass for myself."

And with that, she took her leave.

She stopped briefly at the lemonade table, just in case Mary was looking, then darted out of the room and into the hall, where she sank onto a cushioned bench about ten yards from the music room, eager to get a bit of air. Lady Bridgerton had left the music room's French doors open to the small garden at the back of the house, but it was such a crush that the air was stifling, even with the slight breeze from outside.

She remained where she sat for several minutes, more than pleased that the other guests had not chosen to spill out into the hall. But then she heard one particular voice rise slightly above the low rumble of the crowd, followed by decidedly musical laughter, and Kate realized with horror that Lord Bridgerton and his would-be mistress were leaving the music room and entering the hall.

"Oh, no," she groaned, trying to keep her voice to herself. The last thing she wanted was for the viscount to stumble across her sitting alone in the hall. She knew she was by herself by choice, but he'd probably think she'd fled the gathering because she was a social failure and all the *ton* shared his opinion of her—that she was an impertinent, unattractive menace to society.

Menace to society? Kate's teeth clamped together. It would take a long, long time before she'd forgive him *that* insult.

But still, she was tired, and she didn't feel like facing him just then, so she hitched up her skirts by a few inches to save her from tripping and ducked into the doorway next to her bench. With any luck, he and his paramour would walk on by, and she could scoot back into the music room, no one being the wiser.

Kate looked around quickly as she shut the door. There was a lighted lantern on a desk, and as her eyes adjusted to the dimness, she realized she was in some sort of office. The walls were lined with books, although not enough for this to be the Bridgertons' library, and the room was dominated by a massive oak desk. Papers lay on top in neat piles, and a quill and inkpot still sat on the blotter.

Clearly this office was not just for show. Someone actually worked here.

Kate wandered toward the desk, her curiosity getting the better of her, and idly ran her fingers along the wooden rim. The air still smelled faintly of ink, and maybe the slightest hint of pipe smoke.

All in all, she decided, it was a lovely room. Comfortable and practical. A person could spend hours here in lazy contemplation.

But just as Kate leaned back against the desk, savoring her quiet solitude, she heard an *awful* sound.

The click of a doorknob.

With a frantic gasp, she dove under the desk, squeezing herself into the empty cube of space and thanking the heavens that the desk was completely solid, rather than the sort that rested on four spindly legs.

Barely breathing, she listened.

"But I had heard this would be the year we would finally see the notorious Lord Bridgerton fall into the parson's mousetrap," came a lilting feminine voice.

Kate bit her lip. It was a lilting feminine voice with an *Italian* accent.

"And where did you hear that?" came the unmistakable voice of the viscount, followed by another awful click of the doorknob.

Kate shut her eyes in agony. She was trapped in the office with a pair of lovers. Life simply could not get any worse than this.

Well, she could be discovered. *That* would be worse. Funny how that didn't make her feel much better about her present predicament, though.

"It is all over town, my lord," Maria replied. "Everyone is saying you have decided to settle down and choose a bride."

There was a silence, but Kate could swear she could *hear* him shrug.

Some footsteps, most probably drawing the lovers closer together, then Bridgerton murmured, "It is probably past time."

"You are breaking my heart, did you know that?"

Kate thought she might gag.

"Now, now, my sweet signorina"—the sound of lips on skin—"we both know that your heart is impervious to any of my machinations."

Next came a rustling sound, which Kate took to be

Maria pulling coyly away, followed by, "But I am not inclined for a dalliance, my lord. I do not look for marriage, of course—that would be most foolish. But when I next choose a protector, it shall be for, shall we say, the long term."

Footsteps. Perhaps Bridgerton was closing the distance between them again?

His voice was low and husky as he said, "I fail to see the problem."

"Your wife may see a problem."

Bridgerton chuckled. "The only reason to give up one's mistress is if one happens to love one's wife. And as I do not intend to choose a wife with whom I might fall in love, I see no reason to deny myself the pleasures of a lovely woman like you."

And you want to marry Edwina? It was all Kate could do not to scream. Truly, if she weren't squatting like a frog with her hands wrapped around her ankles, she probably would have emerged like a Fury and tried to murder the man.

Then followed a few unintelligible sounds, which Kate dearly prayed were not the prelude to something considerably more intimate. After a moment, though, the viscount's voice emerged clearly. "Would you care for something to drink?"

Maria murmured her assent, and Bridgerton's forceful stride echoed along the floor, growing closer and closer, until . . .

Oh, *no.*

Kate spied the decanter, sitting on the windowsill, directly opposite her hiding spot under the desk. If he just kept his face to the window as he poured, she might escape detection, but if he turned so much as halfway . . .

She froze. Utterly froze. Completely stopped breathing.

Eyes wide and unblinking (could eyelids make a sound?) she watched with utter and complete horror as

Bridgerton came into view, his athletic frame displayed to surprising benefit from her vantage point on the floor.

The tumblers clinked slightly together as he set them down, then he pulled the stopper from the decanter and poured two fingers of amber liquid into each glass.

Don't turn around. Don't turn around.

"Is everything all right?" Maria called out.

"Perfect," Bridgerton answered, although he sounded vaguely distracted. He lifted the glasses, humming slightly to himself as his body slowly began to turn.

Keep walking. Keep walking. If he walked away from her while he turned, he'd go back to Maria and she'd be safe. But if he turned, and *then* walked, Kate was as good as dead.

And she had no doubt that he *would* kill her. Frankly, she was surprised he hadn't made an attempt last week at The Serpentine.

Slowly, he turned. And turned. And didn't walk.

And Kate tried to think of all the reasons why dying at the age of twenty-one was really not such a bad thing.

Anthony knew quite well why he'd brought Maria Rosso back to his study. Surely no warm-blooded man could be immune to her charms. Her body was lush, her voice was intoxicating, and he knew from experience that her touch was equally potent.

But even as he took in that silky sable hair and those full, pouting lips, even as his muscles tightened at the memory of other full, pouting parts of her body, he knew that he was using her.

He felt no guilt that he would be using her for his own pleasure. In that regard, she was using him as well. And she at least would be compensated for it, whereas he would be out several jewels, a quarterly allowance, and the rent on a fashionable townhouse in a fashionable (but not too fashionable) part of town.

No, if he felt uneasy, if he felt frustrated, if he felt like he wanted to put his damned fist through a brick wall, it was because he was using Maria to banish the nightmare that was Kate Sheffield from his mind. He never wanted to wake up hard and tortured again, knowing that Kate Sheffield was the cause. He wanted to drown himself in another woman until the very memory of the dream dissolved and faded into nothingness.

Because God knew he was never going to act on that particular erotic fantasy. He didn't even *like* Kate Sheffield. The thought of bedding her made him break out in a cold sweat, even as it swirled a ripple of desire right through his gut.

No, the only way that dream was going to come true was if he were delirious with fever . . . and maybe she'd have to be delirious as well . . . and perhaps they would both have to be stranded on a desert isle, or sentenced to be executed in the morning, or . . .

Anthony shuddered. It simply wasn't going to happen.

But bloody hell, the woman must have bewitched him. There could be no other explanation for the dream—no, make that a nightmare—and besides that, even now he could swear that he could *smell* her. It was that maddening combination of lilies and soap, that beguiling scent that had washed over him while they were out in Hyde Park last week.

Here he was, pouring a glass of the finest whiskey for Maria Rosso, one of the few women of his acquaintance who knew how to appreciate both a fine whiskey and the devilish intoxication that followed, and all he could smell was the damned scent of Kate Sheffield. He knew she was in the house—and he was half ready to kill his mother for that—but this was ridiculous.

"Is everything all right?" Maria called out.

"Perfect," Anthony said, his voice sounding tight to his ears. He began to hum, something he'd always done to relax himself.

He turned and started to take a step forward. Maria was waiting for him, after all.

But there was that damned scent again. Lilies. He could swear it was lilies. And soap. The lilies were intriguing, but the soap made sense. A practical sort of woman like Kate Sheffield would scrub herself clean with soap.

His foot hesitated in midair, and his step forward proved to be a small one instead of his usual long stride. He couldn't quite escape the smell, and he kept turning, his nose instinctively twisting his eyes toward where he knew there couldn't be lilies, and yet the scent was, impossibly, there.

And then he saw her.

Under his desk.

It was impossible.

Surely this was a nightmare. Surely if he closed his eyes and opened them again, she'd be gone.

He blinked. She was still there.

Kate Sheffield, the most maddening, irritating, diabolical woman in all England, was crouching like a frog under his desk.

It was a wonder he didn't drop the whiskey.

Their eyes met, and he saw hers widen with panic and fright. Good, he thought savagely. She *should* be frightened. He was going to tan her bloody hide until her hide was bloody well bloody.

What the *hell* was she doing here? Wasn't dousing him with the filthy water of The Serpentine enough for her bloodthirsty spirit? Wasn't she satisfied with her attempts to stymie his courtship of her sister? Did she need to spy on him as well?

"Maria," he said smoothly, moving forward toward the desk until he was stepping on Kate's hand. He didn't step hard, but he heard her squeak.

This gave him immense satisfaction.

"Maria," he repeated, "I have suddenly remembered an

urgent matter of business that must be dealt with immediately."

"This very night?" she asked, sounding quite dubious.

"I'm afraid so. Euf!"

Maria blinked. "Did you just grunt?"

"No," Anthony lied, trying not to choke on the word. Kate had removed her glove and wrapped her hand around his knee, digging her nails straight through his breeches and into his skin. Hard.

At least he hoped it was her nails. It could have been her teeth.

"Are you sure there is nothing amiss?" Maria inquired.

"Nothing . . . at"—whatever body part Kate was sinking into his leg sank a little farther—"all!" The last word came out as more of a howl, and he kicked his foot forward, connecting with something he had a sneaking suspicion was her stomach.

Normally, Anthony would die before striking a woman, but this truly seemed to be an exceptional case. In fact, he took not a little bit of pleasure in kicking her while she was down.

She was biting his leg, after all.

"Allow me to walk you to the door," he said to Maria, shaking Kate off his ankle.

But Maria's eyes were curious, and she took a few steps forward. "Anthony, is there an animal under your desk?"

Anthony let out a bark of laughter. "You could say that."

Kate's fist came down on his foot.

"Is it a dog?"

Anthony seriously considered answering in the affirmative, but even he was not that cruel. Kate obviously appreciated his uncharacteristic tact, because she let go of his leg.

Anthony took advantage of his release to quickly step out from behind the desk. "Would I be unforgivably rude," he asked, striding to Maria's side and taking her arm, "if I merely walked you to the door and not back to the music room?"

She laughed, a low, sultry sound that should have seduced him. "I am a grown woman, my lord. I believe I can manage the short distance."

"Forgive me?"

She stepped through the door he held open for her. "I suspect there isn't a woman alive who could deny you forgiveness for that smile."

"You are a rare woman, Maria Rosso."

She laughed again. "But not, apparently, rare enough."

She floated out, and Anthony shut the door with a decisive click. Then, some devil on his shoulder surely prodding him, he turned the key in the lock and pocketed it.

"You," he boomed, eliminating the distance to the desk in four long strides. "Show yourself."

When Kate didn't scramble out quickly enough, he reached down, clamped his hand around her upper arm, and hauled her to her feet.

"Explain yourself," he hissed.

Kate's legs nearly buckled as the blood rushed back to her knees, which had been bent for nearly a quarter of an hour. "It was an accident," she said, grabbing on to the edge of the desk for support.

"Funny how those words seem to emerge from your mouth with startling frequency."

"It's true!" she protested. "I was sitting in the hall, and—" She gulped. He had stepped forward and was now very, very close. "I was sitting in the hall," she said again, her voice sounding crackly and hoarse, "and I heard you coming. I was just trying to avoid you."

"And so you invaded my private office?"

"I didn't know it was your office. I—" Kate sucked in her breath. He'd moved even closer, his crisp, wide lapels now only inches from the bodice of her dress. She knew his proximity was deliberate, that he sought to intimidate rather than seduce, but that didn't do anything to quell the frantic beating of her heart.

"I think perhaps you did know that this was my office," he murmured, letting his forefinger trail down the side of her cheek. "Perhaps you did not seek to avoid me at all."

Kate swallowed convulsively, long past the point of trying to maintain her composure.

"Mmmm?" His finger slid along the line of her jaw. "What do you say to that?"

Kate's lips parted, but she couldn't have uttered a word if her life had depended on it. He wore no gloves—he must have removed them during his tryst with Maria—and the touch of his skin against hers was so powerful it seemed to control her body. She breathed when he paused, stopped when he moved. She had no doubt that her heart was beating in time to his pulse.

"Maybe," he whispered, so close now that his breath kissed her lips, "you desired something else altogether."

Kate tried to shake her head, but her muscles refused to obey.

"Are you sure?"

This time, her head betrayed her and gave a little shake.

He smiled, and they both knew he had won.

Chapter 7

*Also in attendance at Lady Bridgerton's musicale: Mrs.
Featherington and the three elder Featherington daughters (Prudence, Philippa, and Penelope, none of whom
wore colors beneficial to their complexions); Mr. Nigel
Berbrooke (who, as usual, had much to say, although no
one save Philippa Featherington seemed interested); and,
of course, Mrs. Sheffield and Miss Katharine Sheffield.*

*This Author assumes that the Sheffields' invitation
had also included Miss Edwina Sheffield, but she was
not present. Lord Bridgerton seemed in fine spirits despite
the younger Miss Sheffield's absence, but alas, his mother
appeared disappointed.*

*But then again, Lady Bridgerton's matchmaking ten-
dencies are legendary, and surely she must be at loose ends
now that her daughter has married the Duke of Hastings.*

LADY WHISTLEDOWN'S SOCIETY PAPERS, 27 APRIL 1814

nthony knew he had to be insane.

There could be no other explanation. He'd meant to
scare her, terrify her, make her understand that she could
never hope to meddle in his affairs and win, and
instead . . .

He kissed her.

Intimidation had been his intention, and so he'd moved closer and closer until she, an innocent, could only be cowed by his presence. She wouldn't know what it was like to have a man so near that the heat of his body seeped through her clothes, so close that she couldn't tell where his breath ended and hers began.

She wouldn't recognize the first prickles of desire, nor would she understand that slow, swirling heat in the core of her being.

And that slow, swirling heat was there. He could see it in her face.

But she, a complete innocent, would never comprehend what he could see with one look of his experienced eyes. All she would know was that he was looming over her, that he was stronger, more powerful, and that she had made a dreadful mistake by invading his private sanctuary.

He was going to stop right there and leave her bothered and breathless. But when there was barely an inch between them, the pull grew too strong. Her scent was too beguiling, the sound of her breath too arousing. The prickles of desire he'd meant to spark within her suddenly ignited within *him,* sending a warm claw of need to the very tips of his toes. And the finger he'd been trailing along her cheek—just to torture her, he told himself— suddenly became a hand that cupped the back of her head as his lips took hers in an explosion of anger and desire.

She gasped against his mouth, and he took advantage of her parted lips by sliding his tongue between them. She was stiff in his arms, but it seemed more to do with surprise than anything else, and so Anthony pressed his suit further by allowing one of his hands to slide down her back and cup the gentle curve of her derriere.

"This is madness," he whispered against her ear. But he made no move to let her go.

Her reply was an incoherent, confused moan, and her body became slightly more pliant in his arms, allowing him to mold her even closer to his form. He knew he should stop, knew he damned well shouldn't have started, but his blood was racing with need, and she felt so . . . so . . .

So *good.*

He groaned, his lips leaving hers to taste the slightly salty skin of her neck. There was something about her that suited him like no woman ever had before, as if his body had discovered something his mind utterly refused to consider.

Something about her was . . . right.

She felt right. She smelled right. She tasted right. And he knew that if he stripped off all of her clothes and took her there on the carpet on the floor of his study, she would fit underneath him, fit around him—just right.

It occurred to Anthony that when she wasn't arguing with him, Kate Sheffield might bloody well be the finest woman in England.

Her arms, which had been imprisoned in his embrace, slowly edged up, until her hands were hesitantly resting on his back. And then her lips moved. It was a tiny thing, actually, a movement barely felt on the thin skin of his forehead, but she was definitely kissing him back.

A low, triumphant growl emerged from Anthony's mouth as he moved his mouth back to hers, kissing her fiercely, daring her to continue what she'd begun. "Oh, Kate," he moaned, nudging her back until she was leaning against the edge of the desk. "God, you taste so good."

"Bridgerton?" Her voice was tremulous, the word more of a question than anything else.

"Don't say anything," he whispered. "Whatever you do, don't say anything."

"But—"

"Not a word," he interrupted, pressing a finger to her lips. The last thing he wanted was for her to ruin this perfectly good moment by opening her mouth and arguing.

"But I—" She planted her hands on his chest and

wrenched herself away, leaving him off balance and panting.

Anthony let out a curse, and not a mild one.

Kate scurried away, not all the way across the room, but over to a tall wingback chair, far enough away so that she was not in arms' reach. She gripped the stiff back of the chair, then darted around it, thinking that it might be a good idea to have a nice solid piece of furniture between them.

The viscount didn't look to be in the best of tempers.

"Why did you do that?" she said, her voice so low it was almost a whisper.

He shrugged, suddenly looking a little less angry and a little more uncaring. "Because I wanted to."

Kate just gaped at him for a moment, unable to believe that he could have such a simple answer to what was, despite its simple phrasing, such a complicated question. Finally, she blurted out, "But you can't have."

He smiled. Slowly. "But I did."

"But you don't like me!"

"True," he allowed.

"And I don't like you."

"So you've been telling me," he said smoothly. "I'll have to take your word for it, since it wasn't particularly apparent a few seconds ago."

Kate felt her cheeks flush with shame. She had responded to his wicked kiss, and she hated herself for it, almost as much as she hated him for initiating the intimacy.

But he didn't have to taunt her. That was the act of a cad. She gripped the back of the chair until her knuckles turned white, no longer certain if she was using it as a defense against Bridgerton or as a means to stop herself from lunging forward to strangle him.

"I am not going to let you marry Edwina," she said in a very low voice.

"No," he murmured, moving slowly forward until he

was just on the other side of the chair. "I didn't think you were."

Her chin lifted a notch. "And *I* am certainly not going to marry you."

He planted his hands on the armrests and leaned forward until his face was only a few inches from hers. "I don't recall asking."

Kate lurched backward. "But you just kissed me!"

He laughed. "If I offered marriage to every woman I'd kissed, I'd have been thrown into jail for bigamy long ago."

Kate could feel herself begin to shake, and she held on to the back of the chair for dear life. "You, sir," she nearly spat out, "have no honor."

His eyes blazed and one of his hands shot out to grip her chin. He held her that way for several seconds, forcing her to meet his gaze. "That," he said in a deadly voice, "is not true, and were you a man, I'd call you out for it."

Kate remained still for what seemed like a very long time, her eyes locked on his, the skin on her cheek burning where his powerful fingers held her motionless. Finally she did the one thing she'd sworn she would never do with this man.

She begged.

"Please," she whispered, "let me go."

He did, his hand releasing her with a startling abruptness. "My apologies," he said, sounding the slightest bit . . . surprised?

No, that was impossible. Nothing could surprise this man.

"I didn't mean to hurt you," he added softly.

"Didn't you?"

He gave his head a small shake. "No. To scare you, perhaps. But not to hurt you."

Kate stepped backward on shaky legs. "You're nothing but a rake," she said, wishing her voice had emerged with a bit more disdain and a bit less quavering.

"I know," he said with a shrug, the intense fire in his eyes draining down to light amusement. "It's in my nature."

Kate took another step back. She didn't have the energy to try to keep up with his abrupt changes of mood. "I'm leaving now."

"Go," he said affably, waving toward the door.

"You can't stop me."

He smiled. "I wouldn't dream of it."

She began to edge away, walking slowly backward, afraid that if she took her eyes off him for one second he might pounce. "I'm leaving now," she said again, unnecessarily.

But when her hand was an inch away from the doorknob, he said, "I suppose I'll see you next time I call upon Edwina."

Kate went white. Not that she could actually see her face, of course, but for the first time in her life, she actually felt the blood drain from her skin. "You said you were going to leave her alone," she said accusingly.

"No," he replied, leaning rather insolently against the side of the chair, "I said that I didn't think you were likely to 'let' me marry her. Which doesn't really signify, as I have no plans to let you manage my life."

Kate suddenly felt as if a cannonball were lodged in her throat. "But you can't possibly want to marry her after you—after I—"

He took a few steps toward her, his movements slow and sleek like a cat. "After you kissed me?"

"I didn't—" But the words burned the back of her throat, because they were so obviously a lie. She had not initiated the kiss, but she had, in the end, participated in it.

"Oh, come now, Miss Sheffield," he said, standing up straight and crossing his arms. "Let's not go down that road. We don't like each other, that much is true, but I do respect you in an odd, perverted sort of way, and I know you're not a liar."

She said nothing. Really, what could she say? How did one respond to a statement that contained the words "respect" *and* "perverted"?

"You kissed me back," he said with a small, satisfied smile. "Not with any great enthusiasm, I'll admit, but that would be just a matter of time."

She shook her head, unable to believe what she was hearing. "How can you talk of such things not even a minute after declaring your intention to court my sister?"

"This does put a bit of a crimp in my plans, that is true," he commented, his voice light and thoughtful, as if he were considering the purchase of a new horse, or perhaps deciding which neckcloth to wear.

Maybe it was his casual posture, maybe it was the way he stroked his chin as if pretending to give the matter some thought. But something ignited a fuse inside of Kate, and without even thinking, she launched forward, all the furies of the world collecting in her soul as she threw herself against him, pounding his chest with her fists. "You will never marry her!" she cried out. "Never! Do you hear me?"

He raised one arm to ward off a blow to his face. "I'd have to be deaf not to." Then he expertly captured her wrists, holding her arms immobile while her body heaved and shook with rage.

"I won't let you make her unhappy. I won't let you ruin her life," she said, the words choking in her throat. "She is everything that is good and honorable and pure. And she deserves better than you."

Anthony watched her closely, his eyes trained on her face, somehow rendered beautiful by the force of her anger. Her cheeks were high with color, her eyes shone with tears she was fighting hard to keep off her face, and he was beginning to feel like he might be the worst sort of cad.

"Why, Miss Sheffield," he said softly, "I do believe you truly love your sister."

"Of course I love her!" she burst out. "Why do you

think I have gone to such efforts to keep her away from *you*? Did you think I did it for amusement? Because I can assure you, my lord, I can think of many things more amusing than being held captive in your study."

Abruptly, he let go of her wrists.

"I should think," she said with a sniffle, rubbing her reddened, abused flesh, "that my love for Edwina would be the one thing about me you could understand with perfect clarity. You, who are supposedly so devoted to your own family."

Anthony said nothing, just watched her, and wondered if perhaps there was a great deal more to this woman than he'd originally estimated.

"If you were Edwina's brother," Kate said with deadly accuracy, "would you allow her to marry a man like you?"

He did not speak for a very long moment, long enough so that the silence rang awkwardly in his own ears. Finally he said, "That is beside the point."

To her credit, she did not smile. She did not crow, nor did she taunt. When she spoke, her words were quiet and true. "I believe I have my answer." Then she turned on her heel and began to walk away.

"My sister," he said, loudly enough to halt her progress toward the door, "married the Duke of Hastings. Are you familiar with his reputation?"

She paused, but she did not turn around. "He is reputed to be quite devoted to his wife."

Anthony chuckled. "Then you are not familiar with his reputation. At least not as it was before he married."

Kate turned slowly around. "If you are attempting to convince me that reformed rakes make the best husbands, you will meet with no success. It was in this very room, not fifteen minutes ago, that you told Miss Rosso that you saw no reason to give up a mistress for a wife."

"I believe I said that was the case only if one does not love one's wife."

A funny little sound emerged from her nose—not quite

a snort, but more than a breath, and it was abundantly clear, in that moment at least, that she had no respect for him. With a sharp amusement in her eyes, she asked, "And do you love my sister, Lord Bridgerton?"

"Of course not," he replied. "And I would never insult your intelligence by saying otherwise. *But*," he said loudly, warding off the interruption he knew was sure to come, "I have known your sister but a week. I have no reason to believe that I would not come to love her were we to spend many years in holy matrimony."

She crossed her arms. "Why is it that I cannot believe a word out of your mouth?"

He shrugged. "I'm sure I do not know." But he did know. The very reason he'd selected Edwina for his wife was that he knew he'd never come to love her. He liked her, he respected her, and he was confident that she'd make an excellent mother to his heirs, but he'd never love her. The spark simply was not there.

She shook her head, disappointment in her eyes. Disappointment that somehow made him feel less of a man. "I hadn't thought you a liar, either," she said softly. "A rake and a rogue, and perhaps a whole host of other things, but not a liar."

Anthony felt her words like blows. Something unpleasant squeezed around his heart—something that made him want to lash out, to hurt her, or at least to show her she hadn't the power to hurt him. "Oh, Miss Sheffield," he called out, his voice a rather cruel drawl, "you won't get far without *this*."

Before she had a chance to react, he reached into his pocket, pulled out the key to the study, and tossed it in her direction, deliberately aiming it at her feet. Given no warning, her reflexes were not sharp, and when she thrust out her hands to catch the key, she missed it entirely. Her hands made a hollow clapping sound as they connected, followed by the dull thud of the key hitting the carpet.

She stood there for a moment, staring at the key, and he

could tell the instant she realized he had not intended for her to catch it. She remained utterly still, and then she brought her eyes to his. They were blazing with hatred, and something worse.

Disdain.

Anthony felt as if he'd been punched in the gut. He fought the most ridiculous impulse to leap forward and grab the key from the carpet, to get down on one knee and hand it to her, to apologize for his conduct and beg her forgiveness.

But he would do none of those things. He did not want to mend this breach; he did not want her favorable opinion.

Because that elusive spark—the one so noticeably absent with her sister, whom he intended to marry—crackled and burned so strongly it seemed the room ought to be as light as day.

And nothing could have terrified him more.

Kate remained motionless for far longer than he would have thought, obviously loath to kneel before him, even if it was to gather up the key that would provide her with the escape she so obviously desired.

Anthony just forced a smile, lowering his gaze to the floor and then back up to her face. "Don't you want to leave, Miss Sheffield?" he said, too smoothly.

He watched as her chin trembled, as her throat worked a convulsive swallow. And then, abruptly, she crouched down and scooped up the key. "You will never marry my sister," she vowed, her low, intense voice sending chills to his very bones. "Never."

And then, with a decisive click of the lock, she was gone.

Two days later, Kate was still furious. It didn't help that the afternoon following the musicale, a large bouquet of flowers had arrived for Edwina, the card reading, "With my wishes for a speedy recovery. Last night was dull indeed without your shining presence. —Bridgerton."

Mary had ooohed and aahed over the note—so poetic, she'd sighed, so lovely, so obviously the words of a man truly smitten. But Kate had known the truth. The note was more of an insult toward her than it was a compliment toward Edwina.

Dull indeed, she fumed, eyeing that note—enshrined now on a table in the sitting room—and wondering how she might make it look an accident if it somehow found itself torn into pieces. She might not know very much about matters of the heart and the affairs of men and women, but she'd bet her life that whatever the viscount had been feeling that night in the study, it had not been boredom.

He hadn't, however, come to call. Kate couldn't imagine why, since taking Edwina out for a drive would be an even bigger slap in the face than the note had been. In her most fanciful moments, she liked to flatter herself that he hadn't stopped by because he was afraid to face her, but she knew that was patently untrue.

That man wasn't afraid of anyone. Least of all, a plain, aging spinster he'd probably kissed out of a mix of curiosity, anger, and pity.

Kate crossed over to a window and gazed out over Milner Street; not the most picturesque view in London, but at least it stopped her from staring at the note. It was the pity that truly ate at her. She prayed that whatever had gone into that kiss, the curiosity and the anger had outweighed the pity.

She didn't think she could bear it if he pitied her.

But Kate didn't have very long to obsess over the kiss and what it might and might not have meant, because that afternoon—the afternoon after the flowers—arrived an invitation far more unsettling than anything Lord Bridgerton might have issued himself. The Sheffields' presence, it seemed, was desired at a country house party being rather spontaneously hosted in one week's time by Lady Bridgerton.

The mother of the devil himself.

And there was no way that Kate could possibly get out of going. Nothing short of an earthquake combined with a hurricane combined with a tornado—none of which were likely to occur in Great Britain, although Kate was still holding out hope for the hurricane, as long as there was no thunder or lightning involved—would prevent Mary from showing up on the Bridgertons' bucolic doorstep with Edwina in tow. And Mary certainly wasn't going to allow Kate to remain alone in London, left to her own devices. Not to mention that there was no way Kate was going to allow Edwina to go without her.

The viscount had no scruples. He'd probably kiss Edwina just as he'd kissed Kate, and Kate couldn't imagine that Edwina would have the fortitude to resist such an advance. She'd probably think it beyond romantic and fall in love with him on the spot.

Even Kate had had difficulty keeping her head when his lips had been on hers. For one blissful moment, she'd forgotten everything. She'd known nothing but an exquisite sensation of being cherished and wanted—no, *needed*—and it had been heady stuff, indeed.

Almost enough to make a lady forget that the man doing the kissing was a worthless cad.

Almost . . . but not quite.

Chapter 8

As any regular reader of this column knows, there are two sects in London who shall forever remain in the utmost opposition: Ambitious Mamas and Determined Bachelors.

The Ambitious Mama has daughters of marriageable age. The Determined Bachelor does not want a wife. The crux of the conflict should be obvious to those with half a brain, or, in other words, approximately fifty percent of This Author's readership.

This Author has not yet seen a guest list for Lady Bridgerton's country house party, but informed sources indicate that nearly every eligible young lady of marriageable age will be gathering in Kent next week.

This surprises no one. Lady Bridgerton has never made a secret of her desire to see her sons favorably married. This sentiment has made her a favorite among the Ambitious Mama set, who despairingly view the Bridgerton brothers as the worst sort of Determined Bachelors.

If one is to trust the betting books, then at least one of the Bridgerton brothers shall be witness to wedding bells before the year is through.

As much as it pains This Author to agree with the betting books (they are written by men, and thus inherently flawed), This Author must concur in the prediction.

Julia Quinn

Lady Bridgerton will soon have her daughter-in-law. But who she will be—and to which brother she shall find herself married—ah, Gentle Reader, that is still anyone's guess.

LADY WHISTLEDOWN'S SOCIETY PAPERS, 29 APRIL 1814

*O*ne week later, Anthony was in Kent— in his private suite of offices, to be precise—awaiting the start of his mother's country house party.

He'd seen the guest list. There could be no doubt that his mother had decided to host this party for one reason and one reason only: to get one of her sons married off, preferably him. Aubrey Hall, the ancestral seat of the Bridgertons, would be filled to the brim with eligible young ladies, each lovelier and more empty-headed than the last. To keep numbers even, Lady Bridgerton had had to invite a number of gentlemen, to be sure, but none were as wealthy or well connected as her own sons, save for the few who were married.

His mother, Anthony thought ruefully, had never been known for her subtlety. At least not when the well-being (*her* definition of well-being, that is) of her children was concerned.

He had not been surprised to see that an invitation had been extended to the Misses Sheffield. His mother had mentioned—several times—how much she liked Mrs. Sheffield. And he had been forced to listen to his mother's "Good Parents Make Good Children" theory too many times not to know what *that* meant.

He'd actually felt a resigned sort of satisfaction upon the sight of Edwina's name on the list. He was eager to propose to her and be done with it. He did feel a measure of uneasiness over what had happened with Kate, but there seemed little to be done now unless he wanted to go to the trouble of finding another prospective bride.

Which he did not. Once Anthony made a decision—in this case to finally get married—he saw no reason in courting delays. Procrastination was for those with a bit more time to live out their lives. Anthony might have avoided the parson's mousetrap for nearly a decade, but now that he'd decided it was time for a bride, there seemed little sense in tarrying.

Marry, procreate, and die. Such was the life of a noble Englishman, even one whose father and uncle had not dropped unexpectedly dead at the ages of thirty-eight and thirty-four, respectively.

Clearly, all he could do at this point was to avoid Kate Sheffield. An apology would probably also be in order. It wouldn't be easy, since the last thing he wanted to do was humble himself to that woman, but the whispers of his conscience had risen to a dull roar, and he knew she deserved the words, "I'm sorry."

She probably deserved more, but Anthony was unwilling to contemplate what that might be.

Not to mention that unless he went and spoke to her, she was likely to block a union between him and Edwina to her dying breath.

Now was clearly the time to take action. If there ever was a romantic spot for a proposal of marriage, Aubrey Hall was it. Built in the early 1700s of warm yellow stone, it sat comfortably on a wide green lawn, surrounded by sixty acres of parkland, a full ten of which were flowering gardens. Later in the summer the roses would be out, but now the grounds were carpeted with grape hyacinths and the brilliant tulips his mother had had imported from Holland.

Anthony gazed across the room and out the window, where ancient elms rose majestically around the house. They shaded the drive and, he liked to think, made the hall seem a bit more like it was a part of nature and a bit less like the typical country homes of the aristocracy—man-made monuments to wealth, position, and power. There were several ponds, a creek, and countless hills and hollows, each one with its own special memories of childhood.

And his father.

Anthony closed his eyes and exhaled. He loved coming home to Aubrey Hall, but the familiar sights and smells brought his father to mind with a clarity so vivid it was almost painful. Even now, nearly twelve years after Edmund Bridgerton's death, Anthony still expected to see him come bounding around the corner, the smallest of the Bridgerton children screaming with delight as he rode on his father's shoulders.

The image made Anthony grin. The child on the shoulders might be a boy or a girl; Edmund had never discriminated between his children when it came to horseplay. But no matter who held the coveted spot at the top of the world, they would surely be chased after by a nurse, insisting that they stop this nonsense at once, and that a child's place was in the nursery and certainly *not* on her father's shoulders.

"Oh, Father," Anthony whispered, looking up at the portrait of Edmund that hung over the fireplace, "how on earth will I ever live up to your achievements?"

And surely that had to have been Edmund Bridgerton's greatest achievement—presiding over a family filled with love and laughter and everything that was so often absent from aristocratic life.

Anthony turned away from his father's portrait and crossed over to the window, watching the coaches pull up the drive. The afternoon had brought a steady stream of arrivals, and every conveyance seemed to carry yet another fresh-faced young lady, her eyes alight with happiness at having been gifted with an invitation to the Bridgerton house party.

Lady Bridgerton didn't often elect to fill her country home with guests. When she did, it was always the event of the season.

Although, truth be told, none of the Bridgertons spent much time at Aubrey Hall any longer. Anthony suspected that his mother suffered the same malady he did—memories of Edmund around every corner. The younger children had few memories of the place, having been raised primarily in London. They certainly didn't recall the long hikes across fields, or the fishing, or the treehouse.

Hyacinth, who was now just eleven, had never even been held in her father's arms. Anthony had tried to fill the gap as best as he could, but he knew he was a very pale comparison.

With a weary sigh, Anthony leaned heavily against the window frame, trying to decide whether or not he wanted to pour himself a drink. He was staring out over the lawn, his eyes focusing on absolutely nothing, when a carriage decidedly shabbier than the rest rolled down the drive. Not that there was anything shoddy about it; it was obviously well made and sturdy. But it lacked the gilded crests that graced the other carriages, and it seemed to bump along a tiny bit more than the rest, as if it weren't quite well sprung enough for comfort.

This would be the Sheffields, Anthony realized. Everyone else on the guest list was in possession of a respectable fortune. Only the Sheffields would have had to hire a carriage for the season.

Sure enough, when one of the Bridgerton footmen, dressed in stylish powder-blue livery, leaped forward to open the door, out stepped Edwina Sheffield, looking a veritable vision in a pale yellow traveling dress and matching bonnet. Anthony was not close enough to see her face clearly, but it was easy enough to imagine. Her cheeks would be soft and pink, and her exquisite eyes would mirror the cloudless sky.

The next to emerge was Mrs. Sheffield. It was only when she took her place next to Edwina that he realized how closely they resembled one another. Both were charmingly graceful and petite, and as they spoke, he could see that they held themselves in the same manner. The tilt of the head was identical, as were their posture and stance.

Edwina would not outgrow her beauty. This would clearly be a good attribute in a wife, although—Anthony threw a rueful glance at his father's portrait—he wasn't likely to be around to watch her age.

Finally, Kate stepped down.

And Anthony realized he'd been holding his breath.

She didn't move like the two other Sheffield women. They had been dainty, leaning on the footman, putting their hands in his with a graceful arch of the wrist.

Kate, on the other hand, practically hopped right down. She took the footman's proffered arm, but she certainly didn't appear to need his assistance. As soon as her feet touched the ground, she stood tall and lifted her face to gaze at the facade of Aubrey Hall. Everything about her was direct and straightforward, and Anthony had no doubt that if he were close enough to gaze into her eyes, he would find them utterly forthright.

Once she saw him, however, they would fill with disdain, and perhaps a touch of hatred as well.

Which was really all he deserved. A gentleman did not treat a lady as he had Kate Sheffield and expect her continued good favor.

Kate turned to her mother and sister and said something, causing Edwina to laugh and Mary to smile indulgently. Anthony realized he hadn't had much opportunity to watch the three of them interact before. They were a true family, comfortable in each other's presence, and there was a warmth one sensed in their faces when they conversed. It was especially fascinating since he knew that Mary and Kate were not blood relatives.

There were some bonds, he was coming to realize, that were stronger than those of blood. These were not bonds he had room for in his life.

Which was why, when he married, the face behind the veil would have to be Edwina Sheffield's.

Kate had expected to be impressed by Aubrey Hall. She had not expected to be enchanted.

The house was smaller than she'd expected. Oh, it was still far, far larger than anything she'd ever had the honor to call home, but the country manor was not a hulking behemoth rising out of the landscape like a misplaced medieval castle.

Rather, Aubrey Hall seemed almost cozy. It seemed a bizarre word to use to describe a house with surely fifty rooms, but its fanciful turrets and crenellations almost made it seem like something out of a fairy story, especially with the late afternoon sun giving the yellow stone an almost reddish glow. There was nothing austere or imposing about Aubrey Hall, and Kate liked it immediately.

"Isn't it lovely?" Edwina whispered.

Kate nodded. "Lovely enough to make a week spent in the company of that awful man almost bearable."

Edwina laughed and Mary scolded, but even Mary could not resist an indulgent smile. But she did say, casting an eye to the footman, who had gone around the back of the coach to unload their luggage, "You should not say such things, Kate. One never knows who is listening, and it is unbecoming to speak thusly about our host."

"Have no fear, he didn't hear me," Kate replied. "And besides, I thought Lady Bridgerton was our hostess. She *did* issue the invitation."

"The viscount owns the house," Mary returned.

"Very well," Kate acceded, motioning to Aubrey Hall with a dramatic wave of her arm. "The moment I enter those hallowed halls, I shall be nothing but sweetness and light."

Edwina snorted. "That will certainly be a sight to behold."

Mary shot Kate a knowing look. " 'Sweetness and light' applies to the gardens as well," she said.

Kate just smiled. "Truly, Mary, I shall be on my best behavior. I promise."

"Just do your best to avoid the viscount."

"I will," Kate promised. *As long as he does his best to avoid Edwina.*

A footman appeared at their side, his arm sweeping toward the hall in a splendid arc. "If you will step inside," he said, "Lady Bridgerton is eager to greet her guests."

The three Sheffields immediately turned and made their way to the front door. As they mounted the shallow steps, however, Edwina turned to Kate with a mischievous grin and whispered, "Sweetness and light begins here, sister mine."

"If we weren't in public," Kate returned, her voice equally hushed, "I might have to hit you."

Lady Bridgerton was in the main hall when they stepped inside, and Kate could see the ribboned hems of walking dresses disappearing up the stairs as the previous carriage's occupants made their way to their rooms.

"Mrs. Sheffield!" Lady Bridgerton called out, crossing over toward them. "How lovely to see you. And Miss Sheffield," she added, turning to Kate, "I am so glad you were able to join us."

"It was kind of you to invite us," Kate replied. "And it is truly a pleasure to escape the city for a week."

Lady Bridgerton smiled. "You are a country girl at heart, then?"

"I'm afraid so. London is exciting, and always worth a visit, but I do prefer the green fields and fresh air of the countryside."

"My son is much the same way," Lady Bridgerton said. "Oh, he spends his time in the city, but a mother knows the truth."

"The viscount?" Kate asked doubtfully. He seemed such the consummate rake, and everyone knew a rake's natural habitat was the city.

"Yes, Anthony. We lived here almost exclusively when he was a child. We went to London during the season, of course, since I do love to attend parties and balls, but never for more than a few weeks. It was only after my husband passed away that we moved our primary residence to town."

"I'm sorry for your loss," Kate murmured.

The viscountess turned to her with a wistful expression in her blue eyes. "That is very sweet of you. He has been gone for many years, but I do still miss him each and every day."

Kate felt a lump forming in her throat. She remembered how well Mary and her father had loved each other, and she knew that she was in the presence of another woman who had experienced true love. And suddenly she felt so very sad. Because Mary had lost her husband and the viscountess had lost hers as well, and . . .

And maybe most of all because she would probably never know the bliss of true love herself.

"But we're becoming so maudlin," Lady Bridgerton suddenly said, smiling a little too brightly as she turned back to Mary, "and here I haven't even met your other daughter."

"Have you not?" Mary asked, her brow furrowing. "I suppose that must be true. Edwina was not able to attend your musicale."

"I have, of course, seen you from afar," Lady Bridgerton said to Edwina, bestowing upon her a dazzling smile.

Mary made the introductions, and Kate could not help but notice the appraising manner in which Lady Bridgerton regarded Edwina. There could be no doubt about it. She'd decided Edwina would make an excellent addition to her family.

After a few more moments of chitchat, Lady Bridgerton offered them tea while their bags were being delivered to their rooms, but they declined, as Mary was tired and wanted to lie down.

"As you wish," Lady Bridgerton said, signaling to a housemaid. "I shall have Rose show you to your rooms. Dinner is at eight. Is there anything else I may do for you before you retire?"

Mary and Edwina both shook their heads no, and Kate started to follow suit, but at the last minute she blurted out, "Actually, if I might ask you a question."

Lady Bridgerton smiled warmly. "Of course."

"I noticed when we arrived that you have extensive flower gardens. Might I explore them?"

"Then you are a gardener as well?" Lady Bridgerton inquired.

"Not a very good one," Kate admitted, "but I do admire the hand of an expert."

The viscountess blushed. "I should be honored if you explored the gardens. They are my pride and joy. I don't have much a hand in them now, but when Edmund was al—" She stopped and cleared her throat. "That is to say, when I spent more time here, I was always up to my elbows in dirt. It used to drive my mother positively mad."

"And the gardener, too, I imagine," Kate said.

Lady Bridgerton's smile erupted into laughter. "Oh, indeed! He was a terrible sort. Always saying that the only thing women knew about flowers was how to accept them as a gift. But he had the greenest thumb you could ever imagine, so I learned to put up with him."

"And he learned to put up with you?"

Lady Bridgerton smiled wickedly. "No, he never did, actually. But I didn't let that stop me."

Kate grinned, instinctively warming to the older woman.

"But don't let me keep you any longer," Lady Bridgerton said. "Let Rose take you up and get you settled in. And Miss Sheffield," she said to Kate, "if you like, I should be happy to give you a tour of the gardens later in the week. I'm afraid I'm too busy greeting guests right now, but I would be delighted to make time for you at a later date."

"I would like that, thank you," Kate said, and then she and Mary and Edwina followed the maid up the stairs.

Anthony emerged from his position behind his ever-so-slightly ajar door and strode down the hall toward his mother. "Was that the Sheffields I saw you greeting?" he asked, even though he knew very well it was. But his offices were too far down the hall for him to have heard anything the quartet of women had actually said, so he decided that a brief interrogation was in order.

"Indeed it was," Violet replied. "Such a lovely family, don't you think?"

Anthony just grunted.

"I'm so glad I invited them."

Anthony said nothing, although he considered grunting again.

"They were a last-minute addition to the guest list."

"I didn't realize," he murmured.

Violet nodded. "I had to scrounge up three more gentlemen from the village to even the numbers."

"So we may expect the vicar at supper this eve?"

"And his brother, who is visiting for a spell, and his son."

"Isn't young John only sixteen?"

Violet shrugged. "I was desperate."

Anthony pondered this. His mother was indeed desperate to have the Sheffields join the house party if it meant inviting a spotty-faced sixteen-year-old to supper. Not that she wouldn't have invited him for a family meal; when not formally entertaining, the Bridgertons broke with accepted standards and had all the children eat in the dining room, regardless of age. Indeed, the first time Anthony had gone to visit a friend, he'd been shocked that he was expected to take his meals in the nursery.

But still, a house party was a house party, and even Violet Bridgerton did not allow children at the table.

"I understand you've made the acquaintance of both Sheffield girls," Violet said.

Anthony nodded.

"I find them both delightful myself," she continued. "They haven't much in the way of fortune, but I've always maintained that when choosing a spouse, fortune is not as important as character, provided, of course, that one isn't in desperate straits."

"Which I," Anthony drawled, "as I am sure you are about to point out, am not."

Violet sniffed and shot him a haughty look. "I should not be so quick to mock me, my son. I merely point out the truth. You should be down on your hands and knees thanking your maker every day that you don't *have* to marry an heiress. Most men don't have the luxury of free will when it comes to marriage, you know."

Anthony just smiled. "I should be thanking my maker? Or my mother?"

"You are a beast."

He clucked her gently under the chin. "A beast you raised."

"And it wasn't an easy task," she muttered. "I can assure you of that."

He leaned forward and dropped a kiss on her cheek. "Have fun greeting your guests, Mother."

She scowled at him, but her heart clearly wasn't in it. "Where are you going?" she asked as he started to move away.

"For a walk."

"Really?"

He turned around, a bit bewildered over her interest. "Yes, really. Is there a problem with that?"

"Not at all," she replied. "Just that you haven't taken a walk—for the simple sake of taking a walk—in ages."

"I haven't been in the country in ages," he commented.

"True," she conceded. "In that case, you should really head out to the flower gardens. The early species are just beginning to bloom, and it's simply spectacular. Like nothing you can ever see in London."

Anthony nodded. "I shall see you for supper."

Violet beamed and waved him off, watching as he disappeared back into his offices, which wrapped around the corner of Aubrey Hall and had French doors leading out to the side lawn.

Her eldest son's interest in the Sheffields was most intriguing. Now, if she could only figure out which Sheffield he was interested in. . . .

About a quarter of an hour later, Anthony was out strolling through his mother's flower gardens, enjoying the contradiction of the warm sun and the cool breeze, when he heard the light sound of a second set of footsteps on a nearby path. This piqued his curiosity. The guests were all settling in their rooms, and it was the gardener's day off. Frankly, he'd been anticipating solitude.

He turned toward the direction of the footfall, moving silently until he reached the end of his path. He looked to the right, then to the left, and then he saw . . .

Her.

Why, he wondered, was he surprised?

Kate Sheffield, dressed in a pale lavender frock, blending in charmingly with the irises and grape hyacinths. She was standing beside a decorative wooden arch, which, later in the year, would be covered with climbing pink and white roses.

He watched her for a moment as she trailed her fingers along some fuzzy plant he could never remember the name of, then bent down to sniff at a Dutch tulip.

"They don't have a scent," he called out, slowly making his way toward her.

She straightened immediately, her entire body reacting before she'd turned to see him. He could tell she'd recognized his voice, which left him feeling rather oddly satisfied.

As he approached her side, he motioned to the brilliant red bloom and said, "They're lovely and somewhat rare in an English garden, but alas, with no perfume."

She waited longer to reply than he would have expected, then she said, "I've never seen a tulip before."

Something about that made him smile. "Never?"

"Well, not in the ground," she explained. "Edwina has received many bouquets, and the bulb flowers are quite the rage this time of year. But I've never actually seen one growing."

"They are my mother's favorite," Anthony said, reaching down and plucking one. "That and hyacinths, of course."

She smiled curiously. "Of course?" she echoed.

"My youngest sister is named Hyacinth," he said, handing her the flower. "Or didn't you know that?"

She shook her head. "I didn't."

"I see," he murmured. "We are quite famously named in alphabetical order, from Anthony right down to Hyacinth. But then, perhaps I know a great deal more about you than you know of me."

Kate's eyes widened in surprise at his enigmatic statement, but all she said was, "That may very well be true."

Anthony quirked a brow. "I'm shocked, Miss Sheffield. I had donned all my armor and was expecting you to return with, 'I know quite enough.' "

Kate tried not to make a face at his imitation of her voice. But her expression was wry in the extreme as she said, "I promised Mary I would be on my best behavior."

Anthony let out a loud hoot of laughter.

"Strangely enough," Kate muttered, "Edwina had a similar reaction."

He leaned one hand against the arch, carefully avoiding the thorns on the climbing rose vine. "I find myself insanely curious as to what constitutes good behavior."

She shrugged and fiddled with the tulip in her hand. "I expect I shall figure that out as I go along."

"But you're not supposed to argue with your host, correct?"

Kate shot him an arch look. "There was some debate

over whether or not you qualify as our host, my lord. After all, the invitation was issued by your mother."

"True," he acceded, "but I do own the house."

"Yes," she muttered, "Mary said as much."

He grinned. "This is killing you, isn't it?"

"Being nice to you?"

He nodded.

"It's not the easiest thing I've ever done."

His expression changed slightly, as if he might be done teasing her. As if he might have something entirely different on his mind. "But it's not the hardest thing, either, now, is it?" he murmured.

"I don't like you, my lord," she blurted out.

"No," he said with an amused smile. "I didn't think you did."

Kate started to feel very strange, much like she had in his study, right before he'd kissed her. Her throat suddenly felt a bit tight, and her palms grew very warm. And her insides—well, there was really nothing to describe the tense, prickly feeling that tightened through her abdomen. Instinctively, and perhaps out of self-preservation, she took a step back.

He looked amused, as if he knew exactly what she was thinking.

She fiddled with the flower some more, then blurted out, "You shouldn't have picked this."

"You should have a tulip," he said matter-of-factly. "It isn't right that Edwina receives all the flowers."

Kate's stomach, already tense and prickly, did a little flip. "Nonetheless," she managed to say, "your gardener will surely not appreciate the mutilation of his work."

He smiled devilishly. "He'll blame one of my younger siblings."

She couldn't help but smile. "I *should* think less of you for such a ploy," she said.

"But you don't?"

She shook her head. "But then again, it's not as if my opinion of you could sink very much lower."

"Ouch." He shook a finger at her. "I thought you were supposed to be on your best behavior."

Kate looked around. "It doesn't count if there is no one nearby to hear me, right?"

"*I* can hear you."

"*You* certainly don't count."

His head dipped a little closer in her direction. "I should think I was the *only* one who did."

Kate said nothing, not wanting even to meet his eyes. Whenever she allowed herself one glimpse into those velvety depths, her stomach started flipping anew.

"Miss Sheffield?" he murmured.

She looked up. Big mistake. Her stomach flipped again.

"Why did you seek me out?" she asked.

Anthony pushed off the wooden post and stood straight. "I didn't, actually. I was just as surprised to see you as you were me." Although, he thought acerbically, he shouldn't have been. He should have realized his mother was up to something the moment she actually suggested where he take his walk.

But could she possibly be steering him to the *wrong* Miss Sheffield? Surely she wouldn't choose Kate over Edwina as a prospective daughter-in-law.

"But now that I have found you," he said, "I did have something I wanted to say."

"Something you haven't already said?" she quipped. "I can't imagine."

He ignored her jibe. "I wanted to apologize."

That got her attention. Her lips parted with shock, and her eyes grew round. "I beg your pardon?" she said. Anthony thought her voice sounded rather like a frog.

"I owe you an apology for my behavior the other night," he said. "I treated you most rudely."

"You're apologizing for the kiss?" she asked, still looking rather dazed.

The kiss? He hadn't even considered apologizing for the kiss. He'd never apologized for a kiss, never before kissed someone for whom an apology might be necessary. He'd actually been thinking more of the unpleasant things he'd said to her after the kiss. "Er, yes," he lied, "the kiss. And for what I said, as well."

"I see," she murmured. "I didn't think rakes apologized."

His hand flexed, then made a tight fist. It was damned annoying, this habit of hers always to jump to conclusions about him. "This rake does," he said in clipped tones.

She took a deep breath, then let it out in a long, steady exhale. "Then I accept your apology."

"Excellent," he said, offering his most winning smile. "May I escort you back to the house?"

She nodded. "But don't think this means that I will suddenly change my mind about you and Edwina."

"I would never dream of considering you so easily swayed," he said, quite honestly.

She turned to him, her eyes startlingly direct, even for her. "The fact remains that you kissed me," she said bluntly.

"And you kissed me," he could not resist returning.

Her cheeks turned a delightful shade of pink. "The fact remains," she repeated determinedly, "that it happened. And should you marry Edwina—regardless of your reputation, which I do not consider inconsequential—"

"No," he murmured, interrupting her with velvet soft tones, "I didn't think you would."

She glared at him. "Regardless of your reputation, *it* would always be between us. Once something happens, you can't take it away."

The devil in Anthony nearly compelled him to drawl the word, "It?" forcing her to repeat the words, "The kiss," but instead he took pity on her and let it go. Besides, she had a good point. The kiss would always be between them. Even now, with her cheeks pinkened by embarrassment and her lips pursed with irritation, he found himself wondering how she'd feel if he pulled her into his arms, how she'd taste if he traced the outline of her lips with his tongue.

Would she smell like the garden? Or would that maddening scent of lilies and soap still cling to her skin?

Would she melt into his embrace? Or would she push him away and run for the house?

There was only one way to find out, and doing so would ruin his chances with Edwina forever.

But as Kate had pointed out, maybe marrying Edwina would bring with it far too many complications. It would not do to be lusting after one's sister-in-law, after all.

Maybe the time had come to search out a new bride, tedious though the prospect may be.

Maybe the time was right to kiss Kate Sheffield again, here in the perfect beauty of Aubrey Hall's gardens, with the flowers grazing their legs and the smell of lilac hanging in the air.

Maybe . . .

Maybe . . .

Chapter 9

*Men are contrary creatures. Their heads and their hearts
are never in agreement. And as women know all too well,
their actions are usually governed by a different aspect
altogether.*

LADY WHISTLEDOWN'S SOCIETY PAPERS, 29 APRIL 1814

*O*r maybe not.

Just as Anthony was plotting the best course to her lips,
he heard the perfectly awful sound of his younger
brother's voice.

"Anthony!" Colin shouted out. "There you are."

Miss Sheffield, blissfully unaware of how close she'd
come to having been kissed utterly senseless, turned to
watch Colin approach.

"One of these days," Anthony muttered, "I'm going to
have to kill him."

Kate turned back. "Did you say something, my lord?"

Anthony ignored her. It was probably his best option,
since *not* ignoring her tended to leave him rather desperately lusting after her, which was, as he well knew, a short,
straight road to utter disaster.

In all truth, he probably should have thanked Colin for

his untimely interruption. A few more seconds, and he would have kissed Kate Sheffield, which would have been the greatest mistake of his life.

One kiss with Kate could probably be excused, especially considering how far she'd provoked him the other night in his study. But two . . . well, two would have required any man of honor to withdraw his courtship of Edwina Sheffield.

And Anthony wasn't quite ready to give up on the concept of honor.

He couldn't believe how close he'd come to tossing aside his plan to marry Edwina. What was he thinking? She was the perfect bride for his purposes. It was only when her meddlesome sister was around that his brain grew confused.

"Anthony," Colin said again as he drew near, "and Miss Sheffield." He eyed them curiously; he well knew they didn't get along. "What a surprise."

"I was just exploring your mother's gardens," Kate said, "and I stumbled upon your brother."

Anthony gave a single nod of agreement.

"Daphne and Simon are here," Colin said.

Anthony turned to Kate and explained, "My sister and her husband."

"The duke?" she inquired politely.

"The very one," he grumbled.

Colin laughed at his brother's pique. "He was opposed to the marriage," he said to Kate. "It kills him that they're happy."

"Oh, for the love of—" Anthony snapped, catching himself just before he blasphemed in front of Kate. "I'm very happy that my sister is happy," he ground out, not sounding particularly happy. "It's simply that I should have had one more opportunity to beat the tar out of that bas—bounder before they embarked on 'happily ever after.'"

Kate choked on a laugh. "I see," she said, fairly certain that she had *not* kept the straight face she'd been aiming for.

Colin shot her a grin before turning back to his brother.

"Daff suggested a game of Pall Mall. What do you say? We haven't played for ages. And, if we set off soon, we can escape the milksop misses Mother has invited for us." He turned back to Kate with the sort of grin that could win forgiveness for anything. "Present company excluded, of course."

"Of course," she murmured.

Colin leaned forward, his green eyes flashing with mischief. "*No one* would make the mistake of calling you a milksop miss," he added.

"Is that a compliment?" she asked acerbically.

"Without a doubt."

"Then I shall accept it with grace and good favor."

Colin laughed and said to Anthony, "I like her."

Anthony didn't look amused.

"Have you ever played Pall Mall, Miss Sheffield?" Colin asked.

"I'm afraid not. I'm not even sure what it is."

"It's a lawn game. Brilliant fun. More popular in France than it is here, although they call it *Paille Maille*."

"How does one play?" Kate asked.

"We set out wickets on a course," Colin explained, "then hit wooden balls through them with mallets."

"That sounds simple enough," she mused.

"Not," he said with a laugh, "when you're playing with the Bridgertons."

"And what does *that* mean?"

"It means," Anthony cut in, "that we've never seen the need to set out a regulation course. Colin sets out the wickets over tree roots—"

"And you aimed yours toward the lake," Colin interrupted. "We never did find the red ball after Daphne sank it."

Kate knew she shouldn't be committing herself to an afternoon in the company of Viscount Bridgerton, but dash it all, Pall Mall sounded fun. "Might there be room for one more player?" she inquired. "Since we've already excluded me from the ranks of the milksops?"

"Of course!" Colin said. "I suspect you'll fit right in with the rest of us schemers and cheaters."

"Coming from you," Kate said with a laugh, "I *know* that was a compliment."

"Oh, for certain. Honor and honesty has its time and place, but *not* in a game of Pall Mall."

"And," Anthony cut in, a smug expression on his face, "we shall have to invite your sister as well."

"Edwina?" Kate choked out. Drat. She'd just played right into his hand. She'd been doing her best to keep the two of them apart, and now she'd practically arranged an afternoon out. There was no way she could exclude Edwina after all but inviting herself into the game.

"Do you have another sister?" he asked mildly.

She just scowled at him. "She might not wish to play. I think she was resting in her room."

"I'll instruct the maid to knock very lightly on her door," Anthony said, obviously lying.

"Excellent!" Colin said brightly. "We shall be evenly matched. Three men and three women."

"Does one play on teams?" Kate asked.

"No," he replied, "but my mother has always been adamant that one must be evenly matched in all things. She'll be quite disturbed if we go out in odd numbers."

Kate couldn't imagine the lovely and gracious woman she'd chatted with just an hour earlier getting upset over a game of Pall Mall, but she figured it wasn't her place to comment.

"I'll see to fetching Miss Sheffield," Anthony murmured, looking insufferably smug. "Colin, why don't you see *this* Miss Sheffield down to the field and I'll meet you there in half an hour?"

Kate opened her mouth to protest the arrangements that would leave Edwina alone in the viscount's company, even for so short a time as a walk down to the field, but in the end she remained silent. There was no reasonable excuse she could give to prevent it, and she knew it.

Anthony caught her fishlike spluttering and quirked one corner of his mouth in the most obnoxious manner before he said, "I'm pleased to see you agree with me, Miss Sheffield."

She just grumbled. If she'd formed words, they wouldn't have been polite ones.

"Excellent," Colin said. "We'll see you then."

And then he looped his arm through hers and led her away, leaving Anthony smirking behind them.

Colin and Kate walked about a quarter of a mile from the house to a somewhat uneven clearing bordered on one side by a lake.

"Home of the prodigal red ball, I presume?" Kate queried, motioning to the water.

Colin laughed and nodded. "It's a pity, because we used to have equipment enough for eight players; Mother had insisted on our purchasing a set that could accommodate all of her children."

Kate wasn't certain whether to smile or frown. "Yours is a very close family, isn't it?"

"The best," Colin said simply, walking over to a nearby shed.

Kate trailed after him, tapping her hand idly against her thigh. "Do you know what time it is?" she called out.

He paused, pulled out his pocket watch, and flipped it open. "Ten minutes past three."

"Thank you," Kate replied, making a mental note of it. They'd probably left Anthony at five to three, and he'd promised to deliver Edwina to the Pall Mall field within thirty minutes, so they should be down at twenty-five past the hour.

Half three at the very latest. Kate was willing to be generous and allow for unavoidable delays. If the viscount had Edwina down by half three, she wouldn't quibble.

Colin resumed his trek to the shed, Kate watching with

interest as he wrenched open the door. "It sounds rusty," she commented.

"It's been a while since we've been out here to play," he said.

"Really? If I had a house like Aubrey Hall, I would never go to London."

Colin turned around, his hand still on the half-open door to the shed. "You're a lot like Anthony, did you know that?"

Kate gasped. "Surely you're joking."

He shook his head, a strange little smile on his lips. "Perhaps it's because you're both the eldest. The Lord knows I'm thankful every day I wasn't born in Anthony's shoes."

"What do you mean?"

Colin shrugged. "I simply wouldn't want his responsibilities, that's all. The title, the family, the fortune—it's a great deal to fit on one man's shoulders."

Kate didn't particularly want to hear how well the viscount had assumed the responsibilities of his title; she didn't want to hear anything that might change her opinion of him, although she had to confess that she'd been impressed by the apparent sincerity of his apology earlier that afternoon. "What has this to do with Aubrey Hall?" she inquired.

Colin stared at her blankly for a moment, as if he'd forgotten that the conversation had started with her innocent comment about how lovely his country home was. "Nothing, I suppose," he said finally. "And everything as well. Anthony loves it here."

"But he spends all his time in London," Kate said. "Doesn't he?"

"I know." Colin shrugged. "Odd, isn't it?"

Kate had no reply, so she just watched as he pulled the door to the shed all the way open. "Here we are," he said, pulling out a wheeled cart that had been specially constructed to fit eight mallets and wooden balls. "A bit musty, but none the worse for the wear."

"Except for the loss of the red ball," Kate said with a smile.

"I blame that entirely on Daphne," Colin replied. "I blame everything on Daphne. It makes my life much easier."

"I heard that!"

Kate turned to see an attractive young couple approaching. The man was devastatingly handsome, with dark, dark hair and light, light eyes. The woman could only be a Bridgerton, with the same chestnut hair as both Anthony and Colin. Not to mention the same bone structure and smile. Kate had heard that all the Bridgertons looked rather alike, but she'd never fully believed it until now.

"Daff!" Colin called out. "You're just in time to help us put out the wickets."

She gave him an arch smile. "You didn't think I'd let you set up the course yourself, do you?" She turned to her husband. "I don't trust him as far as I can throw him."

"Don't listen to her," Colin said to Kate. "She's very strong. I'd wager she could toss me clear into the lake."

Daphne rolled her eyes and turned to Kate. "Since I'm sure my miserable brother won't do the honors, I'll introduce myself. I am Daphne, Duchess of Hastings, and this is my husband Simon."

Kate bobbed a quick curtsy. "Your grace," she murmured, then turned to the duke and said again, "Your grace."

Colin waved his hand toward her as he bent down to retrieve the wickets from the Pall Mall cart. "This is Miss Sheffield."

Daphne looked confused. "I just passed by Anthony at the house. I thought he said he was on his way to fetch Miss Sheffield."

"My sister," Kate explained. "Edwina. I am Katharine. Kate to my friends."

"Well, if you are brave enough to play Pall Mall with the Bridgertons, I definitely want you as my friend," Daphne said with a wide smile. "Therefore you must call me Daphne. And my husband Simon. Simon?"

"Oh, of course," he said, and Kate had the distinct

impression that he would have said the same had she just declared the sky orange. Not that he wasn't listening to her, just that it was clear he adored her to distraction.

This, Kate thought, was what she wanted for Edwina.

"Let me take half of those," Daphne said, reaching for the wickets in her brother's hand. "Miss Sheffield and I . . . that is, Kate and I"—she flashed Kate a friendly grin—"will set up three of them, and you and Simon can do the rest."

Before Kate could even venture an opinion, Daphne had taken her by the arm and was leading her toward the lake.

"We have to make absolutely certain that Anthony loses his ball in the water," Daphne muttered. "I have never forgiven him for last time. I thought Benedict and Colin were going to die laughing. And Anthony was the worst. He just stood there smirking. Smirking!" She turned to Kate with a most beleaguered expression. "No one smirks quite like my eldest brother."

"I know," Kate muttered under her breath.

Thankfully, the duchess hadn't heard her. "If I could have killed him, I vow I would have."

"What will happen once all your balls are lost in the lake?" Kate couldn't resist asking. "I haven't played with you lot yet, but you do seem rather competitive, and it seems . . ."

"That it would be inevitable?" Daphne finished for her. She grinned. "You're probably right. We have no sense of sportsmanship when it comes to Pall Mall. When a Bridgerton picks up a mallet, we become the worst sorts of cheaters and liars. Truly, the game is less about winning than making sure the other players lose."

Kate fought for words. "It sounds . . ."

"Awful?" Daphne grinned. "It's not. You'll never have more fun, I guarantee it. But at the rate we're going, the entire set will end up in the lake ere long. I suppose we'll have to send to France for another set." She jammed a wicket into the ground. "It seems a waste, I know, but worth it to humiliate my brothers."

Kate tried not to laugh, but she didn't succeed.

"Do you have any brothers, Miss Sheffield?" Daphne asked.

Since the duchess had forgotten to use her given name, Kate deemed it best to revert to formal manners. "None, your grace," she replied. "Edwina is my only sibling."

Daphne shaded her eyes with her hand and scanned the area for a devilish wicket location. When she spied one— sitting right atop a tree root—she marched away, leaving Kate no choice but to follow.

"Four brothers," Daphne said, shoving the wicket into the ground, "provide quite a marvelous education."

"The things you must have learned," Kate said, quite impressed. "Can you give a man a black eye? Knock him to the ground?"

Daphne grinned wickedly. "Ask my husband."

"Ask me what?" the duke called out from where he and Colin were placing a wicket on a tree root on the opposite side of the tree.

"Nothing," the duchess called out innocently. "I've also learned," she whispered to Kate, "when it's best just to keep one's mouth shut. Men are much easier to manage once you understand a few basic facts about their nature."

"Which are?" Kate prompted.

Daphne leaned forward and whispered behind her cupped hand, "They're not as smart as we are, they're not as intuitive as we are, and they certainly don't need to know about fifty percent of what we do." She looked around. "He didn't hear that, did he?"

Simon stepped out from behind the tree. "Every word."

Kate choked on a laugh as Daphne jumped a foot. "But it's true," Daphne said archly.

Simon crossed his arms. "I'll let you think so." He turned to Kate. "I've learned a thing or two about women over the years."

"Really?" Kate asked, fascinated.

He nodded and leaned in, as if imparting a grave state secret. "They're much easier to manage if one allows them to believe that they are smarter and more intuitive than men. And," he added with a superior glance at his wife, "our lives are much more peaceful if we pretend that we're only aware of about fifty percent of what they do."

Colin approached, swinging a mallet in a low arc. "Are they having a spat?" he asked Kate.

"A discussion," Daphne corrected.

"God save me from such discussions," Colin muttered. "Let's choose colors."

Kate followed him back to the Pall Mall set, her fingers drumming against her thigh. "Do you have the time?" she asked him.

Colin pulled out his pocket watch. "A bit after half three, why?"

"I just thought that Edwina and the viscount would be down by now, that's all," she said, trying not to look too concerned.

Colin shrugged. "They should be." Then, completely oblivious to her distress, he motioned to the Pall Mall set. "Here. You're the guest. You choose first. What color do you want?"

Without giving it much thought, Kate reached in and grabbed a mallet. It was only when it was in her hand that she realized it was black.

"The mallet of death," Colin said approvingly. "I knew she'd make a fine player."

"Leave the pink one for Anthony," Daphne said, reaching for the green mallet.

The duke pulled the orange mallet out of the set, turning to Kate as he said, "You are my witness that I had nothing to do with Bridgerton's pink mallet, yes?"

Kate smiled wickedly. "I noticed that *you* didn't choose the pink mallet."

"Of course not," he returned, his grin even more devious than hers. "My wife had already chosen it for him. I could not gainsay her, now, could I?"

"Yellow for me," Colin said, "and blue for Miss Edwina, don't you think?"

"Oh, yes," Kate replied. "Edwina loves blue."

The foursome stared down at the two mallets left: pink and purple.

"He's not going to like either one," Daphne said.

Colin nodded. "But he'll like pink even less." And with that, he picked up the purple mallet and tossed it into the shed, then reached down and sent the purple ball in after it.

"I say," the duke said, "where *is* Anthony?"

"That's a very good question," Kate muttered, tapping her hand against her thigh.

"I suppose you'll want to know what time it is," Colin said slyly.

Kate flushed. She'd already asked him to check his pocket watch twice. "I'm fine, thank you," she answered, lacking a witty retort.

"Very well. It's just that I've learned that once you start moving your hand like that—"

Kate's hand froze.

"—you're usually about ready to ask me what time it is."

"You've learned quite a lot about me in the past hour," Kate said dryly.

He grinned. "I'm an observant fellow."

"Obviously," she muttered.

"But in case you wanted to know, it's a quarter of an hour before four."

"They're past due," Kate said.

Colin leaned forward and whispered, "I highly doubt that my brother is ravishing your sister."

Kate lurched back. "Mr. Bridgerton!"

"What are you two talking about?" Daphne asked.

Colin grinned. "Miss Sheffield is worried that Anthony is compromising the other Miss Sheffield."

"Colin!" Daphne exclaimed. "That isn't the least bit funny."

"And certainly not true," Kate protested. Well, almost not true. She didn't think the viscount was compromising Edwina, but he was probably doing his very best to charm her silly. And *that* was dangerous in and of itself.

Kate pondered the mallet in her hand and tried to figure out how she might bring it down upon the viscount's head and make it look like an accident.

The mallet of death, indeed.

Anthony checked the clock on the mantel in his study. Almost half three. They were going to be late.

He grinned. Oh, well, nothing to do about it.

Normally he was a stickler for punctuality, but when tardiness resulted in the torture of Kate Sheffield, he didn't much mind a late arrival.

And Kate Sheffield was surely writhing in agony by now, horrified at the thought of her precious younger sister in his evil clutches.

Anthony looked down at his evil clutches—hands, he reminded himself, hands—and grinned anew. He hadn't had this much fun in ages, and all he was doing was loitering about his office, picturing Kate Sheffield with her jaw clenched together, steam pouring from her ears.

It was a highly entertaining image.

Not, of course, that this was even his fault. He would have left right on time if he hadn't had to wait for Edwina. She'd sent word down with the maid that she would join him in ten minutes. That was twenty minutes ago. He couldn't help it if she was late.

Anthony had a sudden image of the rest of his life—waiting for Edwina. Was she the sort who was chronically late? That might grow vexing after a while.

As if on cue, he heard the patter of footsteps in the hall, and when he looked up, Edwina's exquisite form was framed by the doorway.

She was, he thought dispassionately, a vision. Utterly lovely in every way. Her face was perfection, her posture the epitome of grace, and her eyes were the most radiant shade of blue, so vivid that one could not help but be surprised by their hue every time she blinked.

Anthony waited for some sort of reaction to rise up within him. Surely no man could be immune to her beauty.

Nothing. Not even the slightest urge to kiss her. It almost seemed a crime against nature.

But maybe this was a good thing. After all, he didn't want a wife with whom he'd fall in love. Desire would have been nice, but desire could be dangerous. Desire certainly had a greater chance of sliding into love than did disinterest.

"I'm terribly sorry I'm late, my lord," Edwina said prettily.

"It was no trouble whatsoever," he replied, feeling a bit brightened by his recent set of rationalizations. She'd still work just fine as a bride. No need to look elsewhere. "But we should be on our way. The others will have the course set up already."

He took her arm and they strolled out of the house. He remarked on the weather. She remarked on the weather. He remarked on the previous day's weather. She agreed with whatever he'd said (he couldn't even remember, one minute later).

After exhausting all possible weather-related topics, they fell into silence, and then finally, after a full three minutes of neither of them having anything to say, Edwina blurted out, "What did you study at university?"

Anthony looked at her oddly. He couldn't remember ever being asked such a question by a young lady. "Oh, the usual," he replied.

"But what," she ground out, looking most uncharacteristically impatient, "is the usual?"

"History, mostly. A bit of literature."

"Oh." She pondered that for a moment. "I love to read."

"Do you?" He eyed her with renewed interest. He wouldn't have taken her for a bluestocking. "What do you like to read?"

She seemed to relax as she answered the question. "Novels if I'm feeling fanciful. Philosophy if I'm in the mood for self-improvement."

"Philosophy, eh?" Anthony queried. "Never could stomach the stuff myself."

Edwina let out one of her charmingly musical laughs. "Kate is the same way. She is forever telling me that she knows perfectly well how to live her life and doesn't need a dead man to give her instructions."

Anthony thought about his experiences reading Aristotle, Bentham, and Descartes at university. Then he thought about his experiences *avoiding* reading Aristotle, Bentham, and Descartes at university. "I think," he murmured, "that I would have to agree with your sister."

Edwina grinned. "*You,* agree with Kate? I feel I should find a notebook and record the moment. Surely this must be a first."

He gave her a sideways, assessing sort of glance. "You're more impertinent than you let on, aren't you?"

"Not half as much as Kate."

"*That* was never in doubt."

He heard Edwina let out a little giggle, and when he looked over at her, she appeared to be trying her hardest to maintain a straight face. They rounded the final corner to the field, and as they came over the rise, they saw the rest of the Pall Mall party waiting for them, idly swinging their mallets to and fro as they waited.

"Oh, bloody hell," Anthony swore, completely forgetting that he was in the company of the woman he planned to make his wife. "She's got the mallet of death."

Chapter 10

The country house party is a very dangerous event. Married persons often find themselves enjoying the company of one other than one's spouse, and unmarried persons often return to town as rather hastily engaged persons.

Indeed, the most surprising betrothals are announced on the heels of these spells of rustication.

LADY WHISTLEDOWN'S SOCIETY PAPERS, 2 MAY 1814

"You certainly took your time getting here," Colin remarked as soon as Anthony and Edwina reached the group. "Here, we're ready to go. Edwina, you're blue." He handed her a mallet. "Anthony, you're pink."

"I'm pink and *she*"—he jabbed a finger toward Kate—"gets to have the mallet of death?"

"I gave her first pick," Colin said. "She is our guest, after all."

"Anthony is usually black," Daphne explained. "In fact, he gave the mallet its name."

"You shouldn't have to be pink," Edwina said to Anthony. "It doesn't suit you at all. Here"—she held out her mallet—"why don't we trade?"

"Don't be silly," Colin interjected. "We specifically decided that you must be blue. To match your eyes."

Kate thought she heard Anthony groan.

"I will be pink," Anthony announced, grabbing the offending mallet rather forcefully from Colin's hand, "and I will still win. Let's begin, shall we?"

As soon as the necessary introductions were made between the duke and duchess and Edwina, they all plopped their wooden balls down near the starting point and prepared to play.

"Shall we play youngest to oldest?" Colin suggested, with a gallant bow in Edwina's direction.

She shook her head. "I should rather go last, so that I might have a chance to observe the play of those more experienced than I."

"A wise woman," Colin murmured. "Then we shall play oldest to youngest. Anthony, I believe you're the most ancient among us."

"Sorry, brother dear, but Hastings has a few months on me."

"Why," Edwina whispered in Kate's ear, "do I get the feeling I am intruding upon a family spat?"

"I think the Bridgertons take Pall Mall very seriously," Kate whispered back. The three Bridgerton siblings had assumed bulldog faces, and they all appeared rather single-mindedly determined to win.

"Eh eh eh!" Colin scolded, waving a finger at them. "No collusion allowed."

"We wouldn't even begin to know where to collude," Kate commented, "as no one has seen fit to even explain to us the rules of play."

"Just follow along," Daphne said briskly. "You'll figure it out as you go."

"I think," Kate whispered to Edwina, "that the object is to sink your opponents' balls into the lake."

"Really?"

"No. But I think that's how the Bridgertons see it."

"You're still whispering!" Colin called out without

sparing a glance in their direction. Then, to the duke, he barked, "Hastings, hit the bloody ball. We haven't all day."

"Colin," Daphne cut in, "don't curse. There are ladies present."

"You don't count."

"There are two ladies present who are not me," she ground out.

Colin blinked, then turned to the Sheffield sisters. "Do you mind?"

"Not at all," Kate replied, utterly fascinated. Edwina just shook her head.

"Good." Colin turned back to the duke. "Hastings, get moving."

The duke nudged his ball a bit forward from the rest of the pile. "You do realize," he said to no one in particular, "that I have never played Pall Mall before?"

"Just give the ball a good whack in that direction, darling," Daphne said, pointing to the first wicket.

"Isn't that the last wicket?" Anthony asked.

"It's the first."

"It *ought* to be the last."

Daphne's jaw jutted out. "I set up the course, and it's the first."

"I think this might get bloody," Edwina whispered to Kate.

The duke turned to Anthony and flashed him a false smile. "I believe I'll take Daphne's word for it."

"She did set up the course," Kate cut in.

Anthony, Colin, Simon, and Daphne all looked at her in shock, as if they couldn't quite believe she'd had the nerve to enter the conversation.

"Well, she did," Kate said.

Daphne looped her arm through hers. "I do believe I adore you, Kate Sheffield," she announced.

"God help me," Anthony muttered.

The duke drew back his mallet, let fly, and soon the orange ball was hurtling along the lawn.

"Well done, Simon!" Daphne cried out.

Colin turned and looked at his sister with disdain. "One never cheers one's opponents in Pall Mall," he said archly.

"He's never played before," she said. "He's not likely to win."

"Doesn't matter."

Daphne turned to Kate and Edwina and explained, "Bad sportsmanship is a requirement in Bridgerton Pall Mall, I'm afraid."

"I'd gathered," Kate said dryly.

"My turn," Anthony barked. He gave the pink ball a disdainful glance, then gave it a good whack. It sailed splendidly over the grass, only to slam into a tree and drop like a stone to the ground.

"Brilliant!" Colin exclaimed, getting ready to take his turn.

Anthony muttered a few things under his breath, none of which were suitable for gentle ears.

Colin sent the yellow ball toward the first wicket, then stepped aside to let Kate try her hand.

"Might I have a practice swing?" she inquired.

"No." It was a rather loud no, coming, as it did, from three mouths.

"Very well," she grumbled. "Stand back, all of you. I won't be held responsible if I injure anyone on the first try." She drew back on her mallet with all her might and slammed it into the ball. It sailed through the air in a rather impressive arc, then smacked into the same tree that had foiled Anthony and plopped on the ground right next to his ball.

"Oh, dear," Daphne said, setting her aim by drawing back on her mallet a few times without actually hitting the ball.

"Why 'oh, dear'?" Kate asked worriedly, not reassured by the duchess's faintly pitying smile.

"You'll see." Daphne took her turn, then marched off in the direction of her ball.

Kate looked over at Anthony. He looked very, very pleased with the current state of affairs.

"What are you going to do to me?" she asked.

He leaned forward devilishly. "What am I *not* going to do to you might be a more appropriate question."

"I believe it's my turn," Edwina said, stepping up to the starting point. She gave her ball an anemic hit, then groaned when it traveled only a third as far as the rest.

"Put a bit more muscle into it next time," Anthony said before stalking over to his ball.

"Right," Edwina muttered at his back. "I never would have figured that out."

"Hastings!" Anthony yelled. "It's your turn."

While the duke tapped his ball toward the next wicket, Anthony leaned against the tree with crossed arms, his ridiculous pink mallet hanging from one hand, and waited for Kate.

"Oh, Miss Sheffield," he finally called out. "Play of the game dictates that one follow one's ball!"

He watched her tromp over to his side. "There," she grumbled. "Now what?"

"You really ought to treat me with more respect," he said, offering her a slow, sly smile.

"After you tarried with Edwina?" she shot back. "What I ought to do is have you drawn and quartered."

"Such a bloodthirsty wench," he mused. "You'll do well at Pall Mall . . . eventually."

He watched, utterly entertained, as her face grew red, then white. "What do you mean?" she asked.

"For the love of God, Anthony," Colin yelled. "Take your bloody turn."

Anthony looked down to where the wooden balls sat

kissing on the grass, hers black, his appallingly pink. "Right," he murmured. "Wouldn't want to keep dear, sweet Colin waiting." And with that, he put his foot atop his ball, drew back his mallet—

"What are you doing?" Kate shrieked.

—and let fly. His ball remained firmly in place under his boot. Hers went sailing down the hill for what seemed like miles.

"You fiend," she growled.

"All's fair in love and war," he quipped.

"I am going to *kill* you."

"You can try," he taunted, "but you'll have to catch up with me first."

Kate pondered the mallet of death, then pondered his foot.

"Don't even think about it," he warned.

"It's so very, very tempting," she growled.

He leaned forward menacingly. "We have witnesses."

"And that is the only thing saving your life right now."

He merely smiled. "I believe your ball is down the hill, Miss Sheffield. I'm sure we'll see you in a half hour or so, when you catch up."

Just then Daphne marched by, following her ball, which had sailed unnoticed past their feet. "That was why I said 'oh, dear,' " she said—rather unnecessarily, in Kate's opinion.

"You'll pay for this," Kate hissed at Anthony.

His smirk said more than words ever could.

And then she marched down the hill, letting out a loud and extremely unladylike curse when she realized her ball was lodged under a hedge.

Half an hour later Kate was still two wickets behind the next-to-last player. Anthony was winning, which irked her to no end. The only saving grace was that she was so far behind she couldn't see his gloating face.

Then as she was twiddling her thumbs and waiting for her turn (there was precious little else to do while waiting for her turn, as no other players were remotely near her), she heard Anthony let out an aggrieved shout.

This immediately got her attention.

Beaming with anticipation at his possible demise, she looked eagerly about until she saw the pink ball hurtling along the grass, straight at her.

"Urp!" Kate gurgled, jumping up and darting quickly to the side before she lost a toe.

Looking back up, she saw Colin leaping into the air, his mallet swinging wildly above him, as he cried out exultantly, "Woo-hoo!"

Anthony looked as if he might disembowel his brother on the spot.

Kate would have done a little victory dance herself—if she couldn't win, the next best thing was knowing that *he* wouldn't—except now it seemed that he'd be stuck back with her for a few turns. And while her solitude wasn't terribly entertaining, it was better than having to make conversation with *him*.

Still, it was difficult not to look just a little bit smug when he came tromping over toward her, scowling as if a thundercloud had just lodged itself in his brain.

"Bad luck there, my lord," Kate murmured.

He glared at her.

She sighed—just for effect, of course. "I'm sure you'll still manage to place second or third."

He leaned forward menacingly and made a sound suspiciously like a growl.

"Miss Sheffield!" came Colin's impatient holler from up the hill. "It's your turn!"

"So it is," Kate said, analyzing her possible shots. She could aim for the next wicket or she could attempt to sabotage Anthony even further. Unfortunately, his ball wasn't touching hers, so she couldn't attempt the foot-on-the-ball maneuver he'd used on her earlier in the game. Which was probably for the best. With her luck, she'd end up missing the ball entirely and instead breaking her foot.

"Decisions, decisions," she murmured.

Anthony crossed his arms. "The only way you're going to ruin my game is to ruin yours as well."

"True," she acceded. If she wanted to send him into oblivion, she'd have to send herself there as well, since she'd have to hit hers with all she was worth just to get his to move. And since she couldn't hold hers in place, heaven only knew where she'd end up.

"But," she said, looking up at him and smiling innocently, "I really have no chance of winning the game, anyway."

"You could come in second or third," he tried.

She shook her head. "Unlikely, don't you think? I'm so far behind as it is, and we are nearing the end of play."

"You don't want to do this, Miss Sheffield," he warned.

"Oh," she said with great feeling, "I *do*. I really, really do." And then, with quite the most evil grin her lips had ever formed, she drew back her mallet and smacked her ball with every ounce of every single emotion within her. It knocked into his with stunning force, sending it hurtling even farther down the hill.

Farther . . .

Farther . . .

Right into the lake.

Openmouthed with delight, Kate just stared for a moment as the pink ball sank into the lake. Then something rose up within her, some strange and primitive emotion, and before she knew what she was about, she was jumping about like a crazy woman, yelling, "Yes! Yes! I win!"

"You don't win," Anthony snapped.

"Oh, it *feels* like I've won," she reveled.

Colin and Daphne, who had come dashing down the hill, skidded to a halt before them. "Well done, Miss

Sheffield!" Colin exclaimed. "I knew you were worthy of the mallet of death."

"Brilliant," Daphne agreed. "Absolutely brilliant."

Anthony, of course, had no choice but to cross his arms and scowl mightily.

Colin gave her a congenial pat on the back. "Are you certain you're not a Bridgerton in disguise? You have truly lived up to the spirit of the game."

"I couldn't have done it without you," Kate said graciously. "If you hadn't hit his ball down the hill . . ."

"I had been hoping you would pick up the reins of his destruction," Colin said.

The duke finally approached, Edwina at his side. "A rather stunning conclusion to the game," he commented.

"It's not over yet," Daphne said.

Her husband gave her a faintly amused glance. "To continue the play now seems rather anticlimactic, don't you think?"

Surprisingly, even Colin agreed. "I certainly can't imagine anything topping it."

Kate beamed.

The duke glanced up at the sky. "Furthermore, it's starting to cloud over. I want to get Daphne in before it starts to rain. Delicate condition and all, you know."

Kate looked in surprise at Daphne, who had started to blush. She didn't look the least bit pregnant.

"Very well," Colin said. "I move we end the game and declare Miss Sheffield the winner."

"I was two wickets behind the rest of you," Kate demurred.

"Nevertheless," Colin said, "any true aficionado of Bridgerton Pall Mall understands that sending Anthony into the lake is far more important than actually sending one's ball through all the wickets. Which makes you our winner, Miss Sheffield." He looked about, then straight at Anthony. "Does anyone disagree?"

No one did, although Anthony looked close to violence.

"Excellent," Colin said. "In that case, Miss Sheffield is our winner, and Anthony, *you* are our loser."

A strange, muffled sound burst from Kate's mouth, half laugh and half choke.

"Well, someone has to lose," Colin said with a grin. "It's tradition."

"It's true," Daphne agreed. "We're a bloodthirsty lot, but we do like to follow tradition."

"You're all mad in the head is what you are," the duke said affably. "And on that note, Daphne and I must bid you farewell. I do want to get her inside before it begins to rain. I trust no one will mind if we leave without helping to clear the course?"

No one minded, of course, and soon the duke and duchess were on their way back to Aubrey Hall.

Edwina, who had kept silent throughout the exchange (although she had been looking at the various Bridgertons as if they'd recently escaped from an asylum), suddenly cleared her throat. "Do you think we should try to retrieve the ball?" she asked, squinting down the hill toward the lake.

The rest of the party just stared at the calm waters as if they'd never considered such a bizarre notion.

"It's not as if it landed in the middle," she added. "It just rolled in. It's probably right by the edge."

Colin scratched his head. Anthony continued to glower.

"Surely you don't want to lose another ball," Edwina persisted. When no one had a reply, she threw down her mallet and threw up arms, saying, "Fine! I'll get the silly old ball."

That certainly roused the men from their stupor, and they jumped to help her.

"Don't be silly, Miss Sheffield," Colin said gallantly as he started to walk down the hill, "I'll get it."

"For the love of Christ," Anthony muttered. "I'll get the bloody ball." He strode down the hill, quickly overtaking his brother. For all his ire, he couldn't really blame Kate for her actions. He would have done the very same thing, although he would have hit the ball with enough force to sink hers in the middle of the lake.

Still, it was damned humiliating to be bested by a female, especially *her*.

He reached the edge of the lake and peered in. The pink ball was so brightly colored that it ought to show through the water, provided it had settled at a shallow enough level.

"Do you see it?" Colin asked, coming to a halt beside him.

Anthony shook his head. "It's a stupid color, anyway. No one ever wanted to be pink."

Colin nodded his agreement.

"Even the purple was better," Anthony continued, moving a few steps to the right so that he could inspect another stretch of shoreline. He looked up suddenly, glaring at his brother. "What the hell happened to the purple mallet, anyway?"

Colin shrugged. "I'm sure I have no idea."

"And I'm sure," Anthony muttered, "that it will miraculously reappear in the Pall Mall set tomorrow evening."

"You might very well be right," Colin said brightly, moving a bit past Anthony, keeping his eyes on the water the whole way. "Perhaps even this afternoon, if we're lucky."

"One of these days," Anthony said matter-of-factly, "I'm going to kill you."

"Of that I have no doubt." Colin scanned the water, then suddenly pointed with his index finger. "I say! There it is."

Sure enough, the pink ball sat in the shallow water, about two feet out from the edge of the lake. It looked to be only a foot or so deep. Anthony swore under his breath. He was going to have to take off his boots and wade in. It seemed Kate Sheffield was forever forcing him to take off his boots and wade into bodies of water.

No, he thought wearily, he hadn't had time to remove

his boots when he'd charged into The Serpentine to save Edwina. The leather had been completely ruined. His valet had nearly fainted from the horror of it.

With a groan he sat on a rock to pull off his footwear. To save Edwina he supposed it was worth a pair of good boots. To save a stupid pink Pall Mall ball—frankly, it didn't even seem worth getting his feet wet.

"You seem to have this well in hand," Colin said, "so I'm going to go help Miss Sheffield pull up the wickets."

Anthony just shook his head in resignation and waded in.

"Is it cold?" came a feminine voice.

Good God, it was *her*. He turned around. Kate Sheffield was standing on the shore.

"I thought you were pulling up wickets," he said, somewhat testily.

"That's Edwina."

"Too bloody many Miss Sheffields," he muttered under his breath. There ought to be a law against letting sisters come out in the same season.

"I beg your pardon?" she asked, cocking her head to the side.

"I said it's freezing," he lied.

"Oh. I'm sorry."

That got his attention. "No, you're not," he finally said.

"Well, no," she admitted. "Not for your losing, anyway. But I didn't intend for you to freeze your toes off."

Anthony was suddenly gripped by the most insane desire to see her toes. It was a horrible thought. He had no business lusting after this woman. He didn't even like her.

He sighed. That wasn't true. He supposed he did like her in an odd, paradoxical sort of way. And he thought, strangely enough, she might be beginning to like him in much the same manner.

"You would have done the same thing if you were me," she called out.

He said nothing, just continued his slow wade.

"You would have!" she insisted.

He leaned down and scooped up the ball, getting his sleeve wet in the process. Damn. "I know," he replied.

"Oh," she said, sounding surprised, as if she hadn't expected him to admit it.

He waded back out, thankful that the ground by the shore was firmly packed, so that dirt didn't stick to his feet.

"Here," she said, holding out what looked like a blanket. "It was in the shed. I stopped by on my way down. I thought you might need something to dry your feet."

Anthony opened his mouth, but oddly enough, no sound emerged. Finally, he managed, "Thank you," and took the blanket from her hands.

"I'm not such a terrible person, you know," she said with a smile.

"Neither am I."

"Perhaps," she allowed, "but you shouldn't have tarried so long with Edwina. I know you did it just to vex me."

He lifted a brow as he sat on the rock so he could dry his feet, dropping the ball onto the ground next to him. "Don't you think it's possible that my delay had anything to do with my wanting to spend time with the woman I'm considering making my wife?"

She colored slightly, but then muttered, "This has to be the most self-centered thing I've ever said, but no, I think you just wanted to vex me."

She was right, of course, but he wasn't going to tell her so. "As it happens," he said, "Edwina was delayed. Why, I do not know. I deemed it impolite to seek her out in her room and demand that she hurry along, so I waited in my study until she was ready."

There was a long moment of silence, then she said, "Thank you for telling me that."

He smiled wryly. "I'm not such a terrible person, you know."

She sighed. "I know."

Something about her resigned expression made him grin. "But maybe a little terrible?" he teased.

She brightened, their return to levity obviously making her much more comfortable with the conversation. "Oh, for certain."

"Good. I'd hate to be boring."

Kate smiled, watching him as he pulled on his stockings and boots. She reached down and picked up the pink ball. "I'd better carry this back to the shed."

"In case I'm overcome by an uncontrollable urge to toss it back in the lake?"

She nodded. "Something like that."

"Very well." He stood. "I'll take the blanket, then."

"A fair trade." She turned to walk up the hill, then spied Colin and Edwina disappearing into the distance. "Oh!"

Anthony turned quickly around. "What is it? Oh, I see. It seems your sister and my brother have decided to head back without us."

Kate scowled at their errant siblings, then shrugged in resignation as she started trudging up the hill. "I suppose I can tolerate your company for a few more minutes if you can tolerate mine."

He didn't say anything, which surprised her. It seemed just the sort of comment to which he'd have a witty and perhaps even cutting comeback. She looked up at him, then drew back slightly in surprise. He was staring at her in the *oddest* manner . . .

"Is—is everything all right, my lord?" she asked hesitantly.

He nodded. "Fine." But he sounded rather distracted.

The rest of the trip to the shed was met with silence. Kate set the pink ball in its spot in the Pall Mall cart, noting that Colin and Edwina had cleared the course and put everything neatly away, including the errant purple mallet and ball. She stole a glance at Anthony and had to smile. It was obvious from his beleaguered frown that he'd noticed as well.

"The blanket goes in here, my lord," she said with a hidden grin, stepping out of his way.

Anthony shrugged. "I'll bring it up to the house. It probably needs a good cleaning."

She nodded in agreement, and they shut the door and were off.

Chapter 11

There is nothing like a spot of competition to bring out the worst in a man—or the best in a woman.
LADY WHISTLEDOWN'S SOCIETY PAPERS, 4 MAY 1814

*A*nthony whistled as they ambled up the path to the house, stealing glances at Kate when she wasn't looking. She really was quite an attractive woman in her own right. He didn't know why this always surprised him, but it did. His memory of her never quite lived up to the enchanting reality of her face. She was always in motion, always smiling or frowning or pursing her lips. She'd never master the placid, serene expression to which young ladies were meant to aspire.

He'd fallen into the same trap as had the rest of society—of thinking of her only in terms of her younger sister. And Edwina was so stunning, so amazingly, startlingly beautiful that anyone near to her couldn't help but fade into the background. It was, Anthony allowed, difficult to look at anyone else when Edwina was in the room.

And yet . . .

He frowned. And yet he'd barely spared Edwina a glance through the entire Pall Mall game. This might have been understandable simply because it was Bridgerton

Pall Mall, and it brought out the worst in anyone named Bridgerton; hell, he probably wouldn't have spared a glance for the Prince Regent if he'd deigned to join the game.

But that explanation wouldn't wash, for his mind was filled with other images. Kate bending over her mallet, her face tense with concentration. Kate giggling as someone missed a shot. Kate cheering on Edwina when her ball rolled through the wicket—a very un-Bridgerton-like trait, that. And, of course, Kate smiling wickedly in that last second before she'd sent his ball flying into the lake.

Clearly, even if he hadn't been able to spare a glance for Edwina, he'd been sparing plenty for Kate.

That ought to have been disturbing.

He glanced back over at her again. This time her face was tilted slightly toward the sky, and she was frowning.

"Is something wrong?" he inquired politely.

She shook her head. "Just wondering if it's going to rain."

He looked up. "Not anytime soon, I imagine."

She nodded slowly in agreement. "I hate the rain."

Something about the expression on her face—rather reminiscent of a frustrated three-year-old—made him laugh. "You live in the wrong country, then, Miss Sheffield."

She turned to him with a sheepish smile. "I don't mind a gentle rain. It's just when it grows violent that I don't like it."

"I've always rather enjoyed thunderstorms," he murmured.

She shot him a startled look but didn't say anything, then returned her gaze to the pebbles at her feet. She was kicking one along the path as they walked, occasionally breaking her stride or stepping to the side just so she could give it a kick and keep it flying ahead of her. There was something charming about it, something rather sweet about the way her booted foot peeked out from under the hem of her dress at such regular intervals and connected with the pebble.

Anthony watched her curiously, forgetting to pull his eyes off her face when she looked back up.

"Do you think— *Why* are you looking at me like that?" she asked.

"Do I think what?" he returned, deliberately ignoring the second part of her question.

Her lips settled into a peevish line. Anthony felt his own quivering, wanting to smile with amusement.

"Are you laughing at me?" she asked suspiciously.

He shook his head.

Her feet ground to a halt. "I think you are."

"I assure you," he said, sounding even to himself as if he wanted to laugh, "that I am not laughing at you."

"You're lying."

"I'm not—" He had to stop. If he spoke any further he knew he'd explode with laughter. And the strangest thing was—he hadn't a clue why.

"Oh, for heaven's sake," she muttered. "What is the problem?"

Anthony sank against the trunk of a nearby elm, his entire body shaking with barely contained mirth.

Kate planted her hands on her hips, the expression in her eyes a little bit curious, a little bit furious. "What's so funny?"

He finally gave in to the laughter and barely managed to lift his shoulders into a shrug. "I don't know," he gasped. "The expression on your face . . . it's . . ."

He noticed that she smiled. He loved that she smiled.

"The expression on your face is not exactly unamusing yourself, my lord," she remarked.

"Oh, I'm sure." He took a few deep breaths and then, when he was satisfied that he had regained control, straightened. He caught sight of her face, still vaguely suspicious, and suddenly he realized that he had to know what she thought of him.

It couldn't wait until the next day. It couldn't wait until that evening.

He wasn't sure how it had come about, but her good opinion meant a great deal to him. Of course he needed her approval in his much-neglected suit of Edwina, but there was more to it than that. She'd insulted him, she'd nearly dunked him in The Serpentine, she'd humiliated him at Pall Mall, and yet he craved her good opinion.

Anthony couldn't remember the last time someone's regard had meant so much, and frankly, it was humbling.

"I think you owe me a boon," he said, pushing off the tree and standing straight. His mind was whirring. He needed to be clever about this. He had to know what she thought. And yet, he didn't want her knowing how much it meant to him. Not until he understood *why* it meant so much to him.

"I beg your pardon?"

"A boon. For the Pall Mall game."

She let out a ladylike snort as she leaned against the tree and crossed her arms. "If anyone owes anyone else a boon, then you owe one to me. I did win, after all."

"Ah, but I was the one humiliated."

"True," she acceded.

"You would not be yourself," he said in an extremely dry voice, "if you resisted the urge to agree."

Kate gave him a demure glance. "A lady should be honest in all things."

When she raised her eyes to his face, one corner of his mouth was curved into a rather knowing smile. "I was hoping you'd say that," he murmured.

Kate felt immediately uneasy. "And why is that?"

"Because my boon, Miss Sheffield, is to ask you a question—any question of my choosing—and you must answer with the utmost honesty." He planted one hand against the tree trunk, rather close to her face, and leaned forward. Kate suddenly felt trapped, even though it would be easy enough to dart away.

With a touch of dismay—and a shiver of excitement—she realized that she felt trapped by his eyes, which were burning rather dark and hot into hers.

"Do you think you can do that, Miss Sheffield?" he murmured.

"Wh-what is your question?" she asked, not realizing that she was whispering until she heard her voice, breathy and crackling like the wind.

He cocked his head slightly to the side. "Now, remember, you have to answer honestly."

She nodded. Or at least she thought she nodded. She *meant* to nod. In all truth, she wasn't entirely convinced of her ability to move.

He leaned forward, not so much that she could feel his breath, but close enough to make her shiver. "Here, Miss Sheffield, is my question."

Her lips parted.

"Do you"—he moved closer—"still"—and another inch—"hate me?"

Kate swallowed convulsively. Whatever she'd been expecting him to ask, it hadn't been this. She licked her lips, preparing to speak, even though she had no idea what she'd say, but not a sound emerged.

His lips curved into a slow, masculine smile. "I'll take that as a no."

And then, with an abruptness that left her head spinning, he pushed off the tree and said briskly, "Well, then, I do believe it's time we went inside and prepared for the evening, don't you?"

Kate sagged against the tree, completely devoid of energy.

"You wish to remain outside for a few moments?" He planted his hands on his hips and looked up at the sky, his demeanor pragmatic and efficient—one hundred and eighty degrees changed from the slow, lazy seducer he'd been just ten seconds earlier. "You might as well. It doesn't look like it's going to rain, after all. At least not in the next few hours."

She just stared at him. Either he'd lost his mind or she'd forgotten how to talk. Or maybe both.

"Very well. I've always admired a woman who appreciates fresh air. I shall see you at supper, then?"

She nodded. She was surprised she even managed that.

"Excellent." He reached out and took her hand, dropping a searing kiss on the inside of her wrist, upon the single band of bare flesh that peeked out between her glove and the hem of her sleeve. "Until tonight, Miss Sheffield."

And then he strode off, leaving her with the oddest feeling that something rather important had just taken place.

But for the life of her, she had no idea what.

At half seven that night, Kate considered falling dreadfully ill. At quarter to eight, she'd refined her goal to an apoplectic fit. But at five minutes to the hour, as the dinner bell sounded, alerting guests that it was time to assemble in the drawing room, she squared her shoulders and walked into the hall outside her bedroom door to meet Mary.

She refused to be a coward.

She *wasn't* a coward.

And she could make it through the evening. Besides, she told herself, she wasn't likely to be seated anywhere near Lord Bridgerton. He was a viscount and the man of the house, and would therefore be at the head of the table. As the daughter of a baron's second son, she held little rank compared to the other guests, and would most certainly be seated so far down the table that she wouldn't even be able to see him without developing a crick in her neck.

Edwina, who was sharing a room with Kate, had already gone to Mary's chamber to help her choose a necklace, and so Kate found herself alone in the hall. She supposed she could enter Mary's room and wait for the two of them there, but she didn't feel terribly conversational, and Edwina had already noticed her odd, reflective mood. The last thing Kate needed was a round of "Whatever can be wrong's" from Mary.

And the truth was—Kate didn't even *know* what was wrong. All she knew was that that afternoon, something had changed between her and the viscount. Something was different, and she freely admitted (to herself, at least) that it frightened her.

Which was normal, right? People always feared what they didn't understand.

And Kate *definitely* didn't understand the viscount.

But just as she was beginning to truly enjoy her solitude, the door across the hall opened, and out walked another young lady. Kate recognized her instantly as Penelope Featherington, the youngest of the three famed Featherington sisters—well, the three who were out in society. Kate had heard that there was a fourth still in the schoolroom.

Unfortunately for the Featherington sisters, they were famed for their lack of success on the marriage mart. Prudence and Philippa had been out for three years now, without a single proposal between the two of them. Penelope was in the midst of her second season and could usually be found at social functions trying to avoid her mother and sisters, who were universally regarded as ninnies.

Kate had always liked Penelope. The two had formed a bond ever since they'd both been skewered by Lady Whistledown for wearing gowns of an unflattering color.

Kate noted with a sad sigh that Penelope's current gown of lemon yellow silk made the poor girl look hopelessly sallow. And if that weren't bad enough, it had been cut with far too many frills and flounces. Penelope wasn't a tall girl, and the gown positively overwhelmed her.

It was a pity, because she might be quite attractive if

someone could convince her mother to stay away from the modiste and let Penelope choose her own clothing. She had a rather pleasing face, with the pale, pale skin of a redhead, except that her hair was truly more auburn than red, and if one really wanted to put a fine point on it, more brownish red than auburn.

Whatever you called it, Kate thought with dismay, it didn't go with lemon yellow.

"Kate!" Penelope called out, after closing her door behind her. "What a surprise. I didn't realize you were attending."

Kate nodded. "I think we might have been issued a late invitation. We met Lady Bridgerton only just last week."

"Well, I know I just said I was surprised, but I'm actually not surprised. Lord Bridgerton has been paying much attention to your sister."

Kate flushed. "Er, yes," she stammered. "He has."

"That is what the gossips say, at least," Penelope continued. "But then again, one can't always trust the gossips."

"I have rarely known Lady Whistledown to be incorrect," Kate said.

Penelope just shrugged and then looked down at her gown with disgust. "She certainly is never incorrect about *me*."

"Oh, don't be silly," Kate said quickly, but they both knew she was just being polite.

Penelope gave her head a weary shake. "My mother is convinced that yellow is a *happy* color and that a *happy* girl will snare a husband."

"Oh, dear," Kate said, snorting a giggle.

"What she doesn't grasp," Penelope continued wryly, "is that such a *happy* shade of yellow makes me look rather *un*happy and positively repels the gentlemen."

"Have you suggested green?" Kate inquired. "I think you'd be smashing in green."

Penelope shook her head. "She doesn't like green. Says it's melancholy."

"Green?" Kate asked with disbelief.

"I don't even try to understand her."

Kate, who was wearing green, held up her sleeve near Penelope's face, blocking the yellow as best as she could. "Your whole face lights up," she said.

"Don't tell me that. It will only make the yellow more painful."

Kate offered her a sympathetic smile. "I would loan you one of mine, but I'm afraid it would drag on the floor."

Penelope waved away her offer. "That's very kind of you, but I'm resigned to my fate. At least it's better than last year."

Kate raised a brow.

"Oh, that's right. You weren't out last year." Penelope winced. "I weighed nearly two stone more than I do now."

"Two stone?" Kate echoed. She couldn't believe it.

Penelope nodded and made a face. "Baby fat. I begged Mama not to force me to come out until I turned eighteen, but she thought a head start might be good for me."

Kate only had to take one look at Penelope's face to know that it hadn't been good for her. She felt a certain kinship with this girl, even though Penelope was nearly three years younger. Both of them knew the singular feeling of not being the most popular girl in the room, knew the exact expression you put on your face when you weren't asked to dance but you wanted to look as if you didn't care.

"I say," Penelope said, "why don't the two of us go down to supper together? It seems your family and mine are both delayed."

Kate wasn't in much of a rush to reach the drawing room and the inevitable company of Lord Bridgerton, but waiting for Mary and Edwina would delay the torture by only a few minutes, so she decided she might as well head down with Penelope.

They both poked their heads into their respective

mother's room, informed them of the change in plans, and linked arms, heading down the hall.

When they reached the drawing room, much of the company was already in attendance, milling about and chatting as they waited for the rest of the guests to come down. Kate, who had never attended a country house party before, noted with surprise that nearly everyone seemed more relaxed and a bit more animated than they did in London. It must be the fresh air, she thought with a smile. Or perhaps distance relaxed the strict rules of the capital. Whatever the case, she decided she preferred this atmosphere to that of a London dinner party.

She could see Lord Bridgerton across the room. Or rather she supposed she could sense him. As soon as she spotted him standing over by the fireplace, she'd kept her gaze scrupulously averted.

But she could feel him nonetheless. She knew she had to be crazy, but she'd swear she knew when he tilted his head, and heard him when he spoke and when he laughed.

And she definitely knew when his eyes were on her back. Her neck felt as if it were about to go up in flames.

"I didn't realize Lady Bridgerton had invited so many people," Penelope said.

Careful to keep her eyes away from the fireplace, Kate did a sweep of the room to see who was there.

"Oh, no," Penelope half whispered, half moaned. "Cressida Cowper is here."

Kate discreetly followed Penelope's gaze. If Edwina had any competition for the role of 1814's reigning beauty, it was Cressida Cowper. Tall, slender, with honey-blond hair and sparkling green eyes, Cressida was almost never without a small bevy of admirers. But where Edwina was kind and generous, Cressida was, in Kate's estimation, a self-centered, ill-mannered witch who took her joy in the torment of others.

"She hates me," Penelope whispered.

"She hates everyone," Kate replied.

"No, she *really* hates me."

"Whyever?" Kate turned to her friend with curious eyes. "What could you possibly have done to her?"

"I bumped into her last year and caused her to spill punch all over herself *and* the Duke of Ashbourne."

"That's all?"

Penelope rolled her eyes. "It was enough for Cressida. She's convinced he would have proposed if she hadn't appeared clumsy."

Kate let out a snort that didn't even pretend to be lady-like. "Ashbourne isn't about to get hitched anytime soon. Everyone knows that. He's nearly as bad a rake as Bridgerton."

"Who is most probably going to get married this year," Penelope reminded her. "If the gossips are correct."

"Bah," Kate scoffed. "Lady Whistledown herself wrote that she doesn't think he'll marry this year."

"That was *weeks* ago," Penelope replied with a dismissive wave of her hand. "Lady Whistledown changes her mind all the time. Besides, it's obvious to everyone that the viscount is courting your sister."

Kate bit her tongue before she muttered, "Don't remind me."

But her wince of pain was drowned out by Penelope's hoarse whisper of, "Oh, *no*. She's coming this way."

Kate gave her arm a reassuring squeeze. "Don't worry about her. She's no better than you."

Penelope shot her a sarcastic look. "I *know* that. But that doesn't make her any less unpleasant. And she always goes out of her way to make sure that I *have* to deal with her."

"Kate. Penelope," Cressida trilled, drawing up alongside them, giving her shiny hair an affected shake. "What a surprise to see you here."

"And why is that?" Kate asked.

Cressida blinked, obviously surprised that Kate had even questioned her pronouncement. "Well," she said slowly, "I suppose it is not such a surprise to see *you* here, as your sister is very much in demand, and we all know that you must go where she goes, but Penelope's presence . . ." She shrugged daintily. "Well, who am I to judge? Lady Bridgerton is a most kindhearted woman."

The comment was so rude that Kate could not help but gape. And while she was staring at Cressida, open-mouthed with shock, Cressida went in for the kill.

"That's a lovely gown, Penelope," she said, her smile so sweet that Kate would swear she could taste sugar in the air. "I do love yellow," she added, smoothing down the pale yellow fabric of her own gown. "It takes a very special complexion to wear it, don't you think?"

Kate ground her teeth together. Naturally Cressida looked brilliant in her gown. Cressida would look brilliant in a sackcloth.

Cressida smiled again, this time reminding Kate of a serpent, then turned slightly to motion to someone across the room. "Oh, Grimston, Grimston! Come over here for a moment."

Kate looked over her shoulder to see Basil Grimston approaching and just barely managed to stifle a groan. Grimston was the perfect male counterpart to Cressida— rude, supercilious, and self-important. Why a lovely lady like Viscountess Bridgerton had invited him, she'd never know. Probably to even up the numbers with so many young ladies invited.

Grimston slithered over and lifted one corner of his mouth in a mockery of a smile. "Your servant," he said to Cressida after sparing Kate and Penelope a fleeting, disdainful glance.

"Don't you think dear Penelope looks fetching in that gown?" Cressida said. "Yellow truly must be the color of the season."

Grimston did a slow, insulting perusal of Penelope, from the top of her head to the tips of her feet and back. He barely moved his head, letting his eyes travel up and down her frame. Kate fought a spasm of revulsion so strong it nearly brought on a wave of nausea. More than anything, she wanted to throw her arms around Penelope and give the poor girl a hug. But such attention would only single her out further as someone who was weak and easily bullied.

When Grimston was finally done with his rude inspection, he turned to Cressida and shrugged, as if he couldn't think of anything complimentary to say.

"Don't you have somewhere else to be?" Kate blurted out.

Cressida looked shocked. "Why, Miss Sheffield, I can hardly countenance your impertinence. Mr. Grimston and I were merely admiring Penelope's appearance. That shade of yellow does so much for her complexion. And it is so nice to see her looking so well after last year."

"Indeed," Grimston drawled, his oily tone making Kate feel positively unclean.

Kate could feel Penelope shaking next to her. She hoped it was with anger, not with pain.

"I can't imagine what you mean," Kate said in icy tones.

"Why, surely you know," Grimston said, his eyes glittering with delight. He leaned forward and then said in a whisper that was louder than his usual voice, loud enough so that a great many people could hear, "She was *fat*."

Kate opened her mouth to give a scathing retort, but before she could make a sound, Cressida added, "It was such a pity, because there were so many more men in town last year. Of course most of us still never lack for a dance partner, but I do feel for poor Penelope when I see her sitting with the dowagers."

"The dowagers," Penelope ground out, "are often the only people in the room with a modicum of intelligence."

Kate wanted to jump up and cheer.

Cressida made a breathy little "Oh" sound, as if she had

any right to be offended. "Still, one cannot help but . . . Oh! Lord Bridgerton!"

Kate moved to the side to allow the viscount into their small circle, noticing with disgust that Cressida's entire demeanor changed. Her eyelids began to flutter and her mouth made a pretty little cupid's bow.

It was so appalling Kate forgot to be self-conscious around the viscount.

Bridgerton shot Cressida a hard look but did not say anything. Instead, he turned quite deliberately to Kate and Penelope and murmured their names in greeting.

Kate nearly gasped with glee. He'd given Cressida Cowper the cut direct!

"Miss Sheffield," he said smoothly, "I hope you will excuse us as I escort Miss Featherington in to dinner."

"But you can't escort her in!" Cressida blurted out.

Bridgerton gave her an icy stare. "I'm sorry," he said in a voice that said he was anything but. "Had I included you in the conversation?"

Cressida shrank back, obviously mortified by her outburst. Still, it was beyond irregular for him to escort Penelope. As the man of the house, it was his duty to escort the highest-ranking woman. Kate wasn't sure who that happened to be this evening, but it certainly wasn't Penelope, whose father had been a mere mister.

Bridgerton offered Penelope his arm, turning his back on Cressida in the process. "I do hate a bully, don't you?" he murmured.

Kate clapped her hand over her mouth, but she couldn't stifle her giggle. Bridgerton offered her a small, secret smile over Penelope's head, and in that moment Kate had the oddest feeling that she understood this man completely.

But even stranger—suddenly she wasn't so certain that he was the soulless, reprehensible rake she'd taken such comfort in believing him.

"Did you see that?"

Kate, who, along with the rest of the assembled company, had been staring openmouthed as Bridgerton led Penelope from the room, his head bent to hers as if she were the most fascinating woman ever to walk the earth, turned to see Edwina standing next to her.

"I saw the whole thing," Kate said in a dazed voice. "I heard the whole thing."

"What happened?"

"He was . . . he was . . ." Kate stumbled over her words, unsure of how to describe what exactly he'd done. And then she said something she'd never thought possible: "He was a hero."

Chapter 12

A man with charm is an entertaining thing, and a man with looks is, of course, a sight to behold, but a man with honor—ah, he is the one, dear reader, to which the young ladies should flock.

LADY WHISTLEDOWN'S SOCIETY PAPERS, 2 MAY 1814

$\mathcal{L}$ater that night, after supper was done and the men went off to drink their port before rejoining the ladies with superior expressions on their faces, as if they had just talked about something weightier than which horse was likely to win the Royal Ascot; after the assembled company had played a sometime tedious and sometime hilarious round of charades; after Lady Bridgerton had cleared her throat and discreetly suggested that it might be time to turn in; after the ladies had taken their candles and headed off to bed; after the gentlemen had presumably followed . . .

Kate couldn't sleep.

Clearly, it was to be one of those stare-at-the-cracks-in-the-ceiling sort of nights. Except that there were no cracks in the ceiling at Aubrey Hall. And the moon wasn't even out, so there wasn't any light filtering through the curtains, which meant that even if there were cracks, she wouldn't be able to see them, and . . .

Kate groaned as she pushed back her covers and rose to her feet. One of these days she was going to have to learn how to force her brain to stop racing in eight different directions at once. She'd already lain in bed for nearly an hour, staring up into the dark, inky night, shutting her eyes every now and then and trying to will herself to sleep.

It wasn't working.

She couldn't stop thinking about the expression on Penelope Featherington's face when the viscount had swooped in to her rescue. Her own expression, Kate was sure, must have been somewhat similar—a bit stunned, a little delighted, and a lot as if she were about to melt onto the floor at that very minute.

Bridgerton had been *that* magnificent.

Kate had spent the entire day either watching or interacting with the Bridgertons. And one thing had become clear: Everything that had been said about Anthony and his devotion to his family—it was all true.

And while she wasn't quite ready to relinquish her opinion that he was a rake and a rogue, she was starting to realize that he might be all that and something else as well.

Something good.

Something that, if she were trying to be utterly objective about the matter, which she admitted was difficult to do, really ought not disqualify him as a potential husband for Edwina.

Oh, why why why did he have to go and be *nice*? Why couldn't he have just stayed the suave but shallow libertine it had been so easy to believe him? Now he was something else altogether, someone she feared she might actually come to care for.

Kate felt her face flush, even in the dark. She had to stop thinking about Anthony Bridgerton. At this rate she wasn't going to get any sleep for a week.

Maybe if she had something to read. She'd seen a rather

large and extensive library earlier that evening; surely the Bridgertons had some tome in there that would be guaranteed to put her to sleep.

She pulled on her robe and tiptoed to the door, careful not to wake Edwina. Not that that would have been an easy task. Edwina had always slept like the dead. According to Mary, she'd even slept through the night as a baby—from the very first day of her birth.

Kate slid her feet into a pair of slippers, then moved quietly into the hall, careful to look this way and that before shutting the door behind her. This was her first country house visit, but she'd heard a thing or two about these sorts of gatherings, and the last thing she wanted to do was run into someone on his way to a bedroom not his own.

If someone was carrying on with someone not his spouse, Kate decided, she didn't want to know about it.

A single lantern lit the hall, giving the dark air a dim, flickering glow. Kate had grabbed a candle on her way out, so she walked over and flipped the lid of the lantern to light her wick. Once the flame was steady, she started toward the stairs, making sure to pause at every corner and check carefully for passersby.

A few minutes later she found herself in the library. It wasn't large by *ton* standards, but the walls were covered floor to ceiling with bookcases. Kate pushed the door until it was almost closed—if someone was up and about, she didn't want to alert them to her presence by letting the door click shut—and made her way to the nearest bookcase, peering at the titles.

"Hmmm," she murmured to herself, pulling out a book and looking at the front cover, "botany." She did love gardening, but somehow a textbook on the subject didn't sound terribly exciting. Should she seek out a novel, which would capture her imagination, or should she go for a dry text, which would be more likely to put her to sleep?

Kate replaced the book and moved over to the next bookcase, setting her candle down on a nearby table. It appeared to be the philosophy section. "Definitely not," she muttered, sliding her candle along the table as she moved one bookcase to the right. Botany might put her to sleep, but philosophy was likely to leave her in a stupor for days.

She moved the candle a bit to the right, leaning forward to peer at the next set of books, when a bright and completely unexpected flash of lightning lit up the room.

A short, staccato scream burst forth from her lungs, and she jumped backward, bumping her behind against the table. *Not now*, she silently pleaded, *not here*.

But as her mind formed the word, "here," the entire room exploded with a dull boom of thunder.

And then it was dark again, leaving Kate shaking, her fingers gripping the table so hard that her joints locked. She hated this. Oh, how she hated this. She hated the noise and the streaks of light, and the crackling tension in the air, but most of all she hated what it made her feel.

So terrified that eventually she couldn't feel anything at all.

It had been this way all her life, or at least as long as she could remember. When she'd been small, her father or Mary had comforted her whenever it had stormed. Kate had many memories of one of them sitting on the edge of her bed, holding her hand and whispering soothing words as thunder and lightning crashed around her. But as she grew older, she managed to convince people that she was over her affliction. Oh, everyone knew that she still hated storms. But she'd managed to keep the extent of her terror to herself.

It seemed the worst sort of weakness—one with no apparent cause, and unfortunately, one with no clear cure.

She didn't hear any rain against the windows; maybe the storm wouldn't be so bad. Maybe it had started far away and was moving even farther. Maybe it was—

Another flash illuminated the room, squeezing out a second scream from Kate's lungs. And this time the thunder had arrived even closer to the lightning, indicating that the storm was pulling closer.

Kate felt herself sink to the floor.

It was too loud. Too loud, and too bright, and too—

BOOM!

Kate huddled under the table, her legs folded up, her arms about her knees, waiting in terror for the next round.

And then the rain began.

It was a bit past midnight, and all the guests (who were keeping somewhat to country hours) had gone to bed, but Anthony was still in his study, tapping his fingers against the edge of his desk in time with the rain beating against his window. Every now and then a bolt of lightning lit up the room in a flash of brilliance, and each clap of thunder was so loud and unexpected, he jumped in his chair.

God, he loved thunderstorms.

Hard to tell why. Maybe it was just the proof of nature's power over man. Maybe it was the sheer energy of the light and sound that pounded around him. Whatever the case, it made him feel alive.

He hadn't been particularly tired when his mother had suggested they all turn in, and so it had seemed silly not to use these few moments of solitude to go over the Aubrey Hall books his steward had left out for him. The Lord knew his mother would have his every minute crammed with activities involving eligible young women on the morrow.

But after an hour or so of painstaking checking, the dry tip of a quill tapping against each number in the ledger as he added and subtracted, multiplied and occasionally divided, his eyelids began to droop.

It had been a long day, he allowed, closing the ledger but leaving a piece of paper sticking out to mark his place. He'd spent much of the morning visiting tenants and inspecting buildings. One family needed a door repaired. Another was having trouble harvesting their crops and paying their rent, due to the father's broken leg. Anthony had heard and settled disputes, admired new babies, and even helped to fix a leaky roof. It was all part of being a landowner, and he enjoyed it, but it was tiring.

The Pall Mall game had been an enjoyable interlude, but once back at the house, he'd been thrust into the role of host for his mother's party. Which had been almost as exhausting as the tenant visits. Eloise was barely seventeen and clearly had needed someone to watch over her, that bitchy Cowper girl had been tormenting poor Penelope Featherington, and someone had had to do something about that, and . . .

And then there was Kate Sheffield.

The bane of his existence.

And the object of his desires.

All at once.

What a muddle. He was supposed to be courting her sister, for God's sake. Edwina. The belle of the season. Lovely beyond compare. Sweet and generous and eventempered.

And instead he couldn't stop thinking about Kate. Kate, who, much as she infuriated him, couldn't help but command his respect. How could he not admire one who clung so steadfastly to her convictions? And Anthony had to admit that the crux of her convictions—devotion to family—was the one principle he held above all else.

With a yawn, Anthony got up from behind his desk and stretched his arms. It was definitely time for bed. With any luck, he'd fall asleep the moment his head hit the pillow. The last thing he wanted was to find himself staring at the ceiling, thinking of Kate.

And of all the things he wanted to do *to* Kate.

Anthony picked up a candle and headed out into the empty hall. There was something peaceful and intriguing about a quiet house. Even with the rain beating against the walls, he could hear every click of his boots against the floor—heel, toe, heel, toe. And except for when the lightning streaked through the sky, his candle provided the only illumination in the hall. He rather enjoyed waving the flame this way and that, watching the play of shadows against the walls and furniture. It was a rather odd feeling of control, but—

One of his brows rose up in question. The library door was a few inches ajar, and he could see a pale strip of candlelight shining from within.

He was fairly certain no one else was up. And there certainly wasn't a sound coming from the library. Someone must have gone in for a book and left a candle burning. Anthony frowned. It was a damned irresponsible thing to do. Fire could devastate a house faster than anything else, even in the middle of a rainstorm, and the library—filled to the brim with books—was the ideal place to spark a flame.

He pushed the door open and entered the room. One entire wall of the library was taken up by tall windows, so the sound of the rain was much louder here than it had been in the hall. A crack of thunder shook the floor, then, practically on top of that, a flash of lightning split the night.

The electricity of the moment made him grin, and he crossed over to where the offending candle had been left burning. He leaned over, blew it out, and then . . .

He heard something.

It was the sound of breath. Panicked, labored, with the slightest touch of a whimper.

Anthony looked purposefully around the room. "Is someone here?" he called out. But he could see no one.

Then he heard it again. From below.

Holding his own candle steady, he crouched down to peer under the table.

And his breath was sucked right out of his body.

"My God," he gasped. "Kate."

She was curled up into a ball, her arms wrapped around her bent legs so tightly it looked as if she were about to shatter. Her head was bent down, her eye sockets resting on her knees, and her entire body was shaking with fast, intense tremors.

Anthony's blood ran to ice. He'd never seen someone shake like that.

"Kate?" he said again, setting his candle down on the floor as he moved closer. He couldn't tell if she could hear him. She seemed to have retreated into herself, desperate to escape something. Was it the storm? She'd said she hated the rain, but this went far deeper. Anthony knew that most people didn't thrive on electrical storms as he did, but he'd never heard of someone being reduced to this.

She looked as if she'd break into a million brittle pieces if he so much as touched her.

Thunder shook the room, and her body flinched with such torment that Anthony felt it in his gut. "Oh, Kate," he whispered. It broke his heart to see her thus. With a careful and steady hand, he reached out to her. He still wasn't sure if she'd even registered his presence; startling her might be like waking a sleepwalker.

Gently he set his hand on her upper arm and gave it the tiniest of squeezes. "I'm here, Kate," he murmured. "Everything will be all right."

Lightning tore through the night, flashing the room with a sharp burst of light, and she squeezed herself into an even tighter ball, if that was possible. It occurred to him that she was trying to shield her eyes by keeping her face to her knees.

He moved closer and took one of her hands in his. Her skin was like ice, her fingers stiff from terror. It was difficult to pry her arm from around her legs, but eventually he was able to bring her hand to his mouth, and he pressed his lips against her skin, trying to warm her.

"I'm here, Kate," he repeated, not really sure what else to say. "I'm here. It will be all right."

Eventually he managed to scoot himself under the table so that he was sitting beside her on the floor, with his arm around her trembling shoulders. She seemed to relax slightly at his touch, which left him with the oddest feeling—almost a sense of pride that he had been the one to be able to help her. That, and a bone-deep feeling of relief, because it was killing him to see her in such torment.

He whispered soothing words in her ear and softly caressed her shoulder, trying to comfort her with his mere presence. And slowly—very, slowly; he had no idea how many minutes he sat under that table with her—he could feel her muscles begin to unwind. Her skin lost that awful clammy feeling, and her breathing, while still rushed, no longer sounded quite so panicked.

Finally, when he felt she might be ready, he touched two fingers to the underside of her chin, using the softest pressure imaginable to lift her face so that he could see her eyes. "Look at me, Kate," he whispered, his voice gentle but suffused with authority. "If you just look at me, you will know that you are safe."

The tiny muscles around her eyes quivered for a good fifteen seconds before her lids finally fluttered. She was trying to open her eyes, but they were resisting. Anthony had little experience with this sort of terror, but it seemed to make sense to him that her eyes just wouldn't want to open, that they simply wouldn't want to see whatever it was that so frightened her.

After several more seconds of fluttering, she finally managed to open her eyes all the way and met his gaze.

Anthony felt as if he'd been punched in the gut.

If eyes were truly the windows to the soul, something had shattered within Kate Sheffield that night. She looked haunted, hunted, and utterly lost and bewildered.

"I don't remember," she whispered, her voice barely audible.

He took her hand, which he'd never relinquished his

hold on, and brought it to his lips again. He pressed a gentle, almost paternal kiss on her palm. "You don't remember what?"

She shook her head. "I don't know."

"Do you remember coming to the library?"

She nodded.

"Do you remember the storm?"

She closed her eyes for a moment, as if the act of keeping them open had required more energy than she possessed. "It's still storming."

Anthony nodded. That was true. The rain was still beating against the windows with just as much ferocity as before, but it had been several minutes since the last bout of thunder and lightning.

She looked at him with desperate eyes. "I can't . . . I don't . . ."

Anthony squeezed her hand. "You don't have to say anything."

He felt her body shudder and relax, then heard her whisper, "Thank you."

"Do you want me to talk to you?" he asked.

She shut her eyes—not as tightly as before—and nodded.

He smiled, even though he knew she could not see it. But maybe she could sense it. Maybe she'd be able to hear his smile in his voice. "Let's see," he mused, "what can I tell you about?"

"Tell me about the house," she whispered.

"This house?" he asked in surprise.

She nodded.

"Very well," he replied, feeling rather absurdly pleased that she was interested in the one pile of stone and mortar that meant so much to him. "I grew up here, you know."

"Your mother told me."

Anthony felt a spark of something warm and powerful in his chest as she spoke. He'd told her she didn't have to say anything, and she'd been quite obviously thankful for that, but now she was actually taking part in the conversation. Surely that had to mean she was beginning to feel better. If she'd open her eyes—if they weren't sitting under a table—it might seem almost normal.

And it was stunning how much he wanted to be the one to make her feel better.

"Shall I tell you about the time my brother drowned my sister's favorite doll?" he asked.

She shook her head, then flinched when the wind picked up, causing the rain to beat against the windows with new ferocity. But she steeled her chin and said, "Tell me something about you."

"All right," Anthony said slowly, trying to ignore the vague, uncomfortable feeling that spread in his chest. It was so much easier to tell a tale of his many siblings than to talk about himself.

"Tell me about your father."

He froze. "My father?"

She smiled, but he was too shocked by her request to notice. "You must have had one," she said.

Anthony's throat began to feel very tight. He didn't often talk about his father, not even with his family. He'd told himself that it was because it was so much water under the bridge; Edmund had been dead for over ten years. But the truth was that some things simply hurt too much.

And there were some wounds that didn't heal, not even in ten years.

"He—he was a great man," he said softly. "A great father. I loved him very much."

Kate turned to look at him, the first time she'd met his gaze since he'd lifted her chin with his fingers many minutes earlier. "Your mother speaks of him with great affection. That was why I asked."

"We all loved him," he said simply, turning his head and staring out across the room. His eyes focused on the leg of a chair, but he didn't really see it. He didn't see anything but the memories in his mind. "He was the finest father a boy could ever want."

"When did he die?"

"Eleven years ago. In the summer. When I was eighteen. Right before I left for Oxford."

"That's a difficult time for a man to lose his father," she murmured.

He turned sharply to look at her. "Any time is a difficult time for a man to lose his father."

"Of course," she quickly agreed, "but some times are worse than others, I think. And surely it must be different for boys and girls. My father passed on five years ago, and I miss him terribly, but I don't think it's the same."

He didn't have to voice his question. It was there in his eyes.

"My father was wonderful," Kate explained, her eyes warming as she reminisced. "Kind and gentle, but stern when he needed to be. But a boy's father—well, he has to teach his son how to be a man. And to lose a father at eighteen, when you're just learning what all that means . . ." She let out a long exhale. "It's probably presumptuous for me even to discuss it, as I'm not a man and therefore couldn't possibly put myself in your shoes, but I think . . ." She paused, pursing her lips as she considered her words. "Well, I just think it would be very difficult."

"My brothers were sixteen, twelve, and two," Anthony said softly.

"I would imagine it was difficult for them as well," she replied, "although your youngest brother probably doesn't remember him."

Anthony shook his head.

Kate smiled wistfully. "I don't remember my mother, either. It's an odd thing."

"How old were you when she died?"

"It was on my third birthday. My father married Mary only a few months later. He didn't observe the proper mourning period, and it shocked some of the neighbors, but he thought I needed a mother more than he needed to follow etiquette."

For the first time, Anthony wondered what would have happened if it had been his mother who had died young, leaving his father with a house full of children, several of them infants and toddlers. Edmund wouldn't have had an easy time of it. None of them would have.

Not that it had been easy for Violet. But at least she'd had Anthony, who'd been able to step in and try to act the role of surrogate father to his younger siblings. If Violet had died, the Bridgertons would have been left completely without a maternal figure. After all, Daphne—the eldest of the Bridgerton daughters—had been only ten at Edmund's death. And Anthony was certain that his father would not have remarried.

No matter how his father would have wanted a mother for his children, he would not have been able to take another wife.

"How did your mother die?" Anthony asked, surprised by the depth of his curiosity.

"Influenza. Or at least that's what they thought. It could have been any sort of lung fever." She rested her chin on her hand. "It was very quick, I'm told. My father said I fell ill as well, although mine was a mild case."

Anthony thought about the son he hoped to sire, the very reason he had finally decided to marry. "Do you miss a parent you never knew?" he whispered.

Kate considered his question for some time. His voice had held a hoarse urgency that told her there was something critical about her reply. Why, she couldn't imagine, but something about her childhood clearly rang a chord within his heart.

"Yes," she finally answered, "but not in the way you would think. You can't really miss her, because you didn't know her, but there's still a hole in your life—a big empty spot, and you know who was supposed to fit there, but you can't remember her, and you don't know what she was like, and so you don't know *how* she would have filled that hole." Her lips curved into a sad sort of smile. "Does this make any sense?"

Anthony nodded. "It makes a great deal of sense."

"I think losing a parent once you know and love them is harder," Kate added. "And I know, because I've lost both."

"I'm sorry," he said quietly.

"It's all right," she assured him. "That old adage—time heals all wounds—it's really true."

He stared at her intently, and she could tell from his expression that he didn't agree.

"It really is more difficult when you're older. You're blessed because you had the chance to know them, but the pain of the loss is more intense."

"It was as if I'd lost an arm," Anthony whispered.

She nodded soberly, somehow knowing that he hadn't spoken of his sorrow to many people. She licked nervously at her lips, which had gone quite dry. Funny how that happened. All the rain in the world pounding outside, and here she was, parched as a bone.

"Perhaps it was better for me, then," Kate said softly, "losing my mother so young. And Mary has been wonderful. She loves me as a daughter. In fact—" She broke off, startled by the sudden wetness in her eyes. When she finally found her voice again, it was an emotional whisper. "In fact, she has never once treated me differently than she has Edwina. I—I don't think I could have loved my own mother any better."

Anthony's eyes burned into hers. "I'm so glad," he said, his voice low and intense.

Kate swallowed. "She's so funny about it sometimes. She visits my mother's grave, just to tell her how I'm doing. It's very sweet, actually. When I was small, I would go with her, to tell my mother how Mary was doing."

Anthony smiled. "And was your report favorable?"

"Always."

They sat in companionable silence for a moment, both staring at the candle flame, watching the wax drip down the taper to the candlestick. When the fourth drop of wax rolled down the candle, sliding along the column until it hardened in place, Kate turned to Anthony and said, "I'm sure I sound insufferably optimistic, but I think there must be some master plan in life."

He turned to her and quirked a brow.

"Everything really does work out in the end," she explained. "I lost my mother, but I gained Mary. And a sister I love dearly. And—"

A flash of lightning lit the room. Kate bit her lip, trying to force slow and even breaths through her nose. The thunder would come, but she'd be ready for it, and—

The room shook with noise, and she was able to keep her eyes open.

She let out a long exhale and allowed herself a proud smile. That hadn't been so difficult. It certainly hadn't been *fun*, but it hadn't been impossible. It might have been Anthony's comforting presence next to her, or simply that the storm was moving away, but she'd made it through without her heart jumping through her skin.

"Are you all right?" Anthony asked.

She looked over at him, and something inside of her melted at the concerned look on his face. Whatever he'd done in the past, however they'd argued and fought, in this moment he truly cared about her.

"Yes," she said, hearing surprise in her voice even though she hadn't intended it. "Yes, I think I am."

He gave her hand a squeeze. "How long have you been like this?"

"Tonight? Or in my life?"

"Both."

"Tonight since the first clap of thunder. I get quite nervous when it begins to rain, but as long as there is no thunder and lightning, I'm all right. It's not the rain, actually, which upsets me, but just the fear that it might grow into something more." She swallowed, licking her dry lips before she continued. "To answer your other query, I can't remember a time I wasn't terrified by storms. It's simply a part of me. It's quite foolish, I know—"

"It's not foolish," he interjected.

"You're very sweet to think so," she said with a sheepish half-smile, "but you're wrong. Nothing could be more foolish than to fear something with no reason."

"Sometimes . . ." Anthony said in a halting voice, "sometimes there are reasons for our fears that we can't quite explain. Sometimes it's just something we feel in our bones, something we know to be true, but would sound foolish to anyone else."

Kate stared at him intently, watching his dark eyes in the flickering candlelight, and catching her breath at the flash of pain she saw in the brief second before he looked away. And she knew—with every fiber of her being—that he wasn't speaking of intangibles. He was talking about his own fears, something very specific that haunted him every minute of every day.

Something she knew she did not have the right to ask him about. But she wished—oh, how she wished—that when he was ready to face his fears, she could be the one to help him.

But that wasn't to be. He would marry someone else, maybe even Edwina, and only his wife would have the right to talk to him about such personal matters.

"I think I might be ready to go upstairs," she said. Suddenly it was too hard to be in his presence, too painful to know that he would belong to someone else.

His lips quirked into a boyish smile. "Are you saying I might finally crawl out from under this table?"

"Oh, goodness!" She clapped one of her hands to her cheek in a sheepish expression. "I'm so sorry. I stopped noticing where we were sitting ages ago, I'm afraid. What a ninny you must think me."

He shook his head, still smiling. "Never a ninny, Kate.

Even when I thought you the most insufferable female creature on the planet, I had no doubts about your intelligence."

Kate, who had been in the process of scooting out from under the table, paused. "I just don't know if I should feel complimented or insulted by that statement."

"Probably both," he admitted, "but for friendship's sake, let's decide upon complimented."

She turned to look at him, aware that she presented an awkward picture on her hands and knees, but the moment seemed too important to delay. "Then we are friends?" she whispered.

He nodded as he stood. "Hard to believe, but I think we are."

Kate smiled as she took his helping hand and rose to her feet. "I'm glad. You're—you're really not the devil I'd originally thought you."

One of his brows lifted, and his face suddenly took on a very wicked expression.

"Well, maybe you are," she amended, thinking he probably was every bit the rake and rogue that society had painted him. "But maybe you're also a rather nice person as well."

"Nice seems so bland," he mused.

"*Nice*," she said emphatically, "is nice. And given what I used to think of you, you ought to be delighted by the compliment."

He laughed. "One thing about you, Kate Sheffield, is that you are never boring."

"Boring is so bland," she quipped.

He smiled—a true grin, not that ironic curve he used at society functions, but the real thing. Kate's throat suddenly felt very tight.

"I'm afraid I cannot walk you back to your room," he said. "If someone should come across us at this hour . . ."

Kate nodded. They'd forged an unlikely friendship, but she didn't want to get trapped into marriage with him, right? And it went without saying that *he* didn't want to marry *her*.

He motioned to her. "And especially with you dressed like that. . . ."

Kate looked down and gasped, yanking her robe more tightly around her. She'd completely forgotten that she wasn't properly dressed. Her nightclothes certainly weren't risqué or revealing, especially with her thick robe, but they *were* nightclothes.

"Will you be all right?" he asked softly. "It's still raining."

Kate stopped and listened to the rain, which had softened to a gentle patter against the windows. "I think the storm is over."

He nodded and peered out into the hall. "It's empty," he said.

"I should go."

He stepped aside to let her pass.

She moved forward, but when she reached the doorway she stopped and turned around. "Lord Bridgerton?"

"Anthony," he said. "You should call me Anthony. I believe I've already called you Kate."

"You did?"

"When I found you." He waved a hand. "I don't think you heard anything I said."

"You're probably right." She smiled hesitantly. "Anthony." His name sounded strange on her tongue.

He leaned forward slightly, an odd, almost devilish light in his eyes. "Kate," he said in return.

"I just wanted to say thank you," she said. "For helping me tonight. I—" She cleared her throat. "It would have been a great deal more difficult without you."

"I didn't do anything," he said gruffly.

"No, you did everything." And then, before she'd be tempted to stay, she hurried down the hall and up the stairs.

Chapter 13

*There is little to report in London with so many people
away in Kent at the Bridgerton house party. This Author
can only imagine all the gossip that will soon reach town.
There will be a scandal, yes? There is always a scandal at
a house party.*

LADY WHISTLEDOWN'S SOCIETY PAPERS, 4 MAY 1814

*T*he following morning was the sort that usually fol-
lows a violent storm—bright and clear, but with a fine,
damp mist that settled cold and refreshing on the skin.

Anthony was oblivious to the weather, having spent
most of the night staring into the darkness and seeing
nothing but Kate's face. He'd finally fallen asleep as the
first streaks of dawn fingered across the sky. By the time
he woke, it was well past noon, but he did not feel rested.
His body was suffused with a strange combination of
exhaustion and nervous energy. His eyes felt heavy and
dull in their sockets, and yet his fingers kept drumming
the bed, inching toward the edge as if they alone could
pull him out and to his feet.

Finally, when his stomach growled so loudly that he
could swear he saw the plaster on the ceiling shake, he
staggered upright and pulled on his robe. With a wide,

loud yawn, he moved to the window, not because he was looking for anyone or anything in particular, but simply because the view was better than anything else in his room.

And yet in the quarter second before he looked down and gazed upon the grounds, he somehow knew what he would see.

Kate. Walking slowly across the lawn, far more slowly than he'd ever seen her walk before. Usually, she walked as if in a race.

She was much too far away for him to see her face—just a sliver of her profile, the curve of her cheek. And yet he could not take his eyes off of her. There was so much magic in her form—a strange grace in the way her arm swung as she walked, an artistry in the posture of her shoulders.

She was walking toward the garden, he realized.

And he knew he had to join her.

The weather remained in its contradictory state for most of the day, dividing the house party neatly in half, between those who insisted the bright sunshine beckoned outdoor play, and those who eschewed the wet grass and damp air for the warmer, drier clime of the drawing room.

Kate was firmly in the former group, although she was not in the mood for company. Her mind was in far too reflective a mood to make polite conversation with people she barely knew, and so she stole away once again to Lady Bridgerton's spectacular gardens and found herself a quiet spot on a bench near the rose arbor. The stone was cold and just a little bit damp beneath her bottom, but she hadn't slept particularly well the night before, and she was tired, and it was better than standing.

And it was, she realized with a sigh, just about the only place where she might be left to her own company. If she remained in the house, she'd surely be roped into joining the group of ladies chatting in the drawing room while they wrote correspondence to friends and family, or worse, she'd be stuck with the coterie who'd retired to the orangery to pursue their embroidery.

As for the outdoor enthusiasts, they'd also broken into two groups. One had hied off to the village to shop and see whatever sights there were to be found, and the other was taking a constitutional walk to the lake. As Kate had no interest in shopping (and she was already quite familiar with the lake) she'd eschewed their company as well.

Hence, her solitude in the garden.

She sat for several minutes, just staring off into space, her eyes focusing somewhat blindly on the tightly furled bud of a nearby rose. It was nice to be alone, where she didn't have to cover her mouth or stifle the loud sleepy noises she made when she yawned. Nice to be alone, where no one was going to comment on the dark circles beneath her eyes or her uncommon quietude and lack of conversation.

Nice to be alone, where she could sit and attempt to sort through her muddle of thoughts about the viscount. It was a daunting task, and one she'd rather put off, but it had to be done.

But there really wasn't all that much to sort out. Because everything she had learned in the past few days pointed her conscience in one, singular direction. And she knew that she could no longer oppose Bridgerton's courtship of Edwina.

In the past few days he'd proven himself sensitive, caring, and principled. Even, she thought with a glimmer of a smile as she recalled the light in Penelope Featherington's eyes when he'd saved her from the verbal talons of Cressida Cowper, heroic.

He was devoted to family.

He had used his social position and power not to lord over others but simply to spare another person insult.

He had helped her through one of her phobic attacks with a grace and sensitivity that, now that she could view it with a clear head, stunned her.

He might have been a rake and a rogue—he might still *be* a rake and a rogue—but clearly his behavior to those ends did not define the man. And the only objection Kate had to his marrying Edwina was . . .

She swallowed painfully. There was a lump the size of a cannonball in her throat.

Because deep in her heart, she wanted him for herself.

But that was selfish, and Kate had spent her life trying to be unselfish, and she knew she could never ask Edwina not to marry Anthony for such a reason. If Edwina knew that Kate was even the tiniest bit infatuated with the viscount, she would put an end to his courtship at once. And what purpose would that serve? Anthony would just find some other beautiful, eligible woman to pursue. There were plenty to choose from in London.

It wasn't as if he were going to ask *her* instead, so what would she have to gain by preventing a match between him and Edwina?

Nothing except the agony of having to see him married to her sister. And that would fade in time, wouldn't it? It had to; she herself had just said the night before that time truly did heal all wounds. Besides, it would probably hurt just as much to see him married to some other lady; the only difference would be that she would not have to see him at holidays and christenings and the like.

Kate let out a sigh. A long, sad, weary sigh that stole every breath from her lungs and left her shoulders sagging, her posture drooping.

Her heart aching.

And then a voice filled her ears. *His* voice, low and smooth, like a warm swirl around her. "My goodness, you sound serious."

Kate stood so suddenly that the backs of her legs knocked into the edge of the stone bench, setting her off balance and causing her to stumble. "My lord," she blurted out.

His lips curved with the barest hint of a smile. "I thought I might find you here."

Her eyes widened at the realization that he'd deliberately sought her out. Her heart started beating faster as well, but at least that was something she could keep hidden from him.

He glanced briefly down to the stone bench, signaling that she should feel free to resume her seat. "Actually, I saw you from my window. I wanted to make certain that you were feeling better," he said quietly.

Kate sat down, disappointment rising in her throat. He was merely being polite. Of *course* he was merely being polite. Silly of her to dream—even for a moment—that there might be something more. He was, she'd finally realized, a nice person, and any nice person would want to make sure that she was feeling better after what had transpired the night before.

"I am," she replied. "Very much. Thank you."

If he thought anything of her broken, staccato sentences, he did not make any discernible reaction of it. "I'm glad," he said as he sat beside her. "I worried about you for much of the night."

Her heart, which had already been pounding much too quickly, skipped a beat. "You did?"

"Of course. How could I not?"

Kate swallowed. There it was, that infernal politeness again. Oh, she didn't doubt that his interest and concern were real and true. It just hurt that they were prompted by his natural kindness of spirit, not any special feeling for her.

Not that she had expected anything different. But she'd found it impossible not to hope, anyway.

"I'm sorry to have bothered you so late at night," she said quietly, mostly because she thought she should. In truth, she was desperately glad that he'd been there.

"Don't be silly," he said, straightening slightly and fixing upon her a rather stern sort of look. "I hate to think of you all alone during a storm. I'm glad I was there to comfort you."

"I'm usually alone during storms," she admitted.

Anthony frowned. "Your family does not offer you comfort during storms?"

She looked a little sheepish as she said, "They do not know that I still fear them."

He nodded slowly. "I see. There are times—" Anthony paused to clear his throat, a diversionary tactic he frequently employed when he wasn't quite certain what it was he wanted to say. "I think you would gain comfort by seeking the aid of your mother and sister, but I know—" He cleared his throat again. He knew well the singularly strange sensation of loving one's family to distraction, and yet not feeling quite able to share one's deepest and most intractable fears. It brought on an uncanny sense of isolation, of being remarkably alone in a loud and loving crowd.

"I know," he said again, his voice purposely even and subdued, "that it can often be most difficult to share one's fears with those one most deeply loves."

Her brown eyes, wise and warm and undeniably perceptive, focused on his. For one split moment he had the bizarre thought that she somehow knew everything about him, every last detail from the moment of his birth to his certainty of his own death. It seemed, in that second, with her face tipped up toward his and her lips slightly parted, that she, more than anyone else who would ever walk this earth, truly *knew* him.

It was thrilling.

But more than that, it was terrifying.

"You're a very wise man," she whispered.

It took him a moment to remember what they'd been talking about. Ah yes, fears. He knew fears. He tried to laugh off her compliment. "Most of the time I'm a very foolish man."

She shook her head. "No. I think you've hit the nail squarely on its proverbial head. Of course I would not tell Mary and Edwina. I do not want to trouble them." She chewed on her lip for a moment—a funny little movement with her teeth that he found oddly seductive.

"Of course," she added, "if I am to be true to myself, I must confess that my motives are not entirely unselfish. Surely, an equal part of my reluctance lies in my desire not to be seen as weak."

"That's not such a terrible sin," he murmured.

"Not as far as sins go, I suppose," Kate said with a smile. "But I would hazard a guess that it is one from which you, too, suffer."

He didn't say anything, just nodded his assent.

"We all have our roles to play in life," she continued, "and mine has always been to be strong and sensible. Cringing under a table during an electrical storm is neither."

"Your sister," he said quietly, "is probably a great deal stronger than you think."

Her eyes flew to his face. Was he trying to tell her that he'd fallen in love with Edwina? He'd complimented her sister's grace and beauty before, but never had he referred to her inner person.

Kate's eyes searched his for as long as she dared, but she found nothing that revealed his true feelings. "I did not mean to imply that she wasn't," she finally replied. "But I am her older sister. I have always had to be strong for her. Whereas she has only had to be strong for herself." She brought her eyes back up to his, only to find that he was staring at her with an odd intensity, almost as if he could see past her skin and into her very soul. "You are the oldest as well," she said. "I'm sure you know what I mean."

He nodded, and his eyes looked amused and resigned at the same time. "Exactly."

She gave him an answering smile, the kind that passed between people who know similar experiences and trials. And as she felt herself growing more at ease next to him, almost as if she could sink into his side and bury herself against the warmth of his body, she knew that she could put off her task no longer.

She had to tell him that she'd withdrawn her opposition to his match with Edwina. It wasn't fair to anyone to keep it to herself, just because she wanted to keep *him* to herself, if only for a few perfect moments right here in the gardens.

She took a deep breath, straightened her shoulders, and turned to him.

He looked at her expectantly. It was obvious, after all, that she had something to say.

Kate's lips parted. But nothing came out.

"Yes?" he asked, looking rather amused.

"My lord," she blurted out.

"Anthony," he corrected gently.

"Anthony," she repeated, wondering why the use of his given name made this all the more difficult. "I did need to speak with you about something."

He smiled. "I'd gathered."

Her eyes became inexplicably fastened on her right foot, which was tracing half-moons on the packed dirt of the path. "It's . . . um . . . it's about Edwina."

Anthony's brows rose and he followed her gaze to her foot, which had left half-moons behind and was now drawing squiggly lines. "Is something amiss with your sister?" he inquired gently.

She shook her head, looking back up. "Not at all. I believe she's in the drawing room, writing a letter to our cousin in Somerset. Ladies like to do that, you know."

He blinked. "Do what?"

"Write letters. I'm not a very good correspondent

myself," she said, her words coming forth in an oddly rushed fashion, "as I rarely have the patience to sit still at a desk long enough to write an entire letter. Not to mention that my penmanship is abysmal. But most ladies spend a goodly portion of every day drafting letters."

He tried not to smile. "You wanted to warn me that your sister likes to write letters?"

"No, of course not," she mumbled. "It's just that you asked if she was all right, and I said of course, and I told you where she was, and then we were entirely off the topic, and—"

He laid his hand across hers, effectively cutting her off. "What is it you needed to tell me, Kate?"

He watched with interest as she steeled her shoulders and clenched her jaw. She looked as if she were preparing for a hideous task. Then, in one big rush of a sentence, she said, "I just wanted you to know that I have withdrawn my objections to your suit of Edwina."

His chest suddenly felt a bit hollow. "I . . . see," he said, not because he did see, just because he had to say something.

"I admit to a strong prejudice against you," she continued quickly, "but I have come to know you since my arrival at Aubrey Hall, and in all conscience, I could not allow you to go on thinking that I would stand in your way. It would—it would not be right of me."

Anthony just stared at her, completely at a loss. There was, he realized dimly, something a bit deflating about her willingness to marry him off to her sister, since he'd spent the better part of the last two days fighting the urge to kiss her rather senseless.

On the other hand, wasn't this what he wanted? Edwina would make the perfect wife.

Kate would not.

Edwina fit all the criteria he'd laid out when he'd finally decided it was time to wed.

Kate did not.

And he certainly couldn't dally with Kate if he meant to marry Edwina.

She was giving him what he wanted—*exactly*, he reminded himself, what he wanted; with her sister's blessing, Edwina would marry him next week if he so desired.

Then why the devil did he want to grab her by the shoulders and shake and shake and shake until she took back every bloody little annoying word?

It was that spark. That damnable spark that never seemed to dim between them. That awful prickle of awareness that burned every time she entered a room, or took a breath, or pointed a toe. That sinking feeling that he could, if he let himself, love her.

Which was the one thing he feared most.

Perhaps the only thing he feared at all.

It was ironic, but death was the one thing he wasn't afraid of. Death wasn't frightening to a man alone. The great beyond held no terror when one had managed to avoid attachments here on earth.

Love was truly a spectacular, sacred thing. Anthony knew that. He'd seen it every day of his childhood, every time his parents had shared a glance or touched hands.

But love was the enemy of the dying man. It was the only thing that could make the rest of his years intolerable—to taste bliss and know that it would all be snatched away. And that was probably why, when Anthony finally reacted to her words, he didn't yank her to him and kiss her until she was gasping, and he didn't press his lips to her ear and burn his breath against her skin, making sure she understood that he was on fire for her, and not her sister.

Never her sister.

Instead, he just looked at her impassively, his eyes far, far steadier than his heart, and said, "I am much relieved," all the while having the strangest feeling that he wasn't really there, but rather watching the entire scene—nothing

more than a farce, really—from outside of his body, all the
while wondering what the hell was going on.

She smiled weakly and said, "I thought you might feel
that way."

"Kate, I—"

She'd never know what he meant to say. In all truth, *he*
wasn't even sure what he intended to say. He hadn't even
realized that he was going to speak until her name passed
over his lips.

But his words would remain forever unspoken, because
at that moment, he heard it.

A low buzz. A whine, really. It was the sort of sound
most people found mildly annoying.

Nothing, to Anthony, could have been more terrifying.

"Don't move," he whispered, his voice harsh with fear.

Kate's eyes narrowed, and of course she moved, trying
to twist about. "What are you talking about? What is
wrong?"

"Just don't move," he repeated.

Her eyes slid to the left, then her chin followed by a
quarter of an inch or so. "Oh, it's just a bee!" Her face
broke out in a relieved grin, and she lifted her hand to swat
it away. "For goodness' sake, Anthony, don't do that
again. You had me scared for a moment."

Anthony's hand shot out and grasped her wrist with
painful force. "I said don't move," he hissed.

"Anthony," she said, laughing, "it's a *bee*."

He held her immobile, his grasp hard and painful, his
eyes never leaving the loathsome creature, watching as it
buzzed purposefully around her head. He was paralyzed
by fear, and fury, and something else he couldn't quite put
his finger on.

It wasn't as if he hadn't come into contact with bees in
the eleven years since his father's death. One couldn't
reside in England, after all, and expect to avoid them altogether.

Until now, in fact, he'd forced himself to flirt with them in an odd, fatalistic manner. He'd always suspected that he might be doomed to follow in his father's footsteps in all respects. If he was going to be brought down by a humble insect, by God he'd do it standing firm and holding his ground. He was going to die sooner or . . . well, sooner, and he wasn't going to run from some bloody bug. And so when one flew by, he laughed, he mocked, he cursed, and he swatted it away with his hand, daring it to retaliate.

And he'd never been stung.

But seeing one fly so dangerously close to Kate, brushing by her hair, landing on the lacy sleeve of her dress—it was terrifying, almost hypnotizing. His mind raced ahead, and he saw the tiny monster sink its stinger into her soft flesh, he saw her gasping for air, sinking to the ground.

He saw her here at Aubrey Hall, laid out on the same bed that had served as his father's first coffin.

"Just be quiet," he whispered. "We're going to stand— *slowly*. Then we're going to walk away."

"Anthony," she said, her eyes crinkling in an impatiently confused manner, "what is *wrong* with you?"

He tugged on her hand, trying to force her to rise, but she resisted. "It's a *bee*," she said in an exasperated voice. "Stop acting so strangely. For heaven's sake, it's not going to kill me."

Her words hung heavy in the air, almost like solid objects, ready to crash to the ground and shatter them both. Then, finally, when Anthony felt his throat relax enough to speak, he said in a low, intense voice, "It might."

Kate froze, not because she meant to follow his orders, but because something in his aspect, something in his eyes, frightened her to the bone. He looked changed, possessed by some unknown demon. "Anthony," she said in what she hoped was an even, authoritative voice, "let go of my wrist this instant."

She pulled, but he did not relent, and the bee kept buzzing relentlessly about her.

"Anthony!" she exclaimed. "Stop this right—"

The rest of her sentence was lost as she somehow managed to yank her hand from his crushing grasp. The sudden freedom left her off balance, and her arm flailed up and about, the inside of her elbow knocking into the bee, which let out a loud, angry buzz as the force of the blow sent it hurtling through space, smashing right into the strip of bare skin above the lace-edged bodice of her afternoon dress.

"Oh, for the love of— Ow!" Kate let out a howl as the bee, no doubt infuriated by its abuse, sank its stinger into her flesh. "Oh, damn," she swore, completely past any pretensions toward proper language. It was just a bee sting, of course, and nothing she hadn't suffered several times before, but bloody hell, it *hurt*.

"Oh, bother," she grumbled, pulling her chin against her chest so she could look down and get the best view of the red welt rising right along the edge of her bodice. "Now I'll have to go inside for a poultice, and it'll get all over my dress." With a disdainful sniff, she brushed the dead carcass of the bee from her skirt, muttering, "Well, at least he's dead, the vexing thing. It's probably the only justice in the—"

That was when she looked up and spied Anthony's face. He'd gone white. Not pale, not even bloodless, but white. "Oh, my God," he whispered, and the oddest thing was that his lips didn't even move. "Oh, my God."

"Anthony?" she asked, leaning forward and momentarily forgetting about the painful sting on her chest. "Anthony, what is wrong?"

Whatever trance he was in suddenly snapped, and he leaped forward, roughly grabbing one of her shoulders with one hand while his other grappled with the bodice of her gown, pulling it down to better expose her wound.

"My lord!" Kate shrieked. "Stop!"

He said nothing, but his breath was ragged and fast as he pinned her against the back of the bench, still holding her dress down, not low enough to expose her, but certainly lower than decency allowed.

"Anthony!" she tried, hoping that the use of his given name might get his attention. She didn't know this man; he wasn't the one who had sat at her side just two minutes earlier. He was crazed, frantic, and completely heedless of her protestations.

"Will you shut up?" he hissed, never once looking up at her. His eyes were focused on the red, swollen circle of flesh on her chest, and with trembling hands he plucked the stinger from her skin.

"Anthony, I'm fine!" she insisted. "You must—"

She gasped. He'd moved one of his hands slightly as he used the other to yank a handkerchief from his pocket, and it now rather indelicately cupped her entire breast.

"Anthony, what are you doing?" She grabbed at his hand, trying to remove it from her person, but his strength was beyond her.

He pinned her even more firmly against the back of the bench, his hand nearly pressing her breast flat. "Be still!" he barked, and then he took the handkerchief and began to press against the swollen sting.

"What are you doing?" she asked, still trying to scoot away.

He didn't look up. "Expressing the venom."

"*Is* there venom?"

"There must be," he muttered. "There has to be. Something is killing you."

Her mouth fell open. "Something is *killing me*? Are you mad? Nothing is killing me. It's a bee sting."

But he ignored her, too focused on his self-appointed task of treating her wound.

"Anthony," she said in a placating voice, trying to reason with him. "I appreciate your concern, but I've been stung by bees at least a half dozen times, and I—"

"He'd been stung before, too," he interrupted.

Something about his voice sent a shiver down her spine. "Who?" she whispered.

He pressed more firmly against the raised hive, dabbing the handkerchief against the clear liquid that oozed out. "My father," he said flatly, "and it killed him."

She couldn't quite believe it. "A bee?"

"Yes, a bee," he snapped. "Haven't you been listening?"

"Anthony, a little bee cannot kill a man."

He actually paused in his ministrations for a brief second to glance up at her. His eyes were hard, haunted. "I assure you that it can," he bit off.

Kate couldn't quite believe that his words were true, but she also didn't think he was lying, and so she held still for a moment, recognizing that he needed to treat her bee sting far more than she needed to scoot away from his attentions.

"It's still swollen," he muttered, pressing harder with the handkerchief. "I don't think I got it all out."

"I'm sure I'll be fine," she said gently, her ire with him turning into an almost maternal concern. His brow was wrinkled with concentration, and his movements still carried an air of frantic energy. He was petrified, she realized, scared that she would drop dead right there on the garden bench, felled by a tiny little bee.

It seemed unfathomable, and yet it was true.

He shook his head. "It's not good enough," he said hoarsely. "I have to get it all out."

"Anthony, I— What are you *doing*?"

He'd tipped her chin back and his head was closing the distance between them, almost as if he meant to kiss her.

"I'm going to have to suck the venom out," he said grimly. "Just hold still."

"Anthony!" she shrieked. "You can't—" She gasped, completely unable to finish her sentence once she felt his lips settling on her skin, applying a gentle, yet inexorable pressure, pulling her into his mouth. Kate didn't know how to respond, didn't know whether to push him away or pull him toward her.

But in the end she just froze. Because when she lifted her head and looked over his shoulder, she saw a group of three women staring at them with equal expressions of shock.

Mary.

Lady Bridgerton.

And Mrs. Featherington, arguably the *ton*'s biggest gossip.

And Kate knew, beyond a shadow of a doubt, that her life would never be the same.

Chapter 14

And indeed, if a scandal does erupt at Lady Bridgerton's party, those of us who remain in London may be assured that any and all titillating news shall reach our tender ears with all possible haste. With so many notorious gossips in attendance, we are all but guaranteed a full and detailed report.

LADY WHISTLEDOWN'S SOCIETY PAPERS, 4 MAY 1814

For a split second, everyone remained frozen as if in a tableau. Kate stared at the three matrons in shock. They stared back at her in utter horror.

And Anthony kept trying to suck the venom from Kate's bee sting, completely oblivious to the fact that they had an audience.

Of the quintet, Kate found her voice—and her strength—first, shoving with all her might against Anthony's shoulder as she let out an impassioned cry of, "Stop!"

Caught off guard, he proved surprisingly easy to dislodge, and he landed on his bum on the ground, his eyes still burning with determination to save her from what he perceived as her deathly fate.

"Anthony?" Lady Bridgerton gasped, her voice quavering on her son's name, as if she couldn't quite believe what she was seeing.

He twisted around. "Mother?"

"Anthony, what were you doing?"

"She was stung by a bee," he said grimly.

"I'm fine," Kate insisted, then yanked up her dress. "I told him I was fine, but he wouldn't listen to me."

Lady Bridgerton's eyes misted over with understanding. "I see," she said in a small, sad voice, and Anthony knew that she did see. She was, perhaps, the only person who *could* see.

"Kate," Mary finally said, choking on her words, "he had his lips on your . . . on your—"

"On her breast," Mrs. Featherington said helpfully, folding her arms over her ample bosom. A disapproving frown crossed her face, but it was clear that she was enjoying herself immensely.

"He did not!" Kate exclaimed, struggling to her feet, which wasn't the easiest task, since Anthony had landed on one of them when she'd shoved him off the bench. "I was stung right here!" With a frantic finger, she pointed at the round red welt that was still rising on the thin skin covering her collarbone.

The three older ladies stared at her bee sting, their skin assuming identical blushes of faint crimson.

"It's not anywhere near my breast!" Kate protested, too horrified by the direction of the conversation to remember to feel embarrassed at her rather anatomical language.

"It isn't *far*," Mrs. Featherington pointed out.

"Will someone shut her up?" Anthony snapped.

"Well!" Mrs. Featherington huffed. "I never!"

"No," Anthony replied. "You *always*."

"What does he mean by that?" Mrs. Featherington demanded, poking Lady Bridgerton in the arm. When the viscountess did not respond, she turned to Mary and repeated the question.

But Mary had eyes only for her daughter. "Kate," she ordered, "come here this instant."

Dutifully, Kate moved to Mary's side.

"Well?" Mrs. Featherington asked. "What are we going to do?"

Four sets of eyes turned on her in disbelief.

" 'We'?" Kate questioned faintly.

"I fail to see how *you* have any say in the matter," Anthony bit off.

Mrs. Featherington just let out a loud, disdainful, and rather nasal sniff. "You have to marry the chit," she announced.

"What?" The word was ripped from Kate's throat. "You must be mad."

"I must be the only sensible one in the garden is what I must be," Mrs. Featherington said officiously. "Lud, girl, he had his mouth on your bubbies, and we all saw it."

"He did not!" Kate moaned. "I was stung by a bee. A bee!"

"Portia," Lady Bridgerton interjected, "I hardly think there is need for such graphic language."

"There's little use for delicacy now," Mrs. Featherington replied. "It's going to make a tidy piece of gossip no matter how you describe it. The *ton*'s most fervent bachelor, brought down by a bee. I must say, my lord, it's not how I imagined it."

"There is not going to be any gossip," Anthony growled, advancing on her with a menacing air, "because no one is going to say a word. I will not see Miss Sheffield's reputation besmirched in any way."

Mrs. Featherington's eyes bugged out with disbelief. "You think you can keep something like this quiet?"

"*I'm* not going to say anything, and I rather doubt that Miss Sheffield will, either," he said, planting his hands on his hips as he glared down at her. It was the sort of stare that brought grown men to their knees, but Mrs. Featherington was either impervious or simply stupid, so he continued with, "Which leaves our respective mothers, who would seem to have a vested interest in protecting our reputations. Which then leaves you, Mrs. Featherington, as the only member of our cozy little group who might prove herself a gossipy, loudmouthed fishwife over this."

Mrs. Featherington turned a dull red. "Anyone could have seen from the house," she said bitterly, clearly loath to lose such a prime piece of gossip. She'd be fêted for a month as the only eyewitness to such a scandal. The only eyewitness who'd talk, that is.

Lady Bridgerton glanced up at the house, her face going pale. "She's right, Anthony," she said. "You were in full view of the guest wing."

"It was a bee," Kate practically wailed. "Just a bee! Surely we can't be forced to marry because of a bee!"

Her outburst was met with silence. She looked from Mary to Lady Bridgerton, both of whom were gazing at her with expressions hovering between concern, kindness, and pity. Then she looked at Anthony, whose expression was hard, closed, and utterly unreadable.

Kate closed her eyes in misery. This wasn't how it was supposed to happen. Even as she had told him he might marry her sister, she'd secretly wished he could be hers, but not like this.

Oh, dear Lord, not like this. Not so he'd feel trapped. Not so he'd spend the rest of his life looking at her and wishing she were someone else.

"Anthony?" she whispered. Maybe if he spoke to her, maybe if he just looked at her she might glean some clue as to what he was thinking.

"We will marry next week," he stated. His voice was firm and clear, but otherwise devoid of emotion.

"Oh, good!" Lady Bridgerton said with great relief, clapping her hands together. "Mrs. Sheffield and I will begin preparations immediately."

"Anthony," Kate whispered again, this time with more

urgency, "are you certain?" She grabbed his arm and tried to pull him away from the matrons. She gained only a few inches, but at least now they weren't facing them.

He gazed at her with implacable eyes. "We will marry," he said simply, his voice that of the consummate aristocrat, brooking no protest and expecting to be obeyed. "There is nothing else to do."

"But you don't want to marry me," she said.

This caused him to raise a brow. "And do you want to marry me?"

She said nothing. There was nothing she could say, not if she wanted to maintain even a shred of pride.

"I suspect we shall suit well enough," he continued, his expression softening slightly. "We've become friends of a sort, after all. That's more than most men and women have at the beginning of a union."

"You can't want this," she persisted. "You wanted to marry Edwina. What are you going to say to Edwina?"

He crossed his arms. "I never made any promises to Edwina. And I imagine we'll simply tell her we fell in love."

Kate felt her eyes rolling of their own volition. "She'll never believe *that*."

He shrugged. "Then tell her the truth. Tell her you were stung by a bee, and I was trying to aid you, and we were caught in a compromising position. Tell her whatever you want. She's your sister."

Kate sank back down onto the stone bench, sighing. "No one is going to believe you wanted to marry me," she said. "Everyone will think you were trapped."

Anthony shot a pointed glare at the three women, who were still staring at them with interest. At his, "Would you mind?" both his and Kate's mothers stepped back several feet and turned around to afford them more privacy. When Mrs. Featherington did not follow immediately, Violet reached forward and nearly pulled her arm out of the socket.

Sitting down next to Kate, he said, "There is little we can do to prevent people from talking, especially with Portia Featherington as a witness. I don't trust that woman to keep her mouth shut any longer than it takes her to return to the house." He leaned back and propped his left ankle on his right knee. "So we might as well make the best of it. I have to get married this year—"

"Why?"

"Why what?"

"Why do you have to get married this year?"

He paused for a moment. There wasn't really an answer to that question. So he said, "Because I decided I would, and that's a good enough reason for me. As for you, you have to get married eventually—"

She interrupted him again with, "To be honest, I rather assumed I wouldn't."

Anthony felt his muscles tense, and it took him several seconds to realize that what he was feeling was rage. "You planned to live your life as a spinster?"

She nodded, her eyes innocent and frank at the same time. "It seemed a definite possibility, yes."

Anthony held himself still for several seconds, thinking he might like to murder all those men and women who had compared her to Edwina and found her lacking. Kate truly had no idea that she might be attractive and desirable in her own right.

When Mrs. Featherington had announced that they must marry, his initial reaction had been the same as Kate's—utter horror. Not to mention a rather pricked sense of pride. No man liked to be forced into marriage, and it was particularly galling to be forced by a *bee*.

But as he stood there, watching Kate howl in protest (not, he thought, the most flattering of reactions, but he supposed she was allowed her pride as well), a strange sense of satisfaction washed over him.

He wanted her.

He wanted her desperately.

He wouldn't, in a million years, have allowed himself to choose her as a wife. She was far, far too dangerous to his peace of mind.

But fate had intervened, and now that it looked like he *had* to marry her . . . well, there didn't seem much use in putting up a big fuss. There were worse fates than finding oneself married to an intelligent, entertaining woman whom one happened to lust after around the clock.

All he had to do was make certain he didn't actually fall in love with her. Which shouldn't prove impossible, right? The Lord knew she drove him crazy half the time with her incessant arguing. He could have a pleasant marriage with Kate. He'd enjoy her friendship and enjoy her body and keep it at that. It didn't have to go any deeper.

And he couldn't have asked for a better woman to serve as mother to his sons after he was gone. That was certainly worth a great deal.

"This will work," he said with great authority. "You'll see."

She looked doubtful, but she nodded. Of course, there was little else she could do. She'd just been caught by the biggest gossip in London with a man's mouth on her chest. If he hadn't offered to marry her, she'd have been ruined forever.

And if she'd refused to marry him . . . well, then she'd be branded a fallen woman *and* an idiot.

Anthony suddenly stood. "Mother!" he barked, leaving Kate on the bench as he strode over to her. "My fiancée and I desire a bit of privacy here in the garden."

"Of course," Lady Bridgerton murmured.

"Do you think that's wise?" Mrs. Featherington asked.

Anthony leaned forward, placed his mouth very close to his mother's ear, and whispered, "If you do not remove her from my presence within the next ten seconds, I shall murder her on the spot."

Lady Bridgerton choked on a laugh, nodded, and managed to say, "Of course."

In under a minute, Anthony and Kate were alone in the garden.

He turned to face her; she'd stood and taken a few steps toward him. "I think," he murmured, slipping his arm through hers, "that we ought to consider moving out of sight of the house."

His steps were long and purposeful, and she stumbled to keep up with him until she found her stride. "My lord," she asked, hurrying along, "do you think this is wise?"

"You sound like Mrs. Featherington," he pointed out, not breaking his pace, even for a second.

"Heaven forbid," Kate muttered, "but the question still stands."

"Yes, I do think it's very wise," he replied, pulling her into a gazebo. Its walls were partially open to the air, but it was surrounded by lilac bushes and afforded them considerable privacy.

"But—"

He smiled. Slowly. "Did you know you argue too much?"

"You brought me here to tell me *that*?"

"No," he drawled, "I brought you here to do *this*."

And then, before she had a chance to utter a word, before she even had a chance to draw breath, his mouth swooped down and captured hers in a hungry, searing kiss. His lips were voracious, taking everything she had to give and then demanding even more. The fire that glowed within her burned and crackled even hotter than what he'd stoked that night in his study, hotter by a tenfold.

She was melting. Dear God, she was melting, and she wanted so much more.

"You shouldn't do this to me," he whispered against her mouth. "You shouldn't. Everything about you is absolutely wrong. And yet . . ."

Kate gasped as his hands stole around to her backside and pressed her harshly against his arousal.

"Do you see?" he said raggedly, his lips moving along

her cheek. "Do you feel?" He chuckled hoarsely, an odd mocking sound. "Do you even understand?" He squeezed mercilessly, then nibbled the tender skin of her ear. "Of course you don't."

Kate felt herself sliding into him. Her skin was starting to burn, and her traitorous arms stole up and around his neck. He was stoking a fire in her, something she could not even begin to control. She'd been possessed by some primitive urge, something hot and molten which needed nothing so much as the touch of his skin against hers.

She wanted him. Oh, how she wanted him. She shouldn't want him, shouldn't desire this man who was marrying her for all the wrong reasons.

And yet she wanted him with a desperation that left her breathless.

It was wrong, so very wrong. She had grave doubts about this marriage, and she knew she ought to maintain a clear head. She kept trying to remind herself of that, but it didn't stop her lips from parting to allow his entry, nor her own tongue from shyly flicking out to taste the corner of his mouth.

And the desire pooling in her belly—and surely that was what this strange, prickly, swirling feeling had to be—it just kept getting stronger and stronger.

"Am I a terrible person?" she whispered, more for her ears than for his. "Does this mean I am fallen?"

But he heard her, and his voice was hot and moist on the skin of her cheek.

"*No.*"

He moved to her ear and made her listen more closely.

"*No.*"

He traveled to her lips and forced her to swallow the word.

"*No.*"

Kate felt her head fall back. His voice was low and seductive, and it almost made her feel like she'd been born for this moment.

"You're perfect," he whispered, his large hands moving urgently over her body, one settling on her waist and the other moving up toward the gentle swell of her breast. "Right here, right now, in this moment, in this garden, you're perfect."

Kate found something unsettling about his words, as if he were trying to tell her—and perhaps himself as well—that she might not be perfect tomorrow, and perhaps even less so the next day. But his lips and hands were persuasive, and she forced the unpleasant thoughts from her head, instead reveling in the heady bliss of the moment.

She felt beautiful. She felt . . . perfect. And right there, right then, she couldn't help but adore the man who made her feel that way.

Anthony slid the hand at her waist to the small of her back, supporting her as his other hand found her breast and squeezed her flesh through the thin muslin of her dress. His fingers seemed beyond his control, tight and spasmodic, gripping her as if he were falling off a cliff and had finally found purchase. Her nipple was hard and tight against his palm, even through the fabric of her dress, and it took everything in him, every last ounce of restraint, not to reach around to the back of her frock and slowly pull each button from its prison.

He could see it all in his mind, even as his lips met hers in another searing kiss. Her dress would slip from her shoulders, the muslin doing a tantalizing slide along her skin until her breasts were bared. He could picture those in his mind, too, and he somehow knew they, too, would be perfect. He'd cup one, lifting the nipple to the sun, and slowly, ever so slowly, he'd bend his head toward her until he could just barely touch her with his tongue.

She'd moan, and he'd tease her some more, holding her tightly so that she couldn't wriggle away. And then, just when her head dropped back and she was gasping, he'd replace his tongue with his lips and suckle her until she screamed.

Dear God, he wanted that so badly he thought he might explode.

But this wasn't the time or the place. It wasn't that he felt a need to wait for his marriage vows. As far as he was concerned, he'd declared himself in public, and she was his. But he wasn't going to tumble her in his mother's garden gazebo. He had more pride—and more respect for her—than that.

With great reluctance, he slowly tore himself away from her, letting his hands rest on her slim shoulders and straightening his arms to keep himself far enough away so that he wouldn't be tempted to continue where he'd left off.

And the temptation was there. He made the mistake of looking at her face, and in that moment he would have sworn that Kate Sheffield was every bit as beautiful as her sister.

Hers was a different sort of attraction. Her lips were fuller, less in fashion but infinitely more kissable. Her lashes—how had he not noticed before how long they were? When she blinked they seemed to rest on her cheeks like a carpet. And when her skin was tinged with the pinks of desire, she glowed. Anthony knew he was being fanciful, but when he gazed upon her face, he could not help thinking of the new dawn, of that exact moment when the sun was creeping over the horizon, painting the sky with its subtle palette of peaches and pinks.

They stood that way for a full minute, both catching their breath, until Anthony finally let his arms drop, and they each took a step back. Kate lifted a hand to her mouth, her fore, middle, and ring fingers just barely touching her lips. "We shouldn't have done that," she whispered.

He leaned back against one of the gazebo posts, looked extremely satisfied with his lot. "Why not? We're betrothed."

"We're not," she admitted. "Not really."

He quirked a brow.

"No agreements have been made," Kate explained hastily. "Or papers signed. And I have no dowry. You should know that I have no dowry."

This caused him to smile. "Are you trying to get rid of me?"

"Of course not!" She fidgeted slightly, shifting her weight from foot to foot.

He took a step toward her. "Surely you're not trying to provide me with a reason to be rid of *you*?"

Kate flushed. "N-no," she lied, even though that was exactly what she had been doing. It was, of course, the utmost stupidity on her part. If he backed out of this marriage, she'd be ruined forever, not just in London, but also in her little village in Somerset. News of a fallen woman always traveled fast.

But it was never easy to be the second choice, and a part of her almost wanted him to confirm all of her suspicions—that he didn't want her as his bride, that he'd much prefer Edwina, that he was only marrying her because he had to. It would hurt dreadfully, but if he would just say it, she would know, and knowing—even if the knowledge was bitter—was always better than not knowing.

At least then she would know exactly where she stood. As it was, she felt as if her feet were planted firmly in quicksand.

"Let us make one thing clear," Anthony said, capturing her attention with his decisive tone. His eyes caught hers, burning with such intensity that she could not look away. "I said I was going to marry you. I am a man of my word. Any further speculation on the subject would be highly insulting."

Kate nodded. But she couldn't help thinking: *Be careful what you wish for . . . be careful what you wish for.*

She'd just agreed to marry the very man with whom she

feared she was falling in love. And all she could wonder was: *Does he think of Edwina when he kisses me?*

Be careful what you wish for, her mind thundered. *You just might get it.*

Chapter 15

*Once again, This Author has been proven correct. Coun-
try house parties do result in the most surprising of
betrothals.*

*Yes indeed, dear reader, you are surely reading it here
first: Viscount Bridgerton is to marry Miss Katharine
Sheffield. Not Miss Edwina, as gossips had speculated,
but Miss Katharine.*

*As to how the betrothal came about, details have been
surprisingly difficult to obtain. This Author has it on the
best authority that the new couple was caught in a compromising position, and that Mrs. Featherington was a
witness, but Mrs. F has been uncharacteristically close-
lipped about the entire affair. Given that lady's propen-
sity for gossip, This Author can only assume that the
viscount (never known for lacking a spine) threatened
bodily injury upon Mrs. F should she even breathe a syllable.*

LADY WHISTLEDOWN'S SOCIETY PAPERS, 11 MAY 1814

*K*ate soon realized that notoriety did not agree with
her.

The remaining two days in Kent had been bad enough;
once Anthony had announced their engagement at supper

following their somewhat precipitous betrothal, she had scarcely a chance to breathe between all the congratulations, questions, and innuendos that were being tossed her way by Lady Bridgerton's guests.

The only time she felt truly at ease was when, a few hours after Anthony's announcement, she finally had a chance to talk privately with Edwina, who'd thrown her arms around her sister and declared herself "thrilled," "overjoyed," and "not even one tiny bit surprised."

Kate had expressed *her* surprise that Edwina was not surprised, but Edwina had just shrugged and said, "It was obvious to me that he was smitten. I do not know why no one else saw it."

Which had left Kate rather puzzled, since she'd been fairly certain that Anthony had had his matrimonial sights set on Edwina.

Once Kate returned to London, the speculation was even worse. Every single member of the *ton*, it seemed, found it imperative to stop by the Sheffields' small rented home on Milner Street to call on the future viscountess. Most managed to infuse their congratulations with a healthy dose of unflattering implication. No one believed it possible that the viscount might actually *want* to marry Kate, and no one seemed to realize how rude it was to say as much to her face.

"My goodness, you were lucky," said Lady Cowper, the mother of the infamous Cressida Cowper, who, for her part, did not say two words to Kate, just sulked in the corner and glared daggers in her direction.

"I had no *idea* he was interested in you," gushed Miss Gertrude Knight, with a facial expression that clearly said she still didn't believe it, and perhaps even hoped that the betrothal might still prove to be a sham, announcement in the *London Times* notwithstanding.

And from Lady Danbury, who'd never been known to mince words: "Don't know how you trapped him, but it must have been a neat trick. There are a few gels out there who wouldn't mind taking lessons from you, mark my words."

Kate just smiled (or tried to, at least; she suspected that her attempts at gracious and friendly response were not always convincing) and nodded, and murmured, "I am a fortunate girl," whenever Mary poked her in the side.

As for Anthony, the lucky man had been able to avoid the harsh scrutiny she'd been forced to endure. He had told her he needed to remain at Aubrey Hall to take care of a few estate details before the wedding, which had been set for the following Saturday, only nine days after the incident in the garden. Mary had worried that such hastiness would lead to "talk," but Lady Bridgerton had rather pragmatically explained that there would be "talk" no matter what, and that Kate would be less subject to unflattering innuendo once she had the protection of Anthony's name.

Kate suspected that the viscountess—who had gained a certain reputation for her single-minded desire to see her adult children married off—simply wanted to get Anthony in front of the bishop before he had the chance to change his mind.

Kate found herself in agreement with Lady Bridgerton. As nervous as she was about the wedding and the marriage to follow, she'd never been the sort to put things off. Once she made a decision—or, in this case, had one made for her—she saw no reason for delay. And as for the "talk," a hasty wedding might increase its volume, but Kate suspected that the sooner she and Anthony were married, the sooner it would die down, and the sooner she might hope to return to the normal obscurity of her own life.

Of course, her life would not be her own for much longer. She was going to have to get used to that.

Not that it felt like her own even now. Her days were a whirlwind of activity, with Lady Bridgerton dragging her from shop to shop, spending an enormous amount of

Anthony's money for her trousseau. Kate had quickly learned that resistance was useless; when Lady Bridgerton—or Violet, as she had now been instructed to call her—made up her mind, heaven help the fool who got in her way. Mary and Edwina had accompanied them on a few of the outings, but they had quickly declared themselves exhausted by Violet's indefatigable energy and gone off to Gunter's for a flavored ice.

Finally, a mere two days before the wedding, Kate received a note from Anthony, asking her to be at home at four that afternoon so that he might pay her a call. Kate was a little nervous at seeing him again; somehow everything seemed different—more formal—in town. Nonetheless, she seized upon the opportunity to avoid another afternoon on Oxford Street, at the dressmaker, and the milliner, and the glovemaker, and to whomever else Violet had it in mind to drag her.

And so, while Mary and Edwina were out running errands—Kate had conveniently forgotten to mention that the viscount was expected—she sat down in the drawing room, Newton sleeping contentedly at her feet, and waited.

Anthony had spent most of the week thinking. Not surprisingly, all of his thoughts were of Kate and their upcoming union.

He'd been worried that he could, if he let himself, love her. The key, it seemed, was simply not to let himself. And the more he thought about it, the more convinced he was that this would not pose a problem. He was a man, after all, and well in control of his actions and emotions. He was no fool; he knew that love existed. But he also believed in the power of the mind, and perhaps even more importantly, the power of the will. Frankly, he saw no reason why love should be an involuntary thing.

If he didn't want to fall in love, then by damn, he wasn't going to. It was as simple as that. It *had* to be as simple as that. If it weren't, then he wasn't much of a man, was he?

He would, however, have to have a talk with Kate on this measure prior to the wedding. There were certain things about their marriage that needed to be made clear. Not rules, exactly, but . . . *understandings*. Yes, that was a good word for it.

Kate needed to understand exactly what she could expect from him, and what he expected in return. Theirs was not a love match. And it wasn't going to grow into one. That simply was not an option. He didn't think she had any delusions on that measure, but just in case, he wanted to make it clear now, before any misunderstandings had the chance to grow into full-fledged disasters.

It was best to lay everything out on the proverbial table so that neither party would be unpleasantly surprised later on. Surely Kate would agree. She was a practical girl. She'd want to know where she stood. She wasn't the sort who liked to be kept guessing.

At precisely two minutes before four, Anthony rapped twice on the Sheffields' front door, trying to ignore the half dozen members of the *ton* who just *happened* to be strolling along Milner Street that afternoon. They were, he thought with a grimace, a bit far from their usual haunts.

But he wasn't surprised. He might be recently returned to London, but he was well aware that his betrothal was the current scandal *du jour*. *Whistledown* was delivered all the way in Kent, after all.

The butler opened the door quickly and ushered him in, showing him to the nearby drawing room. Kate was waiting on the sofa, her hair swept up into a neat something-or-other (Anthony never could remember the names of all those coiffures the ladies seemed to favor) and topped with a ridiculous little cap of some sort that he supposed was meant to match the white trim on her pale blue afternoon dress.

The cap, he decided, would be the first thing to go once they were married. She had lovely hair, long and lustrous and thick. He knew that good manners dictated that she wear bonnets when she was out and about, but really, it seemed a crime to cover it up in the comfort of her own home.

Before he could open his mouth, however, even in greeting, she motioned to a silver tea service on the table in front of her and said, "I took the liberty of ordering tea. There's a slight chill in the air and I thought you might like some. If you don't, I'd be happy to ring for something else."

There hadn't been a chill in the air, at least not one that Anthony had detected, but he nonetheless said, "That would be lovely, thank you."

Kate nodded and picked up the pot to pour. She tipped it about an inch, then righted it, frowning as she said, "I don't even know how you take your tea."

Anthony felt one corner of his mouth tipping up slightly. "Milk. No sugar."

She nodded, setting the pot down in favor of the milk. "It seems a thing a wife should know."

He sat down in a chair that sat at a right angle to the sofa. "And now you do."

She took a deep breath and then let it go. "Now I do," she murmured.

Anthony cleared his throat as he watched her pour. She wasn't wearing gloves, and he found he liked to watch her hands as she worked. Her fingers were long and slender, and they were incredibly graceful, which surprised him, considering how many times she'd trod on his toes while dancing.

Of course some of those missteps had been done on purpose, but not, he suspected, as many as she would have liked to have him believe.

"Here you are," she murmured, holding out his tea. "Be careful, it's hot. I've never been one for lukewarm tea."

No, he thought with a smile, she wouldn't be. Kate wasn't the sort to do anything in half measures. It was one of the things he liked best about her.

"My lord?" she said politely, moving the tea a few inches farther in his direction.

Anthony grasped the saucer, allowing his gloved fingers to brush against her bare ones. He kept his eyes on her face, noticing the faint pink stain of blush that touched her cheeks.

For some reason that pleased him.

"Did you have something specific you wanted to ask me, my lord?" she asked, once her hand was safely away from his and her fingers wrapped around the handle of her own teacup.

"It's Anthony, as I'm sure you recall, and I can't call upon my fiancée merely for the pleasure of her company?"

She gave him a shrewd look over the rim of her cup. "Of course you can," she replied, "but I don't think you are."

He raised a brow at her impertinence. "As it happens, you're right."

She murmured something. He didn't quite catch it, but he had a sneaking suspicion it had been, "I usually am."

"I thought we ought to discuss our marriage," he said.

"I beg your pardon?"

He leaned back in his chair. "We're both practical people. I think we'll find ourselves more at ease once we understand what we can expect from one another."

"Of—of course."

"Good." He set his teacup down in the saucer, then set both down on the table in front of him. "I'm glad you feel that way."

Kate nodded slowly but didn't say anything, instead choosing to keep her eyes trained on his face as he cleared his throat. He looked as if he were preparing for a parliamentary speech.

"We did not get off to the most favorable of starts," he said, scowling slightly when she nodded her agreement, "but I feel—and I hope that you do as well—that we have since reached a friendship of sorts."

She nodded again, thinking that she might make it all the way through the conversation doing nothing but nodding.

"Friendship between the husband and the wife is of the utmost importance," he continued, "even more important, in my opinion, than love."

This time she didn't nod.

"Our marriage will be one based on mutual friendship and respect," he pontificated, "and I for one could not be more pleased."

"Respect," Kate echoed, mostly because he was looking at her expectantly.

"I will do my best to be a good husband to you," he said. "And, provided that you do not bar me from your bed, I shall be faithful to both you and our vows."

"That's rather enlightened of you," she murmured. He was saying nothing she did not expect, and yet she found it somewhat needling all the same.

His eyes narrowed. "I hope you're taking me seriously, Kate."

"Oh, very much so."

"Good." But he gave her a funny look, and she wasn't sure if he believed her. "In return," he added, "I expect that you will not behave in any manner that will sully my family's name."

Kate felt her spine stiffen. "I would not dream of it."

"I didn't think you would. That is one of the reasons I am so pleased with this marriage. You will make an excellent viscountess."

It was meant as a compliment, Kate knew, but still it felt a bit hollow, and maybe a touch condescending. She'd much rather have been told that she'd make an excellent wife.

"We shall have friendship," he announced, "and we

shall have mutual respect, and children—intelligent children, thank God, since you are quite the most intelligent woman of my acquaintance."

That made up for his condescension, but Kate had barely time to smile at his compliment before he added, "But you should not expect love. This marriage will not be about love."

An awful lump rose in Kate's throat, and she found herself nodding yet again, except this time every movement of her neck somehow brought pain to her heart.

"There are certain things I cannot give you," Anthony said, "and love, I'm afraid, is one of them."

"I see."

"Do you?"

"Of course," she practically snapped. "You could not make it any plainer if you wrote it on my arm."

"I had never planned to marry for love," he said.

"That is not what you told me when you were courting Edwina."

"When I was courting Edwina," he returned, "I was trying to impress *you.*"

Her eyes narrowed. "You are not impressing me now."

He let out a long breath. "Kate, I did not come here to argue. I merely thought it best if we were honest with one another before the wedding on Saturday morning."

"Of course," she sighed, forcing herself to nod. His intention hadn't been to insult her, and she shouldn't have overreacted. She knew him well enough now to know that he was merely acting out of concern. He knew he would never love her; better to make that clear in the beginning.

But still it hurt. She didn't know if she loved him, but she was fairly certain she *could* love him, and deathly afraid that after a few weeks of marriage, she *would* love him.

And it would be so nice if he could just love her back.

"It is best that we understand each other now," he said softly.

Kate just kept nodding. A body in motion tended to

remain in motion, and she was afraid that if she stopped, she might do something really stupid, like cry.

He reached across the table and took her hand, which made her flinch. "I didn't want you to enter this marriage with any delusions," he said. "I didn't think you'd want that."

"Of course not, my lord," she said.

He frowned. "I thought I told you to call me Anthony."

"You did," she said, "my lord."

He withdrew his hand. Kate watched as he returned it to his own lap, feeling strangely bereft.

"Before I go," he said, "I have something for you." Without taking his eyes off of her face, he reached into his pocket and pulled out a small jeweler's box. "I must apologize for being so delayed in presenting you with a betrothal ring," he murmured, handing it to her.

Kate smoothed her fingers over the blue velvet covering before flipping the box open. Inside lay a rather simple gold ring, adorned by a single round-cut diamond.

"It's a Bridgerton heirloom," he said. "There are several betrothal rings in the collection, but I thought you'd like this one best. The others were rather heavy and fussy."

"It's beautiful," Kate said, quite unable to take her eyes off of it.

He reached out and took the box from her. "May I?" he murmured, plucking the ring from its velvet nest.

She held out her hand, cursing at herself when she realized she was trembling—not a great deal, but surely enough for him to notice. He didn't say a word, though, just steadied her hand with his as he used the other to slip the ring on her finger.

"Looks rather nice, don't you think?" he asked, still holding the tips of her fingers with his.

Kate nodded, unable to take her eyes off of it. She'd never been one for rings; this would be the first she wore with any regularity. It felt strange on her finger, heavy and cold and very, very solid. It somehow made everything

that had happened in the past week seem more real. More
final. It occurred to her as she was staring at the ring that
she'd been half expecting a bolt of lightning to come
down from heaven and stop the proceedings before they
actually said their vows.

Anthony moved closer, then brought her newly adorned
fingers to his lips. "Perhaps we should seal the bargain
with a kiss?" he murmured.

"I'm not sure. . . ."

He pulled her onto his lap and grinned devilishly. "I am."

But as Kate tumbled onto him, she accidentally kicked
Newton, who let out a loud, whiny bark, obviously dis-
tressed at having his nap so rudely interrupted.

Anthony raised a brow and peered over Kate at Newton. "I didn't even see him here."

"He was taking a nap," Kate explained. "He's a very
sound sleeper."

But once awake, Newton refused to be left out of the
action, and with a slightly more awake bark, he leaped up
onto the chair, landing on Kate's lap.

"Newton!" she squealed.

"Oh, for the love of—" But Anthony's mutterings were
cut short by a big, sloppy kiss from Newton.

"I think he likes you," Kate said, so amused by
Anthony's disgusted expression that she forgot to be self-
conscious about her position on his lap.

"Dog," Anthony ordered, "get down on the floor this
instant."

Newton hung his head and whined.

"Now!"

Letting out a big sigh, Newton turned about and
plopped down onto the floor.

"My goodness," Kate said, peering down at the dog,
who was now moping under the table, his snout lying sor-
rowfully on the carpet, "I'm impressed."

"It's all in the tone of voice," Anthony said archly,

snaking a viselike arm around her waist so that she could not get up.

Kate looked at his arm, then looked at his face, her brows arching in question. "Why," she mused, "do I get the impression you find that tone of voice effective on women as well?"

He shrugged and leaned toward her with a heavy-lidded smile. "It usually is," he murmured.

"Not this one." Kate planted her hands on the arms of the chair and tried to wrench herself up.

But he was far too strong. "Especially this one," he said, his voice dropping to an impossibly low purr. With his free hand, he cupped her chin and turned her face to his. His lips were soft but demanding, and he explored her mouth with a thoroughness that left her breathless.

His mouth moved along the line of her jaw to her neck, pausing only to whisper, "Where is your mother?"

"Out," Kate gasped.

His teeth tugged at the edge of her bodice. "For how long?"

"I don't know." She let out a little squeal as his tongue dipped below the muslin and traced an erotic line on her skin. "Good heavens, Anthony, what are you doing?"

"How long?" he repeated.

"An hour. Maybe two."

Anthony glanced up to make sure he'd shut the door when he had entered earlier. "Maybe two?" he murmured, smiling against her skin. "Really?"

"M-maybe just one."

He hooked a finger under the edge of her bodice up near her shoulder, making sure to catch the edge of her chemise as well. "One," he said, "is still quite splendid." Then, pausing only to bring his mouth to hers so that she could not utter any protest, he swiftly pulled her dress down, taking the chemise along with it.

He felt her gasp into his mouth, but he just deepened

the kiss as he palmed the round fullness of her breast. She was perfect under his fingers, soft and pert, filling his hand as if she'd been made for him.

When he felt the last of her resistance melt away, he moved his kiss to her ear, nibbling softly on her lobe. "Do you like this?" he whispered, squeezing gently with his hand.

She nodded jerkily.

"Mmmm, good," he murmured, letting his tongue do a slow sweep of her ear. "It would make things very difficult if you did not."

"H-how?"

He fought the bubble of mirth that was rising in his throat. This absolutely wasn't the time to laugh, but she was so damned innocent. He'd never made love to a woman like her before; he was finding it surprisingly delightful. "Let's just say," he said, "that I like it very much."

"Oh." She offered him the most tentative of smiles.

"There's more, you know," he whispered, letting his breath caress her ear.

"I'm sure there must be," she replied, her voice mere breath.

"You are?" he asked teasingly, squeezing her again.

"I'm not so green that I think one can make a baby from what we've been doing."

"I'd be happy to show you the rest," he murmured.

"Not— Oh!"

He'd squeezed again, this time allowing his fingers to tickle her skin. He loved that she couldn't think when he touched her breasts. "You were saying?" he prompted, nibbling on her neck.

"I—I was?"

He nodded, the faint stubble of his beard brushing her throat. "I'm sure you were. But then again, perhaps I'd rather not hear. You'd begun with the word 'not.' Surely," he added with a flick of his tongue against the underside of her chin, "not a word that belongs between us at a time like this. But"—his tongue moved down the line of her throat to the hollow above her collarbone—"I digress."

"You—you do?"

He nodded. "I believe I was trying to determine what pleases you, as all good husbands should do."

She said nothing, but her breathing quickened.

He smiled against her skin. "What, for example, about this?" He flattened his hand so that he was no longer cupping her, instead just letting his palm graze lightly over her nipple.

"Anthony!" she choked out.

"Good," he said, moving to her neck, nudging her chin up so that she was more open to him. "I'm glad we're back to Anthony. 'My lord' is so formal, don't you think? Far too formal for *this*."

And then he did what he'd been fantasizing about for weeks. He lowered his head to her breast and took her into his mouth, tasting, suckling, teasing, reveling in each gasp he heard spill forth from her lips, each spasm of desire he felt shivering across her body.

He loved that she reacted this way, thrilled that he did this to her. "So good," he murmured, his breath hot and moist against her skin. "You taste so damn good."

"Anthony," she said, her voice hoarse, "Are you sure—"

He put a finger to her lips without even lifting his face to look at her. "I have no idea what you're asking, but whatever it is"—he moved his attention to her other breast—"I'm sure."

She made a soft little moaning sound, the sort that came from the very bottom of one's throat. Her body arched under his ministrations, and with renewed fervor, he teased her nipple, grazing it gently between her teeth.

"Oh, my—oh, Anthony!"

He ran his tongue around the aureole. She was perfect, simply perfect. He loved the sound of her voice, hoarse and broken with desire, and his body tingled at the thought of their wedding night, of her cries of passion and need. She'd be an inferno beneath him, and he relished the prospect of making her explode.

He pulled away so that he could see her face. She was flushed and her eyes were dazed and dilated. Her hair was starting to come undone from that hideous cap.

"This," he said, plucking it from her head, "has got to go."

"My lord!"

"Promise me you'll never wear it again."

She twisted in her seat—on his lap, actually, which did little to help the rather urgent state of his groin—to look over the edge of the chair. "I'll do no such thing," she retorted. "I quite like that cap."

"You can't possibly," he said in all seriousness.

"I can and— Newton!"

Anthony followed her line of vision and broke out into loud laughter, shaking the both of them in their seats. Newton was happily munching away on Kate's cap. "Good dog!" he said on a laugh.

"I would make you buy me another," Kate muttered, yanking her dress back up, "except that you've already spent a fortune on me this week."

This amused him. "I have?" he inquired mildly.

She nodded. "I've been shopping with your mother."

"Ah. Good. I'm sure she didn't let you pick out anything like *that*." He motioned toward the now mangled cap in Newton's mouth.

When he looked back at her, her mouth was twisted into a fetchingly disgruntled line. He couldn't help but smile. She was so easy to read. His mother hadn't let her buy such an unattractive cap, and it was killing her that she couldn't offer a retort to his last statement.

He sighed rather contentedly. Life with Kate wasn't going to be dull.

But it was getting late, and he should probably be going. Kate had said her mother wasn't expected for at least an hour, but Anthony knew better than to trust the female sense of time. Kate could be wrong, or her mother could have changed her mind, or any number of things might have happened, and even though he and Kate were due to be married in just two days, it didn't seem particularly prudent to get caught in the drawing room in such a compromising position.

With great reluctance—sitting in the chair with Kate and doing nothing but hold her was surprisingly satisfying—he stood, lifting her in his arms as he did so, and then set her back in the chair.

"This has been a delightful interlude," he murmured, leaning down to drop a kiss on her forehead. "But I fear your mother's early return. I shall see you Saturday morning?"

She blinked. "Saturday?"

"A superstition of my mother's," he said with a sheepish smile. "She thinks it's bad luck for the bride and groom to see one another the day before the wedding."

"Oh." She rose to her feet, self-consciously smoothing her dress and hair. "And do you believe it as well?"

"Not at all," he said with a snort.

She nodded. "It's very sweet of you to indulge your mother, then."

Anthony paused for a moment, well aware that most men of his reputation did not want to appear tied to apron strings. But this was Kate, and he knew that she valued devotion to family as much as he did, so he finally said, "There is little I would not do to keep my mother content."

She smiled shyly. "It is one of the things I like best about you."

He made some sort of gesture designed to change the subject, but she interrupted with, "No, it's true. You're far more caring a person than you'd like people to believe."

Since he wasn't going to be able to win the argument with her—and there was little point in contradicting a woman when she was being complimentary—he put a finger to his lips and said, "Shhh. Don't tell anyone." And then, with one last kiss to her hand and a murmured, "Adieu," he made his way out the door and outside.

Once on his horse and on his way back to his small townhouse across town, he allowed himself to assess the visit. It went well, he thought. Kate had seemed to understand the limits he had set upon their marriage, and she'd reacted to his lovemaking with a desire that was sweet and fierce at the same time.

All in all, he thought with a satisfied smile, the future looked bright. His marriage would be a success. As for his previous concerns—well, it was clear he had nothing to worry about.

Kate was worried. Anthony had been practically tripping over himself to make certain that she understood that he would never love her. And he certainly didn't seem to want her love in return.

Then he'd gone and kissed her as if there were no tomorrow, as if she were the most beautiful woman on earth. She'd be the first to admit that she had little experience with men and their desires, but he'd certainly seemed to desire her.

Or was he simply wishing she was someone else? She was not his first choice for a wife. She'd do well to remember that fact.

And even if she did fall in love with him—well, she'd simply have to keep it to herself. There was really nothing else to do.

Chapter 16

It has come to This Author's attention that the wedding of Lord Bridgerton and Miss Sheffield is to be a small, intimate, and private affair.

In other words, This Author is not invited.

But have no fear, dear reader, This Author is at her most resourceful at times such as these, and promises to uncover the details of the ceremony, both the interesting and the banal.

The wedding of London's most eligible bachelor is surely something which must be reported in This Author's humble column, don't you agree?

LADY WHISTLEDOWN'S SOCIETY PAPERS, 13 MAY 1814

The night before the wedding, Kate was sitting on her bed in her favorite dressing gown, looking dazedly at the multitude of trunks strewn across the floor. Her every belonging was packed away, neatly folded or stored, ready for transport to her new home.

Even Newton had been prepared for the journey. He'd been bathed and dried, a new collar had been affixed to his neck, and his favorite toys were loaded into a small satchel that now sat in the front hall, right next to the delicately carved wooden chest Kate had had since she was a baby.

The chest was filled with Kate's childhood toys and treasures, and she'd found tremendous comfort in their presence here in London. It was silly and sentimental, but to Kate it made her upcoming transition a little less scary. Bringing her things—funny little items that meant nothing to anyone but her—to Anthony's home made it seem more like it would truly be her home as well.

Mary, who always seemed to understand what Kate needed before she understood it herself, had sent word to friends back in Somerset as soon as Kate had become betrothed, asking them to ship the chest to London in time for the wedding.

Kate stood and wandered about the room, stopping to run her fingers across a nightgown that was folded and laid upon a table, awaiting transfer to the last of her trunks. It was one that Lady Bridgerton—Violet, she had to start thinking of her as Violet—had picked out, modest in cut but sheer in fabric. Kate had been mortified throughout the entire visit to the lingerie maker. This was her betrothed's mother, after all, selecting items for the wedding night!

As Kate picked up the gown and set it carefully in a trunk, she heard a knock at the door. She called out her greeting, and Edwina poked her head in. She, too, was dressed for bed, her pale hair pulled back into a sloppy bun at the nape of her neck.

"I thought you might like some hot milk," Edwina said.

Kate smiled gratefully. "That sounds heavenly."

Edwina reached down and picked up the ceramic mug she'd set on the floor. "Can't hold two mugs and twist the doorknob at the same time," she explained with a smile. Once inside, she kicked the door shut and handed one of the mugs to Kate. Eyes trained on Kate, Edwina asked without preamble, "Are you scared?"

Kate took a gingerly sip, checking the temperature before gulping it down. It was hot but not scalding, and it somehow comforted her. She'd been drinking hot milk since childhood, and the taste and feel of it always made her feel warm and secure.

"Not scared precisely," she finally replied, sitting down on the edge of her bed, "but nervous. Definitely nervous."

"Well, of course you're nervous," Edwina said, her free hand waving animatedly through the air. "Only an idiot wouldn't be nervous. Your whole life is going to change. Everything! Even your name. You'll be a married woman. A viscountess. After tomorrow, you will not be the same woman, Kate, and after tomorrow *night*—"

"That's enough, Edwina," Kate interrupted.

"But—"

"You are *not* doing anything to ease my mind."

"Oh." Edwina offered her a sheepish smile. "Sorry."

"It's all right," Kate assured her.

Edwina managed to hold her tongue for about four seconds before she asked, "Has Mother been in to speak with you?"

"Not yet."

"She must, don't you think? Tomorrow is your wedding day, and I'm sure there are all sorts of things one needs to know." Edwina took a big gulp of her milk, leaving a rather incongruous white mustache on her upper lip, then perched on the edge of the bed across from Kate. "I know there are all sorts of things *I* don't know. And unless you've been up to something I don't know about, I don't see how *you* could know them, either."

Kate wondered if it would be impolite to muzzle her sister with some of the lingerie Lady Bridgerton had picked out. There seemed to be some rather nice poetic justice in such a maneuver.

"Kate?" Edwina asked, blinking curiously. "Kate? Why are you looking at me so strangely?"

Kate gazed at the lingerie longingly. "You don't want to know."

"Hmmph. Well, I—"

Edwina's mutterings were cut short by a soft knock at

the door. "That'll be Mother," Edwina said with a wicked grin. "I can't wait."

Kate rolled her eyes at Edwina as she rose to open the door. Sure enough, Mary was standing in the hall, holding two steaming mugs. "I thought you might like some hot milk," she said with a weak smile.

Kate lifted her mug in response. "Edwina had the same notion."

"What is Edwina doing here?" Mary asked, entering the room.

"Since when do I need a reason to talk with my sister?" Edwina asked with a snort.

Mary shot her a peevish look before turning her attention back to Kate. "Hmmm," she mused. "We do seem to have a surfeit of hot milk."

"This one's gone lukewarm, anyway," Kate said, setting her mug down on one of the already-closed-up trunks and replacing it with the warmer one in Mary's hand. "Edwina can take the other one down to the kitchen when she leaves."

"Beg pardon?" Edwina asked, vaguely distracted. "Oh, of course. I'm happy to help." But she didn't rise to her feet. In fact, she didn't even twitch, save for the back and forth of her head as she looked from Mary to Kate and back again.

"I need to speak with Kate," Mary said.

Edwina nodded enthusiastically.

"Alone."

Edwina blinked. "I have to leave?"

Mary nodded and held out the lukewarm mug.

"Now?"

Mary nodded again.

Edwina looked stricken, then her expression melted into a wary smile. "You're joking, right? I may stay, right?"

"Wrong," Mary replied.

Edwina turned pleading eyes to Kate.

"Don't look to me," Kate said with a barely suppressed smile. "It's her decision. She'll be doing the talking, after all. I'll just be listening."

"And asking questions," Edwina pointed out. "And I have questions, too." She turned to her mother. "Lots of questions."

"I'm sure you do," Mary said, "and I'll be happy to answer them all the night before you get married."

Edwina groaned her way upright. "This isn't fair," she grumbled, snatching the mug out of Mary's hand.

"Life isn't fair," Mary said with a grin.

"I'll say," Edwina muttered, dragging her feet as she crossed the room.

"And no listening at the door!" Mary called out.

"I wouldn't dream of it," Edwina drawled. "Not that you'd talk loudly enough for me to hear a thing, anyway."

Mary sighed as Edwina stepped out into the hall and shut the door, her movements punctuated by a constant stream of unintelligible grumbles. "We shall have to whisper," she said to Kate.

Kate nodded, but she did feel enough loyalty toward her sister to say, "She *might* not be eavesdropping."

The look Mary gave her was dubious in the extreme. "Do you want to swing the door open to find out?"

Kate grinned despite herself. "Point taken."

Mary sat down in the spot Edwina had just vacated and gave Kate a rather direct look. "I'm sure you know why I'm here."

Kate nodded.

Mary took a sip of her milk and was silent for a long moment before she said, "When I married—for the first time, not to your father—I knew nothing of what to expect in the marriage bed. It was not—" She closed her eyes briefly, and for a moment she looked to be in pain. "My lack of knowledge made it all the more difficult," she finally said, the slowness of her carefully chosen words telling Kate that "difficult" was probably a euphemism.

"I see," Kate murmured.

Mary looked up sharply. "No, you don't see. And I hope you never do. But that is beside the point. I always swore that no daughter of mine would enter into marriage ignorant of what occurs between a husband and wife."

"I'm already aware of the basics of the maneuver," Kate admitted.

Clearly surprised, Mary asked, "You are?"

Kate nodded. "It can't be very much different from animals."

Mary shook her head, her lips pursed into a slightly amused smile. "No, it's not."

Kate pondered how best to phrase her next question. From what she'd seen on her neighbor's farm back in Somerset, the act of procreation didn't look terribly enjoyable at all. But when Anthony kissed her, she felt as if she were losing her mind. And when he kissed her twice, she wasn't even sure if she wanted it back! Her entire body tingled, and she suspected that if their recent encounters had occurred in more suitable locales, she would have let him have his way with her with nary a protest.

But then there was that awful screaming mare at the farm. . . . Frankly, the various pieces of the puzzle didn't seem to reconcile.

Finally, after much clearing of her throat, she said, "It doesn't look very pleasant."

Mary closed her eyes again, her face taking on that same look as before—as if she were remembering something she'd rather keep tucked away in the darkest recesses of her mind. When she opened her eyes again, she said, "A woman's enjoyment depends entirely on her husband."

"And a man's?"

"The act of love," Mary said, blushing, "can and should be a pleasant experience for both man and woman. But—" She coughed and took a sip of her milk. "I would be remiss if I did not tell you that a woman does not always find pleasure in the act."

"But a man does?"

Mary nodded.

"That doesn't seem fair."

Mary's smile was wry. "I believe I just told Edwina that life wasn't always fair."

Kate frowned, staring down into her milk. "Well, this *really* doesn't seem fair."

"This doesn't mean," Mary hastened to add, "that the experience is necessarily distasteful to the woman. And I'm certain it won't be distasteful to you. I assumed the viscount has kissed you?"

Kate nodded without looking up.

When Mary spoke, Kate could hear the smile in her voice. "I'll assume from your blush," Mary said, "that you enjoyed it."

Kate nodded again, her cheeks now burning.

"If you enjoyed his kiss," Mary said, "then I am certain you won't be upset by his further attentions. I'm sure that he will be gentle and attentive with you."

"Gentle" didn't quite capture the essence of Anthony's kisses, but Kate didn't think that was the sort of thing one was meant to share with one's mother. Truly, the entire conversation was embarrassing enough as it was.

"Men and women are very different," Mary continued, as if that weren't completely obvious, "and a man—even one who is faithful to his wife, which I'm sure the viscount will be to you—can find his pleasure with almost any woman."

This was disturbing, and not what Kate had wanted to hear. "And a woman?" she had prompted.

"It is different for a woman. I have heard that wicked women find their pleasure like a man, in the arms of any who will satisfy, but I do not believe it. I think that a woman must care for her husband in order to enjoy the marriage bed."

Kate was silent for a moment. "You did not love your first husband, did you?"

Mary shook her head. "It makes all the difference, sweet one. That, and a husband's regard for his wife. But I have seen the viscount in your company. I realize that your match was sudden and unexpected, but he treats you with care and respect. You will have nothing to fear, I'm sure of it. The viscount will treat you well."

And with that, Mary kissed Kate upon the forehead and bade her good night, picking up both empty milk mugs as she left the room. Kate sat on her bed, staring sightlessly at the wall for several minutes.

Mary was wrong. Kate was sure of it. She had much to fear.

She hated that she was not Anthony's first choice for a wife, but she was practical, and she was pragmatic, and she knew that certain things in life simply had to be accepted as fact. But she'd been consoling herself with the memory of the desire she had felt—and she thought Anthony had felt—when she was in his arms.

Now it seemed that this desire wasn't even necessarily for her, but rather some primitive urge that every man felt for every woman.

And Kate would never know if, when Anthony snuffed the candles and took her to bed, he closed his eyes . . .

And pictured another woman's face.

The wedding, which was held in the drawing room of Bridgerton House, was a small, private affair. Well, as small as one could expect with the entire Bridgerton family in attendance, from Anthony all the way down to little eleven-year-old Hyacinth, who'd taken her role as flower girl *very* seriously. When her brother Gregory, aged thirteen, had tried to tip her basket of rose petals, she'd walloped him in the chin, delaying the ceremony by a good ten minutes but interjecting a much-needed note of levity and laughter.

Well, for everyone except Gregory, who'd been quite put out by the entire episode and certainly *wasn't* laughing, even though he was, as Hyacinth was quick to point out to anyone who would listen (and her voice was loud enough so that one didn't really have the option of *not* listening), the one who'd started it.

Kate had seen it all from her vantage point in the hall, where she'd been peeking through a crack in the door. It had made her smile, which was much appreciated, since her knees had been knocking for over an hour. She could only thank her lucky stars that Lady Bridgerton had not insisted upon a large, grand affair. Kate, who'd never thought of herself as a nervous sort of person before, would probably have passed out from fright.

Indeed, Violet had mentioned the possibility of a huge wedding as a method by which to combat the rumors that were circulating about Kate, Anthony, and their rather sudden engagement. Mrs. Featherington was, true to her word, remaining mostly silent on the details of the matter, but she'd let enough innuendo slip that *everyone* knew that the betrothal had not come about in the usual matter.

As a result, *everyone* was talking, and Kate knew it was only a matter of time before Mrs. Featherington could no longer restrain herself and everyone learned the true story of her downfall at the hands—or rather, the stinger—of a bee.

But in the end Violet had decided that a quick marriage was best, and since one couldn't throw together a grand party in one week, the guest list had been limited to family. Kate was attended by Edwina, Anthony by his brother Benedict, and in due course they were man and wife.

It was strange, Kate thought later that afternoon as she stared at the gold band that had joined the diamond on her left hand, how quickly one's life could change. The ceremony had been brief, rushing by in a crazy blur, and yet her life was forever altered. Edwina had been correct. Everything was different. She was a married woman now, a viscountess.

Lady Bridgerton.

She chewed on her lower lip. It sounded like someone else. How long would it take before someone said, "Lady Bridgerton," and she actually thought they were talking to *her*, and not Anthony's mother?

She was a wife now, with a wife's responsibilities.

It terrified her.

Now that the wedding was done, Kate reflected upon Mary's words from the previous night and knew that she was right. In many respects, she was the luckiest woman alive. Anthony would treat her well. He would treat any woman well. And that was the problem.

And now she was in a carriage, traveling the short distance between Bridgerton House, where the reception had been held, and Anthony's private residence, which she supposed could no longer be referred to as "bachelor's lodgings."

She stole a glance at her new husband. He was facing straight ahead, his face oddly serious.

"Do you plan to move into Bridgerton House now that you are married?" she inquired quietly.

Anthony started, almost as if he'd forgotten she was there. "Yes," he replied, turning to face her, "although not for several months. I thought we could do with a bit of privacy at the start of our marriage, don't you think?"

"Of course," Kate murmured. She looked down at her hands, which were fidgeting in her lap. She tried to still them, but it was impossible. It was a wonder she had not burst out of her gloves.

Anthony followed the line of her gaze and placed one of his large hands over both of hers. She went still instantly.

"Are you nervous?" he inquired.

"Did you think I wouldn't be?" she replied, trying to keep her voice dry and ironic.

He smiled in response. "There is nothing to fear."

Kate nearly burst out in jittery laughter. It seemed she

was destined to hear that platitude over and over again. "Perhaps," she allowed, "but still much about which to be nervous."

His smile broadened. "Touché, my dear wife."

Kate swallowed convulsively. It was strange to be someone's wife, especially strange to be this man's wife. "And are *you* nervous?" she countered.

He leaned in toward her, his dark eyes hot and heavy with the promise of things to come. "Oh, desperately," he murmured. He closed the rest of the distance between them, his lips finding the sensitive hollow of her ear. "My heart is pounding," he whispered.

Kate's body seemed to stiffen and melt at the same time. And then she blurted out, "I think we should wait."

He nibbled on her ear. "Wait for what?"

She tried to wiggle away. He didn't understand. If he'd understood, he'd be furious, and he didn't seem particularly upset.

Yet.

"F-for the marriage," she stammered.

That seemed to amuse him, and he playfully wiggled the rings that now rested on her gloved fingers. "It's a bit late for that, don't you think?"

"For the wedding night," she clarified.

He drew back, his dark brows flattening into a straight, and perhaps a little bit angry, line. "No," he said simply. But he did not move to embrace her again.

Kate tried to think of words that would make him understand, but it wasn't easy; she wasn't so sure that she understood herself. And she was rather certain that he would not believe her if she told him that she'd not intended to make this request; it had just burst forth from within her, born of a panic she hadn't even known was there until that very moment.

"I'm not asking for forever," she said, hating the tremor that shook her words. "Just a week."

This caught his attention, and one of his brows rose in ironic query. "And what, pray tell, do you hope to gain by a week?"

"I don't know," she answered quite honestly.

His eyes focused onto hers, hard, hot, and sardonic. "You're going to have to do better than that," he said.

Kate didn't want to look at him, didn't want the intimacy he forced upon her when she was caught in his dark gaze. It was easy to hide her feelings when she could keep her focus on his chin or his shoulder, but when she had to look straight into his eyes . . .

She was afraid he could see into her very soul.

"This has been a week of a great many changes in my life," she began, wishing she knew where she was going with the statement.

"For me as well," he interjected softly.

"Not so much for you," she returned. "The intimacies of marriage are nothing new to you."

One corner of his mouth quirked into a lopsided, slightly arrogant smile. "I assure you, my lady, that I have never before been married."

"That's not what I meant, and you know it."

He did not contradict her.

"I simply would like a bit of time to prepare," she said, primly folding her hands in her lap. But she couldn't keep her thumbs still, and they twiddled anxiously, giving proof to the state of her nerves.

Anthony stared at her for a long moment, then leaned back, propping his left ankle rather casually on his right knee. "Very well," he allowed.

"Really?" She straightened with surprise. She had not expected him to capitulate with such ease.

"Provided . . ." he continued.

She slumped. She should have known that there would be a contingency.

". . . that you edify me on one point."

She gulped. "And what would that be, my lord?"

He leaned forward, the very devil in his eyes. "How, precisely, do you plan to prepare?"

Kate glanced out the window, then swore under her breath when she realized they weren't even to Anthony's street. There would be no escaping his question; she was stuck in the carriage for at least another five minutes. "We-e-e-e-ll," she stalled, "I'm sure I don't understand what you mean."

He chuckled. "I'm sure you don't, either."

Kate scowled at him. There was nothing worse than being the butt of someone else's joke, and it seemed especially inappropriate when one happened to be a bride on her wedding day. "Now you're having fun with me," she accused.

"No," he said with what could only have been called a leer, "I'd *like* to have fun with you. There's quite a difference."

"I wish you wouldn't talk like that," she grumbled. "You know I don't understand."

His eyes focused on her lips as his tongue darted out to wet his own. "You would," he murmured, "if you'd simply give in to the inevitable and forget your silly request."

"I don't enjoy being condescended to," Kate said stiffly.

His eyes flashed. "And I don't like being denied my rights," he returned, his voice cold and his face a harsh rendition of aristocratic power.

"I'm not denying you anything," she insisted.

"Oh, really?" His drawl lacked all humor.

"I'm just asking for a reprieve. A brief, temporary, *brief*"—she repeated the word, just in case his brain was too dulled by single-minded male pride to have understood her the first time—"reprieve. Surely you would not deny me such a simple request."

"Of the two of us," he said, his voice clipped, "I don't think I'm the one doing the denying."

He was right, drat the man, and she had no idea what else to say. She knew she hadn't a leg to stand on with her spur-of-the-moment request; he had every right to toss her over his shoulder, drag her off to bed, and lock her in the room for a week if he so desired.

She was acting foolishly, a prisoner of her own insecurities—insecurities she hadn't even known she possessed until she'd met Anthony.

All her life, she'd been the one who'd received the second glance, the second greeting, the second kiss on the hand. As the elder daughter, it should have been her due to be addressed before her younger sister, but Edwina's beauty was so stunning, the pure and perfect blue of her eyes so startling, that people simply forgot themselves in her presence.

Introductions to Kate were usually met with an embarrassed, "Of course," and a polite murmured greeting while their eyes slid back to Edwina's pure and shining face.

Kate had never minded it much. If Edwina had been spoiled or bad-tempered it might have been difficult, and in all truth, most of the men she'd met were shallow and silly, and she hadn't much cared if they only took the time to acknowledge her after her sister.

Until now.

She wanted Anthony's eyes to light up when *she* entered the room. She wanted him to scan a crowd until he saw *her* face. She didn't need him to love her—or at least that's what she was telling herself—but she desperately wanted to be first in his affections, first in his desires.

And she had an awful, terrible feeling that all this meant she was falling in love.

Falling in love with one's husband—who would have thought it could be such a disaster?

"I see you have no response," Anthony said quietly.

The carriage rolled to a halt, thankfully sparing her from having to make a reply. But when a liveried footman rushed forward and attempted to open the door, Anthony yanked it back shut, never once taking his eyes off of her face.

"How, my lady?" he repeated.

"How . . ." she echoed. She'd quite forgotten what he was asking.

"How," he said yet again, his voice hard as ice but hot as flame, "do you plan to prepare for your wedding night?"

"I—I had not considered," Kate replied.

"I thought not." He let go of the door handle, and the door swung open, revealing the faces of two footmen who were obviously trying very hard not to look curious. Kate remained silent as Anthony helped her down and led her into the house.

His household staff was assembled in the small entry hall, and Kate murmured her greetings as each member was introduced to her by the butler and housekeeper. The staff wasn't very extensive, as the house was small by *ton* standards, but the introductions took a good twenty minutes.

Twenty minutes which, unfortunately, did little to calm her nerves. By the time he placed his hand at the small of her back and guided her toward the stairs, her heart was racing, and for the first time in her life, she thought she might actually pass out.

It wasn't that she feared the marriage bed.

It wasn't even that she feared not pleasing her husband. Even an innocent virgin such as herself could tell that his actions and reactions when they kissed were proof enough of his desire. He would show her what to do; of that she had no doubt.

What she feared . . .

What she feared . . .

She caught her throat closing, choking, and she brought her fist to her mouth, biting on the knuckle to steady her stomach, as if that might actually do something to help the awful churning that had her in knots.

"My God," Anthony whispered as the reached the landing. "You're terrified."

"No," she lied.

He took her by the shoulders and twisted her to face him, staring deeply into her eyes. Cursing under his breath, he grabbed her hand and pulled her into his bedroom, muttering, "We need privacy."

When they reached his chamber—a richly appointed, masculine room exquisitely decorated in shades of burgundy and gold—he planted his hands on his hips and demanded, "Didn't your mother tell you about . . . ah . . . about . . ."

Kate would have laughed at his flailings if she hadn't been so nervous. "Of course," she said quickly. "Mary explained everything."

"Then what the hell is the problem?" He cursed again, then apologized. "I beg your pardon," he said stiffly. "That certainly is not the way to set you at ease."

"I can't say," she whispered, her eyes sliding to the floor, focusing on the intricate pattern of the carpet until they swam with tears.

A strange, horrible choking noise emerged from Anthony's throat. "Kate?" he asked hoarsely. "Did someone . . . has a man . . . ever forced unwelcome attentions on you?"

She looked up, and the concern and terror on his face nearly made her heart melt. "No!" she cried out. "It isn't that. Oh, don't look that way, I can't bear it."

"*I* can't bear it," Anthony whispered, closing the distance between them as he took her hand and raised it to his lips. "You must tell me," he said, his voice oddly choked. "Do you fear me? Do I repulse you?"

Kate shook her head frantically, unable to believe that he could possibly think any woman would find him repulsive.

"Tell me," he whispered, his lips pressing against her ear. "Tell me how to make it right. For I don't think I can grant you your reprieve." He molded his body against hers, his strong arms holding her close as he groaned, "I can't wait a week, Kate. I simply cannot do it."

"I . . ." Kate made the mistake of looking up into his eyes, and she forgot everything she'd meant to say. He was staring at her with a burning intensity that forged a fire in the very center of her being, leaving her breathless, hungry, and desperate for something she did not quite understand.

And she knew that she could not make him wait. If she looked into her own soul, and looked with honesty and without delusion, she was forced to admit that she did not wish to wait, either.

For what could be the point? Maybe he would never love her. Maybe his desire would never be focused as single-mindedly on her as hers was for him.

But she could pretend. And when he held her in his arms and pressed his lips to her skin, it was so, so easy to pretend.

"Anthony," she whispered, his name a benediction, a plea, a prayer all in one.

"Anything," he replied raggedly, dropping to his knees before her, his lips trailing a hot path along her skin as his fingers frantically worked to release her from her gown. "Ask me anything," he groaned. "Anything in my power, I give to you."

Kate felt her head fall back, felt the last of her resistance melting away. "Just love me," she whispered. "Just love me."

His only answer was a low growl of need.

Chapter 17

The deed is done! Miss Sheffield is now Katharine, Viscountess Bridgerton.

This Author extends the very best of wishes to the happy couple. Sensible and honorable people are surely scarce among the ton, and it's certainly gratifying to see two of this rare breed joined in marriage.

LADY WHISTLEDOWN'S SOCIETY PAPERS, 16 MAY 1814

Until that moment, Anthony had not even realized just how badly he'd needed for her to say yes, to admit to her need. He clutched her to him, his cheek pressing against the gentle curve of her belly. Even in her wedding gown she smelled of lilies and soap, that maddening scent that had haunted him for weeks.

"I need you," he growled, not sure if his words were getting lost in the layers of silk that still kept her from him. "I need you now."

He rose to his feet and lifted her in his arms, taking remarkably few steps to reach the large four-poster bed that dominated his bedroom. He'd never taken a woman there before, always preferring to conduct his liaisons elsewhere, and suddenly he was absurdly glad of that fact.

Kate was different, special, his wife. He wanted no

other memories to intrude upon this or any night.

He laid her down on the mattress, his eyes never leaving her charmingly disheveled form as he methodically stripped off his clothing. First his gloves, one by one, then his coat, already rumpled by his ardor.

He caught her eyes, dark and large and filled with wonder, and he smiled, slowly and with satisfaction. "You've never seen a naked man before, have you?" he murmured.

She shook her head.

"Good." He leaned forward and plucked one of her slippers from her foot. "You'll never see another."

He moved to the buttons of his shirt, slowly slipping each from its buttonhole, his desire increased tenfold when he saw her tongue dart out to wet her lips.

She wanted him. He knew enough of women to be positive of that. And by the time this night was through, she wouldn't be able to live without him.

That *he* might not be able to live without *her* was something he refused to consider. What smoldered in the bedroom and what whispered in his heart were two different things. He could keep them separate. He *would* keep them separate.

He might not wish to love his wife, but that did not mean they could not enjoy each other thoroughly in bed.

His hands slid to the top button of his trousers and unfastened it, but stopped there. She was still fully clothed, and still fully an innocent. She wasn't yet ready to see the proof of his desire.

He climbed onto the bed and, like a feral cat, crawled toward her, inching closer and closer until her elbows, which had been propping her up, slid out from under her and she was flat on her back, staring up at him, her breath coming fast and shallow through her parted lips.

There was nothing, he decided, more breathtaking than Kate's face when flushed with desire. Her hair, dark and silky and thick, was already pulling free of the pins and fasteners that had held her elaborate wedding day coiffure in place. Her lips, always a bit too full for conventional beauty, had taken on a dusky pink color in the slanted light of the late afternoon. And her skin—never had it seemed so flawless, so luminescent. A pale blush tinted her cheeks, denying her the bloodless complexion that the fashionable ladies always seemed to desire, but Anthony found the color enchanting. She was real, human, and trembling with desire. He couldn't have wished for more.

With a reverent hand, he stroked her cheek with the backs of his fingers, then slid them down her neck to the tender skin that peeked above the edge of her bodice. Her gown was fastened by a maddening row of buttons at the back, but he'd already undone nearly a third of them, and it was now loose enough to slide the silken fabric over her breasts.

If anything, they looked even more beautiful than they had two days earlier. Her nipples were rosy pink, cresting breasts that he knew fit his hands to perfection. "No chemise?" he murmured appreciatively, running his finger along the prominent line of her collarbone.

She shook her head, her voice breathy as she answered, "The cut of the gown didn't allow it."

One side of his mouth lifted into a very male smile. "Remind me to send a bonus to your modiste."

His hand moved ever lower, and he cupped one of her breasts, squeezing it softly, feeling a groan of desire rise up within him as he heard a similar moan escape her lips.

"So lovely," he murmured, lifting his hand and letting his eyes caress her. It had never occurred to him that there could be such pleasure from the simple act of gazing at a woman. Lovemaking had always been about touch and taste; for the first time sight was equally seductive.

She was so perfect, so utterly beautiful to him, and he felt a rather strange and primitive sense of satisfaction that most men were blind to her beauty. It was as if a certain side of her were visible only to him. He loved that her charms were hidden to the rest of the world.

It made her seem more *his*.

Suddenly eager to be touched as he was touching, he lifted one of her hands, still wrapped in a long satin glove, and brought it to his chest. He could feel the heat of her skin even through the fabric, but it wasn't enough. "I want to feel you," he whispered, then removed the two rings that rested on her fourth finger. He laid them in the hollow between her breasts, a space made shallow by her supine position.

Kate gasped and shivered at the touch of the cold metal against her skin, then watched with breathless fascination as Anthony went to work on her glove, tugging gently at each finger until it was loose, then sliding the length of it down her arm and over her hand. The rush of satin was like an endless kiss, raising goose bumps over her entire body.

Then, with a tenderness that nearly brought tears to her eyes, he replaced the rings on her finger, one by one, stopping only to kiss the sensitive palm of her hand in between.

"Give me your other hand," he gently ordered.

She did, and he repeated the same exquisite torture, tugging and sliding the satin along her skin. But this time, when he was through, he brought her pinkie finger to his mouth, then drew it between his lips and sucked, swirling his tongue around the tip.

Kate felt an answering tug of desire pulling through her arm, shivering through her chest, snaking through her until it pooled, hot and mysterious, between her legs. He was awakening something within her, something dark and maybe just a little bit dangerous, something that had lain dormant for years, just waiting for a single kiss from this man.

Her entire life had been preparation for this very moment, and she didn't even know what to expect next.

His tongue slid down the inner length of her finger, then traced the lines on her palm. "Such lovely hands," he murmured, nibbling on the fleshy part of her thumb as his fingers entwined with hers. "Strong, and yet so graceful and delicate."

"You're talking nonsense," Kate said self-consciously. "My hands—"

But he silenced her with a finger to her lips. "Shhh," he admonished. "Haven't you learned that you should never ever contradict your husband when he is admiring your form?"

Kate shivered with delight.

"For example," he continued, the very devil in his voice, "if I want to spend an hour examining the inside of your wrist"—with lightning-quick movements, his teeth grazed the delicate thin skin on the inside of her wrist—"it is certainly my prerogative, don't you think?"

Kate had no response, and he chuckled, the sound low and warm in her ears.

"And don't think I won't," he warned, using the pad of his finger to trace the blue veins that pulsed under her skin. "I may decide to spend *two* hours examining your wrist."

Kate watched with fascination as his fingers, touching her so softly that she tingled from the contact, made their way to the inside of her elbow, then stopped to twirl circles on her skin.

"I can't imagine," he said softly, "that I could spend two hours examining your wrist and *not* find it lovely." His hand made the jump to her torso, and he used his palm to lightly graze the tip of her puckered breast. "I should be most aggrieved were you to disagree."

He leaned down and captured her lips in a brief, yet searing kiss. Lifting his head just an inch, he murmured, "It is a wife's place to agree with her husband in all things, hmmm?"

His words were so absurd that Kate finally managed to find her voice. "If," she said with an amused smile, "his opinions are agreeable, my lord."

One of his brows arched imperiously. "Are you arguing with me, my lady? And on my wedding night, no less."

"It's my wedding night, too," she pointed out.

He made a clucking noise and shook his head. "I may have to punish you," he said. "But how? By touching?" His hand skimmed over one breast, then the next. "Or not touching?"

He lifted his hands from her skin, but he leaned down, and through pursed lips, blew a soft stream of air over her nipple.

"Touching," Kate gasped, arching off the bed. "Definitely touching."

"You think?" He smiled, slowly like a cat. "I never thought I'd say this, but not touching has its appeal."

Kate stared up at him. He loomed over her on his hands and knees like some primitive hunter coming in for the final kill. He looked feral, triumphant, and powerfully possessive. His thick chestnut hair fell over his forehead, giving him an oddly boyish air, but his eyes burned and gleamed with a very adult desire.

He wanted her. It was thrilling. He might be a man, and thus able to find his satisfaction with any woman, but right now, in this moment, he wanted her. Kate was sure of it.

And it made her feel like the most beautiful woman alive.

Emboldened by the knowledge of his desire, she reached up and cupped one hand around the back of his head, drawing him down until his lips were just a whisper away from hers. "Kiss me," she ordered, surprised by the imperiousness of her voice. "Kiss me now."

He smiled in vague disbelief, but his words, in that last second before their lips met, were, "Anything you wish, Lady Bridgerton. Anything you wish."

And then it all seemed to happen at once. His lips were on hers, teasing and devouring, while his hands were lifting her up into a seated position. His fingers worked nimbly at the buttons of her gown, and she could feel the cool brush of the air on her skin as the fabric slipped down, inch by inch, exposing her rib cage, then her navel, and then . . .

And then his hands slid beneath her hips, and he was lifting her up, yanking the dress out from underneath her. Kate gasped at the intimacy of it. She was clad only in her unmentionables, stockings, and garters. She'd never felt so exposed in her life, and yet she thrilled in every moment, every sweep of his eyes over her body.

"Lift your leg," Anthony ordered softly.

She did, and with a slowness that was exquisite and agonizing at the same time, he rolled one of her silk stockings down to her toes. The other soon followed, and then her drawers came next, and before she knew it she was nude, completely bared before him.

His hand skimmed softly over her stomach, then he said, "I think I'm a little overdressed, don't you?"

Kate's eyes widened as he left the bed and stripped off the rest of his clothing. His body was perfection, his chest finely muscled, his arms and legs powerful, and his—

"Oh, my God," she gasped.

He grinned. "I'll take that as a compliment."

Kate swallowed convulsively. No wonder those animals on her neighbor's farm hadn't looked as if they were enjoying the act of procreation. At least not the female ones. Surely this wasn't going to work.

But she didn't want to seem naive and foolish, so she didn't say anything, just gulped and tried to smile.

Anthony caught the flash of terror in her eyes and smiled gently. "Trust me," he murmured, sliding onto the bed beside her. His hands settled on the curve of her hip as he nuzzled her neck. "Just trust me."

He felt her nod, and he propped himself up on one of his elbows, using his free hand to idly trace circles and swirls on her abdomen, moving lower and lower, until he brushed the edge of the dark thatch of hair nestling between her legs.

Her muscles quivered, and he heard a rush of indrawn breath pass over her lips. "Shhhh," he said soothingly, leaning down to distract her with a kiss. The last time he'd lain with a virgin he'd been one himself, and he was relying on instinct to guide him with Kate. He wanted this, her first time, to be perfect. Or if not perfect, then at least damn good.

While his lips and tongue explored her mouth, his hand dipped ever lower, until he reached the moist heat of her womanhood. She gasped again, but he was relentless, teasing and tickling, delighting in each of her squirms and moans.

"What are you doing?" she whispered against his lips.

He gave her a lopsided grin, as one of his fingers slid inside. "Making you feel really, really good?"

She moaned, which pleased him. If she'd managed intelligible speech he would have known he wasn't doing his job correctly.

He moved over her, nudging her legs farther apart with one of his thighs, and letting out a moan of his own as his manhood settled against her hip. Even there, she felt perfect, and he was nearly bursting at the thought of sinking within her.

He was trying to hold his control, trying to make sure that he remained slow and gentle, but his need was getting stronger and stronger, and his own breath was growing fast and ragged.

She was ready for him, or at least as ready as she was going to be. He knew that this first time would bring her pain, but he prayed it wouldn't last more than a moment.

He fitted himself against her opening, using his arms to brace his body a few inches above hers. He whispered her name, and her dark eyes, hazed by passion, focused on his.

"I'm going to make you mine now," he said, inching forward as he spoke. Her body tightened spasmodically around him; the feeling was so exquisite he had to grit his teeth against it. It would be so, so easy to lose himself in the moment, to plunge forward and seek only his own pleasure.

"Tell me if it hurts," he whispered hoarsely, allowing himself to move forward only by tiny increments. She was certainly aroused, but she was very small, and he knew he needed to give her time to adjust to his intimate invasion.

She nodded.

He froze, barely able to comprehend the stab of pain in his chest. "It hurts?"

She shook her head. "No, I only meant I'll tell you if it does. It doesn't hurt, but it feels so very . . . odd."

Anthony fought a smile and he leaned down to kiss the tip of her nose. "I don't know that I've ever been called odd while making love to a woman before."

For a moment it looked as if she were afraid that she'd insulted him, then her mouth quivered into a small smile. "Perhaps," she said softly, "you've been making love to the wrong women."

"Perhaps so," he replied, moving forward yet another inch.

"May I tell you a secret?" she asked.

He nudged farther. "Of course," he murmured.

"When I first saw you . . . tonight, I mean . . ."

"In all my glory?" he teased, lifting his brows into an arrogant arch.

She shot him a rather enchanting scowl. "I didn't think this could possibly work."

He moved forward. He was close, so close to embedding himself fully within her. "May I tell *you* a secret?" he returned.

"Of course."

"Your secret"—one more little thrust and he was resting against her maidenhead—"wasn't very much of a secret."

Her brows drew together in question.

He grinned. "It was written all over your face."

She scowled again, and it made him want to explode in

laughter. "But now," he said, keeping a scrupulously straight face, "I have a question for you."

She gazed at him in response, clearly waiting for him to elucidate further.

He leaned down, brushed his lips against her ear, and whispered, "What do you think now?"

For a moment she didn't respond in any way, then he felt her start in surprise when she finally figured out what he was asking. "Are we done?" she asked in clear disbelief.

This time he did burst out in laughter. "Far from it, my dear wife," he gasped, wiping his eyes with one hand as he tried to hold himself up with the other. "Far, far from it." His eyes growing serious, he added, "This is where it might hurt a little, Kate. But I promise you, the pain will never be repeated."

She nodded, but he could feel her body tense up, which he knew would only make it worse. "Shhh," he crooned. "Relax."

She nodded, her eyes shut. "I am relaxed."

He was glad she couldn't see him smile. "You are most definitely *not* relaxed."

Her eyes flew open. "Yes, I am."

"I can't believe this," Anthony said, as if there were someone else in the room to hear him. "She's arguing with me on our wedding night."

"I'm—"

He cut her off with a finger to her lips. "Are you ticklish?"

"Am I *ticklish*?"

He nodded. "Ticklish."

Her eyes narrowed suspiciously. "Why?"

"That sounds like a yes to me," he said with a grin.

"Not at— Oooohhh!" She let out a squeal as one of his hands found a particularly sensitive spot under arm. "Anthony, stop!" she gasped, squirming desperately beneath him. "I can't bear it! I—"

He plunged forward.

"Oh," she breathed. "Oh, my."

He groaned, barely able to believe just how good it felt to be buried completely within her. "Oh, my, indeed."

"We're not done now, are we?"

He shook his head slowly as his body began to move in an ancient rhythm. "Not even close," he murmured.

His mouth took hers as one of his hands snaked up to caress her breast. She was utter perfection beneath him, her hips rising to meet his, moving tentatively at first, then with a vigor that matched her rising passion.

"Oh, God, Kate," he moaned, his ability to form flowery sentences completely lost in the primitive heat of the moment. "You're so good. So good."

Her breath was coming faster and faster, and each little wispy gasp inflamed his passion even more. He wanted to possess her, to own her, to hold her beneath him and never let her go. And with each thrust it was getting more difficult to put her needs before his. His mind screamed that this was her first time and he had to have a care for her, but his body demanded release.

With a ragged groan, he forced himself to stop thrusting and catch his breath. "Kate?" he said, barely recognizing his own voice. It sounded hoarse, detached, desperate.

Her eyes, which had been closed as her head tossed from side to side, flew open. "Don't stop," she gasped, "please don't stop. I'm so close to something . . . I don't know what."

"Oh, God," he groaned, plunging back in to the hilt, throwing his head back as his spine arched. "You're so beautiful, so unbelievably— Kate?"

She'd stiffened beneath him, and not in climax.

He froze. "What's wrong?" he whispered.

He saw a brief flash of pain—the emotional sort, not the physical—flash across her face before she hid it and whispered, "Nothing."

"That's not true," he said in a low voice. His arms were

straining from holding himself above her, but he barely noticed. Every fiber of his being was focused on her face, which was shuttered and pained, despite her obvious attempts to hide it.

"You called me beautiful," she whispered.

For a good ten seconds he just stared at her. For the life of him, he couldn't understand how that was a bad thing. But then again, he'd never professed to understand the female mind. He thought he should simply reaffirm the statement, that she *was* beautiful, and what the hell was the problem, but a little voice inside warned him that this was one of *those* moments, and no matter what he said, it would be the wrong thing, so he decided to tread very, very carefully, and he just murmured her name, which he had a feeling might be the only word guaranteed not to get him into trouble.

"I'm not beautiful," she whispered, her eyes meeting his. She looked shattered and broken, but before he could contradict her, she asked, "Who were you picturing?"

He blinked. "I beg your pardon?"

"Who do you think of when you make love to me?"

Anthony felt as if he'd been punched in the gut. The breath whooshed from his body. "Kate," he said slowly. "Kate, you're mad, you're—"

"I know a man doesn't have to feel desire for a woman to find pleasure with her," she cried out.

"You think I don't desire you?" he choked out. God in heaven, he was ready to explode right now within her and he hadn't even moved for the last thirty seconds.

Her lower lip trembled between her teeth, and a muscle spasmed in her neck. "Do you—do you think of Edwina?"

Anthony froze. "How could I *possibly* confuse the two of you?"

Kate felt her face crumple, felt hot tears stinging at her eyes. She didn't want to cry in front of him, oh, God, especially not now, but it hurt, it hurt so much, and—

His hand grasped her cheeks with stunning speed, forcing her to look up at him.

"Listen to me," he said, his voice even and intense, "and listen well, because I'm only going to say this once. I desire you. I burn for you. I can't sleep at night for wanting you. Even when I didn't *like* you, I lusted for you. It's the most maddening, beguiling, damnable thing, but there it is. And if I hear one more word of nonsense from your lips, I'm going to have to tie you to the bloody bed and have my way with you a hundred different ways, until you finally get it through your silly skull that you are the most beautiful and desirable woman in England, and if everyone else doesn't see that, then they're all bloody fools."

Kate wouldn't have thought it possible for her mouth to fall open while she was lying down, but somehow it did.

One of his brows arched into what had to be the most arrogant expression ever to grace a face. "Is that understood?"

She just stared at him, not quite able to form a response.

He leaned down until his nose was a mere inch from hers. "Is that understood?"

She nodded.

"Good," he grunted, and then, before she had a moment even to catch her breath, his lips were devouring hers in a kiss so fierce she was clutching the bed just to keep from screaming. His hips ground into hers, frenzied in their power, thrusting, rotating, stroking her until she was certain she must be on fire.

She clutched at him, not certain whether she was trying to bind him to her or tear him away. "I can't do this," she moaned, certain she would shatter. Her muscles were stiff, tense, and it was getting hard to breathe.

But if he'd heard her, he didn't care. His face was a harsh mask of concentration, sweat beading on his brow.

"Anthony," she gasped, "I can—"

One of his hands slipped between them and touched her intimately, and she screamed. He slammed forward one last time, and her world simply fell apart. She was stiff, then shaking, then she thought she must be falling. She couldn't breathe, couldn't even gasp. Her throat had to be closing, and her head fell back as her hands grabbed at the mattress with a ferocity she'd never have believed she possessed.

He went utterly still above her, his mouth open in a silent scream, and then he collapsed, the weight of him pressing her farther into the mattress.

"Oh, my God," he gasped, his body now shaking. "Never . . . it's never . . . so good . . . it's never been so good."

Kate, who'd had a few seconds longer to recover, smiled as she smoothed his hair. A wicked thought came to her, a perfectly wonderful wicked thought. "Anthony?" she murmured.

How he lifted his head she would never know, because it looked like it took a Herculean effort just to open his eyes and grunt his response.

She smiled, slowly, and with a womanly seductiveness she'd learned just that evening. Letting one of her fingers trail down the angular edge of his jaw, she whispered, "Are we done yet?"

For a second he made no response, then his lips broke into a smile far more devilish than she could ever have imagined. "For now," he murmured huskily, rolling onto his side and pulling her along with him. "But only for now."

Chapter 18

Although gossip still surrounds the hasty marriage of Lord and Lady Bridgerton (formerly Miss Katharine Sheffield, for those of you who have been in hibernation for these past few weeks), This Author is of the firm opinion that theirs was a love match. Viscount Bridgerton does not escort his wife to every society function (but then again, what husband does?), but when he is present, This Author cannot fail to note that he always seems to be murmuring something in his lady's ear, and that something always seems to make her smile and blush.

Furthermore, he always dances with her one more time than is considered de rigueur. Considering how many husbands don't like to dance with their wives at all, this is romantic stuff, indeed.

LADY WHISTLEDOWN'S SOCIETY PAPERS, 10 JUNE 1814

The next few weeks flew by in a delirious rush. After a brief stay in the country at Aubrey Hall, the newlyweds returned to London, where the season was in full swing. Kate had hoped to use her afternoons to resume her flute lessons, but she quickly discovered that she was in great demand, and her days were filled with social calls, shopping excursions with her family, and the occasional ride in the park. Her evenings were a whirlwind of balls and parties.

But her nights were for Anthony alone.

Marriage, she decided, agreed with her. She saw less of Anthony than she would have liked, but she understood and accepted that he was a very busy man. His many concerns, both in Parliament and on his estates, took up a great deal of his time. But when he returned home at night and met her in the bedroom (no separate bedchambers for Lord and Lady Bridgerton!) he was marvelously attentive, asking about her day, telling her of his, and making love to her until the wee hours of the night.

He'd even taken the time to listen to her practice her flute. She'd managed to hire a musician to come and tutor her two mornings a week. Considering the (not very expert) level of play which Kate had achieved, Anthony's willingness to sit through an entire thirty minutes of rehearsal could only be interpreted as a sign of great affection.

Of course, it did not escape her notice that he'd never repeated the gesture.

Hers was a fine existence, a far better marriage than most women of her station could expect. If her husband did not love her, if he would never love her, then at least he did a good job of making her feel cared for and appreciated. And for now Kate was able to content herself with that.

And if he seemed distant during the day, well, he certainly wasn't distant at night.

The rest of society, however, and Edwina in particular, had gotten it into their heads that Lord and Lady Bridgerton's marriage was a love match. Edwina had taken to visiting in the afternoons, and this day was no exception. She and Kate were sitting in the drawing room, sipping tea and nibbling on biscuits, enjoying a rare moment of privacy now that Kate had bidden farewell to her daily swarm of visitors.

Everyone, it seemed, wanted to see how the new viscountess was getting along, and Kate's drawing room was almost never empty in the afternoon.

Newton had hopped up onto the sofa beside Edwina, and she was idly stroking his fur as she said, "Everyone is talking about you today."

Kate didn't even pause as she lifted her tea to her lips and took a sip. "Everyone is always talking about me," she said with a shrug. "They'll soon find another topic."

"Not," Edwina replied, "as long as your husband keeps looking at you the way he did last night."

Kate felt her cheeks grow warm. "He did nothing out of the ordinary," she murmured.

"Kate, he was positively smoldering!" Edwina shifted her position as Newton shifted his, letting her know with a little whine that he wanted his belly rubbed. "I personally saw him push Lord Haveridge out of the way in his haste to reach your side."

"We arrived separately," Kate explained, although her heart was filling with a secret—and most probably foolish—joy. "I'm sure he just had something he needed to tell me."

Edwina looked dubious. "And did he?"

"Did he what?"

"*Tell* you something," Edwina said with palpable exasperation. "You just said you were sure he just had something he needed to tell you. If that were the case, wouldn't he have told you whatever it was? And then you'd *know* he had something to tell you, right?"

Kate blinked. "Edwina, you're making me dizzy."

Edwina's lips smooshed together in a disgruntled frown. "You never tell me anything."

"Edwina, there's nothing to tell!" Kate reached forward, grabbed a biscuit, and took a large, extremely uncouth bite so that her mouth would be too full to speak. What was she supposed to say to her sister—that before they'd even wed, her husband had informed her in a most matter-of-fact and straightforward manner that he would never love her?

That would make for charming conversation over tea and biscuits.

"Well," Edwina finally announced, after watching Kate chew for an improbable full minute, "I actually had another reason for coming here today. I have something I wish to tell you."

Kate swallowed gratefully. "Really?"

Edwina nodded, then blushed.

"What is it?" Kate implored, sipping at her tea. Her mouth was awfully dry after all that chewing.

"I think I'm in love."

Kate nearly spit out her tea. "With whom?"

"Mr. Bagwell."

Try as she might, Kate could not for the life of her recall who Mr. Bagwell was.

"He's a scholar," Edwina said with a dreamy sigh. "I met him at Lady Bridgerton's country house party."

"I don't recall meeting him," Kate said, her brow knitting into thoughtful lines.

"You were rather busy throughout the visit," Edwina replied in an ironic voice. "Getting yourself betrothed and all that."

Kate pulled the sort of face one could only display with a sibling. "Just tell me about Mr. Bagwell."

Edwina's eyes grew warm and bright. "He's a second son, I'm afraid, so he cannot expect much in the way of income. But now that you've married so well, I needn't worry about that."

Kate felt an unexpected welling of tears in her eyes. She hadn't realized just how pressured Edwina must have felt earlier that season. She and Mary had been careful to assure Edwina that she might marry anyone she liked, but they had all known exactly where their finances stood, and they had certainly all been guilty of making jokes about how it was just as easy to fall in love with a wealthy man as it was with a poor one.

It only took one look at Edwina's face to realize that a huge burden had been lifted from her shoulders.

"I'm glad you've found someone who suits you," Kate murmured.

"Oh, he does. I know that we shall not have much in the way of money, but truly, I don't need silks and jewels." Her eyes fell on the glittering diamond on Kate's hand. "Not that I think you do, of course!" she quickly interjected, her face growing red. "Just that—"

"Just that it's nice not to have to worry about supporting your sister and mother," Kate finished for her in a gentle voice.

Edwina let out a huge sigh. "Exactly."

Kate reached across the table and took her sister's hands in hers. "You certainly needn't worry about me, and I'm sure that Anthony and I will always be able to provide for Mary, should she ever need assistance."

Edwina's lips curved into a wobbly smile.

"As for you," Kate added, "I think it's high time you were able to think only of yourself for a change. To make a decision based on what *you* desire, not what you think others need."

Edwina pulled one of her hands free to brush back a tear. "I really like him," she whispered.

"Then I am certain I will like him as well," Kate said firmly. "When may I meet him?"

"He is in Oxford for the next fortnight, I'm afraid. He has prior commitments which I should not want him to break on my account."

"Of course not," Kate murmured. "You wouldn't want to marry the sort of gentleman who does not honor his commitments."

Edwina nodded in agreement. "I received a letter from him this morning, though, and he says he will come down to London at the end of the month and hopes that he might call on me."

Kate smiled wickedly. "He's already sending you letters?"

Edwina nodded and blushed. "Several per week," she admitted.

"And what is his area of study?"

"Archaeology. He's quite brilliant. He has been to Greece. Twice!"

Kate hadn't thought that her sister—already renowned throughout the land for her beauty—could possibly grow any lovelier, but when Edwina spoke of her Mr. Bagwell, her face shone with a radiance that was nothing short of heart-stopping.

"I cannot wait to meet him," Kate announced. "We must have an informal dinner party with him as our guest of honor."

"That would be wonderful."

"And perhaps the three of us might go for a ride in the park ahead of time so that we might become better acquainted. Now that I am an old married lady, I qualify as a suitable chaperone." Kate let out a little laugh. "Isn't that funny?"

A very amused, very male voice sounded from the doorway: "Isn't what funny?"

"Anthony!" Kate exclaimed, surprised to see her husband in the middle of the day. He always seemed to have appointments and meetings that kept him from their home. "How delightful to see you."

He smiled slightly as he nodded toward Edwina in greeting. "I found myself with an unexpected block of free time."

"Would you care to join us for tea?"

"I'll join you," he murmured as he crossed the room and picked up a crystal decanter that sat on a mahogany side table, "but I believe I'll have a brandy instead."

Kate watched as he poured himself a drink, then

swirled it absently in his hand. It was at times like these that she found it so difficult to keep her heart out of her eyes. He was so handsome in the late afternoon. She wasn't sure why; maybe it was the faint hint of stubble on his cheeks or the fact that his hair was always slightly mussed from whatever it was he did all day. Or maybe it was simply that she didn't often get to see him this time of day; she'd once read a poem that said the unexpected moment was always sweeter.

As Kate gazed upon her husband, she rather thought that poet might be right.

"So," Anthony said after taking a sip of his drink, "what have you two ladies been discussing?"

Kate looked to her sister for permission to share her news, and when Edwina nodded, she said, "Edwina has met a gentleman she fancies."

"Really?" Anthony asked, sounding interested in a strangely paternal sort of manner. He perched on the arm of Kate's chair, a relaxed, overstuffed piece of furniture that was not at all in fashion but well loved nonetheless in the Bridgerton household for its uncommon comfort. "I should like to meet him," he added.

"You should?" Edwina echoed, blinking like an owl. "You would?"

"Of course. In fact, I insist upon it." When neither lady commented, he scowled a bit and added, "I am the head of the family, after all. That's what we do."

Edwina's lips parted with surprise. "I—I hadn't realized you felt a responsibility toward me."

Anthony looked at her as if she'd gone momentarily insane. "You're Kate's sister," he said, as if that should explain everything.

Edwina's blank expression remained fixed on her face for another second, and then it melted into a rather radiant delight. "I have always wondered what it would be like to have a brother," she said.

"I hope I pass muster," Anthony grunted, not entirely comfortable with the sudden outpouring of emotion.

She beamed at him. "Brilliantly. I vow I do not understand why Eloise complains so much."

Kate turned to Anthony and explained, "Edwina and your sister have become fast friends since our marriage."

"God help us," he muttered. "And what, may I ask, could Eloise possibly have to complain about?"

Edwina smiled innocently. "Oh, nothing, really. Just that you can, at times, be a touch overprotective."

"That's ridiculous," he scoffed.

Kate choked on her tea. She was quite certain that by the time their daughters were of marriageable age, Anthony would have converted to Catholicism just so that he could lock them in a convent with twelve-foot walls!

Anthony glanced at her with narrowed eyes. "What are you laughing about?"

Kate quickly patted her mouth with a napkin, mumbling, "Nothing," under the folds of the cloth.

"Hmmmph."

"Eloise says that you were quite the bear when Daphne was being courted by Simon," Edwina said.

"Oh, did she?"

Edwina nodded. "She says the two of you dueled!"

"Eloise talks too much," Anthony grumbled.

Edwina nodded happily. "She always knows everything. Everything! Even more than Lady Whistledown."

Anthony turned to Kate with an expression that was one part beleaguered and one part pure irony. "Remind me to buy a muzzle for my sister," he said drolly. "And one for your sister as well."

Edwina let out a musical laugh. "I never dreamed a brother would be as much fun to tease as a sister. I'm so glad you decided to marry him, Kate."

"I didn't have much choice in the matter," Kate said

with a dry smile, "but I'm rather pleased with the way things turned out myself."

Edwina stood, waking up Newton, who had fallen into blissful sleep next to her on the sofa. He let out an affronted whine and toddled to the floor, where he promptly curled up under a table.

Edwina watched the dog and chuckled before saying, "I should be going. No, don't see me out," she added when both Kate and Anthony stood to escort her to the front door. "I can make my own way."

"Nonsense," Kate said, linking her arm in Edwina's. "Anthony, I shall be right back."

"I shall be counting the seconds," he murmured, and then, as he took another sip of his drink, the two ladies left the room, followed by Newton, who was now barking enthusiastically, presumably guessing that someone was going to take him for a walk.

Once the two sisters were gone, he settled into the comfortable chair so recently vacated by Kate. It was still warm from her body, and he rather fancied that he could smell her scent in the fabric. More soap than lilies this time, he thought with a careful sniff. Perhaps the lilies were a perfume, something she added at night.

He wasn't entirely sure why he'd returned home this afternoon; he certainly hadn't intended to. Contrary to what he'd been telling Kate, his many meetings and responsibilities did not require him to be away from the house all the day long; quite a few of his appointments could easily have been scheduled at home. And while he was indeed a busy man—he'd never subscribed to the indolent lifestyle of so many of the *ton*—he'd spent many a recent afternoon at White's, reading the paper and playing cards with his friends.

He'd thought it best. It was important to keep a certain distance from one's wife. Life—or at least *his* life—was meant to be compartmentalized, and a wife fit rather neatly in the sections he'd mentally labeled "society affairs" and "bed."

But when he'd reached White's that afternoon, there was no one there with whom he felt a particular urge to converse. He'd skimmed through the paper, but there was very little of interest in the most recent edition. And as he sat by the window, trying to enjoy his own company (but finding it pathetically lacking), he'd been struck by the most ridiculous urge to return home and see what Kate was up to.

One afternoon couldn't hurt. He wasn't likely to fall in love with his wife for having spent one afternoon in her presence. Not that he thought there was a danger of his falling in love with her at all, he reminded himself sternly. He'd been married nearly a month now and he'd managed to keep his life blessedly free of such entanglements. There was no reason to think that he could not maintain the status quo indefinitely.

Feeling rather satisfied with himself, he took another sip of his brandy, looking up when he heard Kate reenter the room.

"I do think Edwina might be in love," she said, her entire face lit up with a radiant smile.

Anthony felt his body tighten in response. It was rather ridiculous, actually, how he reacted to her smiles. Happened all the time, and it was a damned nuisance.

Well, most of the time it was a nuisance. He didn't mind it much when he was able to follow it with a nudge and a trip to the bedroom.

But Kate's mind was obviously not lodged as firmly in the gutter as his, since she chose to sit in the chair opposite him, even though there was plenty of room in his chair, provided they didn't mind squeezing next to each other. Even the chair kitty-corner to his would have been better; at least then he could have yanked her up and hauled her onto his lap. If he tried that maneuver where she was seated across the table, he'd have to drag her through the middle of the tea service.

Anthony narrowed his eyes as he assessed the situation, trying to guess exactly how much tea would spill on the rug, and then how much it would cost to replace the rug, and then whether he really cared about such a piddling amount of money, anyway . . .

"Anthony? Are you listening to me?"

He looked up. Kate was resting her arms on her knees as she leaned forward to talk with him. She looked very intent and just a little bit irritated.

"Were you?" she persisted.

He blinked.

"Listening to me?" she ground out.

"Oh." He grinned. "No."

She rolled her eyes but didn't bother to scold him any further than that. "I was saying that we should have Edwina and her young man over for dinner one night. To see if we think they suit. I have never before seen her so interested in a gentleman, and I do so want her to be happy."

Anthony reached for a biscuit. He was hungry, and he'd pretty much given up on the prospect of getting his wife into his lap. On the other hand, if he managed to clear off the cups and saucers, yanking her across the table might not have such messy consequences . . .

He surreptitiously pushed the tray bearing the tea service to the side. "Hmmm?" he grunted, chewing on the biscuit. "Oh, yes, of course. Edwina should be happy."

Kate eyed him suspiciously. "Are you certain you don't want some tea with that biscuit? I'm not a great aficionado of brandy, but I would imagine that tea would taste better with shortbread."

Actually, Anthony thought, the brandy did quite well with shortbread, but it certainly couldn't hurt to empty out the teapot a bit, just in case he toppled it over. "Capital idea," he said, grabbing a teacup and thrusting it toward her. "Tea's just the thing. Can't imagine why I didn't think of it earlier."

"I can't imagine, either," she murmured acerbically—if one could murmur in an acerbic manner, and after hearing Kate's low sarcasm, Anthony rather thought one could.

But he just gave her a jovial smile as he reached out and took his teacup from her outstretched hand. "Thank you," he said, checking to see that she'd added milk. She had, which didn't surprise him; she was very good at remembering such details.

"Is it still hot enough?" Kate asked politely.

Anthony drained the cup. "Perfect," he replied, letting out a satisfied exhale. "Might I trouble you for some more?"

"You seem to be developing quite a taste for tea," she said dryly.

Anthony eyed the teapot, wondering how much was left and whether he'd be able to finish it off without being attacked by an urgent need to relieve himself. "You should have some more, too," he suggested. "You look a bit parched."

Her eyebrows shot up. "Is that so?"

He nodded, then worried he might have laid it on a little too thick. "Just a bit, of course," he said.

"Of course."

"Is there enough tea left for me to have another cup?" he asked, as nonchalantly as he could manage.

"If there isn't, I'm sure I could have Cook brew another pot."

"Oh, no, I'm sure that won't be necessary," he exclaimed, probably a little too loudly. "I'll just take whatever is left."

Kate tipped the pot until the last dregs of tea swirled in his cup. She added a dollop of milk, then handed it back to him in silence, although her arched eyebrows spoke volumes.

As he sipped at his tea—his belly was a little too full to gulp it down as quickly as the last cup—Kate cleared her throat and asked, "Do you know Edwina's young man?"

"I don't even know who he *is*."

"Oh. I'm sorry. I must have forgotten to mention his name. It's Mr. Bagwell. I don't know his Christian name, but Edwina said he's a second son, if that's helpful. She met him at your mother's party."

Anthony shook his head. "Never heard of him. He's probably one of the poor chaps my mother invited to even out the numbers. My mother invited a bloody lot of women. She always does, hoping that one of us might actually fall in love, but then she has to find a pack of unremarkable men to even up the numbers."

"Unremarkable?" Kate echoed.

"So that the women don't fall in love with them instead of us," he replied, his grin rather lopsided.

"She's rather desperate to marry the lot of you off, isn't she?"

"All I know," Anthony said with a shrug, "is that my mother invited so many eligible women last time that she had to go down to the vicar's and beg his sixteen-year-old son to come up for supper."

Kate winced. "I think I met him."

"Yes, he's painfully shy, poor fellow. The vicar told me he had hives for a week after ending up seated next to Cressida Cowper at supper."

"Well, that would give anyone hives."

Anthony grinned. "I knew you had a mean streak in you."

"I'm not being mean!" Kate protested. But her smile was sly. "It was nothing more than the truth."

"Don't defend yourself on my account." He finished the tea; it was bitterly strong from having sat in the pot for so long, but the milk made it almost palatable. Setting the cup down, he added, "Your mean streak is one of the things I like best about you."

"Goodness," she muttered, "I should hate to know what you like least."

Anthony just waved a dismissive hand in the air. "But getting back to your sister and her Mr. Bugwell—"

"Bagwell."

"Pity."

"Anthony!"

He ignored her. "I've actually been thinking I ought to provide Edwina with a dowry."

The irony of the gesture was not lost on him. Back when he'd intended to wed Edwina, he'd planned to provide a dowry for *Kate*.

He peeked over at Kate to see her reaction.

He hadn't, of course, made the offer just to gain her good favor, but he wasn't so noble that he couldn't admit to himself that he'd been hoping for a little more than the stunned silence she was displaying.

Then he realized she was near tears.

"Kate?" he asked, not certain whether to be delighted or worried.

She wiped her nose rather inelegantly with the back of her hand. "That's the nicest thing anyone has ever done for me," she sniffled.

"I actually did it for Edwina," he mumbled, never comfortable with weepy females. But inside, she was making him feel about eight feet tall.

"Oh, Anthony!" she practically wailed. And then, much to his extreme surprise, she jumped to her feet and leaped across the table and into his arms, the heavy hem of her afternoon dress sweeping three teacups, two saucers, and a spoon onto the floor.

"You are so sweet," she said, wiping at her eyes as she landed rather solidly in his lap. "The nicest man in London."

"Well, I don't know about that," he returned, sliding his arm around her waist. "The most dangerous, perhaps, or handsome—"

"Nicest," she interrupted firmly, tucking her head into the crook of his neck. "Definitely the nicest."

"If you insist," he murmured, not at all unhappy with the recent turn of events.

"It's a good thing we finished that tea," Kate said, eyeing the cups on the floor. "It would have made a dreadful mess."

"Oh, indeed." He smiled to himself as he pulled her closer. There was something warm and comfortable about holding Kate. Her legs were dangling over the arm of the chair and her back was resting against the curve of his arm. They fit together nicely, he realized. She was just the right size for a man of his proportions.

There were a lot of things about her that were just right. It was the sort of realization that usually terrified him, but at that moment he was so damned *happy* just sitting here with her in his lap that he simply refused to think about the future.

"You are so good to me," she murmured.

Anthony thought of all the times he'd purposely stayed away, all the times he'd left her to her own devices, but he pushed away the guilt. If he was forcing a distance between them, it was for her own good. He didn't want her to fall in love with him. It would make it that much harder for her when he died.

And if he fell in love with her . . .

He didn't even want to think about how much harder it would be for him.

"Do we have any plans for this evening?" he whispered in her ear.

She nodded; the motion caused her hair to tickle his cheek. "A ball," she said. "At Lady Mottram's."

Anthony couldn't resist the soft silkiness of her hair, and he threaded two fingers through it, letting it slide across his hand and wrap around his wrist. "Do you know what I think?" he murmured.

He heard her smile as she asked, "What?"

"I think I've never cared that much for Lady Mottram. And do you know what else I think?"

Now he heard her trying not to giggle. "What?"

"I think we should go upstairs."

"You do?" she asked, clearly feigning ignorance.

"Oh, indeed. This very minute, as a matter of fact."

She wiggled her bottom, the minx, ascertaining for herself just how quickly he needed to go upstairs. "I see," she murmured gravely.

He pinched her hip lightly. "I rather thought you *felt*."

"Well, that, too," she admitted. "It was quite enlightening."

"I'm sure it was," he muttered. Then, with a very wicked smile, he nudged her chin until they were nose to nose. "Do you know what *else* I think?" he said huskily.

Her eyes widened. "I'm sure I can't imagine."

"I think," he said, one of his hands creeping under her dress and slithering up her leg, "that if we don't go upstairs this instant, I might be content to remain right here."

"Here?" she squeaked.

His hand found the edge of her stockings. "Here," he affirmed.

"Now?"

His fingers tickled her soft thatch of hair, then sank into the very core of her womanhood. She was soft and wet and felt like heaven. "Oh, most definitely now," he said.

"Here?"

He nibbled on her lips. "Didn't I already answer that question?"

And if she had any further questions, she didn't voice them for the next hour.

Or maybe it was just that he was trying his damnedest to rob her of speech.

And if a man could judge from the little squeals and mewls that slipped from her mouth, he was doing a ripping good job.

Chapter 19

Lady Mottram's annual ball was a crush, as always, but society watchers could not fail to note that Lord and Lady Bridgerton did not make an appearance. Lady Mottram insists that they had promised to attend, and This Author can only speculate as to what kept the newlyweds at home . . .

LADY WHISTLEDOWN'S SOCIETY PAPERS, 13 JUNE 1814

*M*uch later that night, Anthony was lying on his side in bed, cradling his wife, who had snuggled her back up to his front and was presently sleeping soundly.

Which was fortunate, he realized, because it had started to rain.

He tried to nudge the covers up over her exposed ear so that she would not hear the drops beating against the windows, but she was as fidgety in sleep as she was when awake, and he could not manage to pull the coverlet much above the level of her neck before she shook it off.

He couldn't yet tell whether the storm would grow electrical in nature, but the force of the rain had increased, and the wind had picked up until it howled through the night, rattling the tree branches against the side of the house.

Kate was growing a little more restless at his side, and

he made shhhh-ing sounds as he smoothed her hair with his hand. The storm hadn't woken her up, but it had definitely intruded upon her slumber. She had begun to mumble in her sleep, tossing and turning until she was curled on her opposite side, facing him.

"What happened to make you hate the rain so?" he whispered, tucking one dark lock of hair behind her ear. But he did not judge her for her terrors; he knew well the frustration of unfounded fears and premonitions. His certainty of his own impending death, for example, had haunted him since the moment he'd picked up his father's limp hand and laid it gently on his unmoving chest.

It wasn't something he could explain, or even something he could understand. It was just something he *knew*.

He'd never feared death, though, not really. The knowledge of it had been a part of him for so long that he merely accepted it, just as other men accepted the other truths that made up the cycle of life. Spring followed winter, and summer after that. For him, death was much the same way.

Until now. He'd been trying to deny it, trying to shut the niggling notion from his mind, but death was beginning to show a frightening face.

His marriage to Kate had sent his life down an alternate path, no matter how much he tried to convince himself that he could restrict their marriage to nothing but friendship and sex.

He cared about her. He cared about her far too much. He craved her company when they were apart, and he dreamed about her at night, even as he held her in his arms.

He wasn't ready to call it love, but it terrified him all the same.

And whatever it was that burned between them, he didn't want it to end.

Which was, of course, the cruelest irony of all.

Anthony closed his eyes as he let out a weary and nervous exhale, wondering what the hell he was going to do about the complication that lay beside him in the bed. But even while his eyes were shut, he saw the flash of lightning that lit up the night, turning the black of the inside of his eyelids into a bloody red-orange.

Opening his eyes, he saw that they'd left the drapes partway open when they'd retired to bed earlier in the evening. He'd have to shut those; they'd help to keep the lightning from illuminating the room.

But when he shifted his weight and tried to nudge his way out from under the covers, Kate grabbed his arm, her fingers pressing frantically into his muscles.

"Shhhh, now, it's all right," he whispered, "I'm only going to close the drapes."

But she did not let go, and the whimper that escaped her lips when a clap of thunder shook the night nearly broke his heart.

A pale sliver of moonlight filtered through the window, just enough to illuminate the tense, drawn lines of her face. Anthony peered down to assure himself that she was still sleeping, then pried her hands from his arm and got up to close the drapes. He suspected that the flashes of lightning would still sneak into the room, though, so when he was done with the drapes, he lit a lone candle and set it on his nightstand. It didn't give off enough light to wake her up—at least he hoped it wouldn't—but at the same time it saved the room from utter blackness.

And there was nothing quite so startling as a streak of lightning cutting through utter blackness.

He crawled back into bed and regarded Kate. She was still sleeping, but not peacefully. She'd curled into a semifetal position and her breathing was labored. The lightning didn't seem to bother her much, but every time the room shook with thunder she flinched.

He took her hand and smoothed her hair, and for several minutes he simply lay with her, trying to soothe her as she slept. But the storm was increasing in intensity, with the thunder and lightning practically coming on top of each other. Kate was growing more restless by the second, and then, as a particularly loud clap of thunder exploded in the air, her eyes flew open, her face a mask of utter panic.

"Kate?" Anthony whispered.

She sat up, scrambling back until her spine was pressed against the solid headboard of the bed. She looked like a statue of terror, her body stiff and frozen into place. Her eyes were still open, barely blinking, and though she did not move her head, they flicked frantically back and forth, scanning the entire room, but not seeing anything.

"Oh, Kate," he whispered. This was far, far worse than what she'd been through that night in the library at Aubrey Hall. And he could feel the force of her pain slicing right through his heart.

No one should feel terror like this. And especially not his wife.

Moving slowly, so as not to startle her, he made his way to her side, then carefully laid an arm over her shoulders. She was shaking, but she did not push him away.

"Are you even going to remember any of this in the morning?" he whispered.

She made no response, but then, he hadn't expected her to.

"There, there," he said gently, trying to remember the soothing nonsense words his mother used whenever one of her children was upset. "It's all right now. You'll be fine."

Her tremors seemed to slow a bit, but she was still very clearly disturbed, and when the next clap of thunder shook the room, her entire body flinched, and she buried her face in the crook of her neck.

"No," she moaned, "no, no."

"Kate?" Anthony blinked several times, then gazed at her intently. She sounded different, not awake but more lucid, if that was possible.

"No, no."

And she sounded very . . .

"No, no, don't go."

. . . young.

"Kate?" He held her tightly, unsure of what to do. Should he wake her? Her eyes might be open, but she was clearly asleep and dreaming. Part of him longed to break her of her nightmare, but once she woke, she'd still be in the same place—in bed in the middle of a horrible electrical storm. Would she even feel any better?

Or should he let her sleep? Perhaps if she rode out the nightmare he might actually gain some idea as to what had caused her terror.

"Kate?" he whispered, as if she herself might actually give him a clue as to how to proceed.

"No," she moaned, growing more agitated by the second. "Nooooo."

Anthony pressed his lips to her temple, trying to soothe her with his presence.

"No, please. . . ." She started to sob, her body racked with huge gasps of air as her tears drenched his shoulder. "No, oh, no . . . *Mama!*"

Anthony stiffened. He knew that Kate always referred to her stepmother as Mary. Could she actually be speaking of her true mother, the woman who had given her life and then died so many years ago?

But as he pondered that question, Kate's entire body stiffened and she let out a shrill, high-pitched scream.

The scream of a very young girl.

In an instant, she turned about, and then she leaped into his arms, grabbing at him, clutching his shoulders with a terrifying desperation. "No, Mama," she wailed, her entire body heaving from the exertion of her cries. "No, you can't go! Oh, Mama Mama Mama Mama Mama Mama . . ."

If Anthony hadn't had his back to the headboard, she would have knocked him over, the force of her fervor was that strong.

"Kate?" he blurted out, surprised by the slight note of panic in his voice. "Kate? It's all right. You're all right. You're fine. Nobody is going anywhere. Do you hear me? No one."

But her words had melted away, and all that was left was the low sound of a weeping that came from deep in her soul. Anthony held her, and then when she'd calmed a bit, he eased her down until she was lying on her side again, and then he held her some more, until she drifted back into sleep.

Which, he noticed ironically, was right about the time the last of the thunder and lightning split the room.

When Kate woke the following morning, she was surprised to see her husband sitting up in bed, staring down at her with the oddest look . . . a combination of concern, and curiosity, and maybe even the barest hint of pity. He didn't say anything when her eyes opened, even though she could see that he was watching her face intently. She waited, to see what he would do, and then finally she just said, somewhat hesitantly, "You look tired."

"I didn't sleep well," he admitted.

"You didn't?"

He shook his head. "It rained."

"It did?"

He nodded. "And thundered."

She swallowed nervously. "And lightninged as well, I suppose."

"It did," he said, nodding again. "It was quite a storm."

There was something very profound in the way he was speaking in short, concise sentences, something that raised the hair on the back of her neck. "H-how fortunate that I missed it, then," she said. "You know I don't do well with strong storms."

"I know," he said simply.

But there was a wealth of meaning behind those two

short words, and Kate felt her heartbeat speed up slightly. "Anthony," she asked, not certain she wanted to know the answer, "what happened last night?"

"You had a nightmare."

She closed her eyes for a second. "I didn't think I had those any longer."

"I didn't realize you'd ever suffered from nightmares."

Kate let out a long exhale and sat up, pulling the covers along with her and tucking them under arms. "When I was small. Whenever it stormed, I'm told. I don't know for a fact; I never remembered anything. I thought I'd—" She had to stop for a moment; her throat felt like it was closing up, and her words seemed to choke her.

He reached out and took her hand. It was a simple gesture, but somehow it touched her heart far more than any words would have done. "Kate?" he asked quietly. "Are you all right?"

She nodded. "I thought I'd stopped, that's all."

He didn't say anything for a moment, and the room was so quiet that Kate was sure she could hear both of their heartbeats. Finally, she heard the slight rush of indrawn breath across Anthony's lips, and he asked, "Did you know that you speak in your sleep?"

She hadn't been facing him, but at that comment, her head jerked quite suddenly to the right, her eyes colliding with his. "I do?"

"You did last night."

Her fingers clutched the coverlet. "What did I say?"

He hesitated, but when his words emerged, they were steady and even. "You called out to your mother."

"Mary?" she whispered.

He shook his head. "I don't think so. I've never heard you call Mary anything but Mary; last night you were crying for 'Mama.' You sounded . . ." He paused and took a slightly ragged breath. "You sounded quite young."

Kate licked her lips, then chewed on the bottom one. "I don't know what to tell you," she finally said, afraid to press into the deepest recesses of her memory. "I have no idea why I'd be calling out to my mother."

"I think," he said gently, "that you should ask Mary."

Kate gave her head a quick and immediate shake. "I didn't even know Mary when my mother died. Neither did my father. She couldn't know why I was calling out to her."

"Your father might have told her something," he said, lifting her hand to his lips and giving it a reassuring kiss.

Kate let her eyes drop to her lap. She wanted to understand why she was so afraid of the storms, but prying into one's deepest fears was almost as terrifying as the fear itself. What if she discovered something she didn't want to know? What if—

"I'll go with you," Anthony said, breaking into her thoughts.

And somehow that made everything all right.

Kate looked to him and nodded, tears in her eyes. "Thank you," she whispered. "Thank you so much."

Later that day, the two of them walked up the steps to Mary's small townhouse. The butler showed them into the drawing room, and Kate sat on the familiar blue sofa while Anthony walked over to the window, leaning on the sill as he peered out.

"See something interesting?" she asked.

He shook his head, smiling sheepishly as he turned to face her. "I just like looking out windows, that's all."

Kate thought there was something awfully sweet about that, although she couldn't really put her finger on what. Every day seemed to reveal some new little quirk to his character, some uniquely endearing habit that bound them ever closer. She *liked* knowing strange little things about him, like how he always doubled up his pillow before going to sleep, or that he detested orange marmalade but adored the lemon.

"You look rather introspective."

Kate jerked to attention. Anthony was staring at her quizzically. "You drifted off," he said with an amused expression, "and you had the dreamiest smile on your face."

She shook her head, blushed, and mumbled, "It was nothing."

His answering snort was dubious, and as he walked over to the sofa, he said, "I'd give a hundred pounds for those thoughts."

Kate was saved from having to comment by Mary's entrance. "Kate!" Mary exclaimed. "What a lovely surprise. And Lord Bridgerton, how nice to see you both."

"You really should call me Anthony," he said somewhat gruffly.

Mary smiled as he took her hand in greeting. "I shall endeavor to remember to do so," she said. She sat across from Kate, then waited for Anthony to take his place on the sofa before saying, "Edwina is out, I'm afraid. Her Mr. Bagwell came rather unexpectedly down to town. They've gone for a walk in the park."

"We should lend them Newton," Anthony said affably. "A more capable chaperone I cannot imagine."

"We actually came to see you, Mary," Kate said.

Kate's voice held an uncommon note of seriousness, and Mary responded instantly. "What is it?" she asked, her eyes flicking back and forth from Kate to Anthony. "Is everything all right?"

Kate nodded, swallowing as she searched for the right words. Funny how she'd been rehearsing what to ask all morning, and now she was speechless. But then she felt Anthony's hand on hers, the weight and the warmth of it strangely comforting, and she looked up and said to Mary, "I'd like to ask you about my mother."

Mary looked a little startled, but she said, "Of course. But you know that I did not know her personally. I only know what your father told me of her."

Kate nodded. "I know. And you might not have the

answers to any of my questions, but I don't know who else to ask."

Mary shifted in her seat, her hands clasped primly in her lap. But Kate noticed that her knuckles had gone white.

"Very well," Mary said. "What is it you wish to learn? You know that I will tell you anything I know."

Kate nodded again and swallowed, her mouth having gone dry. "How did she die, Mary?"

Mary blinked, then sagged slightly, perhaps with relief. "But you know that already. It was influenza. Or some sort of lung fever. The doctors were never certain."

"I know, but . . ." Kate looked to Anthony, who gave her a reassuring nod. She took a deep breath and plunged on. "I'm still afraid of storms, Mary. I want to know why. I don't want to be afraid any longer."

Mary's lips parted, but she was silent for many seconds as she stared at her stepdaughter. Her skin slowly paled, taking on an odd, translucent hue, and her eyes grew haunted. "I didn't realize," she whispered. "I didn't know you still—"

"I hid it well," Kate said softly.

Mary reached up and touched her temple, her hands shaking. "If I'd known, I'd have . . ." Her fingers moved to her forehead, smoothing over worry lines as she fought for words. "Well, I don't know what I'd have done. Told you, I suppose."

Kate's heart stopped. "Told me what?"

Mary let out a long breath, both of her hands at her face now, pressing against the upper edge of her eye sockets. She looked as if she had a terrible headache, the weight of the world pounding against her skull, from the inside out.

"I just want you to know," she said in a choked voice, "that I didn't tell you because I thought you didn't remember. And if you didn't remember, well, it didn't seem right to *make* you remember."

She looked up, and there were tears streaking her face.

"But obviously you do," she whispered, "or you wouldn't be so afraid. Oh, Kate. I'm so sorry."

"I am sure there is nothing for you to be sorry about," Anthony said softly.

Mary looked at him, her eyes momentarily startled, as if she'd forgotten he was in the room. "Oh, but there is," she said sadly. "I didn't know that Kate was still suffering from her fears. I should have known. It's the sort of thing a mother should sense. I may not have given her life, but I have tried to be a true mother to her—"

"You have," Kate said fervently. "The very best."

Mary turned back to her, holding her silence for a few seconds before saying, in an oddly detached voice, "You were three when your mother died. It was your birthday, actually."

Kate nodded, mesmerized.

"When I married your father I made three vows. There was the vow I made to him, before God and witnesses, to be his wife. But in my heart I made two other vows. One was to you, Kate. I took one look at you, so lost and forlorn with those huge brown eyes—and they were sad, oh, they were so sad, eyes no child should have—and I vowed that I would love you as my own, and raise you with everything I had within me."

She paused to wipe her eyes, gratefully accepting the handkerchief that Anthony handed to her. When she continued, her voice was barely a whisper. "The other vow was to your mother. I visited her grave, you know."

Kate's nod was accompanied by a wistful smile. "I know. I went with you on several occasions."

Mary shook her head. "No. I mean before I married your father. I knelt there, and that was when I made my third vow. She had been a good mother to you; everyone said so, and any fool could see that you missed her with everything in your heart. So I promised her all the same things I promised you, to be a good mother, to love and cherish you as if you were of my own flesh." She lifted her head, and her eyes were utterly clear and direct when she said, "And I'd like to think that I brought her some peace. I don't think any mother can die in peace leaving behind a child so young."

"Oh, Mary," Kate whispered.

Mary looked at her and smiled sadly, then turned to Anthony. "And that, my lord, is why I am sorry. I should have known, should have seen that she suffered."

"But Mary," Kate protested, "I didn't want you to see. I hid in my room, under my bed, in the closet. Anything to keep it from you."

"But why, sweetling?"

Kate sniffed back a tear. "I don't know. I didn't want to worry you, I suppose. Or maybe I was afraid of appearing weak."

"You've always tried to be so strong," Mary whispered. "Even when you were a tiny thing."

Anthony took Kate's hand, but he looked at Mary. "She is strong. And so are you."

Mary gazed at Kate's face for a long minute, her eyes nostalgic and sad, and then, in a low, even voice, she said, "When your mother died, it was . . . I wasn't there, but when I married your father, he told the story to me. He knew that I loved you already, and he thought it might help me to understand you a bit better.

"Your mother's death was very quick. According to your father, she fell ill on a Thursday and died on a Tuesday. And it rained the whole time. It was one of those awful storms that never ends, just beats the ground mercilessly until the rivers flood and the roads become impassable.

"He said that he was sure she would turnabout if only the rain would stop. It was silly, he knew, but every night he'd go to bed praying for the sun to peek out from the clouds. Praying for anything that might give him a little hope."

"Oh, Papa," Kate whispered, the words slipping unbidden from her lips.

"You were confined to the house, of course, which apparently rankled you to no end." Mary looked up and smiled at Kate, the sort of smile that spoke of years of memories. "You've always loved to be outdoors. Your father told me that your mother used to bring your cradle outside and rock you in the fresh air."

"I didn't know that," Kate whispered.

Mary nodded, then continued with her story. "You didn't realize your mother was ill right away. They kept you from her, fearing contagion. But eventually you must have sensed that something was wrong. Children always do.

"The night she died the rain had grown worse, and I'm told the thunder and lightning were as terrifying as anyone had ever seen." She paused, then tilted her head slightly to the side as she asked, "Do you remember the old gnarled tree in the back garden—the one you and Edwina always used to scramble on?"

"The one that was split in two?" Kate whispered.

Mary nodded. "It happened that night. Your father said it was the most terrifying sound he'd ever heard. The thunder and lightning were coming on top of each other, and a bolt split the tree at the exact moment that the thunder shook the earth.

"I suppose you couldn't sleep," she continued. "I remember that storm, even though I lived in the next county. I don't know how anyone could have slept through it. Your father was with your mother. She was dying, and everyone knew it, and in their grief they'd forgotten about you. They'd been so careful to keep you out, but on that night, their attention was elsewhere.

"Your father told me that he was sitting by your mother's side, trying to hold her hand as she passed. It wasn't a gentle death, I'm afraid. Lung disease often isn't." Mary looked up. "My mother died the same way. I know. The end wasn't peaceful. She was gasping for breath, suffocating before my very eyes."

Mary swallowed convulsively, then trained her eyes on

Kate's. "I can only assume," she whispered, "that you witnessed the same thing."

Anthony's hand tightened on Kate's.

"But where I was five and twenty at my mother's death," Mary said, "you were but three. It's not the sort of thing a child should see. They tried to make you leave, but you would not go. You bit and clawed and screamed and screamed and screamed, and then—"

Mary stopped, choking on her words. She lifted the handkerchief Anthony had given her to her face, and several moments passed before she was able to continue.

"Your mother was near death," she said, her voice so low it was nearly a whisper. "And just as they found someone strong enough to remove such a wild child, a flash of lightning pierced the room. Your father said—"

Mary stopped and swallowed. "Your father told me that what happened next was the most eerie and awful moment he'd ever experienced. The lightning—it lit the room up as bright as day. And the flash wasn't over in an instant, as it should be; it almost seemed to hang in the air. He looked at you, and you were frozen. I'll never forget the way he described it. He said it was as if you were a little statue."

Anthony jerked.

"What is it?" Kate asked, turning to him.

He shook his head disbelievingly. "That's how you looked last night," he said. "Exactly how you looked. I thought those very words."

"I . . ." Kate looked from Anthony to Mary. But she didn't know what to say.

Anthony gave her hand another squeeze as he turned to Mary and urged, "Please, go on."

She nodded once. "Your eyes were fixed on your mother, and so your father turned to see what had horrified you so, and that's when he . . . when he saw . . ."

Kate gently disengaged her hand from Anthony's grasp and got up to sit beside Mary, pulling an ottoman down next to her chair. She took one of Mary's hands in both of her own. "It's all right, Mary," she murmured. "You can tell me. I need to know."

Mary nodded. "It was the moment of her death. She sat upright. Your father said she hadn't lifted her body from the pillows for days, and yet she sat bolt upright. He said she was stiff, her head thrown back, and her mouth was open as if she were screaming, but she couldn't make a sound. And then the thunder came, and you must have thought the sound came from her mouth, because you screamed like nothing anyone had ever heard and came running forward, jumping onto the bed and throwing your arms around her.

"They tried to pry you off, but you just wouldn't let go. You kept screaming and screaming and calling her name, and then there was a terrible crash. Glass shattering. A bolt of lightning severed a branch from a tree, and it crashed right through the window. There was glass everywhere, and wind, and rain, and thunder, and more lightning, and through the whole thing you didn't stop screaming. Even after she was dead and had fallen back onto the pillows, your little arms were still clutched around her neck, and you screamed and sobbed and begged for her to wake up, and not to leave.

"And you just wouldn't let go," Mary whispered. "Finally they had to wait until you wore yourself out and fell asleep."

The room was hung with silence for a full minute, and then Kate finally whispered, "I didn't know. I didn't know that I'd witnessed that."

"Your father said you wouldn't speak of it," Mary said. "Not that you could, right away. You slept for hours and hours, and then when you woke up, it was clear that you'd caught your mother's illness. Not with the same gravity; your life was never in danger. But you were ill, and not in any state to talk about your mother's death. And when you were well, you *wouldn't* talk about it. Your father tried, but he said that every time he mentioned it, you shook your head and clamped your hands over your ears. And eventually he stopped trying."

Mary gave Kate an intent gaze. "He said you seemed happier when he stopped trying. He did what he thought was best."

"I know," Kate whispered. "And at the time, it probably *was* best. But now I needed to know." She turned to Anthony, not for reassurance exactly, but for some sort of validation, and she repeated, "I needed to know."

"How do you feel now?" he asked, his words soft and direct.

She thought about that for a moment. "I don't know. Good, I think. A little lighter." And then, without even realizing what she was doing, she smiled. It was a hesitant, slow thing, but nonetheless a smile. She turned to Anthony with astonished eyes. "I feel as if a huge weight has been lifted from my shoulders."

"Do you remember now?" Mary asked.

Kate shook her head. "But I still feel better. I can't explain it, really. It's good to know, even if I can't remember."

Mary made a choked sort of sound and then she was out of her chair and next to Kate on the ottoman, embracing her with all her might. And they both were crying, the odd, energetic sort of sobs that were mixed with laughter. There were tears, but they were happy tears, and when Kate finally pulled away and looked at Anthony, she saw that he, too, was wiping at the corner of his eye.

He pulled his hand away, of course, and assumed a dignified mien, but she'd seen him. And in that moment, she knew she loved him. With every thought, every emotion, every piece of her being, she loved him.

And if he never loved her back—well, she didn't want to think about that. Not now, not in this profound moment.

Probably not ever.

Chapter 20

Has anyone besides This Author noticed that Miss Edwina Sheffield has been very distracted of late? Rumor has it that she has lost her heart, although no one seems to know the identity of the lucky gentleman.

Judging from Miss Sheffield's behavior at parties, however, This Author feels it is safe to assume that the mystery gentleman is not someone currently residing here in London. Miss Sheffield has shown no marked interest in any one gentleman, and indeed, even sat out the dancing at Lady Mottram's ball Friday last.

Could her suitor be someone she met in the country last month? This Author will have to do a bit of sleuthing to uncover the truth.

LADY WHISTLEDOWN'S SOCIETY PAPERS, 13 JUNE 1814

"Do you know what I think?" Kate asked, as she sat at her vanity table later that night, brushing her hair.

Anthony was standing by the window, one hand leaning against the frame as he gazed out. "Mmmm?" was his reply, mostly because he was too distracted by his own thoughts to formulate a more coherent word.

"I think," she continued in a cheery voice, "that next time it storms, I'm going to be just fine."

He turned slowly around. "Really?" he asked.

She nodded. "I don't know why I think that. A gut feeling, I suppose."

"Gut feelings," he said, in a voice that sounded strange and flat even to his own ears, "are often the most accurate."

"I feel the strangest sense of optimism," she said, waving her silver-backed hairbrush in the air as she spoke. "All my life, I've had this awful thing hanging over my head. I didn't tell you—I never told anyone—but every time it stormed, and I fell to pieces, I thought . . . well, I didn't just *think*, I somehow *knew* . . ."

"What, Kate?" he asked, dreading the answer without even having a clue why.

"Somehow," she said thoughtfully, "as I shook and sobbed, I just knew that I was going to die. I knew it. There was just no way I could feel that awful and live to see the next day." Her head cocked slightly to the side, and her face took on a vaguely strained expression, as if she weren't sure how to say what she needed to say.

But Anthony understood all the same. And it made his blood run to ice.

"I'm sure you'll think it's the silliest thing imaginable," she said, her shoulders rising and falling in a sheepish shrug. "You're so rational, so levelheaded and practical. I don't think you could understand something like this."

If she only knew. Anthony rubbed at his eyes, feeling strangely drunk. He staggered to a chair, hoping she wouldn't notice how off balance he was, and sat down.

Luckily, her attention had returned to the various bottles and trinkets on her vanity table. Or maybe she was just too embarrassed to look at him, thinking he'd scoff at her irrational fears.

"Whenever the storm passed," she continued, talking down at her table, "I knew how foolish I'd been and how ridiculous the notion was. After all, I'd endured thunderstorms before, and none had ever killed me. But knowing

310 Julia Quinn

that in my rational mind never seemed to help. Do you know what I mean?"

Anthony tried to nod. He wasn't sure if he actually did.

"When it rained," she said, "nothing really existed except for the storm. And, of course, my fear. Then the sun would come out, and I'd realize again how silly I'd been, but the next time it stormed, it was just like before. And once again, I knew I would die. I just knew it."

Anthony felt sick. His body felt strange, not his own. He couldn't have said anything if he'd tried.

"In fact," she said, raising her head to look at him, "the only time I felt I might actually live to see the next day was in the library at Aubrey Hall." She stood and walked to his side, resting her cheek on his lap as she knelt before him. "With you," she whispered.

He lifted his hand to stroke her hair. The motion was more out of reflex than anything else. He certainly wasn't conscious of his actions.

He'd had no idea that Kate had any sense of her own mortality. Most people didn't. It was something that had lent Anthony an odd sense of isolation through the years, as if he understood some basic, awful truth that eluded the rest of society.

And while Kate's sense of doom wasn't the same as his—hers was fleeting, brought on by a temporary burst of wind and rain and electricity, whereas his was with him always, and would be until the day he died—she, unlike him, had beaten it.

Kate had fought her demons and she had won.

And Anthony was so damned jealous.

It was not a noble reaction; he knew that. And, caring for her as he did, he was thrilled and relieved and over-joyed and every good and pure emotion imaginable that she had beaten the terrors that came with the storms, but he was still jealous. So goddamned jealous.

Kate had won.

Whereas he, who had acknowledged his demons but

refused to fear them, was now petrified with terror. And all because the one thing he swore would never happen had come to pass.

He had fallen in love with his wife.

He had fallen in love with his wife, and now the thought of dying, of leaving her, of knowing that their moments together would form a short poem and not a long and lusty novel—it was more than he could bear.

And he didn't know where to set the blame. He wanted to point his finger at his father, for dying young and leaving him as the bearer of this awful curse. He wanted to rail at Kate, for coming into his life and making him fear his own end. Hell, he would have blamed a stranger on the street if he'd thought there'd be any use to it.

But the truth was, there was no one to blame, not even himself. It would make him feel so much better if he could point his finger at someone—anyone—and say, "This is *your* fault." It was juvenile, he knew, this need to assign blame, but everyone had a right to childish emotions from time to time, didn't they?

"I'm so happy," Kate murmured, her head still resting on his lap.

And Anthony wanted to be happy, too. He wanted so damned much for everything to be uncomplicated, for happiness just to be happiness and nothing more. He wanted to rejoice in her recent victories without any thought to his own worries. He wanted to lose himself in the moment, to forget about the future, to hold her in his arms and . . .

In one abrupt, unpremeditated movement, he hauled them both to their feet.

"Anthony?" Kate queried, blinking in surprise.

In answer, he kissed her. His lips met hers in an explosion of passion and need that blurred the mind until he could be ruled by body alone. He didn't want to think, he didn't want to be *able* to think. All he wanted was this very moment.

And he wanted this moment to last forever.

He swept his wife into his arms and stalked to the bed, depositing her on the mattress half a second before his body came down to cover hers. She was stunning beneath him, soft and strong, and consumed by the same fire that raged within his own body. She might not understand what had prompted his sudden need, but she felt it and shared it all the same.

Kate had already dressed for bed, and her nightrobe fell open easily under his experienced fingers. He had to touch her, to feel her, to assure himself that she was there beneath him and he was there to make love to her. She was wearing a silky little confection of ice blue that tied at the shoulders and hugged her curves. It was the sort of gown designed to reduce men to liquid fire, and Anthony was no exception.

There was something desperately erotic about the feel of her warm skin through the silk, and his hands roamed over her body relentlessly, touching, squeezing, doing anything he could to bind her to him.

If he could have drawn her within him, he would have done it and kept her there forever.

"Anthony," Kate gasped, in that brief moment when he removed his mouth from hers, "are you all right?"

"I want you," he grunted, bunching her gown up around the tops of her legs. "I want you now."

Her eyes widened with shock and excitement, and he sat up, straddling her, his weight on his knees so as not to crush her. "You are so beautiful," he whispered. "So unbelievably gorgeous."

Kate glowed at his words, and her hands went up to his face, smoothing her fingers over his faintly stubbled cheeks. He caught one of her hands and turned his face into it, kissing her palm as her other hand trailed down the muscled cords of his neck.

His fingers found the delicate straps at her shoulders, tied into loose bow-tie loops. It took the barest of tugs to release the knots, but once the silky fabric slid over her breasts, Anthony lost all semblance of patience, and he yanked at the garment until it pooled at her feet, leaving her completely and utterly naked under his gaze.

With a ragged groan he tore at his shirt, buttons flying as he pulled it off, and it took mere seconds to divest himself of his trousers. And then, when there was finally nothing in the bed but glorious skin, he covered her again, one muscular thigh nudging her legs apart.

"I can't wait," he said hoarsely. "I can't make this good for you."

Kate let out a fevered groan as she grabbed him by the hips, steering him toward her entrance. "It *is* good for me," she gasped. "And I don't want you to wait."

And at that point, words ceased. Anthony let out a primitive, guttural cry as he plunged into her, burying himself fully with one long and powerful stroke. Kate's eyes flew wide open, and her mouth formed a little *Oh* of surprise at the shock of his swift invasion. But she'd been ready for him—more than ready for him. Something about the relentless pace of his lovemaking had stirred a passion deep within her, until she needed him with a desperation that left her breathless.

They weren't delicate, and they weren't gentle. They were hot, and sweaty, and needy, and they held on to each other as if they could make time last forever by sheer force of will. When they climaxed, it was fiery and it was simultaneous, both their bodies arching as their cries of release mingled in the night.

But when they were done, curled in each other's arms as they fought for control over their labored breath, Kate closed her eyes in bliss and surrendered to an overwhelming lassitude.

Anthony did not.

He stared at her as she drifted off, then watched her as she slumbered. He watched the way her eyes sometimes moved under her sleepy eyelids. He measured the pace of her breathing by counting the gentle rise and fall of her chest. He listened for each sigh, each mumble.

There were certain memories a man wanted to sear on his brain, and this was one of them.

But just when he was sure that she was totally and completely asleep, she made a funny, warm sort of noise as she snuggled more deeply into his embrace, and her eyelids fluttered slowly open.

"You're still awake," she murmured, her voice scratchy and mellow with sleep.

He nodded, wondering if he was holding her too tightly. He didn't want to let go. He never wanted to let go.

"You should sleep," she said.

He nodded again, but he couldn't seem to make his eyes close.

She yawned. "This is nice."

He kissed her forehead, making an "Mmmm" sound of agreement.

She arched her neck and kissed him back, full on the lips, then settled into her pillow. "I hope we'll be like this always," she murmured, yawning yet again as sleep overtook her. "Always and forever."

Anthony froze.

Always.

She couldn't know what that word meant to him. Five years? Six? Maybe seven or eight.

Forever.

That was a word that had no meaning, something he simply couldn't comprehend.

Suddenly he couldn't breathe.

The coverlet felt like a brick wall atop him, and the air grew thick.

He had to get out of there. He had to go. He had to—

He vaulted from the bed, and then, stumbling and choking, he reached for his clothes, tossed so recklessly to the floor, and started thrusting his limbs into the appropriate holes.

"Anthony?"

His head jerked up. Kate was pushing herself upright in

the bed, yawning. Even in the dim light, he could see that her eyes were confused. And hurt.

"Are you all right?" she asked.

He gave her one curt nod.

"Then why are you trying to put your leg into the armhole of your shirt?"

He looked down and bit off a curse he'd never before even considered uttering in front of a female. With yet another choice expletive, he balled the offending piece of linen into a wrinkled mess and threw it on the floor, pausing for barely a second before yanking his trousers on.

"Where are you going?" Kate asked anxiously.

"I have to go out," he grunted.

"Now?"

He didn't answer because he didn't know how to answer.

"Anthony?" She stepped out of bed and reached for him, but a split second before her hand touched his cheek he flinched, stumbling backward until his back hit the bedpost. He saw the hurt on her face, the pain of his rejection, but he knew that if she touched him in tenderness, he'd be lost.

"Damn it all," he bit off. "Where the hell are my shirts?"

"In your dressing room," she said nervously. "Where they always are."

He stalked off in search of a fresh shirt, unable to bear the sound of her voice. No matter what she said, he kept hearing *always* and *forever*.

And it was killing him.

When he emerged from his dressing room, coat and shoes on their proper places on his body, Kate was on her feet, pacing the floor and anxiously fidgeting with the wide blue sash on her dressing gown.

"I have to go," he said tonelessly.

She didn't make a sound, which was what he'd thought he wanted, but instead he just found himself standing there, waiting for her to speak, unable to move until she did.

"When will you be back?" she finally asked.

"Tomorrow."

"That's . . . good."

He nodded. "I can't be here," he blurted out. "I have to go."

She swallowed convulsively. "Yes," she said, her voice achingly small, "you've said as much."

And then, without a backward glance and without a clue as to where he was going, he left.

Kate walked slowly to the bed and stared at it. Somehow it seemed wrong to climb in alone, to pull the covers around her and make a little huddle of one. She thought she should cry, but no tears pricked her eyes. So finally she moved to the window, pushed aside the drapes, and stared out, surprising herself with a soft prayer for a storm.

Anthony was gone, and while she was certain he'd return in body, she was not so confident about his spirit. And she realized that she needed something—she needed the storm—to prove to herself that she could be strong, by herself and for herself.

She didn't want to be alone, but she might not have a choice in that matter. Anthony seemed determined to maintain a distance. There were demons within him— demons she feared he would never choose to face in her presence.

But if she was destined to be alone, even with a husband at her side, then by God she'd be alone and strong.

Weakness, she thought as she let her forehead rest against the smooth, cool glass of her window, never got anyone anywhere.

Anthony had no recollection of his off-balance stumble through the house, but somehow he found himself tripping down the front steps, made slippery by the light fog that hung in the air. He crossed the street, not having a clue where he was going, only knowing that he needed to be *away*. But when he reached the opposite pavement, some devil within him forced his eyes upward toward his bedroom window.

He shouldn't have seen her was his rather inane thought. She should have been in bed or the drapes should have been pulled or he should have been halfway to his club by now.

But he did see her and the dull ache in his chest grew sharper, more viciously unrelenting. His heart felt as if it had been sliced wide open—and he had the most unsettling sensation that the hand wielding the knife had been his own.

He watched her for a minute—or maybe it was an hour. He didn't think she saw him; nothing in her posture gave any indication that she was aware of his presence. She was too far away for him to see her face, but he rather thought her eyes were closed.

Probably hoping it doesn't storm, he thought, glancing up at the murky sky. She'd most likely be out of luck. The mist and fog were already coalescing into drops of moisture on his skin, and it seemed only a quick transition to out-and-out rain.

He knew he should leave, but some invisible cord kept him rooted to the spot. Even after she'd left her position at the window, he remained in place, staring up at the house. The pull back inside was nearly impossible to deny. He wanted to run back into the house, fall to his knees before her, and beg her forgiveness. He wanted to sweep her into his arms and make love to her until the first streaks of dawn touched the sky. But he knew he couldn't do any of those things.

Or maybe it was that he *shouldn't*. He just didn't know anymore.

And so, after standing frozen in place for nearly an hour, after the rain came, after the wind blew gusts of chilly air down the street, Anthony finally left.

He left, not feeling the cold, not feeling the rain, which had begun to fall with surprising force.

He left, not feeling anything.

Chapter 21

It has been whispered that Lord and Lady Bridgerton were forced to marry, but even if that is true, This Author refuses to believe that theirs is anything but a love match.

LADY WHISTLEDOWN'S SOCIETY PAPERS, 15 JUNE 1814

It was strange, Kate thought as she looked at the morning repast laid upon the side table in the small dining room, how one could feel utterly famished and at the same time have no appetite. Her stomach was rumbling and churning, demanding food now, and yet everything—from the eggs to the scones to the kippers to the roast pork—looked awful.

With a dejected sigh, she reached for a solitary triangle of toast and sank into her chair with a cup of tea.

Anthony had not come home last night.

Kate took a nibble of the toast and forced it down. She'd been hoping that he might at least make an appearance in time for breakfast. She'd delayed the meal as long as she could—it was already nearly eleven in the morning and she usually ate at nine—but her husband was still absent.

"Lady Bridgerton?"

Kate looked up and blinked. A footman was standing

before her bearing a small cream-colored envelope.

"This arrived for you a few minutes ago," he said.

Kate murmured her thanks and reached for the envelope, which had been secured with a neat dollop of pale pink sealing wax. Bringing it closer to her eyes, she made out the initials *EOB*. One of Anthony's relations? The E would be Eloise, of course, since all of the Bridgertons had been named in alphabetical order.

Kate carefully broke the seal and slipped out the contents—a single piece of paper, neatly folded in half.

Kate—

Anthony is here. He looks a wreck. It is, of course, none of my business, but I thought you might like to know.

Eloise

Kate stared at the note a few seconds longer, then shoved her chair back and stood. It was time she paid a call upon Bridgerton House.

Much to Kate's surprise, when she knocked at Bridgerton House, the door was swung open not by the butler but by Eloise, who immediately said, "That was fast!"

Kate looked around the hall, half expecting another Bridgerton sibling or two to jump out at her. "Were you waiting for me?"

Eloise nodded. "And you don't have to knock at the door, you know. Bridgerton House belongs to Anthony, after all. And you *are* his wife."

Kate smiled weakly. She didn't feel much like a wife this morning.

"I hope you don't think me a hopeless meddler," Eloise continued, linking her arm through Kate's and guiding her down the hall, "but Anthony does look awful, and I had a sneaking suspicion you didn't know he was here."

"Why would you think that?" Kate couldn't help asking.

"Well," Eloise said, "he didn't go to any great pains to tell any of *us* that he was here."

Kate eyed her sister-in-law suspiciously. "Meaning?"

Eloise had the grace to blush a faint pink. "Meaning, ah, that the only reason I know he's here is that I was spying upon him. I don't think my mother even knows he's in residence."

Kate felt her eyelids blink in rapid succession. "You've been spying upon us?"

"No, of course not. But I happened to be up and about rather early this morning, and I heard someone come in, and so I went to investigate and I saw light coming from under the door in his study."

"How, then, do you know he looks awful?"

Eloise shrugged. "I figured he'd have to emerge eventually to eat or relieve himself, so I waited on the steps for an hour or so—"

"Or so?" Kate echoed.

"Or three," Eloise admitted. "It's really not that long when one is interested in one's subject, and besides, I had a book with me to while away the time."

Kate shook her head in reluctant admiration. "What time did he come in last night?"

"Around four or so."

"What were you doing up so late?"

Eloise shrugged again. "I couldn't sleep. I often can't. I'd gone down to get a book to read from the library. Finally, at around seven—well, I suppose it was a bit before seven, so it wasn't quite three hours I waited—"

Kate began to feel dizzy.

"—he emerged. He didn't head in the direction of the breakfast room, so I can only assume it was for other reasons. After a minute or two, he reemerged and headed back into his study. Where," Eloise finished with a flourish, "he has been ever since."

Kate stared at her for a good ten seconds. "Have you

ever considered offering your services to the War Department?"

Eloise grinned, a smile so like Anthony's Kate almost cried. "As a spy?" she asked.

Kate nodded.

"I'd be brilliant, don't you think?"

"Superb."

Eloise gave Kate a spontaneous hug. "I'm so glad you married my brother. Now go and see what is wrong."

Kate nodded, straightened her shoulders, and took a step toward Anthony's study. Turning around, she pointed a finger at Eloise and said, "You will not be listening at the door."

"I wouldn't dream of it," Eloise replied.

"I mean it, Eloise!"

Eloise sighed. "It's time I went up to bed, anyway. I could use a nap after staying up all night."

Kate waited until the younger girl had disappeared up the stairs, then made her way to Anthony's study door. She put her hand on the knob, whispering, "Don't be locked," as she gave it a twist. To her extreme relief, it turned, and the door swung open.

"Anthony?" she called out. Her voice was soft and hesitant, and she found she didn't like the sound of it. She wasn't used to being soft and hesitant.

There was no reply, so Kate stepped farther into the room. The drapes were tightly closed, and the heavy velvet admitted little light. Kate scanned the room until her eyes fell on the figure of her husband, slouched over his desk, sound asleep.

Kate walked quietly across the room to the windows and pulled the drapes partway open. She didn't want to blind Anthony when he woke up, but at the same time, she wasn't going to conduct such an important conversation in the dark. Then she walked back over to his desk and gently shook his shoulder.

"Anthony?" she whispered. "Anthony?"

His reply was closer to a snore than anything else.

Frowning impatiently, she shook a little harder. "Anthony?" she said softly. "Anthon—"

"Yibbledeedad—!" He came awake in one sudden movement, an incoherent rush of speech bursting forth as his torso snapped upright.

Kate watched as he blinked himself into coherency, then focused on her. "Kate," he said, his voice hoarse and husky with sleep and something else—maybe alcohol. "What are you doing here?"

"What are *you* doing here?" she countered. "The last time I checked, we lived nearly a mile away."

"I didn't want to disturb you," he mumbled.

Kate didn't believe that for one second, but she decided not to argue the point. Instead, she opted for the direct approach and asked, "Why did you leave last night?"

A long stretch of silence was followed by a weary, tired sigh, and Anthony finally said, "It's complicated."

Kate fought the urge to cross her arms. "I'm an intelligent woman," she said in a purposefully even voice. "I'm generally able to grasp complex concepts."

Anthony didn't look pleased by her sarcasm. "I don't want to go into this now."

"When *do* you want to go into it?"

"Go home, Kate," he said softly.

"Do you plan to come with me?"

Anthony let out a little groan as he raked a hand through his hair. Christ, she was like a dog with a bone. His head was pounding, his mouth tasted like wool, all he really wanted to do was splash some water on his face and clean his teeth, and here his wife would not stop *interrogating him.* . . .

"Anthony?" she persisted.

That was *enough.* He stood so suddenly that his chair tipped back and slammed into the floor with a resounding crash. "You will cease your questions this instant," he bit off.

Her mouth settled into a flat, angry line. But her eyes. . . .

Anthony swallowed against the acidic taste of guilt that flooded his mouth.

Because her eyes were awash with pain.

And the anguish in his own heart grew tenfold.

He wasn't ready. Not yet. He didn't know what to do with her. He didn't know what to do with himself. All his life—or at least since his father had died—he'd known that certain things were true, that certain things *had* to be true. And now Kate had gone and turned his world upside down.

He hadn't wanted to love her. Hell, he hadn't wanted to love anyone. It was the one thing—the only thing—that could make him fear his own mortality. And what about Kate? He'd promised to love and protect her. How could he do that, all the while knowing he would leave her? He certainly couldn't tell her of his odd convictions. Aside from the fact that she'd probably think he was crazy, all it would do was subject her to the same pain and fear that wracked him. Better to let her live in blissful ignorance.

Or was it even better if she didn't love him at all?

Anthony just didn't know the answer. And he needed more time. And he couldn't think with her standing there before him, those pain-filled eyes raking his face. And—

"Go," he choked out. "Just go."

"No," she said with a quiet determination that made him love her all the more. "Not until you tell me what is bothering you."

He strode out from behind his desk and took her arm. "I can't be with you right now," he said hoarsely, his eyes avoiding hers. "Tomorrow. I'll see you tomorrow. Or the next day."

"Anthony—"

"I need time to think."

"About *what*?" she cried out.

"Don't make this any harder than—"

"How could it possibly get any harder?" she demanded. "I don't even know what you're talking about."

"I just need a few days," he said, feeling like an echo. Just a few days to think. To figure out what he was going to do, how he was going to live his life.

But she twisted around until she was facing him, and then her hand was on his cheek, touching him with a tenderness that made his heart ache. "Anthony," she whispered, "please . . ."

He couldn't form a word, couldn't make a sound.

Her hand slipped to the back of his head, and then she was drawing him closer . . . closer . . . and he couldn't help himself. He wanted her so damned badly, wanted to feel her body pressed against his, to taste the faint salt of her skin. He wanted to smell her, to touch her, to hear the rasp of her breath in his ear.

Her lips touched his, soft and seeking, and her tongue tickled the corner of her mouth. It would be so easy to lose himself in her, to sink down to the carpet and . . .

"No!" The word was ripped from his throat, and by God, he'd had no idea it was there until it burst forth.

"No," he said again, pushing her away. "Not now."

"But—"

He didn't deserve her. Not right now. Not yet. Not until he understood how he was meant to live out the rest of his life. And if it meant he had to deny himself the one thing that might bring him salvation, so be it.

"Go," he ordered, his voice sounding a bit more harsh than he'd intended. "Go now. I'll see you later."

And this time, she did go.

She went, without looking back.

And Anthony, who'd only just learned what it was to love, learned what it was to die inside.

By the following morning, Anthony was drunk. By afternoon, he was hungover.

His head was pounding, his ears were ringing, and his

brothers, who had been surprised to discover him in such a state at their club, were talking *far* too loudly.

Anthony put his hands over his ears and groaned. *Everyone* was talking far too loudly.

"Kate boot you out of the house?" Colin asked, grabbing a walnut from a large pewter dish in the middle their table and splitting it open with a viciously loud crack.

Anthony lifted his head just far enough to glare at him.

Benedict watched his brother with raised brows and the vaguest hint of a smirk. "She definitely booted him out," he said to Colin. "Hand me one of those walnuts, will you?"

Colin tossed one across the table. "Do you want the crackers as well?"

Benedict shook his head and grinned as he held up a fat, leather-bound book. "Much more satisfying to smash them."

"Don't," Anthony bit out, his hand shooting out to grab the book, "even think about it."

"Ears a bit sensitive this afternoon, are they?"

If Anthony had had a pistol, he would have shot them both, hang the noise.

"If I might offer you a piece of advice?" Colin said, munching on his walnut.

"You might not," Anthony replied. He looked up. Colin was chewing with his mouth open. As this had been strictly forbidden while growing up in their household, Anthony could only deduce that Colin was displaying such poor manners only to make more noise. "Close your damned mouth," he muttered.

Colin swallowed, smacked his lips, and took a sip of his tea to wash it all down. "Whatever you did, apologize for it. I know you, and I'm getting to know Kate, and knowing what I know—"

"What the hell is he talking about?" Anthony grumbled.

"I think," Benedict said, leaning back in his chair, "that he's telling you you're an ass."

"Just so!" Colin exclaimed.

Anthony just shook his head wearily. "It's more complicated than you think."

"It always is," Benedict said, with sincerity so false it almost managed to sound sincere.

"When you two idiots find women gullible enough to actually marry you," Anthony snapped, "then you may presume to offer me advice. But until then . . . *shut up.*"

Colin looked at Benedict. "Think he's angry?"

Benedict quirked a brow. "That or drunk."

Colin shook his head. "No, not drunk. Not anymore, at least. He's clearly hungover."

"Which would explain," Benedict said with a philosophical nod, "why he's so angry."

Anthony spread one hand over his face and pressed hard against his temples with his thumb and middle finger. "God above," he muttered. "What would it take to get you two to leave me alone?"

"Go home, Anthony," Benedict said, his voice surprisingly gentle.

Anthony closed his eyes and let out a long breath. There was nothing he wanted to do more, but he wasn't sure what to say to Kate, and more importantly, he had no idea how he'd feel once he got there.

"Yes," Colin agreed. "Just go home and tell her that you love her. What could be more simple?"

And suddenly it *was* simple. He had to tell Kate that he loved her. Now. This very day. He had to make sure she *knew,* and he vowed to spend every last minute of his miserably short life proving it to her.

It was too late to change the destiny of his heart. He'd tried not to fall in love, and he'd failed. Since he wasn't likely to fall back *out* of love, he might as well make the best of the situation. He was going to be haunted by the premonition of his own death whether or not Kate knew of his love for her. Wouldn't he be happier during these last few years if he spent them loving her openly and honestly?

He was fairly certain she'd fallen in love with him as well; surely she'd be glad to hear that he felt the same way. And when a man loved a woman, truly loved her from the depths of her soul to the tips of her toes, wasn't it his God-given duty to try to make her happy?

He wouldn't tell her of his premonitions, though. What would be the point? He might suffer the knowledge that their time together would be cut short, but why should she? Better she be struck by sharp and sudden pain at his death than suffer the anticipation of it beforehand.

He was going to die. Everyone died, he reminded himself. He was just going to have to do it sooner rather than later. But by God, he was going to enjoy his last years with every breath of his being. It might have been more convenient not to have fallen in love, but now that he had, he wasn't going to hide from it.

It was simple. His world was Kate. If he denied that, he might as well stop breathing right now.

"I have to go," he blurted out, standing up so suddenly that his thighs hit the edge of the table, sending walnut shell shards skittering across the tabletop.

"I thought you might," Colin murmured.

Benedict just smiled and said, "Go."

His brothers, Anthony realized, were a bit smarter than they let on.

"We'll speak to you in a week or so?" Colin asked.

Anthony had to grin. He and his brothers had met at their club every day for the past fortnight. Colin's oh-so-innocent query could only imply one thing—that it was obvious that Anthony had completely lost his heart to his wife and planned to spend at least the next seven days proving it to her. And that the family he was creating had grown as important as the one he'd been born into.

"Two weeks," Anthony replied, yanking on his coat. "Maybe three."

His brothers just grinned.

* * *

But when Anthony pushed through the door of his home, slightly out of breath from taking the front steps three at a time, he discovered that Kate was not in.

"Where did she go?" he asked the butler. Stupidly, he'd never once considered that she might not be at home.

"Out for a ride in the park," the butler replied, "with her sister and a Mr. Bagwell."

"Edwina's suitor," Anthony muttered to himself. Damn. He supposed he ought to be happy for his sister-in-law, but the timing was bloody annoying. He'd just made a life-altering decision regarding his wife; it would have been nice if she'd been home.

"Her *creature* went as well," the butler said with a shudder. He'd never been able to tolerate what he considered the corgi's invasion into his home.

"She took Newton, eh?" Anthony murmured.

"I imagine they'll be back within an hour or two."

Anthony tapped his booted toe against the marble floor. He didn't want to wait an hour. Hell, he didn't want to wait even a minute. "I'll find them myself," he said impatiently. "It can't be that difficult."

The butler nodded and motioned through the open doorway to the small carriage in which Anthony had ridden home. "Will you be needing another carriage?"

Anthony gave his head a single shake. "I'll go on horseback. It'll be quicker."

"Very well." The butler bent into a small bow. "I'll have a mount brought 'round."

Anthony watched the butler make his slow and sedate way toward the rear of the house for about two seconds before impatience set in. "I'll take care of it myself," he barked.

And the next thing he knew, he was dashing out of the house.

Anthony was in jaunty spirits by the time he reached Hyde Park. He was eager to find his wife, to hold her in his arms and watch her face as he told her he loved her. He prayed that she would offer words returning the sentiment. He thought she would; he'd seen her heart in her eyes on more than one occasion. Perhaps she was just waiting for him to say something first. He couldn't blame her if that was the case; he'd made a rather big fuss about how theirs would *not* be a love match right before their wedding.

What an idiot he'd been.

Once he entered the park, he made the decision to turn his mount and head over to Rotten Row. The busy path seemed the most likely destination for the threesome; Kate certainly would have no reason to encourage a more private route.

He nudged his horse into as fast a trot as he could safely manage within the confines of the park, trying to ignore the calls and waves of greeting that were directed his way by other riders and pedestrians.

Then, just when he thought he'd made it through without delay, he heard an aged, female, and very imperious voice call out his name.

"Bridgerton! I say, Bridgerton! Stop at once. I'm speaking to you!"

He groaned as he turned about. Lady Danbury, the dragon of the *ton*. There was simply no way he could ignore her. He had no idea how old she was. Sixty? Seventy? Whatever her age, she was a force of nature, and *no one* ignored her.

"Lady Danbury," he said, trying not to sound resigned as he reined in his mount. "How nice to see you."

"Good gad, boy," she barked, "you sound as if you've just taken an antidote. Perk up!"

Anthony smiled weakly.

"Where's your wife?"

"I'm looking for her right now," he replied, "or at least I *was*."

Lady Danbury was far too sharp to miss his pointed

hint, so he could only deduce that she ignored him apurpose when she said, "I like your wife."

"I like her, too."

"Never could understand why you were so set on courting her sister. Nice gel, but clearly not for you." She rolled her eyes and let out an indignant huff. "The world would be a much happier place if people would just listen to me before they up and got married," she added. "I could have the entire Marriage Mart matched up in a week."

"I'm sure you could."

Her eyes narrowed. "Are you patronizing me?"

"I wouldn't dream of it," Anthony said with complete honesty.

"Good. You always seemed like the sensible sort. I . . ." Her mouth fell open. "What the devil is that?"

Anthony followed Lady Danbury's horrified gaze until his eyes fell on an open-topped carriage careening out of control as it rounded a corner on two wheels. It was still too far to see the faces of the occupants, but then he heard a shriek, and then the terrified bark of a dog.

Anthony's blood froze in his veins.

His wife was in that carriage.

With nary a word to Lady Danbury, he kicked his horse into motion and galloped full speed ahead. He wasn't sure what he'd do once he reached the carriage. Maybe he'd grab the reins from the hapless driver. Maybe he'd be able to pull someone to safety. But he knew that he could not sit still and watch while the vehicle crashed before his eyes.

And yet that was exactly what happened.

Anthony was halfway to the drunken carriage when it veered off the path and ran up over a large rock, upsetting the balance and sending it tumbling onto its side.

And Anthony could only watch in horror as his wife died before his eyes.

Chapter 22

Contrary to popular opinion, This Author is aware that she is viewed as something of a cynic.

But that, Dear Reader, could not be further from the truth. This Author likes nothing better than a happy ending. And if that makes her a romantic fool, so be it.

LADY WHISTLEDOWN'S SOCIETY PAPERS, 15 JUNE 1814

$\mathcal{B}$y the time Anthony reached the overturned carriage, Edwina had managed to crawl from the wreckage and was clawing at a mangled piece of wood, trying to open a hole on the other side of the carriage. The sleeve of her dress was torn, and the hem was ragged and dirty, but she seemed not to notice as she tugged frantically at the door. Newton was jumping and squirming at her feet, his barks sharp and frenzied.

"What happened?" Anthony asked, his voice curt and panicked as he leapt from his horse.

"I don't know," Edwina gasped, wiping at the streaky tears that ran down her face. "Mr. Bagwell's not such an experienced driver, I think, and then Newton got loose, and then I don't know *what* happened. One minute we were rolling along, and the next—"

"Where is Bagwell?"

She motioned to the other side of the carriage. "He was thrown. He hit his head. But he'll be all right. But Kate . . ."

"What about Kate?" Anthony dropped to his knees as he tried to peer into the wreckage. The entire carriage had overturned, smashing the right side of the vehicle as it had rolled. "Where is she?"

Edwina swallowed convulsively, and her voice barely rose above a whisper as she said, "I think she's trapped beneath the carriage."

In that moment Anthony tasted death. It was bitter in his throat, metallic and hard. It scraped his flesh like a knife, choking and squeezing, pulling the air from his very lungs.

Anthony yanked viciously at the wreckage, trying to open a wider hole. It wasn't as bad as it had looked during the crash, but that did little to calm his racing heart. "Kate!" he yelled, trying to sound calm and unworried. "Kate, can you hear me?"

The only sound he heard in reply, however, was the frantic whinny of the horses. Damn. He'd have to get them unharnessed and loose before they panicked and started trying to drag the debris. "Edwina?" Anthony called sharply, looking over his shoulder.

She hurried over, wringing her hands. "Yes?"

"Do you know how to unharness the horses?"

She nodded. "I'm not very fast, but I can do it."

Anthony flicked his head toward the onlookers who were hurrying over. "See if you can find someone to help you."

She nodded again and quickly got to work.

"Kate?" Anthony yelled again. He couldn't see anyone; a dislodged bench was blocking the opening. "Can you hear me?"

Still no response.

"Try the other side," came Edwina's frantic voice. "The opening isn't as crushed."

Anthony jumped to his feet and ran around the back of the carriage to the other side. The door had already come off its hinges, leaving a hole just large enough for him to stuff his upper body into. "Kate?" he called out, trying not to notice the sharp sound of panic in his voice. Every breath from his lips seemed overloud, reverberating in the tight space, reminding him that he wasn't hearing the same sounds from Kate.

And then, as he carefully moved a seat cushion that had turned sideways, he saw her. She was terrifyingly still, but her head didn't appear to be stuck in an unnatural position, and he didn't see any blood.

That had to be a good sign. He didn't know much of medicine, but he held on to that thought like a miracle.

"You can't die, Kate," he said as his terrified fingers yanked away at the wreckage, desperate to open the hole until it was wide enough to pull her through. "Do you hear me? *You can't die!*"

A jagged piece of wood sliced open the back of his hand, but Anthony didn't notice the blood running over his skin as he pulled on another broken beam. "You had better be breathing," he warned, his voice shaking and precariously close to a sob. "This wasn't supposed to be you. It was never supposed to be you. It isn't your time. Do you understand me?"

He tore away another broken piece of wood and reached through the newly widened hole to grasp her hand. His fingers found her pulse, which seemed steady enough to him, but it was still impossible to tell if she was bleeding, or had broken her back, or had hit her head, or had . . .

His heart shuddered. There were so many ways to die. If a bee could bring down a man in his prime, surely a carriage accident could steal the life of one small woman.

Anthony grabbed the last piece of wood that stood in his way and heaved, but it didn't budge. "Don't do this to me," he muttered. "Not now. It isn't her time. Do you hear me? It isn't her time!" He felt something wet on his cheeks and dimly realized that it was tears. "It was supposed to be me," he said, choking on the words. "It was always supposed to be me."

And then, just as he was preparing to give that last piece of wood another desperate yank, Kate's fingers tightened like a claw around his wrist. His eyes flew to her face, just in time to see her eyes open wide and clear, with nary a blink.

"What the devil," she asked, sounding quite lucid and utterly awake, "are you talking about?"

Relief flooded his chest so quickly it was almost painful. "Are you all right?" he asked, his voice wobbling on every syllable.

She grimaced, then said, "I'll be fine."

Anthony paused for the barest of seconds as he considered her choice of words. "But are you fine right now?"

She let out a little cough, and he fancied he could hear her wince with pain. "I did something to my leg," she admitted. "But I don't think I'm bleeding."

"Are you faint? Dizzy? Weak?"

She shook her head. "Just in pain. What are you doing here?"

He smiled through his tears. "I came to find you."

"You did?" she whispered.

He nodded. "I came to— That is to say, I realized . . ." He swallowed convulsively. He'd never dreamed that the day would come when he'd say these words to a woman, and they'd grown so big in his heart he could barely squeeze them out. "I love you, Kate," he said chokingly. "It took me a while to figure it out, but I do, and I had to tell you. Today."

Her lips wobbled into a shaky smile as she motioned to the rest of her body with her chin. "You've bloody good timing."

Amazingly, he found himself grinning in return. "Almost makes you glad I waited so long, eh? If I'd told you last week, I wouldn't have followed you out to the park today."

She stuck out her tongue, which, considering the circumstances, made him love her even more. "Just get me out," she said.

"Then you'll tell me you love me?" he teased.

She smiled, wistful and warm, and nodded.

It was, of course, as good as a declaration, and even though he was crawling through the wreckage of an overturned carriage, even though Kate was *stuck* in the cursed carriage, with what might very well be a broken leg, he was suddenly consumed with an overwhelming sense of contentment and peace.

And he realized he hadn't felt that way for nearly twelve years, not since that fateful afternoon when he'd walked into his parents' bedroom and seen his father laid out on the bed, cold and still.

"I'm going to pull you through now," he said, sliding his arms beneath her back. "It'll hurt your leg, I'm afraid, but it can't be avoided."

"My leg already hurts," she said, smiling bravely. "I just want to get out."

Anthony gave her a single, serious nod, then curved his hands around her side and began to pull. "How is that?" he asked, his heart stopping every time he saw her wince with pain.

"Fine," she gasped, but he could tell she was merely putting up a brave front.

"I'm going to have to turn you," he said, eyeing a broken and jagged piece of wood that stuck down from above. It was going to be difficult to maneuver her around it. He couldn't care less if he tore her clothing—hell, he'd buy her a hundred new dresses if she'd only promise never again to step into a carriage if it was being driven by anyone other than himself. But he couldn't bear the thought of scratching even an inch of her skin. She'd been through enough already. She didn't need more.

"I need to pull you out headfirst," he told her. "Do you think you can wiggle yourself around? Just enough so I can grasp under your arms."

She nodded, gritting her teeth as she painstakingly turned herself inch by inch, lifting herself up on her hands as she scooted her hips around clockwise.

"There you are," Anthony said encouragingly. "Now I'm going to—"

"Just do it," Kate ground out. "You don't need to explain."

"Very well," he replied, inching backward until his knees found purchase on the grass. On a mental count of three, he gritted his teeth and began to pull her out.

And stopped a second later, as Kate let out an earsplitting scream. If he hadn't been so convinced that he'd die within the next nine years, he would have sworn she'd just taken ten off his life.

"Are you all right?" he asked urgently.

"I'm fine," she insisted. But she was breathing hard, puffing through pursed lips, and her face was tense with pain.

"What happened?" came a voice from just outside the carriage. It was Edwina, done with the horses and sounding frantic. "I heard Kate scream."

"Edwina?" Kate asked, twisting her neck as she tried to see out. "Are you all right?" She yanked on Anthony's sleeve. "Is Edwina all right? Is she hurt? Does she need a doctor?"

"Edwina's fine," he replied. "*You* need a doctor."

"And Mr. Bagwell?"

"How's Bagwell?" Anthony asked Edwina, his voice curt as he concentrated on maneuvering Kate around the debris.

"A bump on his head, but he's back on his feet."

"It's nothing. Can I help?" came a worried male voice.

Anthony had a feeling that the accident had been as much Newton's fault as Bagwell's, but still, the young man had been in control of the reins, and Anthony wasn't inclined to feel charitable toward him just now. "I'll let you know," he said curtly, before turning back to Kate and saying, "Bagwell's fine."

"I can't believe I forgot to ask after them."

"I'm sure your lapse will be pardoned, given the circumstances," Anthony said, edging farther back until he was nearly entirely out of the carriage. Kate was now positioned at the opening, and it would take only one more—rather long and almost certainly painful—tug to get her out.

"Edwina? Edwina?" Kate was calling out. "Are you sure you're not injured?"

Edwina jammed her face into the opening. "I'm fine," she said reassuringly. "Mr. Bagwell was thrown clear, and I was able to—"

Anthony elbowed her out of the way. "Grit your teeth, Kate," he ordered.

"What? I— *Aaaaaaaargh!*"

With one single tug, he freed her completely from the wreckage, both of them landing on the ground, both of them breathing hard. But where Anthony's hyperventilation was from exertion, Kate's was obviously from intense pain.

"Good God!" Edwina nearly yelled. "Look at her leg!"

Anthony glanced over at Kate and felt his stomach drop down clear to his toes. Her lower leg was crooked and bent, and more than obviously broken. He swallowed convulsively, trying not to let his concern show. Legs could be set, but he'd also heard of men who'd lost limbs due to infection and bad medical care.

"What's wrong with my leg?" Kate asked. "It hurts, but— Oh, my God!"

"Best not to look," Anthony said, trying to tip her chin in the other direction.

Her breathing, which was already rapid from trying to control the pain, grew erratic and panicked. "Oh, my

God," she gasped. "It hurts. Didn't realize how much it hurt until I saw—"

"Don't look," Anthony ordered.

"Oh, my God. Oh, my God."

"Kate?" Edwina asked in a concerned voice, leaning in. "Are you all right?"

"Look at my leg!" Kate nearly shrieked. "Does it look all right?"

"I was actually speaking of your face. You look a bit green."

But Kate couldn't reply. She was hyperventilating too hard. And then, with Anthony, Edwina, Mr. Bagwell, and Newton all staring down at her, her eyes rolled back in her head, and she fainted.

Three hours later, Kate was installed in her bed, certainly not comfortable but at least in a bit less pain thanks to the laudanum Anthony had forced down her throat the minute they'd gotten home. Her leg had been expertly set by the three surgeons Anthony had summoned (not, as all three surgeons had pointed out, that more than one was needed to set a bone, but Anthony had crossed his arms implacably and stared them all down until they'd shut up), and a physician had stopped by to leave several prescriptions that he swore would hasten the bone-knitting process.

Anthony had fussed over her like a mother hen, second-guessing every move from every doctor until one of them had actually had the audacity to ask him when he'd received his license from the Royal College of Physicians.

Anthony had not been amused.

But after much haranguing, Kate's leg was set and splinted, and she was told to look forward to at least a month of confinement in bed.

"Look forward?" she groaned to Anthony once the last of the surgeons had gone. "How can I look forward to that?"

"You'll be able to catch up on your reading," he suggested.

She let out an impatient exhale through her nose; it was hard to breathe through her mouth while clenching her teeth. "I wasn't aware I was behind on my reading."

If he'd been tempted to laugh, he did a good job of hiding it. "Perhaps you could take up needlework," he suggested.

She just glared at him. As if the prospect of needlework were going to make her feel better.

He sat gingerly on the edge of her bed and patted the back of her hand. "I'll keep you company," he said with an encouraging smile. "I'd already decided to cut back on the time I spent at my club."

Kate sighed. She was tired and cranky and in pain, and she was taking it out on her husband, which really wasn't fair. She turned her hand over so that their palms met and then entwined her fingers through his. "I love you, you know," she said softly.

He squeezed her hands and nodded, the warmth of his eyes on hers saying more than words ever could.

"You told me not to," Kate said.

"I was an ass."

She didn't argue; a quirk of his lips told her that he noticed her lack of contradiction. After a moment of silence, she said, "You were saying some odd things in the park."

Anthony's hand remained in hers, but his body pulled back slightly. "I don't know what you mean," he replied.

"I think you do," she said softly.

Anthony closed his eyes for a moment, then stood, his fingers trailing through her grasp until finally they were no longer touching at all. For so many years he'd been careful to keep his odd convictions to himself. It seemed best. Either people would believe him and then worry or they wouldn't and then think him insane.

Neither option was particularly appealing.

But now, in the heat of one terrified moment, he'd blurted it out to his wife. He couldn't even remember exactly what he'd said. But it had been enough to make her curious. And Kate wasn't the sort to let go of a curiosity. He could practice all the avoidance he wanted, but eventually she'd get it out of him. A more stubborn woman had never been born.

He walked to the window and leaned against the sill, gazing blankly in front of him as if he could actually see the streetscape through the heavy burgundy drapes that had long since been pulled shut. "There is something you should know about me," he whispered.

She didn't say anything, but he knew she'd heard. Maybe it was the sound of her changing her position in bed, maybe it was the sheer electricity in the air. But somehow he knew.

He turned around. It would have been easier to speak his words to the curtains, but she deserved better from him. She was sitting up in bed, her leg propped up on pillows, her eyes wide and filled with a heartbreaking mix of curiosity and concern.

"I don't know how to tell you this without sounding ridiculous," he said.

"Sometimes the easiest way is just to say it," she murmured. She patted an empty spot on the bed. "Do you want to sit beside me?"

He shook his head. Proximity would only make it that much more difficult. "Something happened to me when my father died," he said.

"You were very close to him, weren't you?"

He nodded. "Closer than I'd ever been to anyone, until I met you."

Her eyes glistened. "What happened?"

"It was very unexpected," he said. His voice was flat, as if he were recounting an obscure news item and not the single most disturbing event of his life. "A bee, I told you."

She nodded.

"Who would have thought a bee could kill a man?" Anthony said with a caustic laugh. "It would have been funny if it weren't so tragic."

She didn't say anything, just looked at him with a sympathy that made his heart break.

"I stayed with him throughout the night," he continued, turning slightly so that he would not have to look into her eyes. "He was dead, of course, but I needed a little more time. I just sat beside him and watched his face." Another short burst of angry laughter escaped his lips. "God, what a fool I was. I think I half expected him to open his eyes at any moment."

"I don't think that's foolish," Kate said softly. "I've seen death, too. It's hard to believe that someone is gone when he looks so normal and at peace."

"I don't know when it happened," Anthony said, "but by morning I was sure."

"That he was dead?" she asked.

"No," he said roughly, "that I would be, too."

He waited for her to comment, he waited for her to cry, to do anything, but she just sat there staring at him with no perceptible change of expression, until finally he had to say, "I'm not as great a man as my father was."

"He might choose to disagree," she said quietly.

"Well, he's not here to do that, is he?" Anthony snapped.

Again, she said nothing. Again, he felt like a heel.

He cursed under his breath and pressed his fingers against his temples. His head was starting to throb. He was starting to feel dizzy, and he realized that he couldn't remember the last time he'd eaten. "It's my judgment to make," he said in a low voice. "You didn't know him."

He sagged against a wall with a long, weary exhale, and said, "Just let me tell you. Don't talk, don't interrupt, don't judge. It's hard enough to get it out as it is. Can you do that for me?"

She nodded.

Anthony took a shaky breath. "My father was the greatest man I've ever known. Not a day goes by when I don't realize that I'm not living up to his standards. I knew that he was everything to which I could aspire. I might not ever match his greatness, but if I could come close I'd be satisfied. That's all I ever wanted. Just to come close."

He looked at Kate. He wasn't sure why. Maybe for reassurance, maybe for sympathy. Maybe just to see her face.

"If there was one thing I knew," he whispered, somehow finding the courage to keep his eyes focused on hers, "it was that I would never surpass him. Not even in years."

"What are you trying to tell me?" she whispered.

He shrugged helplessly. "I know it makes no sense. I know I can offer no rational explanation. But since that night when I sat with my father's dead body, I knew I couldn't possibly live any longer than he had."

"I see," she said quietly.

"Do you?" And then, as if a dam had burst, the words poured forth. It all gushed out of him—why he'd been so dead set against marrying for love, the jealousy he'd felt when he'd realized that she'd managed to fight her demons and win.

He watched as she brought one of her hands to her mouth and bit the end of her thumb. He'd seen her do that before, he realized—whenever she was disturbed or deep in thought.

"How old was your father when he died?" she asked.

"Thirty-eight."

"How old are you now?"

He looked at her curiously; she knew his age. But he said it anyway. "Twenty-nine."

"So by your estimation, we have nine years left."

"At most."

"And you truly believe this."

He nodded.

She pursed her lips and let out a long breath through her nose. Finally, after what felt like an endless silence, she looked back up at him with clear, direct eyes, and said, "Well, you're wrong."

Oddly enough, the straightforward tone of her voice was rather reassuring. Anthony even felt one corner of his mouth lift up in the palest of smiles. "You think I'm unaware of how ludicrous it all sounds?"

"I don't think it sounds ludicrous at all. It sounds like a perfectly normal reaction, actually, especially considering how much you adored your father." She lifted her shoulders in a rather self-aware shrug as her head tipped to the side. "But it's still wrong."

Anthony didn't say anything.

"Your father's death was an accident," Kate said. "An accident. A terrible, horrible twist of fate that no one could have predicted."

Anthony shrugged fatalistically. "I'll probably go the same way."

"Oh, for the love of—" Kate managed to bite her tongue a split second before she blasphemed. "Anthony, I could die tomorrow as well. I could have died today when that carriage rolled on top of me."

He paled. "Don't ever remind me of that."

"My mother died when she was my age," Kate reminded him harshly. "Did you ever think of that? By your laws, I should be dead by my next birthday."

"Don't be—"

"Silly?" she finished for him.

Silence reigned for a full minute.

Finally, Anthony said, his voice barely above a whisper, "I don't know if I can get past this."

"You don't have to get past it," Kate said. She caught her lower lip, which had begun to tremble, between her teeth, and then laid her hand on an empty spot on the bed. "Could you come over here so I can hold your hand?"

Anthony responded instantly; the warmth of her touch

flooded him, seeping through his body until it caressed his very soul. And in that moment he realized that this was about more than love. This woman made him a better person. He'd been good and strong and kind before, but with her at his side, he was something more.

And together they could do anything.

It almost made him think that forty might not be such an impossible dream.

"You don't have to get past it," she said again, her words blowing softly between them. "To be honest, I don't see how you *could* get completely past it until you turn thirty-nine. But what you *can* do"—she gave his hand a squeeze, and Anthony somehow felt even stronger than he had just moments before—"is refuse to allow it to rule your life."

"I realized that this morning," he whispered, "when I knew I had to tell you I loved you. But somehow now—now I *know* it."

She nodded, and he saw that her eyes were filling with tears. "You have to live each hour as if it's your last," she said, "and each day as if you were immortal. When my father grew ill, he had so many regrets. There were so many things he wished he'd done, he told me. He'd always assumed he had more time. That's something I've always carried with me. Why on earth do you think I decided to attempt the flute at such an advanced age? Everyone told me I was too old, that to be truly good at it I had to have started as a child. But that's not the point, really. I don't need to be truly good. I just need to enjoy it for myself. And I need to know I tried."

Anthony smiled. She was a terrible flutist. Even Newton couldn't bear to listen.

"But the opposite is true as well," Kate added softly. "You can't shun new challenges or hide yourself from love just because you think you might not be here to carry your dreams to completion. In the end, you'll have just as many regrets as did my father."

"I didn't want to love you," Anthony whispered. "It was

the one thing I feared above all. I'd grown rather used to my rather odd little outlook on life. Almost comfortable, actually. But love—" His voice caught; the choking sound seemed unmanly, it made him vulnerable. But he didn't care, because this was Kate.

And it didn't matter if she saw his deepest fears, because he knew she'd love him no matter what. It was a sublimely freeing feeling.

"I've seen true love," he continued. "I wasn't the cynical jade society made me out to be. I knew love existed. My mother—my father—" He stopped, sucking in a ragged breath. This was the hardest thing he'd ever done. And yet he knew the words had to be said. He knew, no matter how difficult it was to get them out, that in the end, his heart would soar.

"I was so sure that it was the one thing that could make this . . . this . . . I don't really know what to call it—this knowledge of my own mortality . . ." He raked his hand through his hair, fighting for words. "Love was the only thing that was going to make that unbearable. How could I love someone, truly and deeply, knowing that it was doomed?"

"But it's not doomed," Kate said, squeezing his hand.

"I know. I fell in love with you, and then I knew. Even if I am right, even if I'm fated to live only as long as my father did before me, I'm not doomed." He leaned forward and brushed a feather-light kiss on her lips. "I have you," he whispered, "and I'm not going to waste a single moment we have together."

Kate's lips spread into a smile. "What does that mean?"

"It means that love isn't about being afraid that it will all be snatched away. Love's about finding the one person who makes your heart complete, who makes you a better person than you ever dreamed you could be. It's about looking in the eyes of your wife and knowing, all the way to your bones, that she's simply the best person you've ever known."

"Oh, Anthony," Kate whispered, tears streaming down her cheeks. "That's how I feel about you."

"When I thought you'd died—"

"Don't say it," she choked out. "You don't have to relive that."

"No," he said. "I do. I have to tell you. It was the first time—even after all these years of expecting my own death—that I truly knew what it meant to die. Because with you gone . . . there was nothing left for me to live for. I don't know how my mother did it."

"She had her children," Kate said. "She couldn't leave you."

"I know," he whispered, "but the pain she must have endured . . ."

"I think the human heart must be stronger than we could ever imagine."

Anthony stared at her for a long moment, his eyes locking with hers until he felt they must be one person. Then, with a shaking hand, he cupped the back of her head and leaned down to kiss her. His lips worshiped hers, offering her every ounce of love and devotion and reverence and prayer that he felt in his soul.

"I love you, Kate," he whispered, his lips brushing the words against her mouth. "I love you so much."

She nodded, unable to make a sound.

"And right now I wish . . . I wish . . ."

And then the strangest thing happened. Laughter bubbled up inside of him. He was overtaken by the pure joy of the moment, and it was all he could do not to pick her up and twirl her grandly through the air.

"Anthony?" she asked, sounding equal parts confused and amused.

"Do you know what else love means?" he murmured, planting his hands on either side of her body and letting his nose rest against hers.

She shook her head. "I couldn't possibly even hazard a guess."

"It means," he grumbled, "that I'm finding this broken leg of yours a damned nuisance."

"Not half so much as I, my lord," she said, casting a rueful glance at her splinted leg.

Anthony frowned. "No vigorous exercise for two months, eh?"

"At least."

He grinned, and in that moment he looked every inch the rake she'd once accused him of being. "Clearly," he murmured, "I shall have to be very, very gentle."

"Tonight?" she croaked.

He shook his head. "Even I haven't the talent to express myself with *that* light a touch."

Kate giggled. She couldn't help herself. She loved this man and he loved her and whether he knew it or not, they were going to grow very, very old together. It was enough to make a girl—even a girl with a broken leg—positively giddy.

"Are you laughing at me?" he queried, one of his brows arching arrogantly as he slid his body into place next to her.

"I wouldn't dream of it."

"Good. Because I have some very important things to tell you."

"Really?"

He nodded gravely. "I may not be able to show you how much I love you this eve, but I can tell you."

"I should never tire of hearing it," she murmured.

"Good. Because when I'm done telling you, I'm going to tell you how I'd like to *show* you."

"Anthony!" she squeaked.

"I think I'd start with your earlobe," he mused. "Yes, definitely the earlobe. I'd kiss it, and then nibble it, and then . . ."

Kate gasped. And then she squirmed. And then she fell in love with him all over again.

And as he whispered sweet nothings in her ear, she had the strangest sensation, almost as if she could see her

entire future laid out before her. Each day was richer and
fuller than the last, and every day she was falling, falling,
falling . . .

Was it possible to fall in love with the same man over
and over again, every single day?

Kate sighed as she settled into the pillows, letting his
wicked words wash over her.

By God, she was going to try.

Epilogue

Lord Bridgerton celebrated his birthday—This Author believes that it was his thirty-ninth—at home with his family.

This Author was not invited.

Nonetheless, details of the fête have reached This Author's always attentive ears, and it sounds to have been a most amusing party. The day began with a short concert: Lord Bridgerton on the trumpet and Lady Bridgerton on the flute. Mrs. Bagwell (Lady Bridgerton's sister) apparently offered to mediate on the pianoforte, but her offer was refused.

According to the dowager viscountess, a more discordant concert has never been performed, and we are told that eventually young Miles Bridgerton stood atop his chair and begged his parents to cease.

We are also told that no one scolded the boy for his rudeness, but rather just heaved huge sighs of relief when Lord and Lady Bridgerton laid down their instruments.

LADY WHISTLEDOWN'S SOCIETY PAPERS, 17 SEPTEMBER 1823

"She must have a spy in the family," Anthony said to Kate, shaking his head.

Kate laughed as she brushed her hair, readying herself

for bed. "She didn't realize that today is your birthday, not yesterday."

"A trifling matter," he grumbled. "She must have a spy. There's no other explanation."

"She did get everything else right," Kate couldn't help noting. "I tell you, I've always admired that woman."

"We weren't that bad," Anthony protested.

"We were dreadful." She set the brush down and walked to his side. "We're always dreadful. But at least we try."

Anthony wound his arms around his wife's waist and settled his chin on the top of her head. There was little that brought him more peace than simply holding her in his arms. He didn't know how any man survived without a woman to love.

"It's almost midnight," Kate murmured. "Your birthday is almost over."

Anthony nodded. Thirty-nine. He'd never thought he'd see the day.

No, that wasn't true. Since the moment he'd let Kate into his heart, his fears had been slowly melting away. But still, it was nice to be thirty-nine. Settling. He'd spent a goodly portion of the day in his study, staring up at his father's portrait. And he'd found himself talking. For hours on end, he'd talked to his father. He told him of his three children, of his siblings' marriages and their children. He told him of his mother, and how she'd recently taken up painting with oils, and that she was actually quite good. And he told him of Kate, and how she'd freed his soul, and how he loved her so damn much.

It was, Anthony realized, what his father had always wanted for him.

The clock on the mantel began to chime, and neither Anthony nor Kate spoke until the twelfth bell rang.

"That's it, then," Kate whispered.

He nodded. "Let's go to bed."

She moved away, and he could see that she was smiling. "That's how you want to celebrate?"

He took her hand and raised it to his lips. "I can think of no better way. Can you?"

Kate shook her head, then giggled as she ran for the bed. "Did you read what else she wrote in her column?"

"That Whistledown woman?"

She nodded.

Anthony planted his hands on either side of his wife and leered down at her. "Was it about us?"

Kate shook her head.

"Then I don't care."

"It was about Colin."

Anthony let out a little sigh. "She does seem to write about Colin a great deal."

"Maybe she has a *tendre* for him," Kate suggested.

"Lady Whistledown?" Anthony rolled his eyes. "That old biddy?"

"She might not be old."

Anthony snorted derisively. "She's a wrinkled old crone and you know it."

"I don't know," Kate said, scooting out of his grasp and crawling under the covers. "I think she might be young."

"And *I* think," Anthony announced, "that I don't much want to talk about Lady Whistledown just now."

Kate smiled. "You don't?"

He slid into place next to her, his fingers settling around the curve of her hip. "I have much better things to do."

"You do?"

"Much." His lips found her ear. "Much, much, *much* better."

And in a small, elegantly furnished chamber, not so very far from Bridgerton House, a woman—no longer in the first blush of youth, but certainly not wrinkled and old—

sat at her desk with a quill and a pot of ink and pulled out
a piece of paper.

Stretching her neck from side to side, she set her quill
to paper and wrote:

> *Lady Whistledown's Society Papers, 19 September, 1823*
> *Ah, Gentle Reader, it has come to This Author's atten-*
> *tion . . .*

Author's Note

$\mathcal{A}$nthony's reaction to his father's untimely death is a very common one, especially among men. (To a much lesser degree, women whose mothers die young react in a similar fashion.) Men whose fathers die at a very young age are very often gripped by a certainty that they, too, will suffer the same fate. Such men usually know their fears are irrational, but it is nearly impossible to get past these fears until one has reached (and passed) the age of one's father's death.

Since my readers are almost exclusively women, and Anthony's issue is such (to use a very modern phrase) a "guy thing," I worried that you might not be able to relate to his problem. As a writer of romance, I constantly find myself walking a fine line between making my heroes utterly and completely heroic, and making them real. With Anthony, I hope I struck a balance. It's easy to scowl at a book and grumble, "Get over it already!" but the truth is, for most men, it's not so easy to "get over" the sudden and premature loss of a beloved father.

Sharp-eyed readers will note that the bee sting that killed Edmund Bridgerton was actually the second sting he'd received in his life. This is medically accurate; bee sting allergies generally don't manifest themselves until the second sting. Since Anthony has only been stung once in his life, it's impossible to know whether or not he's allergic. As the author of this book, however, I'd like to think I have a certain creative control over the medical conditions of my characters, so I've decided that Anthony has no allergies of any kind, and furthermore will live to the ripe old age of 92.

My very best wishes,

Julia Q

Welcome to the world
of the Avon Romance Superleader
Where anything is possible . . .
and dreams really do come true

We all know there are unspoken rules that govern the acts of
courtship. There are the rules of today (if he doesn't call by
Wednesday he won't, even if he says he will!) and the rules of
days gone by (a lady should never dance more than three
times with a gentleman).

But often, what is expected is at odds with what is longed
for . . . and how you're allowed to act is different from the
way you feel. Heaven help you if you take a wrong step . . .
but sometimes it's better to toss the rules away, take matters
into your own hands—just as the heroines of these upcoming Avon Romance Superleaders are about to do.

~

HERE COMES THE BRIDE
Pamela Morsi
JULY AVON ROMANCE SUPERLEADER

Gussie Mudd, the proprietor of a small ice business in Cottonwood, Texas, has determined that at some point in a woman's life she must get herself a man, or give up on the idea entirely. To get her man she decides to play by the rules ... the rules of business. And she makes a business proposition to her employee, Mr. Rome Akers.

"PEOPLE, MR. AKERS, ARE JUST LIKE BUSINESSES. THEY act and think and evolve in the same way as commercial enterprise. People want and need things. But when they are vastly available, they prize them differently."

"Well, yes, I guess so," Rome agreed.

"So when we consider Mr. Dewey's hesitancy to marry me," she continued, "we must avoid emotionalism and try to consider the situation logically."

"Logically?"

Rome was not sure that logic was a big consideration when it came to love.

"Mr. Dewey has been on his own for some time now," she said. "He has a nice home, a hired woman to cook and clean, a satisfying business venture, good friends and myself, a pleasant companion to escort to community events. Basically all his needs as a man are met. He has a virtual monopoly on the things that he requires."

Rome was not certain that *all* of a man's *needs* had been stated, but after his embarrassing foray in that direction, he chose not to comment.

"He is quite comfortable with his life as it is," Miss Gussie continued. "Whyever should he change?"

"Why indeed?" Rome agreed.

She smiled then. That smile that he'd seen often before. That smile that meant a new idea, a clever innovation, an expansion of the company. He had long admired Miss Gussie's good business sense and the very best of her money-making notions came with this smile.

"I can do nothing about Mr. Dewey's nice home, the woman hired to cook and clean, his business, or his friends," Miss Gussie said. "But I can see that he no longer has a monopoly upon my pleasant companion-ship."

"I'm not sure I understand you," Rome said.

"In our business if Purdy Ice began delivering smaller blocks twice a week, we would be forced to do the same."

Rome nodded. "Yes, I suppose you are right about that."

"We would be forced to change, compelled to pro-vide more service for the same money," she said.

"Yes, I suppose that's right."

"That's exactly what we're going to do to Amos Dewey," she declared.

Rome was listening, but still skeptical.

"You are going to pretend to be in love with me," she said as if that were going to be the simplest thing in the world. "You will escort me about town. Sit evenings on this porch with me. Accompany me to civic events."

That seemed not too difficult, Rome thought. He did not normally attend a lot of public functions, but, of course, he could.

"I don't see how that will change Dewey's mind," he told her honestly.

"You will also let it be known that you are madly in love with me," she said, "and that you are determined to get me to the altar as soon as possible."

Rome got a queasy feeling in his stomach.

"Amos Dewey will no longer have a monopoly. *You* will be the competition that will force him to provide the service he is not so willing to provide—marrying me."

Gussie raised her hands in a gesture that said that the outcome was virtually assured.

Rome had his doubts.

"I'm not sure this will work, Miss Gussie," he told her. "Men . . . men don't always behave like businesses. They are not all that susceptible to the law of supply and demand."

"Don't be silly," she said. "Of course they are."

"I'm not sure I'm the right man to be doing this. Perhaps you should think of someone who would seem more . . . well more suited to the task."

Her response was crisp and cool.

"I was hoping for a late-spring wedding," she told

him. "When the flowers are at their peak. But I suppose, in this instance midsummer would be fine. Let's say the Fourth of July; that sounds like an auspicious day for a wedding. It is going to be absolutely perfect. The most perfect wedding this town has ever seen. I do hope you will be there, Mr. Akers."

HEAVEN ON EARTH
Constance O'Day-Flannery

AUGUST AVON ROMANCE SUPERLEADER

For Casey O'Reilly the world was supposed to be an orderly place where you met, married, and had children with the man you love. But nothing had gone according to plan. Mr. Right never made an appearance, and now, at "thirtysomething," Casey figured she had a better chance at being struck by lightning than struck by love . . . but then the unthinkable happened . . .

SHE WAS MAKING THIS UP. WHATEVER WAS HAPPENING was all in her mind. *It had to be!*

Desperately, Casey rubbed at her eyes and then cupped her hands around them to shelter her face as more lightning, familiar narrow streaks, flashed around her and thunder rumbled.

There was no time for questions as a man slowly, deliberately, walked closer, as though he had no fear of the lightning or the sandstorm. Casey's voice was stuck in her throat. She wanted to ask him who he was, but only garbled noises emerged from her mouth as she watched him unbutton his dark coat above her. His face was hidden by a wide turned-up collar and the cowboy hat pulled low over his brow, but somehow the closer he came, the less she feared him.

He knelt before her and, without a word, wrapped the edges of the raincoat around her, pulling her to his chest and sheltering her from the sandstorm. She could feel the strength of his arms around her back, and immediately sensed peace as she was gathered into the sanctuary of his body. She felt the strong beat of his heart reverberating against her face. She smelled something citrusy, very earthy, about him, and lifted her hand to cling to his soft shirt.

"You are all right, Casey O'Reilly."

She almost jumped at the close proximity of his voice resonating from his chest and into her ear. The low soothing tone sent shivers throughout her body and she found herself clinging even more tightly to his shirt.

"Who . . . Who are you?" she managed to mutter.

"I've come to help," he answered, holding her tighter as another crash of thunder made the ground shake violently beneath them.

"Thank heavens," she sobbed.

Somehow she felt incredibly safe, more so than she had ever felt in her life. Her body was tingling with some strange and powerful energy that was unfamiliar and yet . . . so perfectly wonderful. She felt a renewed strength welling up in her muscles, spreading through her body down to her burning foot. Her chest stopped aching and her headache eased as she held this man who had just walked out of a bolt of lightning and into her life . . .

~⌒⌒~

HIS WICKED PROMISE
Samantha James
September Avon Romance Superleader

Glenda knew what was expected of a Highland lass—she must wed a man bold and strong enough to protect her. Love could come later . . . if it came at all. But although she was now without a husband, she had once known the joy of the marriage bed . . . and the pleasure that Laird Egan was willing to reacquaint her with . . .

"WELL, YOU ARE EVER AT THE READY, ARE YOU NOT?"

He cocked a brow. "What do you mean?"

"I think you know quite well what I mean!"

He was completely unfazed by the fire of her glare. A slow smile rimmed his lips. "Glenda, do you speak of my manly appetites?"

"Your words, sir, not mine," she snapped. Her resentment blazed higher with his amusement. "Though I must say, your appetite seems quite hearty!"

"And what of yours, Glenda?"

"Whatever do you mean?"

"You are a woman without a husband. A woman

without a man. I am not a fool. Women . . . well, women have appetites, too. Especially those who know the pleasure that can be found in another's body."

And well she knew. She had lost her maidenhead on the marriage bed, but she had never found lovemaking a chore or a duty, as she'd heard some women were wont to do. Instead, she had found it a vastly pleasurable experience . . . All at once she was appalled. She couldn't believe what they were discussing! To speak of her lying with a man . . . of his lying with a woman . . . and to each other yet!

He persisted. "Come, Glenda, what of you? I asked you once and you would not answer. Do you not find yourself lonely? Do you not miss the closeness of a man's body, the heat of lips warm upon yours?"

Suddenly she was the one who was on the defensive. "Nay," she gasped.

"Nay?" he feigned astonishment. "What, Glenda! Did you not love Niall then?"

Glenda's breath grew short; it seemed there was not enough air to breathe, for he was so close. *Too* close. So close that she could see the tiny droplets of water which glistened in the dense forest of hair on his chest. Niall's chest had been smooth and nearly void of hair, and it was all she could do not to stare in mingled shock and fascination.

She was certain her face flamed scarlet. "Of course I did! You know I did! But I"—she made a valiant stab at reasoning—"I have put aside such longings."

He did not take his eyes from her mouth. "Have you?" he said softly. "Have you indeed?"

A strong hand settled on her waist. In but a half breath, it was joined by the other. His touch seemed to burn through the layers of clothing to the flesh beneath.

"Egan," she floundered. "Egan, please!"

"What, Glenda? What is it?"

She shook her head. Her eyes were wide and dark. Her head had lifted. Her lips hovered but a breath beneath his. The temptation to give in, to kiss her, to trap her lips beneath his and taste the fruit of her mouth was all-consuming. Almost more than he could stand.

She wanted it, too. He sensed it with every fiber of his being, but she was fighting it, damn her! Yet still he wanted to hear her say it. He *needed* it.

"Tell me, Glenda. What is it you want?"

She shook her head. Her hands came up between them. Her fingers opened and closed on his chest . . . his *naked* chest. Dark, bristly hairs tickled her palm; to her the sensation was shockingly intimate. Yet she did not snatch back her hands—she did not push him away—as she should have.

As she could have.

"Egan? Are you here, lad?"

It was Bernard. They jerked apart. Egan moved first, stepping back from her. Did he curse beneath his breath? Glenda did not wait to find out.

She fled. Her heart was pounding and her lungs labored as if the devil himself nipped at her heels. Her feet did not stop until she was safe in her own chamber and the door was shut.

'Twas then that her strength deserted her. She pressed her back against it and slumped, landing in a heap on the floor.

Thrice now, Egan had almost kissed her. *Thrice.*

What madness possessed him? Sweet heaven, what madness possessed *her*?

For Glenda could not deny the yearning that still burned deep in her heart. Just once she longed to feel the touch of his mouth on hers. Just once . . .

~

RULES OF ENGAGEMENT
Christina Dodd

OCTOBER AVON ROMANCE SUPERLEADER

Miss Pamela Lockhart knew that proper behavior could guide a governess through any trying situation. The rules were straight-forward: never become too familiar with your employer, always take your meals upstairs on a tray, and remember your station at all times. But what happens when your employer is devastatingly handsome . . . and his behavior is anything but proper?

"YOU CONSIDER MARRIAGE THE SURE ROUTE TO MISERY."

"Not really." He stroked his chin, a gesture he had adopted from his grandfather. "The trick to marriage is not letting expectations get in the way. A man needs to understand why women get married, that's all."

Her mouth drew down in typical Miss Lockhart censure. "Why, pray tell, do women get married?"

"For money, usually." He could tell she was offended again, but with Miss Lockhart he didn't have to worry overly much about offense. After all, she didn't. Besides, he thought his assessment quite fair. "I don't blame them. The world is not fair to a spinster. She has no recourse but to work or starve. So if she's asked, she marries."

Obviously, *Miss Lockhart* did not consider his assessment fair. She slapped her mug on the table so hard the crockery rattled. "Do you have any idea how insulting you are? To think a woman is single because she has never been asked, or if she is married she has done so for monetary security?"

He found himself entertained and very, very interested. "Ah, I've touched a nerve. Are you telling me there is a man alive who dared to propose to you?"

"I am not telling you anything." But swept along by her passion, she did. "A man can convey financial security, but whither thou goest, I shall go, and all that rot. A woman has to live where her husband wishes, let him waste her money, watch as he humiliates her with other women, and never say a word."

"Men are not the only ones who break their vows."

"So fidelity is a vow *you* intend to keep?"

Of course he had no intention of keeping that vow when he was forced to make it, and falling into that trap which had so neatly snared his father. "I've supported more women than Madame Beauchard's best corset maker. If I let marriage stop me, think of the poor actresses who would be without a patron."

She wasn't amused. "So nothing about your wife would be sacrosanct, not even her body. Your wife will cherish dreams that you never know about, and even if you did they would be less than a puff of wind to you."

Women had dreams? About *what*? A new pair of shoes? Seeing a rival fail? Dancing with a foreign prince? But Miss Lockhart wasn't speaking of the trivial, and he found himself asking, "What are your dreams?"

"You don't care. Until I spoke, it never occurred to you that a woman could have her dreams."

"That's true, but you are a teacher, and already you

have taught me otherwise." Leaning back in his chair, he gazed at her and with absolute sincerity, and then said the most powerful words in the universe. "Tell me what you want. I want to know about you."

She had no defense to withstand him. She leaned back, too, and closed her eyes as if she could see her fantasy before her. "I want a house in the country. Just a cottage, with a fence and cat to sit in my lap and a dog to sleep at my feet. A spot of earth for a garden with flowers as well as vegetables, food on the table, and a little leisure time in which to read the books I've not had time to read or just sit . . . in the sunshine."

The candles softened the stark contrast between her white complexion and that hideous rouge. Light and shadow delineated her pale lips, showing them in their fullness. Her thick lashes formed a ruffled half-circle on her skin. When she was talking like this, imagining her perfect life, she looked almost . . . pretty. "That's all?"

"Oh, yes."

"That's simple enough."

"Yes, very simple. And mine."

Careful not to break into her reverie, he quietly placed his mug next to hers. "Why do you want that?"

"That's what I had before—"

She stopped speaking so suddenly he knew what she had been about to say. Moving to the side of her chair, he knelt on the carpet. "Before your father left?"

At the sound of his voice, her eyes flew open and she stared at him in dismay. She *had* been dreaming, he realized, seeing that cottage, those pets, that garden, and imagining a time when she could sit in the sunshine. Her countenance was open and vulnerable, and his instincts were strong. As gently as a whisper he placed his fingertips on her cheek. "There's one dream you didn't mention, and I can make it come true." Slowly, giving her time to turn if she wished, he leaned forward . . . and kissed her.

JUST THE WAY YOU ARE
Barbara Freethy

November Avon Romance Superleader

Allison Tucker knew that today's women were supposed to face their ex-husbands in a modern way—cordially, friendly, and with the attitude that you didn't have a care in the world. But every time she looked into Sam's eyes, she still felt a longing for what might have been if they stayed together—and what could still be . . .

"Did you ever love Mommy?"

Allison Tucker caught her breath at the simple, heartfelt question that had come from her eight-year-old daughter's lips. She took a step back from the doorway and leaned against the wall, her heart racing in anticipation of the answer. She'd thought she'd explained the separation to her daughter, the reasons why Mommy and Daddy couldn't live together anymore, but apparently Megan still had some questions, and this time it was up to Sam to answer.

Sam cleared his throat, obviously stalling for time. For the life of her, Alli couldn't move away. She hadn't meant to eavesdrop, but when she'd arrived to pick up Megan after her weekend with her father, she had been caught by the cozy scene in the family room.

Sam sat in the brown leather reclining chair looking endearingly handsome in his faded blue jeans and navy-blue rugby shirt. Megan was on his lap, her blond hair a mess in mismatched braids, her clothes almost exactly the same as Sam's, faded blue jeans and a navy-blue T-shirt. Megan adored dressing like her father.

"Did I show you the picture of Mommy when she dressed up like a giant pumpkin for the Halloween dance?" Sam asked, obviously trying to change the subject.

They were looking at a yearbook, Alli realized with dismay. There weren't just pictures of Sam and Alli in the yearbook, there were other people in there, too.

"Did you, Daddy? Did you ever love Mommy?" Megan persisted.

Answer the question, Sam. Tell her you never really loved me, that you only married me because I was pregnant, that your heart still belongs to—my sister.

Alli held her breath, waiting for Sam's answer, knowing the bitter truth, but wondering, hopelessly, impossibly wondering . . .

"I love your mother very much—for giving me you," Sam replied.

Alli closed her eyes against a rush of emotion. It wasn't an answer, but an evasion. She didn't know why she felt even the tiniest bit of surprise. Sam would never admit to loving her. She couldn't remember ever hearing those three simple words cross his lips, not even after Megan's birth. Or after, in the days and weeks and years that followed, not even when they made love, when they shared a passion that was perhaps the only honest part of their relationship. Sam always held a part of himself back, a portion of his heart and his soul that he would never give to her.

Alli clenched her fists, wanting to feel anger, not pain. She'd spent more than half of her twenty-seven years of life in love with Sam Tucker, but he didn't love her and he never would.

∾

THE VISCOUNT
WHO LOVED ME
Julia Quinn

DECEMBER AVON ROMANCE SUPERLEADER

If there's one place a proper young lady should not be, it's in an unmarried gentleman's private study . . . crouched under his desk, desperate to escape discovery. Yet that's exactly where (and in what position) Kate Sheffield finds herself. Even worse, Anthony Bridgerton has brought a potential paramour back with him, and Kate is forced to wait out the entire encounter . . .

ANTHONY KNEW HE HAD TO BE A FOOL. HERE HE WAS, pouring a glass of whiskey for Maria Rosso, one of the few women of his acquaintance who knew how to appreciate both a fine whiskey and the devilish intoxication that followed, and all he could smell was the damned lilies-and-soap scent of Kate Sheffield. He knew she was in the house—he was half ready to kill his mother for inviting her to the musicale—but this was ridiculous.

And then he saw Kate.

Under his desk.

It was impossible.

Surely this was a nightmare. Surely if he closed his eyes and opened them again, she'd be gone.

He blinked. She was still there.

Kate Sheffield, the most maddening, irritating, diabolical woman in all England, was crouching like a frog under his desk.

"Maria," he said smoothly, moving forward toward the desk until he was stepping on Kate's hand. He didn't step hard, but he heard her wince.

This gave him immense satisfaction.

"Maria," he repeated, "I have suddenly remembered an urgent matter of business that must be dealt with immediately."

"This very night?" she asked, sounding dubious.

"I'm afraid so. *Euf!*"

Maria blinked. "Did you just grunt?"

"No," Anthony lied, trying not to choke on the word. Kate had removed her glove and wrapped her hand around his knee, digging her nails straight through his breeches and into his skin. Hard.

At least he hoped it was her nails. It could have been her teeth.

Maria's eyes were curious. "Anthony, is there an animal under your desk?"

Anthony let out a bark of laughter. "You could say that."

Kate let go of his leg, and her fist came down on his foot.

Anthony took advantage of his release to step quickly out from behind the desk. "Would I be unforgivably rude," he asked, striding to Maria's side and taking her arm, "if I merely walked you to the door and not back to the music room?"

She laughed, a low, sultry sound that should have seduced him. "I am a grown woman, my lord. I believe I can manage the short distance."

She floated out, and Anthony shut the door with a decisive click. "You," he boomed, eliminating the distance to the desk in four long strides. "Show yourself."

When Kate didn't scramble out quickly enough, he reached down, clamped his hand around her upper arm, and hauled her to her feet.

"It was an accident," she said, grabbing onto the edge of the desk for support.

"Funny how those words seem to emerge from your mouth with startling frequency."

"It's true!" she gulped. He had stepped forward and was now very, very close. "I was sitting in the hall," she said, her voice sounding crackly and hoarse, "and I heard you coming. I was just trying to avoid you."

"And so you invaded my private office?"

"I didn't know it was your office. I—" Kate sucked in her breath. He'd moved even closer, his crisp, wide lapels now only inches from the bodice of her dress. She knew his proximity was deliberate, that he sought to intimidate rather than seduce, but that didn't do anything to quell the frantic beating of her heart.

"I think perhaps you did know that this was my office," he murmured, letting his forefinger trail down the side of her cheek. "Perhaps you did not seek to avoid me at all."

Kate's lips parted, but she couldn't have uttered a word if her life had depended on it. She breathed when he paused, stopped when he moved. She had no doubt that her heart was beating in time to his pulse.

"Maybe," he whispered, so close now that his breath kissed her lips, "you desired something else altogether."